Henry Seton Merriman

Flotsam

The Study of a Life

Henry Seton Merriman

Flotsam
The Study of a Life

ISBN/EAN: 9783337111694

Printed in Europe, USA, Canada, Australia, Japan

Cover: Foto ©Andreas Hilbeck / pixelio.de

More available books at **www.hansebooks.com**

"THE GLINT OF A WHIRLING SWORD."

FLOTSAM

THE STUDY OF A LIFE

BY

HENRY SETON MERRIMAN

AUTHOR OF 'WITH EDGED TOOLS,' 'THE SOWERS,' ETC.

'Poor flotsam on the human tide!'

NEW EDITION

LONGMANS, GREEN, AND CO.

LONDON, NEW YORK, AND BOMBAY

1896

FLOTSAM.

CHAPTER I.

THE EVIL GENIUS.

THE sun was setting behind some palm-trees, and threw golden shafts of light down the ridges of the paddy fields where the green rice stood lush in water. The Hooghly was stealing past the quiet bungalow built on the bank opposite to the spot where now stands the palace of the King of Oude.

The great river flashed and gleamed greasily in the pink haze of Indian sunset, bearing on its sacred bosom sundry mysterious objects half afloat, half submerged. These were the bodies of the elect floating down to that Paradise where no flesh-eating Feringhee will mar the Oriental peace and luxury of life. The year was at its prime—the monsoon was steady. It was June, and eighteen hundred and thirty-one. No bodies float down the Ganges now; for European energy has set aside the religious growth of the ages. Eighteen hundred and thirty-one! Before the child-queen in the far island of the north had gathered into her firm little hands the reins of a great government—before the profoundest statesman had dreamt of an Indian Empire with its imperial crown on a head six thousand miles away. Before—twenty-five years before—the sorest strait that ever Englishmen were in. For the men who were to fight the Indian Mutiny were mostly children still, throwing pebbles from the bank of the sacred river at the floating corpses and the crocodiles.

The shadows of the palms cast by the lowering sun stretched almost across the sleek water. It was very still, except for the distant song of boatmen who were creeping up the swift river in the shallows by the bank. A strange song this, and full of some racial trouble which touches European ears uneasily. An Englishman in the bungalow garden looked up from a letter he was reading, as if the wail of the thin Hindu voices disturbed him.

He was a young man with an aquiline nose, which seemed to dominate his face. There was something sculptural and clean-cut about this nose which put it out of place upon an ordinary physiognomy. The face was not an unpleasant one in full view, and the profile was striking and attractive. The man was of medium height, with a long-shaped head, somewhat abnormally developed at the back. His eyes were of a greeny grey—his mouth was too small.

He listened to the weird chant of the boatmen, who made more noise than progress, and then turned again with a frown to the letter in his hand. This was written on the thin blue-laid paper still in use among old-established firms for foreign mail correspondence. It was dated four months earlier, and bore the address: 91 St. Helen's Place, London. It was addressed to Phillip Lamond, Esq., Goojera Reach, Hooghly River, Calcutta. And Phillip Lamond read as follows:—

' Dear Sir,—I have your letter of December 4 last, and carefully note contents. Again I beg to assure you that I have every confidence in your kind intentions towards the child thrown upon your hands by the untimely death of my poor cousin and his young wife. Your reasons for suggesting that the boy Henry be allowed to remain in India under your care have received my careful consideration, and I have only to reiterate my former request that the child be sent home without delay. It appears to me that the risks you fear as attaching to a voyage home under the care of a native nurse are less urgent than those which are run by European children remaining in India. Let me assure you that I fully appreciate the kindness you have shown

my little relative. At the same time I must inform
you that I should consider myself, as his next of
kin, deficient in my sense of duty if I allowed the
child, Henry, to pass the next ten or twelve years
in India. His life is, as you know, a valuable one.
He is the heir to considerable riches, and as the son
of a valued servant of the Honourable East India
Company he will step into a position of some
importance in society. It is therefore right and
expedient that he should be sent home at once, and
it will be my personal care and happiness to see
that he receives a good education, such as befits his
future station in life. I shall therefore be obliged
if you will make arrangements with Captain Farr,
of the barque *Golden Horn*, who carries this to you,
that the child and his nurse be put on board that
vessel on her departure from Calcutta.

'Captain Farr has a duplicate of this letter; he
also possesses written instructions to take over in
my name the custody of the child, Henry Charles
Wylam. I beg that you will place no further
difficulty in his way, and that you will accede without demur to my request that the nurse and child
be shipped home to me in the *Golden Horn*. Captain Farr has plenary power from me to take such
steps as he may think necessary to secure obedience
to my desire.

'I note your remarks respecting the affairs of my
late cousin, and thank you for the care you have
devoted to these matters. The remittances may be
forwarded regularly, as you suggest, in drafts pay-

able to myself and Mr. Henry Candler, of this city, joint guardians of the child.

> 'I am, Sir, your obedient servant,
>> 'JOHN GRESHAM.'

Phillip Lamond folded the letter with a shrug of the shoulders, and slipped it into the pocket of his thin tussore silk jacket.

'One of your pompous old city magnates,' he said. 'Big waistcoat, big balance at his bank, as narrow-minded as he is broad in the beam. Old boy wants to have the fingering of the money, I can see that.'

Especially as regards a motive do we judge others by ourselves.

Phillip Lamond was not held, by such as knew him, to be overburdened by that virtue which covereth a multitude of sins. And yet he had just returned from Delhi, whither he had journeyed to watch the interests of Henry Charles Wylam, a waif of tender years, cast upon the great world.

Lamond was the agent of the late Captain Wylam, in so much as he collected the rents accruing to that gentleman from a considerable tract of land lying to the south of Delhi.

Captain and Mrs. Wylam had been cut off in youth and health by him who is no respecter of either and came in the form of virulent cholera.

Phillip Lamond had found Henry Charles Wylam a year earlier in the act of beating his ayah with the leg of a rocking-horse—gay, in a frock and a careless half-humorous access of temper. The child knew nothing of his own bereaved condition, and as little of his prospects in life. He only knew that the near hind leg of the rocking-horse had come off, and formed a convenient instrument of chastisement. He looked with disapproving eyes upon Phillip Lamond, but presently entered into the question of travelling in a boat with unfeigned delight.

It would appear that in children the hereditary character shows itself early. Harry's father had been an adventurous soul. The living Harry laid aside the leg of the rocking-horse and expressed himself ready to start on a long journey. With all the insolence of the dominant race he gave his orders to the ayah in his prattling Hindustani, and Phillip Lamond, while laughing good-naturedly at his haste, threw no obstacle in its way.

So expeditiously, indeed, were the arrangements carried out, that a start was effected the next morning, and in due course Phillip Lamond reached his own home on the banks of the Hooghly, where he installed his charge.

While the agent read the missive in the compound, the master slept the sleep of innocence on a mat

stretched upon the floor of the bungalow, and the
ayah slowly waved a palm-leaf fan over his recum-
bent form.

The child lay with careless outstretched limbs, a
fair scion of the northern race which knows no rest
or fear, which has laid its dead in every part of
the earth, beneath the wave of every sea. The boy
was fair of skin, with golden hair, and cupid lips
half open. The dusky woman bending over him
smiled with very pride as her deep eyes rested on
him.

Thus, Harry Wylam slept amidst the turmoil of
this first stage of his journey through life—careless, fearless, happy with a woman loving him and
men quarrelling over him—a subtle prophecy of
things to come. Indeed, the life of every child is
nothing but a prophecy, for those who know the
interpretation.

Phillip Lamond sat down to think. Presently he
stretched his thin legs down the elongated arms of
the lounge. He lighted a cigar and frowned as he
did so. He beckoned to the silent black servant
who was watching him in the shadow of the verandah, and ordered a brandy and soda, which was
presently brought to him foaming in a long glass.

He was tired after his quick journey to Delhi and
back in the height of the hot season. He was wor-

ried by the London merchant's courteously firm letter. He had grown fond of the high-spirited child during the last few months, a fact of which Mr. Gresham had been informed, although he chose to ignore it.

Lamond was a rising man in India, and in those days men rose fast. By a smart piece of social manœuvring he had a year earlier constituted himself the guardian of Harry Wylam, and this tended to assure to him a position he had not hitherto enjoyed. It is so easy to claim friendship with the dead. With Captain Wylam died the small fact that Phillip Lamond had been his servant. For Lamond had only lately begun to call himself a solicitor. He was a man of many irons—of great and varied knowledge, of small and easy scruple. The very man to get on in India before the Mutiny. Indeed, the very man to get on in any part of this world. He had written home to Mr. Gresham a long account of the sudden death of Captain Wylam and his wife: 'my dear friend Harry Wylam,' he had written with the assurance of the worldling. In reply Mr. Gresham wrote a letter full of gratitude, noting with a business-like exactitude the details relating to the worldly possessions of the late Harry Wylam, and courteously suggesting that the three-year-old son should be sent home at once.

Phillip Lamond replied at some length, setting
forth many good reasons why the child should
remain under his care. And thus a year slipped
away. During that time Lamond administered the
estate near Delhi with wisdom and discretion. He
remitted home to Mr. Gresham quarterly sums, the
rents collected by his native colleague in Delhi. He
informed the English merchant that he had retained
for himself the fitting remuneration attendant on
his duties as agent, in addition to one hundred
pounds per annum for the maintenance and lodging
of the child.

India is a land of overgrown vitality. Life is so
abundant that death is treated cavalierly, and the
dead are soon forgotten. Mr. Gresham in London
had reason to congratulate himself that the affairs of the Wylams were in the hands of a prompt
man of business such as Phillip Lamond, acting
in conjunction with the respectable native firm of
H. Alaraka, Sajin & Co., of Delhi. The Wylams
appeared to have had many acquaintances and a
few friends who could, if they had taken the trouble,
have given details of their life and death. Mr.
Gresham never, however, happened to meet any of
these friends, who naturally moved in a different
circle from his own, and when in England failed to
discover that there was a London east of Temple

Bar. He made careful inquiries none the less respecting the firm of native merchants in Delhi who collected the rents and supervised the affairs of Captain Wylam in that city, and learnt nothing to their discredit.

The sums remitted to Mr. Gresham amounted to fifteen hundred odd pounds per annum, which modest income was duly invested by the careful London merchant in safe affairs.

These and other matters were moving to and fro within the brain of Phillip Lamond as he lay at length and gazed out between his own feet across the river. This man passed for a bachelor, and his small household was conducted on the somewhat Bohemian principles which obtained in India in the olden days. The bungalow stood between the road and the river—a small white house with green shutters in sore need of a coat of paint. A few years earlier Lamond had come from the south, had bought this bungalow from a river-pilot, and had painted it without and furnished it within quite regardless of expense.

He seemed to take it for granted that he should get into society, and for a few months had actually hung on the outskirts of that vague bourne. But society had dropped him—slowly, surely, inexorably. He bore no goodwill towards Anglo-Indians.

From the upper circle he slid imperceptibly to
the second range. He began to haunt the billiard-
rooms of the hotels. His name, after figuring for
months upon the list of more than one club-board
as a candidate for election, disappeared therefrom.
Among such friends as he succeeded in making in
public billiard-rooms and drinking-bars he dissemi-
nated the opinion that Anglo-Indians were a narrow-minded race.

When a man begins to complain of narrow-
mindedness in others the worldly wise gather in
their skirts.

Yet Phillip Lamond did not drink, neither did he
swear. He was ever ready to assist the new-comer,
and even to warn him against such dangers as might
beset his social path.

'But,' he would say with a wave of his cigar,
'don't say I told you. I'm no gossip. I hate a
mischief-maker. I like to live at peace with my
neighbours!''

He laughed his jolly laugh—went his way, and in
due time the new-comer dropped him.

Lamond could not understand it. No more than
he could understand why each succeeding letter
from Mr. Gresham was colder and more polite.
That which he now held in his hand was final. For
Phillip Lamond knew, as certainly as if the mer-

chant had told him, that Captain Farr, of the
barque *Golden Horn*, had a power of attorney from
Harry Wylam's guardians to assume custody of the
child.

He knew Captain Farr by sight. During the last
year or so his friends had mostly been numbered
among the officers of the ships at anchor in the
river. These mariners were in the habit of coming ashore in the evening—brown, well-washed and
soapy in their rough serge clothes, to seek such en-
tertainment as the city afforded, and their haunts
became also the haunts of Phillip Lamond.

Captain Farr was known to be a red-headed skipper of the old school, with a rough tongue further
accentuated by a Glasgow brogue. An honest
man, who thrashed his ship backwards and forwards
round the Cape, making no very quick passages
and few mistakes. He was the sort of man to obey
orders to the letter—a suspicious Scotchman, who
had seen the world and the wickedness thereof.

Phillip Lamond went indoors and wrote a note to
this mariner, asking him to dinner the next evening,
and expressing considerable relief that his charge,
Harry Wylam, was at last to be removed from his
over-burdened hands. 'The truth is,' he wrote, ' a
bachelor like myself is unfit for the management of
a child, and it was only in obedience to my dear

old friend Wylam's desire that I undertook the
thing at all.'

A queer smile hovered beneath the Captain's red
moustache as he read this simple-minded epistle an
hour later.

Phillip Lamond, over his solitary dinner, was perhaps beginning to realise that in India a dog may do
worse than have a bad name—he may have none
at all. For the old order changeth, giving place to
new. If a dog be given a bad name nowadays, he
usually gets into society with it.

CHAPTER II.

THERE is nothing in this world so desolate as the waste of ocean lying to the south of the Cape of Good Hope—the home of the albatross and of his smaller, duskier brethren of the mighty wing.

The loneliness of it all is overwhelming, the silence of it full of melancholy. Here are the mighty works of God and the silence of them. The albatross is a taciturn bird. He sails along on his weird wings—self-absorbed, mysterious, incomprehensible. The Cape pigeon flits by half scared, the dainty petrel trips on the wave, and they one and all have no voice. The great sperm whale lumbers along with a strange air of attending to his own affairs. And the waves, as high as the Sussex Downs, roll unbroken around the world.

Captain Farr was of the old school of mariners, and a navigator always rounds the Cape as he was taught in his apprenticeship. The modern dashing skipper, intent on a quick passage, breaks into that silent sea below the forties. He forces his ship into

the great waste, and boldly sights Prince Edward
Island and the lone Crozets. On the homeward voyage he sails in shoal water and sights Table Mountain. This is the whole art of rapid navigation—to
go where the wind blows steadily.

But the *Golden Horn* rounded the Cape on either
voyage in a safe old medium latitude, sighting no
land, breaking into no unknown waters in search of
a fair wind.

She was now rolling easily on a glassy sea, her
great sails flapping sleepily. As she tumbled to
windward, the canvas filled with a solemn flap.
On the leeward roll, the sails suddenly flattening,
dropped the sheet-blocks with a clatter on the deck.
The regularity of it, the sleepy monotony of the
rattling block-sheaves, the grave flap of the filling
sail, were maddening or sleep-inducing according to
the nerve of the hearer.

It was a Sunday afternoon, and in the shadow of
the deck-house the watch on deck lay prone in
strong attitudes. Some were reading, others slept.
The ayah squatting on the upper deck with her
back against the white rail was wrapped in a deep
Oriental meditation. A monkey sat on the lower
ratlines of the mizzen rigging, engaged in an un-
blushing effort at personal cleanliness. In the intervals of his occupation he glanced with blinking,

affectionate eyes at the gentle native woman, as if
reminding her that they had the tie of a common
country amidst these fair-faced aliens. At times
he looked hurriedly around him, impelled to precaution not so much by the evil conscience hereditary
to his kind, as by the knowledge that his chief tor-
mentor, little Harry Wylam, was about the decks.

The child had as a matter of fact clambered down
from the poop to the main-deck, where he was
peeping wonderingly over the combing of the main-
hatch. The hatches were off, and a warm odour of
Indian produce—of indigo and rapeseed, of cocoa-
nut oil and coir-yarn, rose from the closely stowed
hold.

Harry Wylam, with the irrepressible energy of
his years, had exhausted his ayah's patience, leaving the woman meditatively somnolent in the sun.
He had been forcibly snubbed by the watch in the
shade of the deck-house. The captain was below,
and the first officer, sitting on the stern rail, was
busy with Sunday thoughts of home. For on blue
water the seventh day is devoted to washing clothes
and thinking of one's home ties.

The monkey had escaped to the mizzen rigging.
Remained therefore for the enterprising Harry his
own neck, to risk on lower rigging and poop gangway, the open hatchways and the wonders of the

hold, and perchance a little sport with a young bear
confined in a rough cage between the foremast and
the deck-house.

Having exhausted his investigations of the hold
as seen over the high, old-fashioned combing of the
hatchway, Harry went forward on tiptoe in his little slippers. The bear provided better sport when
aroused from a comfortable nap. With some exultation Harry found that the peace of a warm afternoon had soothed his victim to profound slumber.
It being Sunday the carpenter was not at work, and
the orderly deck provided no suitable arm where-
with to goad the sleeping bear. A belaying-pin
was too short to reach him where he lay at the
back of the cage, the capstan-bars in their rack
against the bulkhead of the deck-house were too
heavy.

With the enterprise of ignorance and a characteristic heedlessness of consequence, Harry determined
to go inside the cage and kick his unconscious foe.
He worked silently and steadily at the door of the
cage with that singular perseverance which in some
natures is only brought to a high perfection by the
knowledge of wrong-doing. At last the door was
open, and clambering on an overturned bucket
Harry Wylam proceeded to carry out his programme to the letter.

2

There was a roar, a shriek,—and the watch hurrying to the spot found a scuffling mass of fur and pinafore and stout bare limbs tossing to and fro in the cage. This was finally extracted, and for a brief moment the fight continued on deck in the centre of a circle of dumbfoundered men. Then some one seized the bear, and immediately the first officer dealt the beast an exceedingly shrewd blow across the eyes with a capstan-bar.

The bear tottered and rolled backwards, opening his great arms as he fell, and dropping from their suffocating embrace Master Harry Wylam—crushed, white, and unconscious. The combatants lay side by side. Some one had already run to the fresh water pump, and presently a pannikin of lukewarm water was sluiced over the child's face, washing away the bloodstains from his pallid cheeks. There was a deep serrated scratch across his forehead, and those who saw it knew that the mark of it would last the child's life.

For a few moments Harry lay motionless, while the ayah knelt on the deck and beat her breast in a terror of suspense. Then the blue eyes opened with a wondering look, which presently gave way to the light of anger. The child scrambled to his feet, and before the onlookers comprehended his intention, he had fallen upon the bear again, literally : tooth and nail. He beat the prostrate animal on the face and head with his tiny fists, he kicked it with his little button-up slippers. It was the sort of thing that appealed to the humour of the British mariner, and the men around him roared again with laughter and admiration of such dauntless pluck.

' That'll be a great man some day,' said a sailor, as they dragged the bear towards its cage.

' Ay,' opined Captain Farr, slowly, as he led the child away, ' or else he'll come to the gallows.'

After this incident a greater vigilance was observed. The child was deemed by the cautious Captain Farr to be too headstrong for such gentle care as the devoted but passive ayah could lavish upon him. Her slim black arms no longer knew how to control his wayward strength of limb. The masterfulness of the dominant race was beginning to override the small moral control which the woman exercised over her charge.

It was probably owing to the Scotchman's suspicious precautions that, when the Start was at length sighted, Harry Wylam was still on board the *Golden Horn*, a merry, heedless child, with a brown face and brave blue eyes—the picture of good health, of happy innocence, and wilful daring.

In due course the great ship crept up the river to the gates of the St. Katherine's Dock—then busy with shipping, alive with commerce; now still and sleepy—the last resting-place of the superseded.

As the *Golden Horn* slowly warped in through the tidal basin, a stout gentleman in tight trousers, in straps, and a black silk choker, walked along the quay, keeping pace with the vessel. Captain Farr on the poop—steady, cautious, infinitely careful, raised his hat at the sight of this gentleman, and received in return a courteous wave of the hand. The old gentleman changed his gold-knobbed malacca cane from the left to the right hand, settled his black silk cravat, and looked the *Golden Horn* up and down—not with the knowing eye of a seaman, but with the possessive pride of an owner.

' Yon's Mr. Gresham,' said the captain curtly to the child at his side, and across the little space of muddy water the fatherless child and sonless man looked hard at each other.

' He's very fat,' said Harry.

' He's varra wealthy,' said the Glasgow captain, sternly.

When the ship was at length moored alongside the quay and the long voyage was at an end, Mr. Gresham walked gravely up the gangway.

' A hearty welcome to you, captain,' he said, with that grand air for which we have no time to-day. And he extended a gracious hand. ' A successful voyage and a clean bill of health I hope,' he added.

And the captain muttered ' Ay, ay !' within his beard.

' Yon's the child,' he said, ' and he's led us a pretty dance.'

Harry was standing in front of his great relative, contemplating the vast silk waistcoat, which had so imperatively commanded his attention.

'Come here, my little man,' said Mr. Gresham kindly—and the two shook hands.

' I am going to be a sailor,' announced Harry, with that blunt arrival at the main issue which we lay aside in later life.

' No doubt, my little man, no doubt,' said the merchant with a smile. ' It is only natural. I hope you have had a nice voyage, and have not given Captain Farr much trouble. And this is your kind nurse. I thank you, my good woman, for your care of this little traveller. And now we will go ashore. My carriage is awaiting us in the Minories. Captain Farr, you will dine with me to-morrow afternoon, I hope.'

The captain expressed a gruff acquiescence, and visiby broke out into a cold perspiration at the thought of the social agonies to come.

As Mr. Gresham walked to the dock-gates, holding the child by the hand, more than one man paused in his work to touch his hat to the great shipowner, and to stare open-mouthed at the black woman, in her dusky reds, meekly walking behind.

The carriage was awaiting them in the shadow of the trees in Trinity Square, for it was St. Martin's summer and a hot October.

The first that Harry saw of England was therefore the great Tower of London, and he abandoned the idea of a maritime career for the red coat the moment he set eyes on the guards drilling in the square.

The carriage rattled away over the cobble stones, past the Mint, through the narrow Minories, where the smell of ships still lingers. And Harry explained to his guardian, in a high, clear voice, the difference between a reef-knot and a bowline, as they drove along; which difference he made clearer by an illustration effected with the check-string attached to the coachman's centre button. Through Leadenhall Street, past the great East India House, all innocent of the Empire within its ledgers, past Crosby Hall—untouched to-day—and through the iron gates of St. Helen's Place.

' You will find a little playmate in the nursery,'

said Mr. Gresham, as he lifted the child to the pavement. ' I have a little girl, younger than you, although you think me a very old man.'

' What is her name ?' asks Harry, stumping up the steps. He has already forgotten Captain Farr and the *Golden Horn.* If we are to have great changes in our life, please God that He may send them in our childhood.

' Her name is Miriam,' replied Mr. Gresham. ' Her mother's name. Her mother is dead, my little man, she has gone to heaven. You must never talk of her. And you must be a brother to my little Miriam.'

' Yes; or else I'll marry her,' replied Harry, sturdily.

The merchant turned and looked down into the child's face with a queer smile. He was rather amused at the independence of spirit displayed by this small traveller, at his grand air acquired in a nursery where he had even been lord and master with cringing servants at his beck and call.

It must be remembered that this was in the thirties, before the drawing-room had begun to advance, much less the nursery; before the mother had begun to shriek and clamour for her rights, much less the child. Mr. Gresham belonged to the older school, and clung to his grand house in St.

Helen's Place in preference to a villa on Clapham Common or at Lewisham. He cherished many quaint ideas, now daily losing ground before the so-called advancement of a generation of women, who hold it higher to be an object of ridicule abroad than the idol of a nursery at home.

Mr. Gresham, in his rigid old-world formality, held very pronounced principles on the bringing up of children—principles in which the nursery figured largely—wherein a wise discipline tempered that parental pride which handicaps many childish virtues. And though we laugh at such to-day, it has yet to be proved by a future generation, whether we are bringing up a better race of men and women than did our grandfathers.

Harry Wylam was led kindly past the open dining-room door—where he glanced wonderingly at the massive, highly polished mahogany—up the grave staircase, where the portraits of many city magnates looked down upon him.

'That,' said the merchant, indicating a steel engraving, ' is the great John Gresham, my second cousin.'

Harry was interested in a picture representing the Duke of Wellington extending his hand to General Blücher.

' Where are we going ?' he asked, as they passed

the drawing-room door, and began to climb the narrower staircase to the upper rooms.

' To the nursery, where your little sister is waiting tea for you,' replied Mr. Gresham, kindly.

' It is very high up,' observed Harry.

Mr. Gresham went into the room first, and Harry arrived in time to see a fair-haired little girl struggle from her high chair to the ground, where she stood respectfully in her father's presence with downcast eyes. The nurse, a respectable middle-aged woman, tightly contained within a black dress, stood at attention behind a highly polished metal teapot.

It was all scrupulously neat and formal; rigidly good, both mentally and physically, for the small lives forming there. The ayah crept in meekly, and her dark eyes fell before the British stare of her compeer.

Harry stood looking at Miriam.

' Here is your little brother, my dear,' said Mr. Gresham to his daughter, ' come all the way from India to live with you. He will make the nursery merrier, Mrs. Down.'

But Mrs. Down had only eyes for the dusky woman, whose clothing struck her as slightly indecorous.

Miriam came shyly forward and kissed Harry.

She led him to a high chair beside her own. Harry clambered up in silent meditation. It was all rather incomprehensible to the boy who had ruled the bungalow by the banks of the Hooghly, and had been allowed as a treat to sip brandy and soda from the tumbler of the indulgent Phillip Lamond.

CHAPTER III.

FOR eight peaceful years Harry Wylam lived in St. Helen's Place. Great events laid their finger upon his little life with that lingering touch which is never obliterated. He was lifted from his cot and carried to an attic window to see the sky all red and shimmering. The Royal Exchange, they told him, was on fire, and he shivered in his nurse's arms with some childish comprehension of a calamity to England. He saw the forked tongues lick the sky; he saw the sparks fly upward. Through the open window he heard the bells of the Royal Exchange ring out a quaint Scotch air. And the maids peering through the windows whispered, awe-struck, that the bells were saying that there was no luck about the burning house.

One morning, when the sun was up betimes, for it was the month of June, Harry was awakened by a wild ringing of bells, and St. Helen's voice was loudest just beneath him. He saw Mr. Gresham in all his city finery--an alderman of his ward, a liveryman of many companies—step into his carriage at seven in the morning. He saw the good people in their best flocking westward, and the nurses told him that England had a new queen who wore a golden crown.

He told little Miriam bravely that he would one day be a soldier and bear a sword for Queen Victoria, and Miriam thought that she would like to be a Court lady.

The ayah had long been sent home, impassive and meek with her torn heart, for this child had been as her own. With her went Harry's last link to distant India—and the palm trees, the meek black faces, the great silent river, faded into a dream.

Life was very real to the child, who was not made of dreaming matter. He lived every moment of his day, a child of quick anger and sudden repentance. At one moment he would laugh at Miriam for a timid girl, and the next defend her against the nurse and all their little world, taking subsequent punishment with a certain grand air of indifference. Once he struck his little playmate because she misunderstood a complicated manœuvre of tin soldiers, which made her whimper, whereupon he suddenly humbled himself to the ground at her little feet, which made her cry the louder—she knew not why.

The nurse—a woman of cold and commanding

presence, the sort of woman one usually finds in
a widower's house—disapproved of him from the
first, and gave him all the love of her repressed
heart after a year. She nursed him through childish
ailments with a severity which is in some natures
the only mode of confessing affection. She piloted
him through childish troubles—very real, very important to him—with a cold justice which she never
meted out to Miriam. And all the while she disapproved of him. Women are strange, and the
colder women the most inconsistent. She was
keenly alive to his faults. She made the worst of
him to that just man, her master, and when at last
the sentence came, it hurt the nurse more than the
culprit.

' There is nothing for it,' said Mr. Gresham, ' but
to send him to school. I will see about it to-day.'

At nursery tea-time came the news that Harry
had been entered for Merchant Taylors' School, and
was to present himself in Suffolk Lane in a week's
time.

Miriam looked up with frightened eyes, and beneath her curls a few hot tears fell upon her little
hands. Harry received his verdict with stubborn
lips pushed forward. He gnawed at his crust—a
punishment tea was his daily fare—in sullen silence.
The nurse poured out the tea with steady hands,

spread thin butter with unflinching severity, and felt strangely angry with Miriam.

' I don't care,' said Harry presently, ' I'm tired of being with—women.'

But he did not want any more bread and butter.

Five minutes later he was in roars of laughter over a struggle with the butler who, having summoned him to the study, refused to let him slide down the banisters.

He pulled his tunic down, drew up his stockings, and walked fearlessly into the study where Mr. Gresham was waiting. Mr. Gresham was grave and kindly as ever. He was somewhat judicial, and the *résumé* of the last five or six years, with which he entertained the small scapegrace, was a genuine surprise to Harry.

Some, indeed, of the boyish crimes set forth in tolerant deliberation by his guardian had been engraved on his memory by the marks they had left upon his person or upon the furniture, but the majority of the charges only came faintly as half-forgotten incidents in a lifetime full of such. Harry had not attributed the blame of these to himself or to any one else. They appeared to him the handiwork of that *force majeure* which, under the name of Fate, shapes the smallest like the largest lives. Harry listened respectfully enough, and presently

a warm tide of shame and self-abnegation welled
up in his heart. His lip quivered, and he bit it
hard.

' I am not blaming you, my little man,' concluded
Mr. Gresham. ' I recognise the force of early circumstance, and endeavour to make allowance for
the irregularity of your infancy. But now you are
going out into a world of little men, which is
very much the same as the world of bigger men
in which I move myself. You will find difficulties
awaiting you—you will find friends there and
enemies. You will have to make your own place
in this little world, and later on in the larger one.
No one else can make that place for you. From
this time forth I shall cease to treat you as a child.
I shall not punish you as a child. You must try
and recognise for yourself the difference between
right and wrong. We will forget the past, Harry.
We will lay aside childish things, and be a man
from to-day. I want you to remember two things
—always. Remember that you are a gentleman —
and an Englishman. As an Englishman do nothing
that is dishonest, as a gentleman nothing that is
mean. Shake hands, my little man. And we will
turn over a new leaf. We will never look at the old
ones again.'

Harry extended a sticky little hand, and withdrew

it. He came forward a step and paused, then he turned suddenly, and throwing his arms on the high window-sill he buried his face in his sleeves, and stood motionless except for the sobs that his new manhood bade him repress.

Mr. Gresham—good merchant-prince—kept his word rigidly. The folded pages of childhood were never reopened—the old misdoings were completely wiped out, and Harry Wylam made a fresh start on the morning that he set out with his satchel and slate for the Merchant Taylors' School.

The novelty of it all lasted six months. Harry fought a few fights, and brought home more than one black eye with the pride attaching to those adornments in early youth. He swaggered considerably as he turned in through the iron gates of St. Helen's Place on these occasions, knowing full well that Miriam would be at the window.

The zest of making his place in the new world was, however, as we have seen, a short-lived pleasure. At the end of two terms the boy's active mind began to look farther afield for an opportunity of distinction. He was never the boy to mope in the corner of the playground with a book, but he drank in greedily enough at second hand the tales of adventure and daring. He had tasted in his infancy the air of the great world, and the flavour of

it lingered still in his memory to the detriment
of the quiet atmosphere of Suffolk Lane and St.
Helen's Place in the city.

Harry, in his thirteenth year, was a fine boy with
tossing fair curls and eyes brimful of mischief. He
was vigorous and active—as successful in the playground as he was unfortunate in the class-room.
The boys admired him for his daring—the masters
had a fondness for his honesty. The sight of his
eager, bright face, coupled with the rumours of
his great wealth, had a marked effect upon the
reports that reached Mr. Gresham. For school-
masters, like the rest of us, are only human. The
brains of a rich boy shine brightly enough in a
school report, and the perjury is wiped out in
extras.

In Harry Wylam's case, however, the brains were
not wanting. He possessed, indeed, a certain brilliancy—a dashing recklessness of consequence which
enabled him to conceal his ignorance and assisted
his tutors in their pious fraud.

Mr. Gresham, like many old-fashioned people,
combined with a great shrewdness a certain simplicity which cannot be attributed to the rising generation. He received the reports of Harry's progress
and conduct with a satisfaction quite unalloyed by
doubt. When, therefore, the old butler from St.

3

Helen's Place sought him at the office one afternoon, with the news that Harry had not put in an
appearance at school, his only thought was that
some accident had befallen the boy.

The butler, who had more worldly wisdom than
his master, suggested at once that Harry had run
away.

'Nonsense, Parks,' said Mr. Gresham, testily
laying aside his pen. 'Some mishap has befallen
the child. You say that he never reported himself
this morning—that is certain?'

'Yes, sir.'

'And you saw him start for school?'

'Closed the door behind him, sir,' replied Parks
in the manner of a man who has arrived at an un-
alterable conclusion.

Clerks and servants were at once sent out to
make inquiries, with the result that Parks the
butler took a seat on the Chatham coach leaving the Borough at four o'clock the same afternoon.

A child answering the description given of Master Harry Wylam had mounted the morning coach
for Rochester, having booked his seat to Chatham.
His luggage consisted of a school satchel and a slate;
his outfit for the journey a bright smile and an
undaunted thirteen-year-old heart—an equipment

some of us engaged on a longer journey may well envy him.

The narrow High Street of Chatham was crowded with soldiers and sailors when the coach arrived. There were the stir and business of life in the very atmosphere, as there always are when red coats and bluejackets are about. Men greeting each other loudly—meeting on a different face of the globe— girls clinging to their frank-hearted mariners, who would sail away the next day and forget them— harpies preying on the simple sons of salt water. The butler, accustomed to London streets, was in no degree flustered, though sorely put about to know which way to look for his small needle in this pottle of human hay.

Like a wise man he went to the principal inn— knowing Harry's grand ways, and shrewdly suspecting that he would there find a servitor willing enough to talk to a gentleman's servant.

He called for a bottle of wine and strolled into the large sitting-room of the 'Harp and Anchor,' with its great windows overlooking the Medway, its organ, its sanded floor, as some of us know it to this day. The waiter, in his rusty black and splaytoed shuffling boots, soon melted to the blandishments of one of the fraternity. He had caught no sight of Harry; but he was not without experience of young gentlemen who ran away and eke of those who did not do it alone.

On hearing that Harry was yet too youthful for the more serious escapade, his face displayed a little loss of interest; for romance is a strange quality, and may oft be found in unlikely hiding-places. Nevertheless, the man had sound advice to offer, and showed the butler the nearest way to the Docks.

It was, however, too late to make prolonged inquiries of the ship captains and dock labourers. At eleven o'clock the butler returned disconsolate to the inn, full of wondering where his charge might be passing the night.

By seven o'clock he was afoot again, making haste to board such vessels as he found getting ready for the sea. It was ten o'clock and past before he clambered up the side of the *Seven Brothers*, sloop of Jersey, and on the deck of the little collier he found Master Harry Wylam talking to the mariners.

'Thought there'd be somebody comin' for 'un before long,' said the captain of the *Seven Brothers*, skilfully ejecting a quid of tobacco, and coming forward to meet the butler. Harry also ran to greet his guardian's servant.

'What—Parks,' cried the child; 'why, you'll never make a sailor.'

'Not likely—Master Harry—but, thank God, I've found you.'

The old man turned in some wrath to the captain, and was met by a broad wink.

'This 'ere young gen'leman,' explained the captain, laying a kindly hand on Harry's shoulder, 'come aboard last evenin' and said he was goin' to be a sailor. Seein' as how it was gettin' late, and havin' just such another at home at Gorey, I thought he'd better ship along of us—in the *Seven Brothers*—and he's a gay good sailor—bless his sperrit.'

'And I slept in a hammock,' said Harry bravely, 'and washed my face in a bucket this morning, just like a sailor.'

He threw up his head and looked round among the crew for confirmatory evidence. But, to judge from the smiling countenances around him, the comparison as to the use of the bucket did not seem very apt.

'I've put his name down in the log-book,' continued the captain with obvious winks, 'for the fust vacancy that occurs. But I'm afraid there ain't no berth for him this voyage.'

The butler's eyes glistened strangely as he took the skipper's broad palm in his fingers, and made no impression on it.

' My master will not forget it, he said, ' and I should like your name and address.'

The captain laughed and shrugged his shoulders, turning at the same time to Harry.

' And so, master, ye'll have to go back and do a little more book-larning before you ship for a sailor.'

' I tried him at figures, last evening,' he continued to the butler, ' and he don't know quite enough about it yet to work out his reckonin's at sea.'

So the evening coach took Harry and the butler back to London, and duly deposited them in the Borough at ten o'clock. Harry slept during most of the journey, and only woke to talk of the *Seven Brothers* of Jersey, and his future intentions with regard to that vessel. The butler endeavoured to make him realise the anxiety and trouble he had caused by his thoughtless escapade, and succeeded to no appreciable extent.

The household was in bed when the travellers reached St. Helen's Place, and Harry, as he crept upstairs, saw only the light beneath his guardian's door.

He came somewhat sheepishly down to breakfast the next morning—which happened to be Sunday—a day when the children breakfasted in the dining-room.

Mr. Gresham looked up gravely when he came into the room.

' Well, Harry,' he said, ' been up to your tricks again ? '

And, for the first time since the leaf was turned, the hot tears rushed to the boy's eyes.

CHAPTER IV.

THROUGH the following years Mr. Gresham continued to the best of his ability the plan of education he had designed for his ward. He steered
Harry through a series of scrapes tending to increase
in importance as the boy grew in mind and stature.
The hand at the helm was as steady and as honest as
could be desired, and had the vessel been a stately
merchantman with plenty of ballast and a well-
stowed cargo, the course would have been straight
enough. But this Harry Wylam was like a brilliant
yacht tossed hither and thither on every wave of life,
bending to every wind of heaven, careening before
a fair breeze, dipping and yawing to each cross sea.
Between them, with every good intention, they
made heavy weather of it.

The boy was not expelled from Merchant Taylors'
School. His tutors thought it better that he should
be sent to a boarding academy, where a stricter discipline was enforced. It had been Mr. Gresham's
intention to send Harry to Oxford, but his orderly

commercial common-sense saw danger in the University life for one of Harry's temperament, and the final stage of a gentleman's education was perforce abandoned.

From school to school this educational waif moved on in search of that discipline which should tame him. And honest John Gresham at his great desk in Eastcheap sat leaning his broad benevolent face in his hand, wondering what was amiss.

' Put the lad into a red coat,' said Mr. Gresham's friends, when he consulted them on 'Change. And truly there seemed no other career for one so full of life and spirits.

His father had carried a sword for King George, why should not Harry do the same by Queen Victoria ? So the commission was bought with the money so ably cared for and administered by Mr. Gresham. The sword was duly delivered at St. Helen's Place carefully enveloped in brown paper, which Mr. Gresham as carefully removed. This good City merchant had a sense of the fitness of a little ceremony. He would not allow the boy to fall upon this parcel like a school-girl on a new dress and tear it from its envelope.

He slowly freed the polished steel from its encumbrances, and holding it by the sheath handed it to Harry.

'See that you bear it with honour, my boy,' he said. And he threw back his own shoulders with honest British pride; for the lad was as his own son. He believed in the goodness of Harry's heart. He was willing to fold over another leaf, and never look at the early pages again.

'Please God to send us many wars,' answered Harry, drawing the bright steel from its sheath. He stood in the old panelled room, a fine figure of a young soldier, and made the light flash again on the burnished blade.

'Please God,' he said, ' to send us many wars.'

And God in the hollow of His hand had the Crimea and the Indian Mutiny for England.

The new uniform duly followed, and Harry went away to his duties at Colchester, regretting that Miriam should not have seen him in his brave red coat and gold braid. The girl was at school at Brighton in the process of being finished by some elderly ladies, who made a specialty of the training of motherless girls, with proportionate charges at the end of the term, and doubtless a commission from the Brighton milliners.

Harry had not seen Miriam for two years, but it was arranged that he should return at Christmas to St. Helen's Place, and it may safely be conjectured that he resolved to bring his finery with him. It

happened, moreover, that his regiment was under
orders to go into barracks at the Tower of London at the beginning of the year, so Mr. Gresham
looked forward to the presence of the young people
in his house again.

Miriam arrived from Brighton with the finish
a little new upon her. A certain prim shyness
towards her father, whom she called ' sir,' very cor-
rectly, bespoke the teaching of maiden ladies, for
whom a father was nevertheless a man. Miriam,
with her curls overshadowing her pretty face, her
crinoline, her prim womanly ways, brought a new
element into the house. The drawing-room was
thrown open, and the chairs, stiffly formal in bright-
coloured wool-work, were sat on after many years of
rest. The city ladies called formally, and one day
the carriage of the Lady Mayoress pulled up at
number ninety-one, to the intense delight of the
neighbours.

Miriam assumed her new position and dignity
with a *savoir-faire* which had not been taught at
Brighton, and John Gresham rubbed his chubby
hands together with benign satisfaction as he
watched her.

Then came Harry one evening with all the dust
and circumstance of war upon him, having marched
with his men from Colchester. Miriam, no doubt,

had never set eyes on so fine a soldier, with his sunburnt merry face, his gay blue eyes looking admiration into hers.

'Egad!' he exclaimed, unbuckling his sword-belt
and laying the virgin weapon aside, 'but I'm
thirsty. Can I have a drink, sir?'

He sat down on a low chair and stretched out his
dusty legs. 'I shouldn't have known you, Miriam,'
he said, 'in your long frock and your grown-up
ways.'

Miriam blushed a little as she rang the bell for
the refreshment he so frankly demanded.

'I would have known you—cousin—anywhere,'
she answered.

'Cousin——! And why not Harry?' settling
his leather stock beneath a chin yet smooth enough.
'If it's going to be cousin I'm bound for the nursery, where I dare say old Mrs. Down will give me
a cup of tea and a piece of bread and scrape. All
scrapes in those days, eh, Guardian?'

'No doubt,' replied Mr. Gresham for Miriam,
who seemed a little tongue-tied; 'it seems a trifle
strange at first to call a great fellow like you by his
Christian name.'

'No more than for me to call a grown-up young
lady Miriam,' protested Harry, with his easy laugh.
'In truth I'm half afraid to come into my lady's

drawing-room, with all this dust on me! But now I'm in I won't evacuate until she calls me Harry.'

Which Miriam presently did unconsciously, in the midst of recalling childish reminiscences.

' And you will often come to see us now that you are quartered so near,' said Mr. Gresham, as Harry rose and looked for his sword and belt.

' You may take your oath on that, Guardian,' replied Harry, with a glance at Miriam, gentle and timid.

They accompanied him to the door, and half St. Helen's Place was at its windows to watch the passage of the boy who had broken more than one of the same panes. At the corner of St. Helen's Place Harry turned and waved his glove, then went clanking down Bishopsgate.

' A fine figure of a soldier,' said Mr. Gresham, contentedly. ' And I really hope he has found his right pigeon-hole at last. We all have a pigeon-hole in this world, my child, and we are never orderly till we get there.'

Miriam made no answer. She went upstairs to the drawing-room, where she took a strange delight in setting in order ornaments and furniture which had been displaced by the free-and-easy young soldier. There was a patch of dust on the tapestry

of a chair where Harry's sleeve had rested. She
dusted it off with a little smile.

'He has not changed,' she said aloud. 'One can
see that he has been in this room.'

Harry came again to St. Helen's Place in redemp-
tion, no doubt, of his emphatic military pledge to
do so. He came often; and, moreover, he came
early, before Mr. Gresham had returned from his
office in Eastcheap.

It was the month of July, and all his drill was
over by nine o'clock in the morning. Number
ninety-one stands on the shady side of St. Helen's
Place, at the far end of that quiet retreat—as far
from the noise and bustle of Bishopsgate as possible. Harry vowed that it was the coolest place in
London on a summer afternoon, and the drawing-
room the pleasantest spot on earth.

When he made statements of such a nature Miriam laughed in her quiet, composed way, and said
that it pleased her to hear him say so. She usually
sat near an open window, hidden from prying eyes
without by a thick lace curtain, which swayed gently in the breeze. As she bent over her needle-
work her brown curls had a way of dropping over
her cheek, so that Harry could not always see her
face. It was her habit to wear the cool brown
tussore dresses, embroidered in white, which her

father's East Indian correspondents sent him annu-
ally. We do not see such tussore now.

' Gad ! ' exclaimed Harry one tropic afternoon ;
' how nice and cool you look in that dress ! '

' It is you who are cool,' replied Miriam demurely,
mindful of her education, ' to make remarks about a
lady's appearance.'

' No harm in calling you cool, Mim, at any rate,'
answered Harry. ' I wonder how it is that you are
always so neat and composed and quiet, as if you
had quite made up your mind about everything,
and meant to abide by the result.'

Miriam looked up with a little smile, and then
her gentle grey eyes returned to the needle-
work, where some difficult stitch commanded her
attention.

' If it was a question of appearance I could say
more than that, by George,' said Harry.

' But it is not,' put in Miriam, in an absurd, old-
fashioned flutter.

' Why not ? ' blurted out Harry. ' Why shouldn't
I tell you that there is not a lady in the land fit to
hold a candle to you ? There is not one of them
worth a moment's thought beside you, Miriam.
When I first came into this house—a little chap in
a frock—I vowed I'd fall in love with you, as your
father has often told. And, faith, I've done it.

I've always been in love with you—Miriam—and, by Heaven, I always will be.'

The girl had risen and was standing half hidden in the curtain, seeking to get away from her impetuous lover, who was already by her chair holding her hand in both of his. This was an emergency unprovided for in the curriculum of the Brighton Academy for young ladies. And it had come to Miriam before her first long dress had lost its delicious novelty.

' Harry, you mustn't,' she protested, white with genuine fright. ' No, you mustn't kiss my hand. It is wrong.'

She tore her hand away and stood before him suddenly blushing rosy red — prettily confused between tears and merriment.

' How dare you !' she exclaimed, regaining her dignity and looking up at him with flashing eyes. ' I'll never let you come to this room again.'

Then suddenly she sat down again, and hid her face in her pocket-handkerchief, a dainty thing not made for woe.

' How was I to know that I should make you cry ?' pleaded Harry full of penitence—standing before her clumsy and abashed.

He touched her shoulder, and gaining courage stroked her bright curls foolishly.

'Miriam—don't cry,' he begged, 'I am very sorry—but I can't help loving you, can I? Was I rough? Did I hurt you?'

She was sitting with her chin in the palm of her hand, looking away from him into the lace curtains.

'No.'

'Did I frighten you?'

'Yes—a little.'

'Then I'm sorry. Deuced sorry. But,' he added, with a little laugh, 'I'm not going to stop loving you for all that.'

Miriam caught her breath. She was beginning to realise how very unfinished she really was. There must have been something wrong about the teaching of the maiden ladies. She had received no tuition for this occasion, and felt herself unequal to it. Yet she was conscious of being less afraid than when the Lady Mayoress called—though in a flutter as our foolish grandmothers were on any provocation.

'I think you had better go away!' she said, with studiously averted face.

'Why?'

'Please go away,' she reiterated, for lack of a valid reason.

'Not till you say you have forgiven me.'

Harry waited for this pardon, and did not receive it.

4

' Do you forgive me—Miriam ? '

There was a faint movement among the curls.

' And you will let me come again ? '

Another faint movement. Miriam had not learnt that delightful ' aplomb ' which schoolgirls bring home with them to-day.

Harry stooped and boldly possessed himself of her right hand, which he raised to his lips with all respect. Within her fingers he discovered a crushed pocket-handkerchief, of which he deliberately possessed himself in his youthful, romantic way—leaving Miriam looking out through the lace curtains.

Mr. Gresham had just finished signing the day's letters when Harry was shown into the room by a clerk.

' Well, my boy, glad to see you,' he said, laying aside his pen. ' Five minutes later and you would have missed me. What can I do for you ? '

Mr. Gresham belonged to the old school of business men, whose business was almost religion, and their office sacred to it.

' I want to marry Mim !' said Harry bluntly, when the clerk had closed the door behind him.

' Come and tell me that two years hence, Harry, and we'll talk it over,' replied Mr. Gresham, who seemed in no way surprised.

'Two years! I can't wait all that time,' cried Harry aghast.

'Is the girl not worth it—Harry?'

'Worth it — by Heaven she is — Guardian! Worth half-a-dozen of me—I know that. But I'm nearly twenty-five. I come into my money in November. What's the good of waiting till I am an old chap?'

'You'll be young enough at twenty-six, my boy,' replied Mr. Gresham.

And all Harry's persuasions fell on stony ground.

CHAPTER V.

On the occasion of his twenty-fifth birthday Harry gave a dinner to his friends, and it may be surmised that he found himself possessed of a larger number of these than he had anticipated. Not only were those simple sons of Mars, his fellow-officers, eager to rejoice with him in that he had found the many pieces of money that had been lost to sight, but from the highways and hedgerows friends, old and young, came trooping.

From over seas there even came a word of kindly congratulation. One signing himself Harry's old friend, Phillip Lamond, wrote from Calcutta with many good wishes.

The dinner took place at a West-end tavern, then much in vogue. This establishment still exists, but has descended the social scale in a day when outward decoration is held to contribute to a greater beatitude than good wine and victuals.

Some of Harry's military friends kindly constituted themselves a tasting committee, and emerged from the hospitable doors of the tavern at three in the morning of Harry's twenty-fifth birthday, informing all and sundry in husky voice that some individual, presumably the hero of the day, was a jolly good fellow.

These friends, now washed and sobered, were grouped round Harry, who received his guests in a sort of drawing-room. Indeed, their presence was somewhat necessary in view of the number of perfect strangers whom Harry was called upon to welcome.

'This,' whispered Montague of the regiment, as a red-faced gentleman swaggered in, 'is Major Meule of the Life Guards—best judge of a horse in London.'

And Major Meule looked it.

'Here comes Tom Calley, who ran away from his American wife—a tip-top chap,' added the gifted Montague.

And Harry shook Mr. Thomas Calley's limp hand.

They all seemed to know Montague, with whom they exchanged a knowing nod. Montague had, by the way, been chairman of the tasting committee. He was now inclined to assume the mastership of the ceremonies, and kindly jogged Harry's elbow whenever that easy-going youth showed a tendency to neglect his duty as host.

They took their seats at table, Montague on Harry's left, and on either side of the long board a row of rubicund faces mostly unknown to the young host. The dinner was a good one; the wines eminently satisfactory. The light of many flickering candles showed the rubicund faces to be verging on cardinal, when the table-cloth was at length removed and the business of the evening began.

Major Meule rose to his feet by arrangement with Montague. He was the great-nephew of a dissolute baronet, which established a certain precedence at this table.

' Gen'lemen,' said the Major, jerking his neck back in his stock and standing in the benign attitude usually assumed by a sworn broker about to sell a horse, ' gen'lemen, charge your glasses. Got a toast to give you. Toast am sure you'll all drink heartily.'

He paused, and looked round on faces that certainly encouraged such a hope.

' Our host, gen'lemen ! It is not the straight thing—gen'lemen—for one gen'leman——'

' Hear, hear,' interrupted the voice of one who owed the Major money.

' To praise another gen'leman before his face. All I can say is that our host has proved himself a thorough —eh—er—gen'leman to-night. He is an acquisition—British Army. Such men as Harry

Wylam—make England—wha' she is. I give you
—Harry Wylam—our host.'

They took their host in bumpers, standing to do
so. Some of them stood a trifle unsteadily. Then,
on a sign from Montague, Harry rose to his feet—
flushed, handsome, excited. He stood nearly six
feet high, a fine upright young Englishman, with a
clear skin and honest eyes, tossing fair hair, and a
weak mouth.

'I am glad to see you, gentlemen, and I hope
that this will not be the last dinner by many that
we shall take together. I am proud to be an
English soldier, and an officer in this regiment. I
am proud to meet many of you who do not belong
to " ours," and I thank you for so kindly drinking
my health. In reply, gentlemen, I give you the
lady we all serve—The Queen.'

Amid shouts the toast was duly drunk. Then
some one called for a song, and Harry rose to his
feet again. He possessed a fine young voice, and
being devoid of affectation sang a good song of a
good old type, now superseded by the ' double
entente ' of the music hall—the subtle humour of the
variety stage. The words of Harry's song only
meant what they said, and the air was more important than the libretto. When he sat down another
rose and lifted up his voice in praise of Bacchus, to

whom, indeed, more than one man present had already poured copious libations.

The evening went merrily enough, and in a jolly voice Harry told the waiters to bring more wine, and be d——d to them for bad waiters. One gentleman volunteered to perform a sailor's horn-pipe on the sideboard, but slipped on a cork which rolled under his foot, and falling heavily, bumped his head against the mahogany, and retired into private life in a corner. Another insisted on reciting Gray's ' Elegy,' to which the assembled guests at first objected, but after useless opposition allowed him to go on, and took no notice of him. Several young warriors slipped quietly under the table as if in search of something, and were lost to sight. Major Meule went quietly to sleep, with his red face appearing above his black leather stock, like a full-blown peony drooping in the sun.

It was not an edifying scene, and need hardly be dwelt upon longer. Every man at the table was a more hardened toper than Harry, who had been in the wildest spirits all the evening—leading song and laughter. His position of host had, perhaps, saved him a little, and indeed it was to no man's advantage that he should take too much. Most of the guests -friends of Montague -lacked such opportunities as this, and made the most of the good wine. There are many men ready enough to get intoxicated if it can be compassed at the expense of another, but stint vice to please avarice if they pay for their own liquor.

The bottles followed each other round the table with a marvellous regularity and speed, while it is to be feared more than one guest forgot his manners in his anxiety to get his fill of good wine. Harry was too young to care for the liquor for its own sake, and in his boisterous way proposed that they should leave the table and go out of doors. Mischief of any sort would suit him, he averred, and plenty of proposals met his suggestion.

' Or shall we go and sing a serenade in St. Helen's Place ? ' cried Montague in a thick voice, glancing at Harry with a devil-may-care leer.

' Where the hell is that ? ' asked some young blade whose father having made a fortune in tallow had taught his sons a fine ignorance of London beyond the Bank.

' Ask Wylam,' answered Montague, who was flushed and incoherent.

' St. Helen's Place is in the City,' replied Harry shortly. And some sly dog gave out a meaning :

' Ah—h ! '

' All right, Harry,' said Montague, with a low-bred wink. ' Mum's the word. I'll not peach.'

He pursed up his coarse lips and looked mysterious.

' I'll only tell 'em that when we go to St. Helen's Place we get ourselves up uncommon smart. I'll only tell 'em that one day on parade we dropped a dainty lace handkerchief out of our sleeve.'

Harry scowled over his wineglass.

But Montague did not notice the indication of a temper never owning to a perfect control.

' And if the City fair be kind, why go to the West-end ?' continued Montague, whose cups conduced to coarseness.

' Drop that, Montague,' said Harry in a warning voice. But as ill-fortune would have it, the joke had just penetrated the muddled brain of a boy fresh from his mother's apron-strings, and therefore anxious to display a deep and depraved knowledge of the world.

' I give you a toast, gentlemen. St. Helen !' he cried with a maddening laugh.

' I give you a better, and yet the same,' shouted Montague. ' Miriam—Saint Miriam of St. Helen's Place ! And no saint, I'll be bound, despite her demure airs—as smart a little maid as——'

He finished with a splutter, for Harry's claret, glass and all, had struck him full in the face; and Harry, sobered, white-lipped, with blazing blue eyes—and none can blaze so fierce—was standing over him.

'If that's not enough for you, take that!' said Harry in a concentrated whisper.

And he struck Montague so heavily on the side of the head that he rolled over sideways, carrying his chair with him.

Montague stood up, his lips twitching, the claret dripping from his whiskers, his face livid, with a red patch where Harry had struck him.

'All right, Mr. Wylam,' he said, 'I'll kill you for that.'

Every man in the room was on his feet. The Major came bustling forward.

'Gentlemen—gentlemen—*if* you please,' he cried in his raucous voice, and the younger men stood aside as in the presence of one who had moved in drunken brawls all his life—a proud distinction.

But another man had already taken Harry by the arm—a tall grey-haired man, a major in his own regiment.

'Come away, Wylam,' he said. 'Montague is drunk.'

'Never soberer in my life,' returned Montague, wiping his face and clothes with a dinner-napkin.

' Then you are a d—— d cad,' said the grey-haired man. ' There would have been some excuse for you if you hadn't been sober.'

' I am not afraid of him,' said Harry, yielding to the pressure of his new friend's hand and going towards the door.

' No, he is afraid of you,' replied the other.

In the passage the landlord came forward, perturbed, in a frock-coat.

' I hope there will be no scandal, gentlemen,' he said, with uplifted hands.

' Get out,' said Harry, passing out into the quiet street.

It was a July morning, and even the streets of the great city looked cleaner and healthier for the passage of the short night. The air was cool, for the sun was not yet up and had only begun to tinge the eastern sky. Over the sordid streets hovered that pearly calm which dawn casts even upon the city.

Harry's eyes were painful after his long vigil, his lips were parched, he tasted the bitterness of that life which young men crave to see.

' I suppose,' he said, huskily, to the man stalking gravely at his side with a solemn clank of spurs, ' that I shall fight him.'

' Yes. You were both too d——d sober.'

Harry gave a short laugh, and pressed his aching head with his two hands as he walked.

' *I* wasn't,' he said.

In a doorway a shadowy form sat up—a night-bird, in his rags, with a homeless face. He sat up and watched the two officers clank past in their red coats, with their swords swinging.

' Poor devil ! ' said Harry.

He paused, fumbled in his pocket, went back and threw the man a half-crown.

The Major watched him, with a smile, and suddenly in the grey light Harry blushed like a boy. There is nothing so difficult as charity.

' Poor devil looked hungry,' he said.

And the shadow in the doorway shrank back, watching the two men in their bright uniforms, with their worn and weary eyes.

A carriage rattled past, and Harry caught a glimpse of two women in ball-dresses. One—the elder woman—sat bolt upright with wide-open eyes staring in front of her. Her face was hard and wise. Her companion—a young girl—was leaning her face against the arm-rest, her lips apart, her pale forehead drawn with weariness, her eyes closed.

The Major saw it too, and made no comment.

The world seemed very hollow. There appeared

to be more fighting in life and against greater odds
than Harry had hitherto imagined.

'I could have done nothing else than stop his talk
with my wine, could I?' he said, half shamedly.

'Nothing,' replied the Major. 'The mistake
dated farther back than that. You should never
have made a friend of Montague.'

'Well,' said Harry, with his reckless laugh, 'I
have made an enemy of him now, and if he wants
to fight I shall not say him nay—d——d if I do.'

Harry swaggered a bit, and held up his aching
head in the morning breeze.

'I'll be ready for him when and where he likes,'
he said.

The Major made no answer, but walked on
gravely, with his great sword clanking on the pavement. The streets were quite deserted. They
were passing through a quiet region between
the Strand and that which is now the Embank-
ment.

'There are no cabs about at this hour,' said the
Major, 'but I dare say the walk will cool our heads.
We must be on parade at six, and it is past three
already. Shall I see you through this business if
Montague challenges?'

'It would be a great kindness,' answered Harry,
touched by this middle-aged man's spontaneous

goodness. 'I do not know anything about such matters—but I'm not afraid of him.'

'It is not Montague you will have to fear,' said the Major gravely, now, or in the future.'

'Who is it?'

'Yourself.'

IT was always a fine sight to see Mr. Gresham enter his orderly office in Eastcheap. The bowing clerks—the grave ledgers ranged tier over tier—the solemn hush—the scrupulous neatness—the inexorable sanctity of business.

'A gentleman is waiting to see you, sir,' one of the clerks told him, as he paused in his stately old-fashioned way to wish them a good morning.

'A gentleman at this hour?' remarked Mr. Gresham, laying aside his stick and hat, scenting no doubt some trouble outside the daily difficulties of commerce.

He went into his private room, and there found awaiting him a grey-haired man of upright carriage and stern demeanour.

'Mr. Gresham?' inquired the stranger.

'The same, sir.'

'My name is Poole—Major Poole, entirely at your service. I am of your nephew's regiment. A scapegrace, I regret to tell you, sir. His own most inveterate enemy.'

'You tell me nothing new, sir. What has my nephew been about now ? '

Mr. Gresham courteously drew forward a chair. He had fought his battles in the world, and had met reverses like the rest of us. It was not likely that he should forget the courtesy due from one gentleman to another, even in a moment of trouble.

'Harry Wylam's quick temper has led him into serious trouble, but nothing more than we soldiers have to face, Mr. Gresham. We have only our lives to play with in the army.'

'How, sir ? Is Harry's life in danger ? ' inquired Mr. Gresham, unsteadily.

'Not at the moment—and we may yet hope that it will only be so from the Queen's enemies, as befits the colour of his jacket. But he is now in expectation of a challenge from the best shot in our regiment, whom he grossly insulted last night.'

The Major drew in his feet and tapped his heel with a smart cane.

'How did it occur—nothing dishonourable, I hope ? ' said Mr. Gresham, fingering his quill-pen uneasily.

'Nothing dishonourable, my good sir, I can answer for that,' replied the Major. 'The lad is a gentleman, whatever be his faults.'

'Thank you,' said Mr. Gresham, quietly.

5

'If you are at liberty,' went on the Major, glancing at the letters on the broad mahogany desk, 'to come with me now, it may serve a good end that you and I call on the boy at his quarters in the Tower.'

Mr. Gresham rose at once.

'For what purpose?' he inquired, pausing.

'We may be able to induce him to offer to Mr. Montague such an apology as will settle the quarrel amicably,' replied the Major.

'I would not have the boy do anything unbefitting his position and his calling,' said Mr. Gresham, with a fine spirit.

'You need have no fear of that, sir,' replied the Major, as they left the room together.

Mr. Gresham's carriage had not been sent away, and in that roomy vehicle the two gentlemen drove down Eastcheap, narrower then than it is to-day, towards the Tower. It was a fine sunny morning, and the Major, grim and hardy, had no appearance of having seen it dawn six hours earlier.

They found Harry, now sobered and grave, in his little room overlooking the leafy quiet of the moat. Through the open windows came the sound of the sharp commands, the tramp of the unwilling feet, of punishment-drill in the square.

Harry rose and bowed to the two gentlemen,

pushing aside some writing materials with which he had been engaged. A letter bearing the words 'Dear Miriam,' and nothing more, lay confessed on the blotting-pad throughout the interview. The boy offered his hand, but Mr. Gresham with fingers stoutly clasped around the knob of his cane did not appear to see the gesture.

'I suppose,' said Harry, addressing his uncle with an engaging smile, 'from the fact of your coming with Major Poole, that you have heard from him of my quarrel with a—a—scoundrel.'

'I suppose, sir,' replied Mr. Gresham, with a severity which entirely failed to impress, 'that you were drunk last night.'

'Not drunk, Guardian,' said Harry, with a laugh. 'Not drunk—that is a nasty word—say jolly.'

Harry laughed, his gay infectious laugh, and Major Poole's lantern jaw relaxed its rigidity. He was, before all, a soldier, this grave pessimist, and the boy who could laugh with his first duel hanging over him would surely find the soft spot in any soldier's heart.

'I presume,' said Mr. Gresham, 'that you will apologise to the gentleman whom you insulted last night.'

'Devil a bit,' answered Harry cheerfully. 'I'll fight him.'

' Then you will never cross my door again,' said Mr. Gresham.

Harry's face dropped. There are some natures so sunny that common sense comes to them as a cold shadow. Your optimist thinks well of all men and best of himself. It never occurred to Harry to question his own wisdom during the proceedings of the last twelve hours. He neither posed as a martyr nor set up for a hero. The blindest man on earth is not he who imagines himself to be what he is not, but that man who is content that he could never be different from what he is.

' Why not ? ' asked Harry blankly.

' Because I do not intend that my quiet home shall be the resort of drunkards and brawlers,' replied Mr. Gresham, looking at him steadily.

' Drunkards and brawlers !' echoed the soldier, who had fondly imagined himself to be inaugurating a career of military glory.

' Yes, such doings as these are not for quiet people like myself,' replied Mr. Gresham inexorably, and at the back of it all was Miriam. His daughter and his daughter's welfare had at last given the good merchant that strength of purpose which had hitherto been lacking in his treatment of Harry Wylam.

' But I want to marry Miriam.'

Mr. Gresham turned away and looked out of the

window on to the quiet prospect of tree and gravel and grey wall.

'And Miriam loves me,' added Harry confidently.

'I hope to God she does not,' said Mr. Gresham, and in saying it he gave Harry Wylam a wound which never healed. We give these little stabs in daily talk, in any passing controversy, and we never know which one of them may bite in and rankle through a lifetime.

'Why do you hope that?' asked Harry in a low voice.

'Because it is not such men as you who make women happy,' replied Mr. Gresham. 'If you are prepared to apologise to the gentleman whom you insulted, I shall be glad to bear such a message to him in company with your kind friend Major Poole. If not '—he drew out his great gold watch and consulted it without being any the wiser, for that Business which we spell with a capital letter must at last go to the wall before the business of life. 'If not—I must be getting back to my office.'

Harry paused, looking from one grave face to the other.

'There is no question of an apology,' he said. 'The nature of the quarrel could hardly allow of it.'

He glanced at the letter which had been begun

half a dozen times, and as yet consisted of only two words.

' I do not wish to know the nature of the quarrel,' said Mr. Gresham, in a voice which perhaps surprised himself as much as it did Harry. ' I wish to know nothing of the affair.'

Harry turned to Major Poole with the obstinate look of a weak man.

' My uncle,' he said, ' does not understand these affairs.'

The Major looked grimly out of the window.

' Pardon me,' he said, finding an answer unavoidable. ' Mr. Gresham no doubt understands the keeping of his own honour as well as you or I, or any other gentleman.'

Mr. Gresham turned round with a slow smile. He bowed gravely and courteously to the Major.

' Young people,' he said, ' are apt to forget that their elders were also young once. In my youthful days we had many foolish notions respecting a gentleman's honour which are to-day fortunately out of date. It was difficult at the end of the century to steer a clear course through the shoals of a young man's life without becoming involved in some disagreeable affair. My nephew has yet to learn that I also have met my man—and killed him.'

The Major nodded curtly, and looked at Harry.

'I regret,' went on the City merchant, in his formal old-fashioned way, which we have to-day exchanged for a carelessness of thought and speech wholly deporable, ' I regret, sir, to inflict upon you these details of a family difference. But, at the same time, I cannot congratulate myself too heartily upon enjoying the advantages of your experience and knowledge in a matter on which my opinion may be antiquated or worthless. Have you ever fought a duel, Major ?'

' Never,' was the grim reply.

' I wonder why,' burst in Harry with irrepressible boyishness and curiosity.

' They were mostly afraid of me—perhaps,' replied the Major with his grim smile.

And indeed he hardly looked inviting.

' May I ask,' said the City magnate, turning to the Major, ' your opinion of this affair ? You know more of the quarrel than I do. It is probably the outcome of some boyish conceit. I beg of you, sir, to tell me outright whether in your view this boy can apologise——'

' No, d——n it, Guardian,' interrupted Harry— and Mr. Gresham waved him aside.

' The two gentlemen,' answered the Major, ' had had too much wine—that is all I know. I consider that Wylam is called upon to apologise.'

' I'll be d——d if I do,' said Harry, and in the same breath he called out ' Come in,' to the firm military knock of his orderly at the door.

The man brought in two letters—the one for Harry and the other for Major Poole. Harry broke the seal, and merely glancing at the note threw it down on the table. The Major read his communication more carefully.

' Calais sands,' he said, folding the paper and looking at Mr. Gresham, ' to-morrow evening, if the wind be fair.'

There was a little pause. Mr. Gresham took up his hat—his stick he had never laid aside.

' You have made your choice,' he said to Harry.

' Yes.'

And the City merchant walked out of the room.

The next morning Harry and the Major went by train to Dover, and crossed thence by the ordinary steamer to Calais, while Montague made for the same port in the yacht of a friend. The wind was fair, and the bells of Calais church were ringing for vespers when the four Englishmen set out on foot towards the dunes that lie between Calais and Boulogne. The keen-eyed hotel proprietor had soon detected the fact that these were not ordinary travellers on their way to Paris, but four gentlemen of the English army engaged in one of those affairs of honour, now daily growing scarcer, which formed no mean source of income to such innkeepers of the Côte du Nord as could hold their tongues.

If the gentlemen wished for a quiet walk after dinner, he could recommend the little path towards Grisnez, which diverged from the Boulogne road across the harbour. Should their lordships be fatigued, would it not be as well to send a carriage round by the road to await their commands at the Chapel of our Lady of Calvary, between the road and the dunes, one mile away from Calais? These and other suggestions were made with that engaging frankness—that inimitable innocence which belongs to France above all nations, and to her innkeepers above all her sons. The suggestions were accepted with a gruff British shamefacedness which did some credit to the honest soldiers engaged in a dishonest affair.

In a little sandy hollow between two wind-swept dunes, with the cool breeze of the Channel playing through their hair, the two young fellows stood facing each other at length, and awaited the word.

'Now!' cried Montague's second, and before the word Montague's pistol had flashed. There was no doubt of it, and the Major's anger so far took possession of him that he cried out, 'Steady, Harry!'

'I'm steady enough,' said Harry, white with

rage, and Montague dropped with a bullet through his neck.

'By God!' whispered Harry, running forward and falling on his knees by the wounded man's side, as quick to repent as he had been to act. 'What have I done—I say, Montague—tell me it's only a scratch?'

'D——n you!' answered Montague with his mouth full of blood. And the Major dragged Harry away.

It was almost dark as Harry and his friend hurried into Calais. 'Will he die?' Harry had asked a hundred times, and the Major could give him little comfort.

'By the merest chance,' the landlord told them, 'there was a boat ready for sea, if the gentlemen wished to leave Calais at once. Their lordships had come merely for the voyage, of course. Many English milords did it—but not so many as in former days. One hundred and fifty francs would tempt the patron of the boat,' he thought.

'Will he die?' asked Harry again, as the two Englishmen crouched on the deck of the unsavoury lugger, and drew their cloaks closer round them.

'I do not know,' answered the Major gloomily. 'But whether he dies or not you will have to leave the regiment and cut the country.'

CHAPTER VII.

TRUTH.

For a week Harry carried on his shoulders, day
and night, the hardest of human burdens, suspense.
He remained within the gates of the Tower the
object of barrack-room and mess whispers, admired by some, pitied by others, avoided by all.
He did his duty with a mechanical alacrity which
raised him to a high level of military discipline.

' If Wylam had a calamity once a week he would
be the finest soldier of us all,' said the Colonel.

And indeed it seemed that a ballasting of trouble
was all that this crank vessel required.

Montague was lying at Calais, and the physicians
would not commit themselves to that ray of hope
for which his adversary longed. The bullet, it
appeared, had displaced some important sinews and
had cut a vein. If the wounded man recovered, he
would, the doctors said, carry his head on one side
for the rest of his days.

For the man lying swathed in his clean little room
overlooking the harbour at Calais, more than one

prayer was daily offered in England, and at last an answer came. The physicians pledged themselves, at length, to set Montague on his feet again, and the news was no less welcome in St. Helen's Place than in the Tower. A great scandal to the regiment had been averted, for no regiment is the better for a court-martial. It was an open secret that Montague and Wylam had fought, and the offence was gravely ignored by those in authority. In India, at this time, duels were of frequent occurrence, but at home they were daily becoming rarer. The articles of war were stringent, but for years had been ignored, and a law which is customarily broken is more difficult to set agoing than new legislation.

Pending the verdict of the French doctors Harry was allowed to continue his daily duties, no sort of restraint being put upon his actions. Montague was on sick leave, and it was understood lay abed at Calais. So the grave farce was carried on, and Harry felt in no way a hero.

After early parade one morning the Colonel drew him aside, and they walked down to the rampart together, the observed of all the rank and file.

' I have had news from Calais,' said the Colonel, and Harry's ruddy face grew pale.

' Montague is now out of danger.'

' Thank God,' said Harry.

'Ay,' said the Colonel, 'thank God. But you'll have to go. We're a quiet-going, hard-up set of fellows, not your sort at all.'

Harry bit his lip, and made no reply.

'You have the making of a good soldier in you, my boy. It isn't that,' went on the old martinet in a kinder tone. 'In some regiments you would get on splendidly, I have no doubt.'

'But not in yours,' said Harry, with a bitter laugh.

'But not in mine. I would suggest India if I may make so bold,' said the Colonel. 'It would be well if they forgot your name at the Horse Guards for a few years. Many a young fellow has begun badly and has got over it all right afterwards.'

'I am the d——dest unlucky fellow that ever lived,' muttered Harry; and, moreover, he meant it. For he was fully convinced that his misfortunes were wholly the outcome of an evil fate that seemed to dog his footsteps.

Side by side they walked backwards and forwards between the grey tower and the busy river, and the Colonel who held fine old-fashioned theories, that the Colonel of a regiment is its father, gave a vast quantity of good advice, which was in no wise heeded. For Harry was desirous of returning to his quarters to send, in answer to an imploring little note from Miriam, the good news that Montague had been pronounced out of danger.

In addition to this Harry wrote a long letter to his Guardian, setting forth the reasons why he had been compelled to fight the duel, and still withholding the cause of the quarrel, which was indeed trivial enough. The writer further expressed contrition for his misdoings; for he was ever soft-hearted, full of self-reproach one moment and laughing again the next. His was a nature demanding and, alas! usually receiving great indulgence from those who loved him. Such having to go out into the world at last find that the world will not love them, and has only indulgence for its own faults.

'I have,' wrote Harry, ' been sufficiently punished for my hastiness, for my Colonel tells me that he can no longer keep me in the regiment, and is at this moment negotiating for me an exchange into an Indian regiment, where I hope by dint of hard work to retrieve the time I have lost and the good name I have endangered. The Colonel says that India is the place for a young fellow to get on, and I am going to have a devilish good try. I am afraid that I have not been living quite within the allowance you and Mr. Chandler made me out of my money, but suppose that now that I am of age it

will be all right. The tailors are a damned dishonest set. I may have had all the clothes they charge
me for, but I do not know where they are now. I
owe Montague four hundred and twenty pounds;
part of it I lost to him at the Derby, backing a horse
I was told of by a mutual friend. Montague himself said the horse ought to have won. The rest I
lost to him at cards. He taught me écarté. He is
not a bad fellow at all, and I am very glad he is
getting better of his wound. It is a great nuisance
about having to exchange, and I am afraid you will
be annoyed about it. It will be a great wrench to
part from you both, especially Miriam. For I love
Miriam, and will never love anybody else. Please
say by the messenger who takes this whether I may
marry Miriam when I come back from India in a
few years, with my majority, perhaps, and a good
name. I love Miriam very much, and will never
marry anybody else. I cannot get on without her.'

So wrote Harry Wylam to his Guardian—contrition, and love, and a wondrous hopefulness all mixed
up together as they are in youth, as indeed they
must be to make life worth the living at all.

In reply he received a note from Miriam, telling
him that her father was ill and had been ordered by
the doctor to keep free from all worry, and not even
to read his letters. She had recognized Harry's

writing on the envelope, and the letter had been placed with others, awaiting her father's attention when he should be sufficiently recovered.

The letter was somewhat stiff and formal—such as young ladies were taught in those days to write to young gentlemen—which, moreover, we should laugh at to-day when young ladies are young women, and behave as such.

Harry read the missive twice, and in the folly of his youth kissed the signature. Then he swore that he would see her if he had to break in the respectable front door of No. 91 St. Helen's Place. He clapped his hat upon his head, took up his smart cane, and stalked off, full of love and those great schemes that belong to life's best adjunct.

The butler 'didn't know as if he rightly ought to admit' him when Harry rang the bell; which, being translated, meant that he had received distinct instructions not to do so. But Harry laughed, and taking the old man by the shoulders threw him playfully against the wall; which display of physical force no doubt solved the easy-going conscience that flourishes in most pantries.

'Master's asleep, Mr. Harry!' whispered the butler, as the young soldier having stormed the fort would have banged the door behind him. And then he stood with a twinkle in his foolish sentimental

eye watching Harry run lightly up the stairs to
the drawing-room, where they both knew Miriam
to be.

Harry burst into the room, and before Miriam
quite realised what was happening she was freeing
herself from her lover's impetuous arms.

'You know you oughtn't to be here,' she said,
repelling him firmly. And he became vaguely
aware that where he had left a child there now
stood a woman. 'My father has forbidden you the
house. Oh, Harry! why are you so thoughtless?
He has been in great trouble. He is very ill, and it
is all your fault.'

Harry's bright face clouded suddenly.

'I'm deuced sorry—Mim—beg pardon, I mean,
I'm *very* sorry. But it could not be helped. And
I say it is a bit hard when everyone is turning
against a fellow that his own people should shut
their door in his face. But I don't mind what they
all do so long as you care a little bit, Miriam. I
have had a bad time—my life has been in danger,
I'm hard up, I've been kicked out of the regiment
—every deuced thing has gone against me, and if
you are going to turn, why I'll just go and put a
bullet through my worthless head. Say, Mim—do
you care—just a little bit?'

'How can anyone care for a person who gets into
6

tap-room quarrels—who disgraces himself and his
regiment—who is a scapegrace and a ne'er-do-
well?' cried Miriam, arguing against herself, which,
mesdames, is a way you have when you will not
acknowledge facts. You place them before your-
selves, and then walk over them.

'Oh—yes,' said Harry, with a hopeless laugh
and no grammar, 'that's me! And I suppose I'll
have to go away and be miserable for the rest of
my life.'

'Go away!' cried Miriam, with a sudden break
in her voice. 'Go away—where?'

'To India,' answered Harry, looking hard at
her.

She turned and looked at him with eyes from
which all youth and hope and reserve had suddenly
vanished. Some men, to their detriment and the
misery of others, have a certain facility for love-
making.

'Miriam,' cried Harry exultingly, 'I believe you
care.'

But the girl recovered herself at once.

'Then you are conceited as well as thoughtless
and inconsiderate,' she replied with spirit. 'What
will father say to your going to India? It will be a
great grief to him.'

'Then he shouldn't shut his door on me. Be-

sides, there is no choice. This country is too hot
for me now.'

Miriam turned away—possibly to conceal her
face, and something that he might have read there.
She stood looking out of the window, having apparently forgotten that her companion deserved to be
turned out of the room and forbidden the house.

' How long will it be ? ' she asked.

' Oh, only a few years,' he replied with that
hopefulness which contributed largely to his
troubles. ' I mean to work confoundedly hard and
make a great name. It is easily done in India,
Mim.'

' I fear it will not be easy for you to do that anywhere,' she said.

' Then you don't care ! ' cried Harry with the
stupendous ignorance of his years. He did not
suspect that the most wonderful and incomprehensible part of a woman's love is its keen perception
of the faults of its object. ' I say, Miriam, if I go
away and do well in India, if I work hard and get
promotion, will you try and care for me a little bit?
I'm not such a hopeless chap as you think.'

' I never said you were,' said Miriam in little
more than a whisper, with a queer little tender smile
which he could not see.

' No—but you think it. And you are right in

part. I am an idle, good-for-nothing fool. I know
it. It is no use your shaking your head. But I'll
try and do better in future—by God, I will. I'll
do anything you tell me, Miriam, if only you will
try and care a bit. Mim, you're crying. Why are
you crying, dear?'

He came close to her, but somehow his impetuous love was held in check by this new womanhood
of Miriam's.

'Is it because I have to go to India?' he asked.

She nodded within her pretty old-world curls.

'Then you do care—a little bit?' he said, following up the advantage.

'A little,' she answered, with a queer laugh which
he never forgot, and of which he did not know the
meaning until his hair was almost white.

'Then,' he cried, 'you've given me something to
work for. And you will see how steady I shall be.
As soon as I have made a name I'll come home and
we'll get married, and I'll never go to India again—
and, Mim, we'll be rich because I shall save up
all the time I'm in India. I'll save up for your
sake.'

'I do not want you to save up,' she answered
with that faint tone of maternal care which is never
wanting in a woman's love. 'But you must take
care of yourself.'

'I'll do that sharp enough—no more duels, I have had enough of them.'

'No,' she said with a sudden gravity, 'no more duels. And now, Harry, you must go. If father wakes up and hears you are in the house, he will be terribly angry, and that will make him ill again. I must not tell him that you have been here, though I hate concealment. But the doctor said your name was not to be mentioned. Go—please, Harry —and very quietly.'

And Harry was in that blissful state that he was ready to do anything to please her, even that which was hardest at the moment, to go away from her.

'Harry,' she said in a grave voice again, and he paused on the threshold.

'People say that duels are always about cards or —or a woman. Which was yours?'

'A woman,' answered Harry with his quick smile.

But Miriam was looking away from him gravely and sadly.

'Whom did you fight for, Harry?'

'For you.'

He stood with his hand almost on the handle of the door, looking at her.

'He mentioned your name disrespectfully at

table,' he explained, ' so I taught him better manners.'

Miriam drew a long breath, but she did not move.

' And you care,' said Harry, summing up, ' and you will wait?'

' I will wait all my life, if need be,' she answered.

CHAPTER VIII.

1854.

MR. GRESHAM, possessing that first commercial requisite—a rapid mind—signified his recovery by sending Miriam to Cheltenham, where his only sister lived a peaceful evening of life, before Harry could see her again.

When Harry heard the news he swore very lustily, with an eloquence acquired in the army, and gave up all idea of effecting a reconciliation with his guardian before sailing for India. It is possible that had the culprit followed up his letter by a visit to the office in Eastcheap he might have made his peace with the man who had been as a father to him. But he made no such effort. Indeed, he harboured considerable resentment against Mr. Gresham, to whom he unreasonably assigned some share of the blame attaching to fate for the mismanagement of a promising career.

Such monetary transactions as were necessary he effected through the army agents instrumental in bringing about the exchange into an Indian regi-

ment. And with a high head Harry Wylam left
England for the land of his birth in the late
autumn of 1853. For the second time in his life he
rounded the Cape of Good Hope, and before his
vessel took on board her Hooghly pilot at the Sand-
heads, far away at home in England Mr. Gresham was
standing on the steps of the Royal Exchange listening to the voice of the Sergeant-at-Arms, who read
aloud to all whom it might concern the declaration
of war against Russia.

The pilot brought letters on board, and among
them one for Harry—full of affection and fatherly
warmth—signed Phillip Lamond. This missive set
forth the fact that the room he had occupied in the
bungalow overlooking the Hooghly was prepared
for Harry's reception, that a warm welcome awaited
him at the hands of his father's oldest friend, and
that Maria, who had always considered him her
brother, from the fact that she had succeeded to
the cradle he had left behind him, was most anxious
to make his acquaintance.

The vessel anchored that night in Diamond Harbour, and at midday following moved into her berth
amid the shipping at Calcutta. Almost immediately she was boarded by the friends and relations
of the passengers, and among them Harry remarked
a grey-haired man, with easy-going side-whiskers

and a pleasant smile, who came forward holding out a slim brown hand.

'Harry, my boy, should have known you anywhere. I'm Phillip Lamond,' he said, with his head slightly on one side.

Since last we met Mr. Lamond the years had been busy with his hair and whiskers, but they had left his form slim and youthful still. He was dressed in the thinnest of tweeds, for the cold season was upon Calcutta, and some there were carrying overcoats. In Calcutta they still keep up the solemn farce of feeling cold in the cool season, when an ordinary Englishman must needs perspire.

' You've grown into a fine big chap,' said Lamond in his easy way, looking up with keen eyes and a guileless smile. ' Poor old Wylam would have been proud of you if he could have lived to see you. Got your traps ready? I've a boat waiting alongside. Let us get away from all these d----d swells.'

And indeed the well-dressed company seemed to take no notice of Phillip Lamond, who crept in and out between their elbows with an air which in any other might have signified abashment.

' First of all,' said Lamond, when they were seated in the boat, ' have you heard the news?'

' No,' answered Harry, with his nose in the air inhaling that subtle scent that hangs over all India.

'Why, we've declared war against Russia, and old Palmerston's in power again. We're going to join with France (for the Germans have backed out) and stand by Turkey. And, by Heaven, we'll give the Russians a d——d good licking. But it's a ticklish time out here. The coloured gentleman is not content with English rule, and it's as likely as not that he'll take the opportunity of letting us know it. Oh, you needn't mind the boatmen; they don't understand a word of English.'

'Seems to me,' said Harry, 'that people are much too careless about talking before the natives. How do you know they don't understand English?'

'My good boy, I don't know. Have a cigar— do. We live on a volcano. You'll soon get accustomed to it! But why are you looking so grave?'

'I was thinking,' answered Harry, strangely at ease with this new-found friend. For there is no man so companionable as he who has something to gain from your companionship.

'What about?' inquired Lamond as he lighted a cheroot.

'I was thinking,' answered Harry, 'that my old regiment was one of the first on the list for active service, and I have missed another chance.'

Thus they chatted as the boat glided down the

swift river, steered rather than propelled by the
quaint round-ended oars. And Harry felt wonder-
fully at home with this man, which feeling he set
down naturally enough to the fact that they had
once been as father and son.

Phillip Lamond's foes—and which of us is without
them?—said that behind his gentle demeanour
there lurked a subtle danger. They averred that,
with that pleasant smile, he would rob the widow
and steal from the orphan—but they had no proof
of it. No man could say for certain that this was
a scoundrel, though many thought it. Some had
even given voice to their surmise in his presence
and to his face—only to be met by the weary,
tolerant, easy-going smile. No one had ever seen
Phillip Lamond roused. In difficulty, in need, in
danger—baffled, beaten, and in the presence of
that most intangible obstacle, the social cold-
shoulder, he was always at his ease—always indifferent and smiling. To him, success and failure
seemed alike of small importance. And it is to be
presumed that of the latter he had come by a full
share. For after twenty years he still lived in the
little bungalow in Goojera Reach, which he had
bought from the Hooghly pilot before Harry was
born. He still dressed with a certain negligent
ease and style, which betokened either a careless-

ness to the result produced or an inability to pay
for better tailoring.

He was still a man commanding a certain popu-
larity when present, and leaving no blank when he
went elsewhere. It was only after Lamond had left
the room that people remembered their dislike of
him.

During those twenty years the social world of
Calcutta had varied with the seasons. For these
were days of quick fortunes, rapid promotions, and
sudden deaths. Life in India had not yet been
reduced to a science. Ice and punkah were not yet
fully comprehended of the people, and the European population passed through quicker changes
than it does to-day.

Many of Lamond's contemporaries had made fortunes and had gone home—others, having developed liver complaints, had departed upon a longer
journey. But Lamond stayed on for ever. Neither
a fortune nor a disease seemed to be his fate. He
did not rise, he did not sink—he merely floated,
waterlogged, a little below the surface of Calcutta life.

'You know,' he said pleasantly, as the boat
swung round to the landing-stage, ' I am a bit of a
fatalist. I have learnt it, I suppose, in this country. I always knew you would come back to us,
Harry.'

And Harry looked curiously at the little bungalow where he had lived as an infant.

At this moment the ripple of music floated
through the afternoon air towards them, and presently the sound of a voice—full, rich, pure, and
innocent—raised in a song, broke the stillness that
ever reigns upon a river.

The two men stopped—Harry, with a muttered
exclamation of surprise and delight, for, like all
impetuous people, he was very liable to the influence of music; Lamond, with a queer smile. They
waited till the song was finished, one of those
frankly sentimental songs which our mothers sang
before the mawkish nonsensical ruled our ballads.

'That is my little girl,' said Lamond, with his
head a little inclined to the left; 'she sings best
when she thinks she is alone.'

They went nearer to the bungalow, of which the
green shutters were half closed upon the open windows to keep out the glare and heat of the afternoon.

'Maria,' cried Lamond. 'My dear——'

The curtain was drawn aside, and in the open
doorway, a picture of youth, of innocent surprise
and perhaps a little shame, as would befit a maiden
caught singing to herself, stood Maria Lamond.
Her surprise was all the more remarkable in face of

the small fact that the boatmen had been singing
as they approached, so that Maria must have been
very deeply absorbed in her maiden meditations to
be astonished at the presence of the two gentlemen.

She came forward with her left hand raised to her
hair, for the afternoon breeze was fresh, and she
had a pretty waist. Either reason or both, according to the reader's fancy.

'This is Harry, my dear,' said Philip Lamond,
with that ease of manner which was a good imitation of good breeding. 'When you were a baby at
home in England, Harry was a baby out here.'

Maria blushed very prettily, and held out her
hand, which Harry took eagerly enough. He was
surprised to find Maria so old, for she was almost
his age. He had vaguely presumed that his father's
friend had never married, and indeed the bungalow
had always been a bachelor establishment until
Maria came from England with her bright dark
eyes, her white skin, her assurance of manner, to
take charge of her father's house.

'I seem to have known you, Harry,' she said,
with a piquant pause before the name, 'all my life.'

Harry laughed, and thought her very pretty,
which no doubt was visible in the glance of his
eyes. He could not claim the same familiarity, for
he had until a few hours earlier been ignorant of

her existence. But he found, nevertheless, this welcome very pleasant.

'And now, my dear,' said Lamond, casting himself down on a long chair, ' I think you had better give us some tea—unless Harry here would like something stronger.'

The tea was set out on a little table, and already the quiet-footed native servant was coming forward with the spirit-lamp and kettle.

'Would Harry like something stronger?' asked Maria, with a glance which would have made teetotallers of most of us.

'Not I,' answered Harry, ready to vow that any cup from such a Hebe would be nectar.

Lamond had given some orders to the servants, who lowered the sun-blinds and sprinkled water on the floor of the verandah, throwing some also on the chunam pillars, where it trickled to the ground and, slowly drying, cooled the air.

Harry listened to the orders which were given in Hindustanee, and understood no word of it.

'And yet you learnt to speak it before you babbled English,' said the Anglo-Indian, when Harry had confessed his forgetfulness.

'And how did you leave Mr. Gresham?' he went on in his pleasant way.

'Oh—he was not very well,' answered Harry

with hesitation; and from behind the bright tea-things a pair of eyes as bright flashed a glance of curiosity.

'Ah!' observed Phillip Lamond with a resigned sigh, 'he is not so young as he was, you see. We are all getting on that way.'

'Please do not talk like that,' broke in Maria with a vivacious shudder. 'You are not going to be allowed to grow old for years and years.'

At which Mr. Lamond laughed affectionately—indeed, the love between father and daughter was very pretty and innocent—and what more natural?

'How old is he?' asked Lamond presently, with that air of indifference which characterized him at times.

'He is getting on for sixty, I believe.'

'Please do not let us talk about age,' broke in the artless representative of youth again; 'I am sure Harry will want cheering up instead of depressing, after leaving home and all his friends.'

She handed him a cup of tea with a little smile, almost, one could have said, of sisterly affection.

'What!' exclaimed Mr. Lamond, 'a soldier depressed at going out to seek his fortune, with all the world before him! Besides—' turning to Harry —'this country is, after all, his home. What has he left in England?'

'Perhaps he has left his heart there,' suggested Miss Lamond with a roguish smile which afforded Harry a gleam of pearly white teeth. And Harry blushed.

'And if he has,' said Lamond in a conclusive way —as if he had some instinct of good feeling of which his daughter was deprived—'and if he has, I have no doubt it is in good keeping. Come, Harry.'

He rose and passed his slim hand across his forehead with a characteristic little gesture of weariness.

'Come in, and I will show you your quarters. I dare say you are tired and want to settle down. We must find you a servant.'

Harry rose and prepared to follow him.

'And remember,' said Lamond, as they passed in by the open window, 'that these rooms will always be at your service so long as you are in Calcutta.'

They went in. The lace curtain dropped behind them, leaving Maria alone on the verandah, with the faintest suspicion of a frown on her brow.

CHAPTER IX.

THE GOOD ANGEL.

'My dear Tom—Fred Marqueray will tell us when he comes.' The lady who propounded this antici- pation was a person of some importance. She was a grey-haired lady of comfortable presence— a pleasant, sweet, wholesome woman of the world, who knew what life was, and had come through it with a pure heart. A great lady this, of long lineage, with a title of her own of which she was less proud than of that which her husband had given her.

Sir Thomas Leaguer, K.C.B. and other things, crossed his dapper legs one over the other, and smiled grimly beneath his shaggy eyebrows. Sir Thomas was not a large man, but upright and square, with the keenest glance in the world. A small brown face, fierce eyebrows, and a pair of glittering blue eyes—a soldier—the son of many soldiers; such was the physical presence of Colonel

Sir Thomas Leaguer. And his moral presence was uprightness, an unflinching courage, a deep insight, and a most perfect comprehension of discipline.

This was Harry Wylam's new Colonel—a man of the quality that has brought a certain small island of the north to the front rank of the nations.

'Yes,' he said, with a movement of the moustache, which the lady knew to indicate a smile. 'Marqueray will know.'

He glanced at the clock. It was five minutes to six.

'At three minutes to—— he will arrive,' said Lady Leaguer, who had seen the glance. The Colonel gave a little grunt, and turned to the open window of the drawing-room in which they sat. They were dressed for dinner, which meal was to be served at six o'clock.

At four minutes to six the sound of wheels made the lady look up with a little smile, at which the Colonel nodded in his thoughtful way.

A smart buggy flashed past the window; a minute later the door opened, and at three minutes to six Fred Marqueray came into the room without haste.

Marqueray, junior captain in the regiment, was a man of twenty-eight, who looked older. His eyes were without expression. To be more correct, they were eyes with one permanent expression. The face was

brown, and sphinxlike in its implacable repose—a
hard nut for physiognomists to crack. The permanent expression of the eyes was that of quiet
observation; of observations made from the summit of an impregnable height, for the face beneath
betrayed nothing.

He shook hands in silence. When he held the
great lady's fingers, he gave a little bow. It was
obvious that these were old friends.

'Before you came,' said the lady. 'I was telling
the Colonel that you would be sure to know something of the new subaltern.'

She spoke as she passed into the dining-room on
his arm, the Colonel following alone. She glanced
at her companion's face, and had hardly to raise her
eyes to do so, for she was tall, and of a queenly
carriage.

'What little I know,' replied Marqueray, ' is now,
as ever, at your service.'

And the Colonel laughed suddenly.

'A very deep well,' commented her ladyship as
she arranged the folds of her skirt, ' with truth at
the bottom, of a certainty, but it never comes to
the top unless it be hauled up by curiosity.'

The remark called for no reply.

'If there is a man in the Indian Army who can
keep his own counsel that man is Frederic Marque-

ray,' the Colonel, himself occupying an unique position in that force, had once said. European and
Native soldiers had fallen into the habit of speaking
of this man as of one destined to greatness—they
knew not why. In the strange lull that had fallen
over India at this time men were fearful of their
neighbours—looking askance at such as held their
tongues, distrusting those who chattered.

'Have you seen him?' asked the Colonel, without
looking up.

'Yes, I saw him on board his ship in the river. I
went to meet him as you suggested. There were a
number of people, and before I had an opportunity
of introducing myself he hurried off with Mr.
Phillip Lamond.'

'The man with the daughter,' said Lady Leaguer.

'Yes,' answered Marqueray, looking at her with
expressionless eyes. 'The man with the daughter.'

'Ah! I have no doubt you admire her as much
as the rest of them.'

'I am her slave,' returned Marqueray, gravely.

'I am sorry Mr. Phillip Lamond has got hold of
Wylam,' said the Colonel, grimly sipping his iced
champagne.

'And yet you know nothing against him,' put in
Lady Leaguer.

The Colonel shrugged his shoulders. His wife looked

at him with her smiling eyes. Then she turned to
Marqueray, who shrugged his shoulders in imitation
of the chief.

'There seems to be some magic in the name of
Lamond,' said her ladyship, lightly setting the subject aside, 'I have noticed that it usually reduces
the men in the room to silence. But tell me something of Mr. Wylam's appearance. I shall be
obliged if you will cast his horoscope.'

Marqueray looked up with his slow grave smile.

'He is tall,' he answered, 'and fair, blue eyes
and wavy hair; the young man in the book who
captivates the hearts of the fair and goes generally
to the dogs.'

'In books,' put in her ladyship, who knew that
world which is not of books but of daily life.

'He has the grand air,' went on Marqueray, who
himself possessed the grander air, which, borrow-
ing nothing from swagger, hovers round the man of
brains who has a purpose in life. 'He carries his
head so high that he will never know what is
beneath his feet. We shall all like him, and we
shall probably have trouble with him.'

The lady classified each item with a little nod of
her head. 'Did he see you?' she asked.

'No,' answered Marqueray, with a smile. He

was as different from Harry as one man could be
from another. Wherever Harry Wylam went he
was seen and heard; his presence was never overlooked. Fred Marqueray, on the contrary, seemed
to move through the world on smooth running
wheels. He never pushed his way in as did Harry,
with a laugh and a word for everybody, seen of
everybody, known of everybody. He never called
the public attention to himself by a display of
that superabundant vitality which marked Harry's
presence.

'Did Mr. Phillip Lamond see you?' asked the
Colonel, in the curt way which had earned for him
the reputation of the sternest commander in the
Bengal Army.

'I imagine so, because he never looked at me.'

There was a little pause, only broken by the sigh
of the swinging punkah.

'I am afraid,' said the Colonel, 'that Wylam is
not the sort of man we want in India '—he paused,
glancing up and noting that the servants had
momentarily left the room—' just now.'

Across the table the eyes of the two men met for
an instant, and it would be hard to say whether the
lady intercepted the glance or not.

'He will, I imagine,' said Marqueray, gravely
fingering some crumbs, ' be a—social acquisition.

He seems prepared to like everybody, and we all like being liked.'

' Question is,' said the Colonel, grimly, ' whether he will get on in this country.'

' I think not,' said Marqueray, after a pause, in his gentle way. ' He has money, and I should imagine that he is possessed of a very keen taste for enjoyment; bad things in India.'

' Well,' said Lady Leaguer, cheerfully, ' we must all combine to make a stand against the temptations that will beset the young man's footsteps. We shall count on you, Fred—you know there is nothing the Colonel dislikes so much as that one of his subalterns should journey towards——'

' The dogs,' supplemented her husband.

And her ladyship nodded.

Presently she looked across the table towards her guest.

' It seems to me,' she said, ' that you know a good deal of Mr. Wylam; too much to have been acquired in a passing glimpse as he climbed down a ship's side.'

' Yes,' admitted Marqueray, ' I have heard about him from home.'

' Nothing to his good, I'll warrant,' said the Colonel.

Marqueray nodded.

'That is why I have forgotten it,' he said, quietly.

Then they fell to talking of home affairs, as exiles love to do, and for a time Harry Wylam and his prospects were laid aside. The Colonel had consented to the exchange, which brought young Wylam into his regiment, chiefly because the name was one of pleasant associations. Harry Wylam's father and this grizzled warrior had been young men together in the early days of annexation, when the Company was growing so rapidly that the whole world seemed to stand watching in surprise.

He had, of course, heard of Harry's quarrel and the subsequent duel with Captain Montague, and had set down the whole affair to a fiery nature which could easily have been inherited. In the days when Colonel Leaguer had known Harry's father duelling was not rare in England, and was common enough in India. During the Colonel's career the practice of thus summarily settling the quarrels which must arise where youth and ambition meet had gradually died out, and with it the decadence of the English officer in India had set in. It is not, of course, to be concluded that the one was the natural consequence of the other, although any practice tending to lower the manhood of Europeans in India cannot be too strictly avoided.

Sir Thomas Leaguer belonged to the old school
of Anglo-Indian, in so much as he held to the doc-
trine that the line of racial demarcation can hardly
be drawn too firmly. But he belonged to the newer
and better school now ruling our Eastern Empire,
in that he deemed that line to be a simple practical
fact, capable of demonstration every time the Asiatic
and the European might come into competition.
It seemed certain that climate and the hundred
subtle influences of daily example had tended to de-
generate men of our race living in India at the time
of Harry Wylam's return to that country, and it is
equally sure that leaders of such material as Colonel
Sir Thomas Leaguer were alive to this degeneration.

The Colonel thought no worse of Harry because
he had revived a dying custom, and that so effectually. In fact, the scrape evinced the presence in
the young soldier of that manliness and energy
which appeared to be dormant in the Anglo-Indian
officers at this period. That the manliness and
energy were to wake up later and leave such a mark
on the Asiatic race as will never be wiped out through
all time we know now, but Colonel Leaguer never
suspected it at this time.

The trio around the Colonel's table had plenty of
news from home to discuss without further dwelling
upon the smaller events of Calcutta life.

Each mail was heavy with news from Europe, where, indeed, the war-cloud was black enough. Lady Leaguer—herself a soldier's daughter—had long learnt to take the change and chance of military life with that unquestioning obedience to discipline which is as good a stimulant as fatalism, and infinitely better suited to the mind of educated men.

England had been at peace for forty years. She had, of course, been engaged in those small colonial wars against savage or semi-barbarous neighbours—the small frontier campaigns—which form such an excellent military school, and keep alive that taste for battle by which we have won our position in the world. But a great war against European troops had seemed at this time almost a thing of the past. Some, indeed, deemed such warfare at an end for ever.

And suddenly there arose a cloud in the East, on the border of that northern empire with which the world has yet to reckon. Russia had grown within the passage of a few generations from a small inland state to a vast empire, with such outlets to the sea as will when her railways are developed raise her to commercial supremacy in the world.

The work of one of the greatest women this planet has ever known—Catherine the Second—had borne

fuller harvest than her wildest dream could have
foreseen. Russia was beginning to awake and
stretch herself. She reached out one hand towards
Constantinople, and lo! the British Lion, asleep
these forty years, must needs get up and roar.

There are times when the world seems strangely
disturbed—when nations are the playthings of Fate,
and man is but grass that is cut down in the morning. Such a time as this had dawned with the year
1854, when Harry Wylam, who had breathed a
prayer over his virgin sword that England might
have many wars, set sail for India.

Strange passions—national passions, which com-
pare with the rage of a man as a thunderstorm
compares to a sneeze—were bestirring themselves
in the hearts of people hitherto peaceful. Nations
were about to arise, impelled by some command
that came they knew not whence, to go down to
the fighting places of the universe, and there to
challenge Fortune.

In England the war was popular. We are shopkeepers—my masters. Let us admit that. But at
times we have a way of laying aside our apron and
our bill-books, our yard-measure and our scales.
We put up the shutters and lock the door—and then
there is usually the devil to pay.

In eighteen hundred and fifty-four such a time as

this came to our country, and far away in Calcutta
— within a stone's throw of that river which has
witnessed the greatest disaster our race has known
two men sniffed the battle wind and talked
together of those things which they saw upon the
horizon.

CHAPTER X.

ON THE SLOPE.

' HOLLOA! Here's old Marks!'

And Master Harry Wylam steadied himself with an effort in front of the long-chair in the verandah of the old Calcutta Field Club.

The rest of the party, engaged as they had been at cards, came to the open window and looked at Marqueray—some of them held long glasses in their hands, and the clink of ice against the rim of these told a tale at every moment. It was nearly midnight. Other revellers still held their cards between unsteady fingers. They had come out for a breath of air, and in the verandah Harry—excited, a little flustered by heavy play, a little heated by many potations—found his friend Marqueray.

Marqueray, it would appear, had been sitting there some time alone—with his thoughts and a cigar. Coming out by another window, he had apparently sat down to watch the fireflies flit in and out among the heavy branches of the Dalmatian cotton trees. The great compound of the Field Club was deserted and still. Below the verandah—at the corner of the kennels—that grave mendicant, the adjutant bird, stood grimly sleeping off the effects of his last heavy meal. For he was a pet at the club, and stood expectant below the windows all day long. The furtive shuffle of a prowling jackal, paying his nocturnal visit to the kitchen refuse-heap, had been the only sound from without, while through the open windows the alternate hush and clamour of voices, which is the unmistakable token of high play, came muffled from the card-room.

'Old Marks, sitting out here with the punkah-wallah,' said Harry, with a laugh. 'You're the d———dest, rummest old fish that ever I've come across! Why don't you come in and have a go at the cards. Believe you've been asleep—*know* the punkah-wallah has, d——-n him.'

He turned to the silent native servant in his white clothes and red-leather belt—a shadowy form crouching against the wall, pulling mechanically at the punkah-rope with one hand—the rest of him was, indeed, asleep. The right arm was a machine.

'Do you hear, you black scum of the earth? You've been asleep. Wake up!'

He poured half a tumbler of iced brandy and soda over him, and Marqueray at the same moment reached out his left foot and sent the glass spinning to the far end of the verandah.

' Don't make an ass of yourself, Wylam,' he said quietly—and in the same breath said something in Hindustance to the servant, who had leapt with flashing eyes to his feet.

There was something in the man's attitude that made Harry turn half threateningly, and glance at him over his shoulder.

' Eh?' he said inquiringly. ' What is the man saying?'

' Nothing,' answered Marqueray, speaking quickly to the servant in Hindustance, which Harry knew very imperfectly, although two years had elapsed since his arrival in India. ' The poor devil was half asleep.'

Harry was still laughing at his own excellent practical joke, and his companions grouped in the window were ready enough to join in his merriment. They had been winning his money.

' He's only a nigger—d——n it,' said Harry, swaggering towards the card-room, while the servant with a little shiver resumed his place at the punkah-cord.

' That's all! ' admitted Marqueray, glancing side-ways at the man under cover of a cloud of smoke. The moon was nearly full—a glorious yellow, Indian moon. It was almost as light as an English winter day when the clouds are low.

Harry went back into the room.

'The best of old Marqueray is,' he said as he resumed his seat, 'that he never preaches. He was in a devilish rage with me then—quite suddenly —I don't know why. Did the punkah-wallah a lot of good I should think—freshened him up—ha! ha! Poor devil, it must have startled him though.'

Harry paused—a heap of rupees lay on the table in front of him. He took up one at random— pushed back his chair, rose and went to the window. 'Here, gye hye, catch!' he shouted, and threw the coin to the man who sat crouching against the wall.

Marqueray seemed to have gone to sleep again. The servant looked towards him with gleaming eyes. The coin had rattled on the stone floor. It lay close to the mat on which the punkah-wallah sat. The man stretched out his slim, nervous hand.

Marqueray was apparently asleep, and the coin whizzed away into the long grass followed by a curse.

Harry Wylam had been two years in India, and in that time had naturally drifted into a 'set' of which social division our Eastern Empire is the

8

natural home. Harry's set was at this moment in
the card-room of the old Field Club, and Fred Marqueray, a member of the club, did not belong to it.

Harry began his sojourn in Calcutta by daily
reviling what he was pleased to call his luck, to
which vague influence he attributed the loss of such
opportunities of promotion as were provided by the
Crimean War. At the beginning also he wrote long
letters home to his guardian and longer effusions to
Miriam, who treasured them up as women do. In
his letters to Miriam he boldly made confession of
his love in such halting phrase as he had at his command, and Mr. Gresham, with a fine old-fashioned
sense of honour and fair-play, never asked his daughter to show him these epistles.

In reply Mr. Gresham wrote sturdy commercial
communications, consisting largely of an enumera-
tion of dates of despatch and receipt of former correspondence, a little news, a little advice; and a
great affection peeping out between the lines.
Miriam penned stiff little letters, giving in a running calligraphy all the small news of St. Helen's
Place, an account of the Christmas decoration of
St. Helen's Church, a nervous synopsis of the warlike news from Russia, and never a word of love.
That which she had to say on the subject she doubtless deemed too sacred to commit to a letter which

might fall into the wrong hands in the hazards of a
long voyage. Or perhaps she had no words to tell
him of that which was within her faithful heart.
It is not always the best love that expresses itself
in the choicest language.

After a few months, however, Harry found himself more absorbed in his immediate environments,
and less interested in such far-off matters as were
treated of in his letters from home. Never a good
correspondent, he began to find it difficult to make
time to write. He played polo, attended race
meetings, was a great favourite in social circles, and
finally his Colonel forced him to attend to his military duties.

'Don't know how the devil it is,' he was wont
to say, ' but all the hard work seems to come my
way.'

And Marqueray at such time would smile his
grave smile, and reply that it was very good for
Harry.

For both the Colonel and Harry's captain had
tamed a young horse in their time, and knew the
beneficial effect of hard work upon a fiery spirit.

The military duties, however, came last, and it
was not to these that Harry could attribute his lack
of time for letter-writing.

Now, at the end of two years, each mail con-

tinued to bring him a letter from one or the other
of his faithful correspondents in St. Helen's Place,
while three out of four homeward despatches left for
London without a scratch from Harry's pen. He
was quite absorbed in the self-indulgent, excite-
ment-seeking life of a subaltern whose duties
towards the regiment were performed by his native
double—the Jemmadar. Each captain had his
native *remplaçant* the Soubahdar—even the European Colonel possessed a double in the shape of the
Soubahdar Major. The native regiments, officered
by Europeans, were complete without their white
chiefs—ready for action, officered, disciplined.

It was assuredly no wonder that such men as
Frederic Marqueray and Colonel Leaguer should
go about their business at this time with grave faces.

'If he is going to the devil,' Marqueray had said
of Harry to the Colonel, 'he must go. We hav'n't
time to stop him.'

And, indeed, they had other matters to attend
to. Marqueray was not always at home. He had
of late developed a taste for sport, and was for ever
vanishing from the busy social life of the city to
some forest fastness in search of big game. After
he came back he seemed always to have much to
tell the Colonel, for these two remained closeted
together for hours.

From such an expedition as this Marqueray had returned this evening, graver than ever. His silent ways, his long, quiet face contributed so little to the merriment of others that he was never missed from club or mess-room when the misanthropic humour happened to be upon him. He had come straight from the Colonel's house to the Field Club, and took, as we have seen, his post unobserved and unobtrusive, on the verandah without the room where Harry was playing away the remnant of a handsome fortune.

The punkah-wallah tugged mechanically at his rope, his deep inscrutable eyes half-closed in a reverie such as only Orientals know. It seemed a part of the glowing, motionless Indian night.

A few yards away Marqueray, in a reverie almost as deep, pondered on the stillness that was over India. Once he turned and looked steadily through the darkness at the white figure crouching against the wall. But he did not speak. He knew, better perhaps than any man in Calcutta, the depth, the utter impenetrability of Oriental silence. Few Europeans knew so much of Brahmin and Moham-medan as Fred Marqueray; few had studied the thousand intricacies of caste and religion; few had attained to such a knowledge of the native charac-ter. He spoke their tongues as one of themselves

—he had passed among them a thousand times as
one of them. He was recalled to himself by a light
footstep, and looked up.

Phillip Lamond stood before him. He had at last
through Harry's influence, been elected to the club.

'Harry Wylam here?' he asked shortly.

'Yes,' answered Marqueray, with a jerk of the
head towards the open window. 'In there.'

'Playing?'

'Yes.'

Phillip Lamond made a step towards the window
from where the clink of silver came to their ears
and stopped.

'He's ruining himself,' he said to Marqueray.
'Do you know that?'

'Yes.'

Marqueray looked up. Lamond looked down.
The shifty eyes, with their indifferent smile, met
the persistent gaze of quiet observation.

'I'll tell you what it is, Captain Marqueray,' said
Lamond with unusual emphasis, 'we must put a
stop to it somehow. That fellow is on the high
road to ruin—going to the devil at a pace only attained in this country. I know it, because I have had
the management of his affairs since he was a baby.'

'Indeed,' said Marqueray indifferently.

'Yes.' Lamond paused with a vague smile, 'and
a very fair fortune he possessed when he landed in

this city two years ago. Got a bit of property up
Delhi way. I remitted the proceeds home to his
guardian—shrewd old business man—not quite a
gentleman, you know, but honest.'

' Same thing,' said Marqueray.

' Yes—ha, ha! of course. Well, sir, Harry
Wylam's squandered all his savings, and now it is a
question of selling some of the property. It's slipping through his fingers. Listen, you can hear it.'

And, indeed, in the silence of the night they
could hear the silver pieces changing hands.

' Well,' said Lamond, ' I'm off home—early man
myself. I wish you would help though, Marqueray. He's a bit of a handful, Master Harry, for an
old chap. Well, will you?'

' Yes,' answered Marqueray, ' I will.'

' Thanks. Just look after him a bit, you know.'

' Yes. Good night.'

Lamond went down the narrow steps, across the
moonlit grass, and disappeared in the shadow of
the trees.

' What's your game, I wonder?' said Marqueray,
rising and stretching himself. He stood for a
moment, a lean, strong figure in a white mess uniform, and then sauntered into the card-room.

' Wylam,' he said, ' I want to walk home with
you. Nearly finished?'

'Yes,' cried Harry, with an oath as he threw
down his cards. 'I've had enough of this. Luck
is dead against me.'

He rose, paid his losses, and followed Marqueray
out of the room.

'Are you going to marry Lamond's daughter?'
asked Marqueray when they were talking down the
avenue of cotton-trees.

'No,' answered Harry with a gay laugh. 'Are
you?'

'No, thank you,' said Marqueray quietly. 'But
if you do not mean to marry her, I should be rather
careful. She is devilish pretty.'

Harry laughed—the somewhat fatuous laugh of a
youthful man of the world.

'Oh, I m all right. You need not be anxious
about me, you straight-laced old badger. There is
nobody out here likely to interfere with my peace
of mind.'

'Oh!' muttered Marqueray.

'No,' went on Harry, who was excited and loqua-
cious; 'I left all that behind me in England. Engaged, you know.'

'Ah!'

'Oh, yes; have been all along. But I kept it
dark—devilish dark.'

'Devilish!' admitted Marqueray, dryly. 'And

the card-playing, and the betting, and the playing ducks and drakes with your money—is all that approved of at home?'

Harry walked along in silence for some time. Then suddenly he stopped.

'You're right, old chap!' he exclaimed penitently. 'By Jove, I'm a blackguard! I'll never touch a card again, by Jove I won't! I mean——'

'I shouldn't, if I were you,' interrupted Marqueray, walking on.

'Well, I've done with play—that's settled,' said Harry. 'And as for Maria—she's all right. She knows, you know. I dine there to-morrow evening. Come in after dinner, and see for yourself.'

'I will. Here we are at your quarters. Good night!'

CHAPTER XI.

COMBINED with that sense of refinement ever imparted to a house by a woman's daily presence, there existed in the atmosphere of Phillip Lamond's bungalow by the Hooghly a certain pleasant sense of Bohemianism. It would be hard to say whether this lingered in the curtains and the furniture in the form of a slight odour of tobacco-smoke, or found its source in a subtle laxity of thought and personal habit enjoyed by the master of the house.

'This is Liberty Hall, you know,' Lamond was wont to say, with his tolerant smile and a shrug of the shoulders, as if to ask who *he* was that he should rail at the weaknesses of his fellow-mortals. 'Liberty Hall. You smoke when and where you like. You drink whatever you can get, and you have merely to ask for anything there is in the house.'

'This is Liberty Hall, you know,' he said to Harry at dessert the following evening. 'Light up whenever you feel inclined—Maria doesn't mind among friends. Do you, my dear?'

And Maria murmured, ' Of course not,' and cast down her eyes, after raising them once to Harry's face in a manner which, in one less naïve and modest, one might almost have suspected of conveying a hint that to the bold and enterprising the privileges of Liberty Hall did not stop at a cigar.

' Not I!' cried Harry, in his jolliest humour; ' it's only when the ladies are not there that I need to smoke.

The repast had been brisk and merry enough; for where Harry was there never lacked laughter and gaiety, and, indeed, Maria had a pretty wit of her own. The viands had been choice, the wine red, and Harry, we may be sure, not afraid to look upon it.

' Fill up, my boy!' Lamond had said half-a-dozen times since the servants had retired. ' It will do you no harm.'

The table was tastefully decorated with flowers, discreetly lighted by shaded candles. The punkah worked smoothly, and there was a gentle breeze from the river which, Maria complained, fluttered one's hair. This was strictly true, as she proved a hundred times with pretty arms upraised and snowy fingers skirmishing over raven curls.

'Then,' she said in reply to Harry's protest, 'I shall be forced to go, because I know papa wants a cigar.'

It was somehow conveyed to Harry that she did not want to go, and at last he yielded—as who would not have done?—to so gentle and kind a desire to make himself at home.

'We must try and persuade him to content himself with a little music and a quiet evening,' said Lamond to his daughter meaningly. 'Dull work, I'm afraid, after the high play we have heard of.'

Maria gave a hopeless little sigh, as if to indicate the fear that no charm or effort of hers could be expected to compete with the fascinations of the gaming table.

'Ah,' said Harry, with a passing gravity, 'I've given up cards. Gave them up last night. Old Marqueray took me in hand. Decent old fellow, Marqueray—you know him, Maria.'

'Yes,' answered Maria demurely, 'I have met him.'

'Well, we walked home together last night, and he persuaded me to turn over a new leaf.'

'Ah, but it will flutter back again,' put in Maria archly, and yet with a grave face and reproving lips.

'Not it!' cried Harry. 'No—I have turned it over in earnest this time.'

' And very glad I am to hear it,' said Lamond.
' Another week or so of such work, and you would
have been a ruined man, I verily believe. No property could stand such a drain upon it——'

' I know—I know,' interrupted Harry. ' Come,
Lamond, don't pull such a long face. I'll go into
the accounts with you some day. In the meantime you've sold, haven't you?'

' Yes—in a bad market. There's a funny feeling
abroad in the country. No one wants to buy
land.'

' Ah,' answered Harry, in his grand, heedless
way, ' more fools they. It is good land.'

But Phillip Lamond was not listening. He had
turned his head to the open window, where the
lights of Garden Reach flickered across the river.

' Thought I heard wheels,' he exclaimed.

At the same moment the door was opened, and
the butler announced, ' Marqueray, sahib.'

'You,' said Lamond, rising and holding out his
hand with an indifferent smile.

' Yes; come to look after Wylam,' answered
Marqueray, with a pleasant laugh, which was not
communicated to his grave observant eyes.

He shook hands with Maria and accorded to her,
as to all women, his stiff little bow. He exchanged
a nod with Harry, and straightway accepted the

chair brought forward by the butler. There was
something soldier-like and straightforward in his
manner of occupying this position without so much
as the usual social untruth.

' We shall have a north-easter to-night,' he said,
calmly. ' There is a cold edge on the wind. Do
you feel them much down here? '

He addressed himself to Lamond, and Maria, as
if to verify his statement, rose and went to the open
window, where Harry presently joined her, engaged
also upon meteorological questions. From the
window it was literally but one step to the verandah; from the verandah to the quiet compound,
bordered by the river, was only another. Marqueray and Lamond were soon left alone.

' Our friend,' said Lamond, in his leisurely way—
half interested in his cigar—' has turned over a new
leaf very quickly. He has just told us that he has
given up play.'

Marqueray nodded.

' Yes '—he pulled out his watch and looked at it
—' twenty hours ago,' he added, without comment.
Phillip Lamond knew very little of Marqueray, and
of that modicum he was afraid. They had met in
the arena of life where men encounter each other
and nod; where they pause and exchange the time
of day, but never know each other's women-folk.

This was the first time that Marqueray had called at the bungalow, although he had met both father and daughter elsewhere.

' I am very glad,' went on Lamond lazily, ignoring the irony, ' that you have succeeded so promptly. I feel more or less responsible for the lad, although I have no authority over him. What are you drinking ? Port ; turn that up and we'll have a fresh bottle. You see, the chap's been going the pace to such an extent during these last two years that he has little or nothing left.'

' He is easily led,' said Marqueray, looking out of the window.

Lamond followed the direction of his glance. Among the shadowy banana trees, between the stems of the palms—a white dress fluttered.

' Yes,' said Lamond, with his usual engaging frankness, ' and to tell you the truth my hands have been rather tied. An old chap like me, with a motherless girl, cannot be too careful. I don't want Maria talked about. What I say is that a girl's name must be kept out of the gossips' mouths at any cost. Suppose I had showed an interest in Harry when he first came over—when he was known to be wealthy—when he seemed to have every chance of a brilliant future ! What would people have said? Why, that I wanted him for Maria.'

Mr. Lamond paused, with his slim brown hand outstretched, his pleasant smile, his engaging innocence of manner. He seemed to lightly draw aside the curtain of his heart, and to say in action if not in words: 'There, my dear Marqueray, you can see right through me!'

'You see,' he went on, 'they do not know what *we* know.'

'And what do *we* know?' inquired Captain Marqueray, calmly.

'Why—about that little girl at home—Miss Gresham.'

'Ah! yes,' replied Marqueray, again looking out of the window towards the mango-grove.

'But now,' went on Maria's father confidentially, 'that the boy is anything but a catch, penniless, and eh—er—not thought very much of in the service, I suppose, I think gossips cannot have much to say.'

'And you are enabled to exercise your parental authority and foresight,' concluded Marqueray, looking at the end of the cigar which he had just lighted.

'Yes,' admitted Lamond rather doubtfully, for it seemed to him that his hearer was slow of comprehension. 'And at the same time I am glad to have an opportunity of thanking you, and Colonel

Leaguer too, as far as that goes, for your kind efforts to keep Harry straight. Believe me, I have been fully aware of your good influence over the boy. At one time I quite hoped that he would develop into a first-class officer, like the Colonel and yourself, but now he seems to have got into the other set—the set that is letting the native service go to the devil.'

Lamond's light grey eyes were watching Marqueray's face.

'India is a very easy country to go to the devil in,' said the soldier pleasantly. 'Wylam is young yet. I dare say he will get over this present phase of Anglo-Indian life. He has the making of a good soldier, but he is lazy, and won't learn the languages.'

The light grey eyes shifted elsewhere.

Marqueray turned again, and looked out of the window in time to see Harry and Maria pass slowly across the face of the river, where the reflections of the stars ran into silver rills. The young people were walking slowly. Harry was bending his head to say something, and across the stillness of the grass there came his jolly laugh.

'You have a very charming daughter,' said Marqueray.

'And you think it rather dangerous,' completed

Lamond, ' allowing her to wander about with our
wild, impecunious young friend yonder.'

' If you don't want more to come of it, certainly.'

' I hope my girl will do better for herself than a
harum-scarum young subaltern of a native regiment,' said Lamond; and, as if acting on the
friendly hint, he went to the window and called the
young people in.

' We want you to sing to us, my dear,' explained
Lamond in his pleasant voice.

And as Maria stepped in between the curtains she
cast a glance of dislike in the direction of the quiet,
grey-haired man who had spoilt this friendly family
party by so untimely a visit.

She led the way to the drawing-room, and there,
with a queer spirit of perversity, set herself the
task of fascinating Frederic Marqueray.

She sang to him and at him. She consulted him
as to the reading of the song, as to the rendering of
certain passages, and regarding the merits of the
composers of the day.

And when Maria Lamond wished to please none
could do so more effectually. Her pretty white
fingers lingered on the tender passages of the accom-
paniment. She swayed a little as she sang. The
music, it was obvious, moved her to the depths of

her heart. One so inexperienced had not yet learnt that such tender ware as a maiden's feelings must be guarded from the eye of the world.

At the beginning it was Harry who turned the pages of her music, but later—no one knew exactly how—the pleasant task fell to Marqueray.

' Are you fond of music?' she asked her new attendant slave between two songs. ' Does Lady Leaguer sing?'

' No, not now,' answered Marqueray, who perhaps knew that when a woman asks two questions at once it is the latter that must be answered.

' You see a great deal of them, do you not?'

' Yes; they are very kind to me.'

He was placing a new song on the music-stand, and, turning, looked down on her with a quiet smile, which somehow had the effect of stopping a flow of questions on the sayings and doings of that world of which Maria was not.

' They have been very kind to Harry also,' she said. ' I suppose Lady Leaguer is a sort of mother to you all?'

' Precisely.'

' He is always raving about her. She seems . . . clever.'

' She is . . . clever.'

Maria looked up quickly. Marqueray was study-

ing the score after the manner of one who, knowing
no music, wishes to make sure of turning over the
page at the right moment.

' Does the scent of these flowers trouble you?'
asked Maria, suddenly changing the subject. She
was referring to a spray of heliotrope, which she
proceeded to remove from the front of her white
dress. The attitude was a pretty one, and the
operation by no means hurried. When at last the
flowers were released she looked up with a quick
side-long glance.

There was nowhere to lay the half-withered blossom. She handed it to him after a little movement
of hesitation, which made the gift the more precious.
She began the prelude. She had, indeed, a musical
touch, and her voice was full and rich.

While she sang Marqueray attached the flower to
the button-hole of his coat. Harry was talking to
Lamond by the open window, and seemed rather
restless. At times he turned and looked towards
the piano.

' You seemed to get on deucedly well with Maria,'
he said rather sullenly, as he drove home in Marqueray's buggy afterwards.

' Deucedly,' answered Marqueray. ' She is not
difficult to get on with.'

Nothing was said of the avowed object of Mar-

queray's visit: namely, to confirm Harry's statement that Maria knew all about Miriam Gresham
at home in England. Indeed, Harry had not very
much to say, and when they reached the sepoy
lines went to his own quarters with a curt good-
night.

CHAPTER XII

A CLOUD.

It is the custom of historians to dwell somewhat dramatically upon the gaieties, the balls, the givings in marriage, and the so-called heedlessness of a city or a country, to be plunged in the next chapter into the misery of war or pestilence or famine—or merely panic.

We do not blame the historian, nor do we grudge him his little stage trick of dramatic contrast. But what does he expect? Is the city to stand still? Would it do for a wine-country to neglect its vineyards, because there may be war in the land before the grapes are picked? Do we reproach the fair white clouds for sailing across the summer sky when the barometer is falling?

If, therefore, it is mentioned that the close of the cool season of 1857 in Calcutta was exceedingly like the close of the same period of 1856 or 1855 we point no moral, neither perhaps do we adorn a tale. We merely state a fact. The race-meetings at Chowringhee were over, the date of the last Bache-

lors' Ball, with which the season always closed, had
arrived. And it happens to be with this ball that
we have to do.

Colonel and Lady Leaguer were there. Frederic
Marqueray's solemn presence was not wanting.
Harry Wylam—the best dancer in Calcutta, the
gayest of the gay, the favourite of men and women
alike—was of course a steward. The Lamonds were
there for the first time. Harry had given Maria
the tickets, and the worldly-wise no doubt suspected
her priceless bouquet of coming from the same
source. Maria's dark eyes flashed a bright welcome or a scornful semi-indifference, according to the
sex of her friend, as she recognised here and there
an acquaintance. Indeed, the change from the one
expression to the other was bewilderingly rapid. If
some fellow-votary at the shrine of Venus possessed
a pretty figure, Maria looked that shapely form up
and down with an imperfectly concealed commisera-
tion. If it happened that the hair of her rival was
fair and soft she noted the dressing of the same
with a pitiful little smile. Whether it happened to
be face or figure, arm or hair, or merely dress, Maria
seemed to discover at one glance the particular
point upon which the possessor prided herself, and
her glance disparaged it.

With regard to the other sex she was marvellously

charitable, overlooking such natural blemishes of face, figure, or intelligence as Nature had bestowed upon them. The youngest subaltern fresh from home, blushing in boyish self-consciousness and an embarrassing inability to keep his hands still, received a firm but kind refusal of a dance with a smile so sweet that he went about for the rest of the evening puffed up with the conviction that he was secretly loved by a grown-up woman. The stoutest and most middle-aged civil servant, provided that he was single, was accorded a ' square,' with a respectful flutter so young and innocent, that he realised once more the fact that a young spark has no chance against a man of the world whenever the latter takes the trouble to compete.

The veriest booby of the Governor's staff found out again that a red-coat ' by gad ' and a pair of spurs carry all before them with a woman.

And all the while she kept half her programme for Harry, and only encroached on that youth's reservation when Frederic Marqueray asked her for a dance.

' I have heard,' she said to him, ' that you dance even better than Harry.'

' Then, Miss Lamond, Sapphira must have told you so,' he answered, with a smile that she did not always understand.

He bowed, returned her engagement-card, and went towards Lady Leaguer, who was talking to Harry.

' I suppose,' that lady was saying to the wildest subaltern in the regiment, ' that you have plenty of friends here. You are sure to——'

' Oh—yes, Lady Leaguer—got a lot of friends.'

' Be sure,' said that lady, slowly fanning herself and looking across the room to where Maria held her little court, ' be sure that they are all you think them.'

Harry laughed re-assuringly, as who would allay all anxiety on that score, and having paid his respects to the Colonel's lady he bowed and withdrew, making room for Frederic Marqueray, who came up at this moment with his usual impassive leisureliness.

' Old Marks,' said Harry in his impulsive way to his next partner, ' goes about the room like a native. Have you noticed it? He has caught their tricks. I believe if you dressed him up in a turban and a blanket no one could tell him from a nigger.'

Frederic Marqueray requested the honour of taking her ladyship down to supper later in the evening, which favour was accorded by the lady at once.

' Any news?' she asked almost immediately, with

a little anxious look about the lips, which she was
in the habit of showing to very few.

They were standing together at the end of the
long room on a daïs raised a few inches above the
dancing floor. Marqueray looked out over the
moving heads of the throng, and did not reply at
once.

' Not yet,' he said at length.

' Where is the Colonel?' asked Lady Leaguer,
with a sharp sigh. She did not look at her companion, but turned her face with a pleasant smile
towards the dancers.

' He will be here presently. Don't be anxious.
If there is a regiment that will stand it is ours.'

' They all say that,' put in the lady forebod-
ingly.

' Yes, and they trust to kindness. We don't, we
trust to fear,' said Marqueray grimly.

The lady raised her fan and turned slowly towards
him. She looked at him with a sort of affection:
for women who love are very tender towards those
who reflect some of the loved one's attributes.

' You and Tom,' she said, ' are the hardest men
in India.'

He turned and met the lady's affectionate glance.
They might have been mother and son.

' There are the others,' he said; ' but we had

better change the subject. It would not do to be overheard.'

Lady Leaguer gave a capable little nod.

'Then tell me,' she said, 'what object Mr. Lamond can have in marrying his daughter to a penniless subaltern like Harry Wylam. Do you know?'

'Not yet,' answered Marqueray, as someone came up and interruped their conversation.

Harry and Maria had in truth disappeared. The room was terribly hot, despite the huge swinging punkahs and the blocks of ice.

'One cannot breathe here,' Maria had said at the end of a waltz. She raised her pretty white shoulders in an exaggerated effort to inhale a breath of air, and looked up at Harry with a face surprisingly cool and composed.

'Deuced hot—let's go out,' ejaculated Harry, fanning her so furiously that her laces fluttered, and she had to set her hair in order.

On the threshold of the long window she paused.

'Ought we?' she asked, in little more than a whisper, pausing with a most engaging hesitation on the brink of an escapade so new and thrilling.

'Yes, come along,' answered her partner, urging her to follow by a movement of his arm, where after all her fingers rested of their own free will. In

the youthful flutter of her perturbation she forgot
no doubt that if she still had misgivings she had
merely to release his sleeve.

The waning moon was lowering over some palm
trees that bordered the large compound of the club
house, where the bachelors gave their last ball of a
memorable season. There is something especially
moving to the human heart—provocative of the
imagination—in the outline of a palm tree against a
moonlit sky. A soft breath, blowing up from the
sea—the shadow of a far-off sea-breeze—rustled
among the small bamboos and stirred the leaves of
the flowering shrubs. The air was scented as only
Indian night-time is, with a thousand competing
odours—each one disturbing in itself. The sound
of the music came softly to those walking on the
parched turf.

Maria cast a quick glance around. She perceived
every point of vantage—like a good general who has
selected his own battle-field.

She drew up her glove. With a little smile she
arranged the flowers at her breast.

' I hope no one saw us come out,' she said.

' Why? Are you engaged for this dance?'

' Yes.'

' Is that why you hope that no one saw us come
out?' asked Harry, who could play this game to

perfection. And, indeed, Maria was marvellously
pretty in her white dress—with a little flush on her
cheeks—her eyes alight with excitement and resolution.

She would not, however, answer him, knowing
that a small thing withheld magnifies its value with
astonishing rapidity. She was looking about, and
at last found a pleasant, secluded seat in the shade
of a clump of jungle grass. Seated here she
returned to the arrangement of the flowers at her
breast. One blossom fell, and Harry immediately
possessed himself of it—unreproved. Indeed, Maria
did not appear to have perceived his impertinence.

' Is that the reason,' he repeated in such a low
voice that he had perforce to go nearer, ' that you
hope we were not seen?'

Maria turned away and looked up at the palms—
leaving, however, her hand not so very far from his.
Her shell-like little ear, moreover, was still at his
disposal.

' Do you not want your next partner to find you?
Is that it?' asked Harry.

' That *may* be it,' she admitted at last, and the
white shoulder, peeping above her frock, swayed—
perhaps one inch—towards him.

Six thousand miles away Miriam, asleep in her
little bed in St. Helen's Place, and dreaming no

doubt of Harry, perhaps turned restlessly at this moment.

In the meantime the Bachelors' Ball was at its height; for those who dance on volcanoes may nevertheless foot it merrily enough while the music lasts.

Colonel Sir Thomas Leaguer had arrived, and the little anxious lines about the kind lips of Lady Leaguer took flight immediately. The Colonel made his way through the thronged rooms, a smart little man in his brilliant uniform—keen eyed, with a firm mouth. He knew everyone in the rooms, and in his curt way greeted them kindly enough.

'No, my dear,' he said to one pert miss who asked him playfully to accept her as a partner. 'I am not going to dance with you. I am an old buffer, and you wouldn't like it if I did.'

A courteous gentleman this—with that tact and knowledge of men and women which goes to make a great commander. Lady Leaguer—on the daïs —watched her husband's face, and knew that he had news, but not for the ears of the revellers. Frederic Marqueray was unobtrusively making his way from another point of the room towards the daïs. They were rallying as it were beside her ladyship

The Colonel nodded affectionately to his wife. He took his stand beside her, and together they looked round upon the gay scene with smiles of approval and enjoyment.

' It has come,' said the Colonel, under his breath.

' Where?' whispered his wife, and all the while she smiled.

' Meerut—where is Marqueray?'

' He is coming towards you—on your left.'

The Colonel exchanged a nod and a wave of the hand with a white-haired general officer, who passed towards the supper-room with a lady on his arm.

On his left he heard the clank of a sword. But he did not look round towards Marqueray, who was standing there studying his engagement-card with a puzzled expression.

' Don't be anxious,' said Sir Thomas to his wife, ' I must go again at once. You get home quietly about one o'clock. It is now nearly twelve. I shall be there soon after. They say it is a small local disturbance, but——'

He paused and shrugged his shoulders.

' No, my lord,' he said to a tall white-faced veteran, who stopped for a moment in passing. ' I'm not dancing to-night. Must retire in favour of the young blood.'

Then he turned to Marqueray.

'As you thought,' he said shortly, 'Meerut, and spreading rapidly. Get the other chaps—Wylam, and the rest of them. Billiard-room, Field Club, ten minutes from now.'

Marqueray stepped down from the daïs and disappeared in the throng, engagement-card in hand. He had apparently succeeded in deciphering the name of his partner for the next dance.

In the compound, under the shadow of the mystic jungle grass, in the witching light of a waning moon, with the sound of the music reaching them through the wizard whisper of the breeze, Harry and Maria still sat side by side.

The hand and arm so negligently left within his reach were still free, but Harry's lips were nearer to the averted cheek. He was talking rapidly and with emphasis, as young men will. And she had admitted, after much persuasion and the sweetest reluctance in the world, that she would be as well pleased should her future partners fail to find her. Perhaps she had admitted other things as well, when Marqueray's firm tread on the gravel startled them both.

'Wylam,' he said, as he approached.

'Yes,' answered Harry angrily, with a muttered oath, which must have shocked Maria sorely.

'One minute, please. Excuse me, Miss Lamond.'

He drew Harry aside, and spoke rapidly in a whisper. Harry's eyes blazed and he began answering excitedly, when Marqueray's gloved fingers closed his mouth.

' I will take you to your father,' he said to Maria the next minute. ' I'm afraid I must go.'

And as Maria took her partner's arm she turned with eyes full of hatred and looked at Marqueray, who returned her gaze steadily.

10

CHAPTER XIII

TO ARMS.

IT is perhaps some small consolation to the survivors to know that those dear to them, and lost perhaps by a death too painful to recall, died not in vain. There are some who would fain wipe the year 1857 out of the British calendar. A year truly of woe and distress and unspeakable horror; a year standing out prominently in great red letters, so long as the world shall remember the English race. But we who now look back, standing as it were farther down the avenue of time, to those days receding fast into the perspective of history, can scarcely fail to recognise that the Indian Mutiny is a corner-stone of our race.

Years such as eighteen hundred and fifty-seven must ever be remembered; such years are the leaven of the ages. A race of human beings is a chain hung down into the centuries. The weather beats upon it, the changes of the seasons try it and chafe and rust it. Prosperity and misfortune alike sap at its strength. It is not only the rain but the sunshine also that deteriorates. Our English chain has hung through fair and foul, and at times a great strain has been put upon it, testing it, proving that its links are not worn yet.

Forty years ago such a strain tugged at us, and we held good. Surely it was well to have been a link of the chain at that time. Surely those men and women, aye, and the children, died to some purpose!

What of Neill and Hodson, of Ewart, of Cooper, who leapt alone through a breach into a stronghold where we killed two thousand; of Adrian Hope, the giant with the gentle smile and the terrible sword; of Nicholson, of Peel, of Inglis, of the clerk Kavanagh, who between sunset and dawn handed his name down to history; of Taylor, of Gubbins, the dauntless civilians; of Neville Chamberlain; of the thousand and one soldiers and civilians who sprang up, like mushrooms in a meadow, wheresoever the need came? What of these? They were Englishmen, and 1857 told us that we had them. Assuredly we may reflect with pride that 1857 was added to our history, that these men were the contemporaries of our fathers, that the women who suffered and were strong, that the men who fought, were the fathers and mothers of some of us.

The news awaiting Harry and Marqueray in the

billiard-room of the Field Club was that of the outbreak at Meerut—the cloud, large only as a man's
hand, which had risen in the north, and was to
spread over all India.

To Harry and to such as he—and they were
many in the Anglo-Indian army in those days—the
news had but little meaning. For the ignorance of
the majority of subalterns was as great as subsequently their courage proved to be.

Harry stood upright by the billiard table with
flashing eyes, with his strong fingers handling the
hilt of his virgin sword, and he was not the only
man in that room who welcomed this news as the
promise of a campaign and promotion.

The gravity of their seniors was scarcely heeded
by these young fellows, who where perhaps a little
tired of the regular and uneventful life of barrack-
yard and mess-room.

' If there is to be any fighting,' said Harry to
Marqueray, with his bold spirit blazing in his eyes,
' by gad, I'll have a fling at it.'

' Yes,' answered Marqueray, with his gentle
smile, ' I've no doubt you will.'

' And you are just the sort of Englishman we
want just now,' he reflected, though he did not say
it. And his eyes rested with something like affection on the dare-devil, reckless face. Frederic Mar-

queray knew somewhat of Asiatic warfare, and that
in such a fight as he perhaps foresaw even then, the
only course for Englishmen was to dare—and dare
—and dare again.

Looking back now to the great Mutiny in the cool
repose of historical reflection, we arrive at the same
conclusion. It was those who dared who saved
India.

Through the thirty days that followed, days
marked by the semi-ridiculous Calcutta panic, by
the windy storm of many counsels, by fear and
pusillanimity on one hand, and a steadfast courage
on the other, days drawn out by suspense and fore-
boding, darkened by news that filtered in from the
North, harassed by the silence that dwelt in the
North-West—through all these the Colonel kept his
men in hand.

' They are faithful, but they are not to be trusted,'
he said grimly in answer to all questions; ' no man
with a dark face is to be trusted in these times.'

' And not all who have white faces,' added Marqueray the cynic.

Then at last Colonel Sir Thomas Leaguer received
permission to dare that bold stroke which he had
long meditated. He paraded his regiment, and
bade the men pile their arms. He sat grimly on
his horse in front of them all, and gave the order,

Marqueray, at the head of his company, repeated
it. There was a silence, a momentary hesitation,
and the life of every European officer hung on a
thread. The pouches were full of ball-cartridge,
the rifles were ready.

Frederic Marqueray's company was the first to
obey the order, in a dazed silence beneath the
unflinching eye of their captain. The others followed suit, and the men were dismissed to their
quarters, while the baggage-waggons, under the
charge of a company of European fusiliers, carried
away the rifles.

Across the parade ground the Colonel and Marqueray exchanged a glance.

'You've ruined the regiment,' said one of the
Majors, with a queer break in his voice. He was
one of those who believed in the integrity of the
sepoy, and it was only by the decree of fortune that
he was saved from paying with his life for his belief.

'No,' answered the Colonel quietly, ' I've saved
it. They would not have held out another day.'

The officers, grave-faced and silent, walked slowly
towards their quarters. Some of them, the younger
subalterns, had queer white patches on their
cheeks. Some of the elders wiped their faces with
their handkerchiefs, as if they had just run a race.

'And what the devil are we to do now?' Harry

asked Marqueray in a low voice, as they strode along side by side.

'Volunteer for active service,' replied the older soldier promptly. 'If it's fighting you want you will get your fill before we have done with this business. The mutineers have Delhi: they will have fifty thousand men in there before we know where we are. We built the fortifications, we trained the men, we have over a hundred big guns there, and the largest stock of ammunition in Upper India. They knew what they were after when they went to Delhi. We shall have to take Delhi, Harry.'

He paused with a queer grim smile, which no doubt was lost upon the eager young soldier, who never dreamt of else than immediate glory for British arms.

'Yes, and we'll give them a d——d good hiding into the bargain,' cried Harry, with his easy laugh. 'What is this about the King of Oudh and two thousand men concealed in Garden Reach?'

'Oh, that is nothing,' replied Marqueray; 'Calcutta knows what we are made of. There will be no trouble down here, because the natives know that we have more at our backs. Up country it is different. They think there that we have no troops left at home, that we show them all we have.'

Harry laughed again.

'How are we to set about getting some work to
do?' he asked as he strode along with a fine martial
swing.

'I advise you to go to the Colonel and tell him.'

'Ah! But he hates me,' exclaimed Harry, 'and
so does she. They think I'm wild and a hopeless
sort of devil altogether, only fit to play cards and
do steward at a dance.'

'I think you're wrong there,' answered Marqueray. 'They like you well enough. Besides, the
Colonel is not the man to withhold a chance from
any young chap who wants to fight. Take my advice, and go now. Tell him you're ready to go off
at once and anywhere.'

'And what about you, you queer old devil? I
thought we should do this campaign together.'

'I've got my own work, Harry,' replied Marqueray quietly. 'Perhaps we'll meet later.'

Harry shrugged his shoulders, and his face
dropped. For he was full of goodwill towards his
fellow-men, and liked their company. This grave-
faced soldier had been his steadiest friend ever since
he had set foot in India, though indeed he had
plenty of others—gay fellows, jolly fellows, who
sang a good song, played a good game, and borrowed money with a fine good fellowship. None of
these things Marqueray did, but he tendered instead

a half cynical, careless advice—he warned him
against the jolly fellows with a fearlessness of consequence and a contempt of personal responsibility,
which left some impression behind.   In Calcutta, in
the gay days of gymkhana and garrison dance, the
other fellows were perhaps the best company, but
as soon as there was question of war, of the trade
which after all was theirs, Harry turned quite naturally to Marqueray, only to meet the disappointment
of a grave statement that the elder soldier had other
work to do.

'I'll see the Colonel this evening,' said Harry
thoughtfully, after a pause.

'No, see him now.'

'But I have several things I want to do.'

'Such as——?'

'Well,' answered Harry, with a slight flush, which
we may be sure was not lost upon his companion.
'Well, I want to go down the river, and say good-
bye to the Lamonds, you know!'

'Yes, I know.   I'll do it for you while you write
home.   I suppose you will be writing——'

Then Harry turned on him with a flash of anger.

'And—d——n it! what about your *own* letters
home?'

'Oh,' replied Marqueray, imperturbably, 'that is
all right, thanks.   I have no one to write to,'

The officers in those days had no quarters in
barracks, nor indeed was there an organised mess-
dinner. The two friends had now reached Marqueray's bungalow, a quiet little house abutting the
native lines.

'I will go down and explain to the Lamonds,' he
said. 'If you take my advice you will go to the
Colonel at once. It is the man who speaks first
who gets the pick in these times.'

Maria was lying in a long chair in the verandah
facing the river, somnolently recovering from the
fatigues of the afternoon heat. Moreover, she was
effecting her ladylike purpose with all grace and a
pretty languor eminently befitting her well-devel-
oped beauty of form and limb. Her dark hair was
just loosely enough bound to betray its length and
luxuriance—her soft white dress was none the less
cunning because its folds were easy. She gave a
little yawn over the book she held in her hand,
but checked it only half enjoyed, for the sound of
wheels set her suddenly alert. She half sat up, and
listened with a little smile. Then she threw herself
back again, and stretching one arm above her head
closed her eyes.

Frederic Marqueray was shown out into the verandah by a native servant, who retired with racial
discretion when he had held aside the scented

curtain of woven grass that hung across the window.

For some moments Maria lay quite still, and Marqueray with a dark smile waited for her to open her eyes. This she presently did with a little cry of surprise and confusion—with white fingers raised to the loosened tresses—with a slipper dropping from an agitated toe.

It was all very pretty and maidenly and natural, but Marqueray, grimly attentive, saw the shade of disappointment in her eyes when they lighted on his worn face instead of the boyish countenance upon which she expected to read the effect of her sweet confusion.

'Ah!' she said, 'I have been asleep.'

'And most becomingly you compassed it,' he answered. 'Pardon me, Miss Lamond, for surprising you. It was, however, a little the fault of your servant. I should not have presumed to come straight through if I had known. Your slipper is beneath the chair; may I—there?'

He handed her the slipper with a grave bow, and drew forward a chair.

'I am the bearer of a message from Harry,' he explained, laying aside his gloves. 'But first— where is your father?'

'Oh, father went away last night suddenly.'

' Ah,' said Marqueray, looking vaguely across the river. ' Where did he go to?'

' I don't know,' replied Maria, half indifferently. She was beginning to feel sleepy again.

' Ah,' said Marqueray again, with a queer look in his eyes, which Harry had described a hundred times as a native look. ' Then you do not know that it is rather unsafe for you to be living alone here with native servants. There is a rising among the men of all the high caste regiments. The mutiny is becoming serious. If I may suggest it, it would be wiser for you to come into Calcutta and stay with friends until your father returns.'

Maria was all attention now, but betrayed no sign of fear. She was, indeed, admirably calm, and not forgetful of her hair. Marqueray told her as much as he knew or as much as he pretended to know, and she learnt his news with due intelligence and some exclamations of anxiety.

' And so,' he finished, ' I have an excuse for my apparent rudeness in not calling since the ball—we have, as you know, been kept in barracks. Harry has, as a matter of fact, commissioned me to tender his apologies—and perhaps make his adieux.'

' And,' said Maria, glancing at him quietly, ' where is he going?'

' He has volunteered for active service. And it

may be that he will leave Calcutta to-night. He is now writing to his people at home.'

Marqueray had risen—had taken her hand to say farewell, and as he said the last words with his grave old-fashioned bow he looked straight into her eyes.

' Indeed,' she answered, with a sudden soft glance from those fine orbs, which it was hard to meet with equanimity.

He turned away and reached the window before her voice arrested him.

' Captain Marqueray!'

' Yes—Miss Lamond.'

He came slowly back, and stood looking down at her.

For a moment she looked into his eyes.

' Will you tell me,' she said with a mystic smile, ' whether it is all women you hate—or only me?'

' I will tell you when we have taken Delhi,' he answered.

CHAPTER XIV

HARRY was hurried away to Delhi, where he took service under General Barnard, and we may be sure raised his voice, together with those of such young fire-eaters as Hodson and Wilberforce Greathed, who were all for daring and a noble recklessness. The former was already known for his great ride from Kurnaul to Umballah, a daring paladin born centuries too late, as brave a man as ever drew a sword—Hodson, of Hodson's Horse, one of the great stained names of our warlike race—Wilberforce Greathed, a man of different metal, an engineer, all brain to conceive, all heart to dare, who drew up a plan of attack wherein science was handmaiden to daring. Among such men as these Harry Wylam found kindred spirits, for there was the making of a great soldier in this happy-hearted subaltern.

All the sternness of war was here suddenly brought before his eyes, and no doubt hardened his heart. He had the good fortune to see Daly ride into the

British camp at the head of his Corps of Guides—
brown-faced warriors, clad in dusky woollen shirts,
with fierce eyes half-shaded by huge dusty turbans—European and Asiatic faces alike tanned by
the sun of an early summer. These men had set
out at half-a-day's notice, had marched twenty-
seven miles a day for twenty-one days, cavalry and
infantry alike: an achievement which holds its place
in the history of the great Mutiny as almost unique.

Harry, too, had his company in the columns that
moved out from the Ridge in the pearly dawn of
the morning of June 12 towards the white walls of
Delhi, in accordance with the wild scheme of assault
forced upon the vacillating General by Greathed
and his colleagues. Wild indeed was this plan to
blow up two of the great gates of the city, and
boldly assault the besieged with two meagre columns of fighting men, but not too wild to have succeeded perhaps had it been attempted. But the
General changed his mind, and the men were called
back—some of them, Harry afterwards said, with
tears of vexation in their eyes.

Thus a great opportunity was lost—and this with
the history of Sebastopol yet fresh in men's minds
—to seize the city by a quick and daring attack.
Instead the troops were withcalled, and began once
more the weary work of besieging a fortified city

with too few men to invest it, and too few heavy guns to batter in its walls.

In the meantime events at Calcutta had been busy with the names of great men. Some in high places had proved themselves unfit to meet the responsibilities attaching to their office, while obscure individuals were beginning to emerge from the rank and file of office holders to set their mark upon the history of India.

The whole city was in a ferment by now, for it was already apparent that the English statesman at the head of Indian affairs lacked some of the qualities necessary in a Governor-General in this great strait. That Lord Canning did well in the storm that raged around him we all know, that a better man might have done better it were folly to ignore. In a multitude of counsellors he failed to assert that authority which is of the mind and not of titles, that divine and heaven-sent spirit of command that made plain John Nicholson, of the Punjaub, quiet Vincent Eyre, of the Royal Artillery, rise like stars in a firmament of mediocrity. That Lord Canning had the courage of his own opinions all Englishmen are ready to admit. He was a brave man—just, conscientious, and merciful. But he lacked the fire of genius. He was without that spark of self-confidence which raises men above the slough of many counsels, and strengthens one hand to hold the helm of a stricken country with daring and a set purpose till the storm be overpast. In the history of the world it has always been written that in moving times a country naturally turns to a fighting leader. At this time all India, all Anglo-Indians, felt that military law was imperative, that the helm should be held by the gauntleted hand. But red-tape reigned supreme, and the anomaly of a civilian organising a great war resulted in Cawnpore and a hundred catastrophes that would have been averted had martial law been declared, and had the aid of civilians tendered with soldier-like promptitude been accepted at once.

The persons with whom we have to deal were thus suddenly dispersed from the capital to work out their destinies with that sequence which to the observant cannot but indicate a pre-ordained scheme.

The Colonel was at Allahabad, where he had found work to do, for in such times no sword needed to be idle nor any scabbard rust, while many mere clerks, both white and coloured, laid aside their pens and handled the heavier steel.

Maria Lamond was staying with friends in Calcutta, where in fact she had taken refuge the day after Marqueray's warning. A letter from her

11

father, bearing no address, doubtless brought about her decision to act upon the advice of a man who, though he obviously disliked her, was moved by a sincere enough sense of chivalry to urge him to seek the good of unprotected youth and beauty. Her father was still absent, as Maria was ready enough to inform inquirers. He had so many irons in the fire that he never remained long at home, and it seemed natural enough that in these troubled days the fire was too hot here and too cold there to suit the astute Mr. Lamond's calculations. The man of many irons usually bears the marks of many burns. Sooner or later he takes hold of something at the wrong end.

' No,' Maria would reply, ' I do not know where he is, and I am of course very anxious about him, although I think that he is quite capable of taking care of himself.'

In which filial sentiment this fond daughter was no doubt correct. She only spoke the truth when she professed a complete ignorance of her father's whereabouts. There were others who felt anxiety on his account, and wondered where the restless and ubiquitous Phillip Lamond might be in these stirring times.

Good-hearted Lady Leaguer had sought out the girl soon after the panic with a fine charity, over-

looking any little characteristics of which she happened to disapprove. In time of war it is only
right that the women who cannot take part in its
action (though it is to be supposed that the coming
generation will appear upon the battle-field in
knickerbockers)—it is only right that they should
bury small social differences, and seek to comfort or
encourage each other. This Lady Leaguer did,
sowing broadcast in the hearts of her more timid
sisters a cheerful courage worthy of a great soldier's
wife.

Frederic Marqueray had been seen in Calcutta.
He had been spoken with in Allahabad. Benares
had known him, and men in the neighbourhood of
Dinapore had exchanged a nod with him. Whatever Marqueray's business happened to be at this
time he went about it with that quiet self-concen-
tration which paralyses curiosity, and sets a seal
upon inquisitiveness. He was never in a hurry,
and yet seemed as ubiquitous as the restless spirit,
Lamond himself.

He was to be found indeed at this time in Calcutta again, leisurely and innocent as to demeanour,
lying at full length on a chair in the smoking-room
of his club. He was alone in the room, and hardly
seemed to notice the entrance of a second member,
a native gentleman in riding-breeches and a small

turban. This man was somewhat remarkable in
the day of which we write, because he had received
an English education, and had learnt to combine
East and West in one keen clear brain in a manner
then little known. He had evidently just returned
from playing polo, of which game he was one of
the finest exponents of his day. His small thin
features relaxed into a sudden smile when his eyes
rested on Marqueray's smooth black hair, just visible over the back of his lounge.

' I have heard strange things about you, Marqueray,' he said, coming forward and laying his riding
whip on the table.

' Ah, Saranj, then don't believe them.'

Marqueray slowly uncurled his long slim legs, and
rose. His movements had that Oriental leisureliness and dignity which it is said comes from the
wearing of flowing robes. He shook hands.

' No, mon prince,' he said with his gentle smile.
' Do not believe them.'

It happened that his interlocutor was a prince in
his own country. At least, the title which his fore-
fathers had borne had no other equivalent in English. The pride, however, of a race that ran back
to the days of the New Testament prevented this
scion from taking the trouble to explain his grade
to every young subaltern fresh from England and a

baronial hall bought by his grandfather; and only
a few Europeans, who happened to know the language and the history of Saranj's country, ever gave
him his rightful title.

' I have heard of a wonderful report drawn up
by a clever officer of a disbanded native regiment.'

' Ah!'

' Yes,' continued the native gentleman, with a
smile almost of affection. ' A report which could
only have been made by one of seven Englishmen
in all the country, of six or seven who know this
country, and our people, and our habits, and our
language, and our thoughts so well that they might
just as well be one of ourselves.'

Marqueray bowed in his abrupt way.

' I have not properly described this paper,' continued the native gentleman, with his well-bred
quiet. ' It is not a report, for it says nothing. It
is merely two columns of names, the names of men
like myself who own large estates, who are mere
sahibs, and who might nevertheless influence a
cause by money or men. The names, I understand are divided into two columns, those under one
heading are to be implicitly trusted at this crisis,
the others—well, the others are not.'

Marqueray was leaning against the table watching

the secretive face, searching the steady bead-like
eyes. He neither admitted nor denied.

' I am told that I head the list on the right side,'
went on the man called Saranj. He had so many
names that the shortest was usually chosen.

Marqueray still admitted and denied nothing.

' I have learnt,' went on the other, ' to keep my
eye on the quiet men, the men who never talk of
themselves or their own achievements, who walk
gently through life in the shadow of the wall of
silence. No one knows who has drawn up this
report.'

' And no one ever will know,' declared Marqueray.

' Precisely,' said the other. ' But whoever he is '
—he paused, looking steadily at the Englishman,
' he has one good friend. There is nothing so
pleasing to a loyal man as the evidence that he is
trusted.'

Marqueray turned round slowly and sat down
again. In those days one could not even think of
one's manners.

' You are not above a friendly hint,' said Saranj,
examining the handle of his riding-whip, which he
nad taken up with the apparent intention of going.

' No.'

' Then let there be a second report, consisting of
European names.'

And he walked quietly out of the room.

For some time Marqueray remained at length in the long cane chair, as if buried in thought. And when he at last arose his face was set and hard, as if his reflections had been the reverse of pleasant or satisfactory.

His horse was awaiting him in the shadow of the trees. He mounted and rode to the bungalow occupied by Lady Leaguer.

That lady was at home, and came into the room where he awaited her, with the smile which this young soldier never failed to receive.

' I am glad to see you,' she said, looking at him keenly. There is a certain maternal scrutiny in the eyes of some women which is not to be deceived by any paltry assumption of cheerfulness or freedom from care.

' Thank you,' he answered. ' My sword has never left its scabbard.'

She gave a little laugh.

' I had a letter from the Colonel yesterday,' she said, ' and in it he wrote —let me see—where is it?'

For she carried the letter in her pocket, and presently she read aloud from the flimsy, close-written sheet :

' If Fred Marqueray is not at the front it is

because he is reserved for work infinitely more dangerous and requiring greater courage, steadier
nerve, and a vaster knowledge than are possessed
by nine out of ten of our younger officers.'

She looked at him, smiled, and shook her head.

'When did you arrive in Calcutta?' she asked.

'Yesterday.'

'And when do you leave?'

'In half-an-hour.'

'For where?'

'For Allahabad first. That is why I came, and
also to say good-bye. If you care to write a letter
I will wait for it.'

Lady Leaguer was already at her writing-table,
and for some minutes the scratching sound of her
quill pen alone broke the silence.

'The mutineers in Delhi and elsewhere,' said
Marqueray at length, 'are receiving information of
our movements. I am going to try and find out
from what source they get it.'

'Which means that you already know,' said Lady
Leaguer, sealing the letter which she handed to
him. 'You are a clever man, Fred. Good-bye,
and don't get killed.'

CHAPTER XV

TREASON.

THE fighting on the Ridge was not of the description to satisfy Harry, who would fain have taken part in some more glorious campaign, such as was accredited to Vincent Eyre on his march to Delhi. For Harry was no patient soldier to lie in camp before a walled city and work out its downfall by stubborn siege.

There was indeed plenty of excitement provided for the little army under General Barnard by an active foe, but it was all of the defensive order. And we may be sure that Harry grumbled sorely at the lack of enterprise displayed by his chief. The truth was, that our men were absurdly outnumbered, and that during the month of June it was as much as they could compass to hold their own. Repeatedly the enemy came out and boldly attacked the British camp, only to be beaten back and pursued to the very gates of the city. This was pretty fighting in its way, but it led to nothing, and the army before Delhi was conscious of the fact that the world was waiting for it to accomplish impossibilities. Such small triumphs as the capture of the Metcalfe house—the holding of Hindoo Rao's house against repeated assault, and finally the taking of the Sammy House, were not sufficient for Harry's hot impetuosity.

It was on the evening of June 23, when Harry, having played his part in the saving of Hindoo Rao's house, was sitting wiping the dust and sweat from his face, that he was surprised by an apparition.

He had hitherto been fortunate enough to escape wounds, although his impetuosity in action had called forth comment more than once from older soldiers who had learnt to guard their own skins. To-day, however, a bayonet-scratch in the wrist had given him considerable pain, and seemed likely to contract the tendons of his left hand. Knowing that medical aid for such a slight wound was out of the question, he was endeavouring to wipe the grime and dust from the torn flesh, when a quiet and pleasant laugh made him look up.

It was Phillip Lamond coming towards him with the air of *débonnaire* leisureliness which did not leave him even in the midst of such a scene as this. He was dressed in clean white clothes, and wore a civilian's sun-helmet. His face was somewhat drawn and thin, but the pleasant smile was upon it.

'Well, Harry,' he said, ' I hope you are not hurt.'

There were many civilians in the camp, and no one noticed Lamond much. He had a pleasant way with him of appearing perfectly at home, wherever he happened to be.

Harry leapt to his feet, and shook the slim hand held out to him with many assurances of delight.

' Well, I'm d———d,' he cried, becoming at length coherent and quite forgetting his wound, ' who would have expected to see you here. How is Maria?'

' Oh, Maria is all right, thank you. At least she was when I left her, except for her anxiety about you.'

And Phillip Lamond gave a little laugh.

' Was she anxious about me?' asked Harry eagerly, and his grimy hand went to his moustache.

' Well,' answered Lamond, with his friendly laugh. ' Naturally.'

' And how the devil did you get here?' asked Harry, slapping his friend on the shoulder. ' And why the devil are you here? And—well, tell me all about yourself.'

Lamond slipped his hand within Harry's arm with a fatherly familiarity, and they walked away from the scene of the conflict together.

'There is not much to tell,' answered Lamond
with gay frankness. 'An old chap spends most
of his time looking after his liver. But it was not
that that brought me here. It was your affairs, my
boy. I came up to see if I could make anything
out of your Oudh estate—of what is left of it, at
any rate.'

'That is not much, I'll be bound,' exclaimed
Harry, with a reckless laugh. 'Where are we?
It's confoundedly dark all of a sudden.'

The short twilight had indeed suddenly given
place to night. They were stumbling along the
Ridge—all broken by the passage of heavy guns and
the recently begun earthworks of the engineers.

'This way,' answered Lamond, guiding his companion skilfully.

'You seem to know your way about here pretty
well,' said Harry. 'So you came up to look after
my affairs. Well, it's devilish good of you. But
I'm afraid it's no go, old fellow. My affairs have
gone to the deuce.'

'There is a bit of the estate left,' said Mr.
Lamond, reflectively, 'which we can re-arrange
when all this trouble is over. It is not much, but
it is all you have to marry Miss Gresham on.'

He gave one of his easy laughs, but did not look
at his companion, who was silent. The arm upon

which Lamond's thin fingers rested affectionately
stiffened a little.

'When will this trouble be over?' asked Harry,
after a pause. 'Not yet a bit, I hope.'

'So do I.'

'Why do you hope that, you who are no soldier?'
asked Harry, looking over the intervening valley
towards the glimmering lights of Delhi.

'Well, I should like you to get a chance before
the mutineers are beaten; and I should like a chance
myself.'

'What sort of a chance? Queer beggar you are,
Lamond.'

'The chance every poor devil wants—of making
a little money.'

'Ah—yes,' cried Harry, with his light laugh.
'But how?'

Lamond shrugged his facile shoulders.

'Goodness knows, something may turn up,' he
replied. 'At all events the niggers will have to pay
someone for all this.'

With which sentiment Harry agreed readily
enough. For at this time it was the fashion among
the men, and even with certain of the officers, to
nourish a cruel and unjust hatred against any man
with a black face. The native servants and the
camp-followers, without whom, indeed, the cam-

paign could never have been prosecuted, went in daily fear of maltreatment at the hands of the masters whom they served faithfully enough.

'When Delhi falls,' said Lamond presently, 'there may be a chance of picking something up. Beggars cannot be choosers of their methods. I shall stay here, and don't you seek to get transferred elsewhere, my boy. You stick to Delhi— stick to Delhi, Harry, to the end.'

'The end seems a deuced long way off,' grumbled the young soldier.

'Not so far as we think perhaps,' replied Lamond airily. 'I came up here with a pretty strong detachment of reinforcements. The siege-train is coming along steadily. Neville Chamberlain will be here to-morrow or the next day. When they get the big guns on to those gates they will soon batter them in. Brind will see to that—he knows his business. And when the city is taken by assault there will be some confusion—and there is plenty of treasure and money inside those walls.'

He turned and waved his slim hand towards the city, standing grey and ghostlike on a hill-top.

'And where the carcase is, there also shall the vultures be gathered together,' laughed Harry, who remembered the solemn daily prayer and Scripture-reading in St. Helen's Place.

But Phillip Lamond failed to perceive the pertinency of the reference. He was gazing uneasily across the hollow towards the walls and minarets of Delhi, now faintly lighted by a waning moon. Beneath them on the broken ground lay many corpses. These were all the slain of the enemy, for the English had brought in their dead, and in the silence between the booming of the heavy guns the picks of the burying party could be heard. The killed lay strewn upon the brown earth, some of them little clad, and others swathed in their dusky whites.

'Looks like washing-day,' said Harry, as he noted the direction of his companion's gaze. But Lamond was absorbed in his own thoughts.

'Do you want to get your V.C.?' he asked suddenly.

'Of course I do.'

'Then I'll put you in the way of it! Sooner or later Delhi will be taken. When the siege guns come up the assault will be decided upon. I am going to stay here. I want to go into the city with the troops. When the time comes you must manage that I be by your side. I know Delhi as I know my own pocket. I know some back ways and by-ways. I'll lead you, my boy, into something good—not only a V.C., but a fortune.'

Harry's eyes glistened. He did not love money for itself, but he loved to spend it. He was open-handed and generous enough. The pinch of poverty was so new to him that it had not yet lost its savour of insult. There was something degrading in the thought that he—Harry Wylam, an officer and a gentleman—should have to think before he put his hand into his pocket.

Some of his friends also had earned their Victoria Cross—it seemed by a chance that never came his way. Some little act of spontaneous daring, some quick seizure of a passing opportunity had gained for others the coveted decoration; and Harry's breast was yet innocent of a medal, though all men knew that the heart beating there was brave enough.

What wonder then that the young soldier never paused to inquire of his father's friend whether the means of gaining such glory and wealth were guaranteed to be legitimate.

'I'm your man,' he cried, with the fervour of battle still running through his blood. 'We ought to have been in there a month ago; and when we do get in, by gad! we'll make 'em pay for it.'

'Yes,' echoed Lamond, 'we'll make them pay for it. You had better go into hospital and get that wound washed. You cannot afford to neglect so

much as a scratch in this climate. I'm going back
to Rao's house.'

He nodded in his careless way, and stood on the
brink of the incline, watching Harry's tall form dis-
appear in the gloom towards the cantonments,
where lights flickered dimly and grey shadows
moved hither and thither in all the stir of camp life
after a battle.

When Harry had left him Phillip Lamond did not
go back towards Hindoo Rao's house, the scene of
the day's conflict. Instead, he sat down where he
was—a shadowy form in the dark—on the deep red
soil. He sat for some minutes as motionless as the
stones around him. Then he moved a few yards
farther down the slope. Below him, huddled up in
a hundred fantastic distortions, lay the dead—each
white-clad corpse looking, as Harry had said, like a
heap of clothes thrown carelessly on a drying-
ground.

A little farther, and Phillip Lamond was within
touch of a dead sepoy. The reek of blood was in
the still air—the nameless scent of death.

Lamond crept forward, and with his foot touched
the nearest body. The man was quite dead, and
as he rolled over displayed a grim, grey-bearded
face. The Englishman crept forward and dragged
off the turban. With infinite caution he waited,

looking quickly round. He was alone with the dead,
who lay on every side of him. He could hear the
shouts and cries, the beating of drums and the boom
of gongs, within the city walls, where a complete
disorder reigned. Behind him the steady sound of
heavy hammering betrayed the whereabouts of an
advanced battery, where the gunners were repairing
a broken carriage.

Phillip Lamond was snake-like and noiseless in his
movements. He was a different man to that Phillip
Lamond known in club and on course at Calcutta.
The leisureliness had vanished, and was indeed re-
placed by a remarkable keenness of glance, a rapid
movement of limb.

In a few moments the Brahmin soldier was
divested of all save his loin-cloth, and Lamond
rapidly threw aside some portions of his own clothing. With feverish haste he rubbed arms, legs,
face, neck, and hands, with a dull red powder which
he carried in his pocket in a small wooden box,
which he subsequently concealed within the folds of
his turban.

He donned the flowing robes of the dead sepoy,
and Phillip Lamond of Calcutta was no more. In
place of him a sepoy, in the robes of his caste, cau-
tiously raised his head and looked around.

The waning moon had set, and the darkness was

further accentuated by a thin mist creeping up from the valley of the Jumna. There was nothing to fear from the rifles of the British sentinels posted on the summit of the Ridge. The sepoy raised himself on his knees, and presently, with great caution, to his feet.

One of the bodies behind him moved a little. Some of these men were not dead yet, but slowly dying, and occasionally one of them groaned. Had Lamond taken the precaution of counting the number of the slain in his immediate vicinity when he first arrived he would have discovered at this time that they had been increased by one.

He stood upright for a moment, listening to the uproar within the city, to the cries of the artillery-men on the walls—men of our own teaching who stood by their guns day and night, and died by them with invincible courage.

The disguise was perfect. Here was a sepoy of Delhi, speaking three or four native tongues with perfect ease.

He moved slowly away down the slope towards the besieged city, and as he did so one of the white-clad forms left for dead upon the battle-field rose up and followed him.

CHAPTER XVI.

ON THE RIDGE.

WHILE Harry and his companions were bewailing
the inactivity of their lot, the grim Messenger came
for their General, and called him away from his half-
finished labours. It was decreed that after many
battles fought the veteran Barnard should die in his
bed, although the voice of the cannon sped his
gentle soul upon its way. Every man in the British camp felt that he had lost a friend and a con-
siderate kindly leader, when the news circulated
among the tents. During his lifetime the younger
soldiers had abused him freely enough for his inactivity, and lack of that wild recklessness which char-
acterised the action of so many Englishmen at this
time. But when he was dead they only remembered his kindliness, his gentle heart, his self-for-
getfulness. And let us remember who look back
through the perspective of history upon one who
perhaps accomplished little when others were doing
much, that he was asked to perform impossibilities,
and in no wise forget that this brave old soldier

refused to abandon the siege of Delhi when that course was suggested to him.

From time to time Harry had word or sight of Phillip Lamond's presence in the camp, where indeed other civilians had business or duty. But the young soldier's duties were naturally somewhat absorbing, and after a long day under a glaring sun he was too tired to set out and seek his friend among the tents. Also it may be confessed at once that Harry Wylam was apt to content himself very well with the company in which he happened to be—to forget, in fact, absent faces and influences no longer nigh. This may be mentioned thus a second time, as serving to show upon what characteristics that solid citizen Mr. Gresham based his judgment of his ward. For Mr. Gresham—and others who have less experience may well learn of him—was of the opinion that the man who is under the influence of the last speaker lacks that stability of character without which it is hard to steer a straight course through life.

At General Barnard's funeral Harry caught sight of Lamond following the military procession with a melancholy mien. It is possible that the enterprising civilian had good reason to mourn the loss of so easy-going and easily-persuaded a commander-in-chief. The authorities had in fact of late experi-

enced some difficulty in restraining the enterprise of
those civilians and unattached officers who were in
the English cantonment under a somewhat vague
appointment. As the Intelligence Department had
more than once profited by the results of individual
daring in the shape of accurate information and an
extended knowledge of the enemy's movements,
discipline was perhaps slightly relaxed in favour of
the primary law that every man has a right to risk
his own life in a good cause.

Ever seeking that fame and glory to be won at
the cannon's mouth, a hundred young fellows vied
with each other in daring, some of them penetrating
so far as the ditch surrounding the city on the
northern side. Others crept up at night within
musket-shot of the walls in the hope of discovering
some weak spot to be indicated subsequently to the
artillerymen for bombardment. Thus private ambition and the public weal worked together so har-
moniously that it was, as it always has been, hard
to separate one from the other in judging of the
results obtained.

It is to be feared that motives less commendable
also stirred men's hearts to action at this time; for
grim war is apt to strip human nature of the fine
apparel of self-restraint in which we deck ourselves
for social purposes. Greed of gain and a bitter thirst

for revenge took hold of hearts at other times charitable and forgiving enough. And many like Harry and Lamond confessed their feelings aloud, and were unashamed.

It was immediately after General Barnard's death, during the first days of the brief command of his successor—a man in broken health—that Harry obtained permission to venture on a small enterprise which he had been meditating for some time. The idea had originally been Phillip Lamond's, and that civilian had drawn out the necessary plans.

To the south of the city, within rifle range of the Delhi Gate, and situated on the smaller road leading through Old Delhi towards Kootubminar, a group of houses and a mosque afforded shelter to the enemy's sharpshooters, who were in the habit of assembling there before making their repeated and harassing attacks on the British right and rear. These suburban positions were so strongly protected by the enemy's heavy guns that they could neither have been taken nor held by the British troops, while to batter them slowly to the ground was a task beyond the power of the besieging artillery, hampered as the gunners were by scarcity of ammunition and the heavy fire from the walls.

Harry's scheme was to blow up these buildings. Phillip Lamond's object was to get into the mosque.

The advantage to be gained was great, while the
risk of life was comparatively small. Harry happened to propose his plan at the right moment, and
received permission to make the attempt.

It was just before dawn one dark morning in the
first weeks of July that Harry crept out of the cantonments with his few picked men at his heels.
Despite the extreme caution that was necessary he
laughed aloud at the accidents attending their
scramble down the slope of the Ridge. He was
more like a boy leading some school escapade than
a man moving towards danger with his life in his
hand. Indeed, Harry Wylam had since the beginning of the great siege displayed so undaunted a
bearing, so reckless and cheerful a courage, that
he was already a marked man among those whose
business it was to select fitting officers for a dangerous mission.

The night had been a dark one, cloudy and sullen. For the rains were at hand, and all nature
seemed to be waiting in breathless suspense for the
relief of cool showers and cloudy skies.

The enemy's guns were silent for a few hours.
The great white city was asleep. At the foot of the
slope a vague form rose from the ground and gave
a cautious whistle. It was Phillip Lamond, who
had been afoot all night prowling like some restless

jackal among the buildings, where lurked a hundred renegades and outcasts ready to sell their nearest friends for a small consideration. Indeed, they would have put a low enough price on their own souls had there been bidders for such damaged wares.

In a whisper Harry halted his men, bidding them set carefully on the ground the bags of powder they carried. Then he moved forward alone to consult with Lamond, who awaited him, motionless.

'There are about twenty of them sleeping in the ground-floor rooms of the large house, there may be more upstairs, I cannot find out,' whispered Lamond, quickly. He was quite calm and collected, in striking contrast to the eager and impatient Harry, who was all alight as it were with the fire of battle before the first shot was fired.

'Twenty,' whispered he, joyously feeling the hilt of his sword. 'And there are seven of us. Yes, we can manage twenty—but what are the twenty doing there?'

'They are guarding the mosque. I am certain that my information is correct. For some reason the money has been secreted in the mosque in preference to taking it into Delhi. They are sepoys from Cawnpore under a subahdar, whom I have seen before somewhere. If it was merely an out-

post they would not have a subahdar in command.
You must lead your men into the house. The
pandies will make no stand. They hate a bayonet
in the dark. I will break open the side door of the
mosque, where you must join me, alone, while your
men are laying the powder and the train.'

'Yes,' answered Harry, somewhat doubtfully.
'But we must not forget that the chief object is to
blow up the buildings!'

'I am not forgetting it. But we are not such
fools as to blow up a lot of bullion that is only waiting there to be taken,' answered Mr. Lamond, in
that fine spirit of commercial enterprise and common sense upon which Englishmen may pride
themselves.

'No,' said Harry, who was thinking more of the
fight than of the gold, 'of course not. But whose
money is it?'

'It will be ours in half-an-hour,' replied Lamond,
with a little laugh at his own readiness of repartee.

Harry, as we know, was in sore need of cash, and
more thoughtful men than he—better men perhaps
deemed it at this time no great disgrace to punish
any with a coloured face by taking his money first
and his life afterwards.

'All is fair,' said Lamond, with a double-sound-
ing laugh, 'in love and war.'

As he spoke he buttoned his jacket across his narrow chest, and tightened up the belt which he wore over it to carry the sword which he, like many other civilians, had assumed. For everyone at this time was a fighting man, and no one knew at what moment he might be called upon to draw and defend his own life. But even these warlike preparations were made by Phillip Lamond with that gentle deprecation of manner which had earned for him a very useful reputation for harmlessness and insignificance. Harry, on the contrary, was full of a hearty British bluster as he struck his sword into the ground and left it quivering there, while he tightened his belt and pulled his khaki tunic down into closer folds across his muscular chest.

He loosened his tunic at the throat, and crammed his forage cap down over his eyes.

' We're going to have a devil of a lark,' he whispered eagerly, ' and a devil of a fight too.'

He prepared himself for this amusement with that glee of anticipation which makes English soldiers what they are. Moreover, it was not mere swagger or the bluster of youth and ignorance. For Harry Wylam had fought in fifteen battles since he had joined the army of Delhi, while the skirmishes in which he had taken part, neither he nor any other had cared to count. It had only been noted vaguely

to his credit that, where the fighting was, Harry
Wylam would be found, and there comporting himself with the courage of an English gentleman and
the daring of a Highlander.

Lamond peered through the darkness at him with
a queer tolerant smile. There was something in
Harry's spirit that Lamond accounted to him for
foolishness.

'Mind,' he said warningly, 'that you do not run
any unnecessary risks. Show the men the way in,
and then let them go. There is nothing so dangerous as fighting hand to hand in a dark room. Let
the men go in first.'

'No,' answered Harry. 'I'm not that sort of man.
The devils volunteered to follow me, and follow me
they shall.'

He turned as he spoke, and called up his men by
a cautious whistle. Two of them were Goorkhas—
one a guide in his dusky shirt and turban—the rest
were Englishmen in trousers and shirt-sleeves, as
they had learnt and been allowed to turn out to
parade or action.

'Remember,' he said to them, 'no firing allowed.
They mustn't know inside the walls that anything
is going on, until the whole place is blown to hell.
Use the bayonet and your kookri. There are twenty
men inside the guard-house—but we are not afraid

of them, eh? Bayonet them, and then lay six bags
inside the house. Keep four bags for the mosque.
Stick close to me, and do not light your fuse until
you have my word. No—better still—no one is to
light the fuse but myself, and if I'm killed—Parsons
here will do it. He's a sapper, and knows the work.
Now, are you ready? Follow me and stick by me
—I'm not asking you to go anywhere I will not go
myself.'

' We know that, sir; d——n yer eyes,' said a
gruff voice, and someone laughed, which sound of
merriment was apparently quashed by a dig in the
ribs. The schoolboy element was not confined to
the leader of this expedition.

They made their way slowly along the valley,
avoiding all buildings, of which there were fewer
without the walls than there are to-day. It was yet
somewhat early to attempt the enterprise, for the
eastern sky was still black. As they crept onward,
Lamond watched continuously for some sign of the
dawn over the trees on the Ridge. He glanced at
his watch impatiently, and seemed to know the exact
moment when the sun should rise. Truly, this
restless spirit seemed of late to have been moving
as much by night as by day.

' A chap followed me for some way,' he whispered
to Harry, looking over his shoulder as he spoke;

' some badmash on the prowl, I expect. There are
plenty of them about down here waiting to strip the
dead.'

' Close up, you fellows,' said Harry to his men—
and the little party crept forward.

They could now distinguish the outline of the
buildings in front of them—a low square house and
the rounded dome of the mosque behind it. The
eastern sky seemed to be a little lighter. The air
had that cool feeling which precedes the dawn of a
new day—something clean and pure, which sweeps
across the face. It was the hour when those who
have watched all night at last give way to sleep—the
moment when the night and its perils seem to rise
up and go away.

'Halt!' whispered Harry, with uplifted sword.

Lamond had laid his hand nervously on his arm.

' There he is,' whispered the elder man. ' Do
you see him, stealing away like a shadow? I have
seen him before with his great turban and his green
scarf—he dogs me.'

And, in truth, something moved away into the
darkness in front of them—something shadowy and
vague.

CHAPTER XVII.

THE little party moved forward and stood in the compound of the square house. It proved to be deserted as Lamond had reported. For the army of Delhi was but ill-disciplined, and few watches were kept. Although technically besieged the mutineers were in fact the besiegers, for they usually attacked, and the British troops were sometimes hard pressed to repel the onslaught.

'They are all asleep within the house,' whispered Lamond. 'Let your men creep in and kill them as they lie.'

'Not I,' returned Harry, with eyes ablaze. For the news of Cawnpore had just reached the army outside Delhi and that word, written in blood in our history for all time, was already becoming a war cry, denoting no quarter and little justice for any coloured man. 'Not I,' said Harry; 'they will have to stand up and be killed. And we'll tell 'em who is doing it.'

They approached the house where silence reigned.

'Come on, you fellows,' cried Harry suddenly.
' Remember Cawnpore, Cawnpore it is!'

Alone he leapt through the window into a room
where twenty bayonets awaited him, his great voice
awaking the sleepers there to the sudden knowledge that their call had come. On his heels the
men crowded in. There was a sound of scuffling in
the dark, the hoarse cursing of the Englishmen, the
wailing of the panic-stricken sepoys. Someone
struck a light, and ignited torches brought for the
purpose. Then followed a broken cry for mercy, a
shriek of agony, a few men scuttling like rabbits
round the walls, slipping on the swimming floor,
and all was still again. A headless body lay near
the window, while the severed skull grinned from a
corner, the result of the first whistling swing of
Harry's sword as he leapt in.

' Lay the bags against the walls and connect the
fuse,' cried Harry, going towards the window again.
' But wait for me to light it.'

Then he stepped out through the open window
into the first grey of dawn to join Lamond, as had
been arranged, at the side door of the mosque. He
ran round the white and sacred building, passing the
chief entrance, which was barricaded. At the side
door he found himself face to face with a tall native
in the dress of a fakir, of whom many hundreds

were abroad at this time preaching the Holy War,
and promising eternal bliss to those who fell fighting the hated Christian rule.

'Out of the way, you d——d nigger,' shouted
Harry, rushing at him with the point.

But the man had a long sword half hidden in the
folds of his robe. With a quick twist of the arm he
turned aside Harry's point, which for a moment
stuck in the wooden jamb of the door. During
that brief moment Harry had time for the uncom-
fortable reflection that had this been a fighting
man instead of a priest, that mistake might have
served to close a wild career. But the native neglected the opportunity, and Harry, wrenching his
sword from the woodwork, stepped back to cut his
adversary down with one whistling stroke. But
here again a slow skill put forth without eagerness
turned the crushing blow aside, and Harry stag-
gered against the defender of the door. He recovered himself with a curse, and tried a feint and a
thrust which Marqueray had taught him in an idle
moment at Calcutta. But this again failed, and
Harry Wylam, who deemed himself one of the best
fencers in India, stood back breathless and dripping
with perspiration.

It seemed impossible to break through the guard
of this silent priest, who contented himself with

merely defending the entrance to his temple.
Harry had pistols in his belt, but gave no thought
to them. Indeed his spirit was aroused, and the
reflection that none would come to interrupt them
had a certain fierce joy in it. He guessed that
Lamond had effected an entrance to the mosque
probably before the priest had been aroused by
the sound of the massacre; but he did not call to
him.

Instead, he ran in again, making use of all his
skill—putting forth the whole of his great strength
and agility. The growing light gleamed on the two
swords—the one whirling and whistling through the
air, the other steady and quick in its short, sharp
turns. Harry could see that his adversary was a
tall man, of slight build. The bare brown arm and
wrist were emaciated, but the muscles stood out
on the forearm like ropes. There was no hope
of fatiguing this spare warrior-priest, who was
cool enough and seemed likely to remain impregnable.

'Lamond!' shouted Harry. 'Where the devil
are you?'

It was getting light. A sortie from Delhi was
almost inevitable, for the shrieks of the dying men
must have reached the ears of the sentinels on the
walls. So Harry, who would not shoot down his

foe, called to Lamond, and almost immediately he
saw the glint of a whirling sword over the turbaned
head of the fakir, who dropped senseless across the
doorway.

'This way!' cried Lamond from within, where
darkness reigned supreme, and his thin white hand
came out from the shadowy background seeking
Harry's. In a few moments they emerged again
into the glimmering twilight, each carrying a bur-
den thrown hastily into a 'praying-carpet' of thin
roughspun cotton of which the four corners had
been gathered together.

They stepped over the body of the fakir, whose
eyes were half-opened in a dazed return to consciousness. Lamond jumped aside hastily when
he saw him.

'That is the man who has dogged me ever since
I have been here,' he said.

And he would have run his sword through the
half-senseless man had not Harry dragged him
away.

'No! no!' he cried, 'not that; that's murder.
Come on!'

The fakir moved a little, and his eyes opened
wider. He saw the two men go away with their
burdens thrown over their shoulders. In a few
minutes Harry returned with two of his company,

who carried bags of powder. He carelessly noted
that the fakir had vanished.

' Poor devil's crawled away,' he said to himself.
' Gad—what a swordsman that was! '

He laid the powder against the walls and con-
nected the bags by a fuse.

' Now,' he said, ' run for your lives; follow the
others. Run like the devil! '

The two laughed, and obeyed his orders. Then
he struck a match, set it to the fuse, and ran back
towards the house with a piece of smoking fuse in
his hand.

He looked up, and across the valley the beating of
drums told him that the city was astir. He lighted
the second fuse, and then ran after his men. As he
began to climb the slope the enemy's guns opened
fire upon him, for their ammunition was practically
inexhaustible. At the same time, the native troops
flocked out of the Lahore Gate. But suddenly the
earth shook and the sky was rent by a glaring
tongue of flame that leapt up from the valley. A
deafening roar silenced the guns—silenced all nature,
which seemed to stand breathless. The enemy's
troops turned and fled back through the gate. For
a time the guns ceased firing. No one knew whether
this was a mine or an accidental explosion of ammunition. The smoke hung motionless in the morning

air, hiding the devastation brought about. And in the meantime the little party of Englishmen made their way back to the summit of the Ridge.

The daylight had developed ere they reached the British cantonment, and Harry, it is to be confessed, swaggered somewhat as he made his way between the neat lines of tents, of which the inmates were astir and anxious to learn the latest news. The hero of the moment had made his carpet full of valuables over to a trusty private, who had gone off quietly with Lamond to another quarter of the camp. Moreover, the treasure had for the moment slipped his memory. He was soaked in blood, for the man whose head he had severed at the window of the bungalow had fallen against him. Harry was wondering whether he would get the coveted Victoria Cross for this. He nodded to a friend here and there, and carried his head high enough to have graced the feathers of a field-marshal.

' Blown up the buildings south of the Lahore Gate,' he answered right and left, as the questions poured in upon him.

And more than one subaltern looked enviously at the handsome young fellow who made his way, laughing, to his tent.

He was fortunate enough too to have performed a deed which bore tangible fruit during the days

that followed, while others, having perhaps displayed greater bravery and a deeper skill, had
nothing to show for their prowess. Fortune thus
ever appears to smile on those who woo her carelessly, while others, seeking her favours more earnestly, must needs go without them.

But Harry did not get his Victoria Cross for this
or any other deed that he did during the Mutiny.
At first he grumbled loudly at the favouritism, as
he was pleased to call the selection for honours
that lighted upon other men and left him undeco-
rated. But he soon forgot his grievance, and sunned
himself very happily in the glow of a present popu-
larity. His was a nature given more to the enjoyment of the present than to thoughts of the future,
and there was no happier man on the Ridge outside
Delhi that morning in July than Harry Wylam.

'I wish,' he said complacently to Lamond—who
breakfasted with him in the tent he shared with two
other officers on volunteered service with the besieging army—'I wish old Marks had been here.'

'Marqueray, you mean,' was the unenthusiastic
answer. 'Why should you wish *him* to be here?'

Harry did not answer at once. It happens to
most of us to meet some other man in our course
through life before whom we have a strange desire
to excel. Marqueray occupied this position in

Harry's existence. When the wild young subaltern
was in disgrace his first instinctive desire was to
conceal the mischance from his captain. When he
happened to distinguish himself—which, as we have
seen, he sometimes did in a reckless, lucky way—it
was somewhat of a grief to him that Marqueray
should never hear of it.

' Oh!' he answered Phillip Lamond hesitatingly;
' because he never thinks any good of me.'

He gave no further explanation. The name of
Marqueray, indeed, was not conducive to a flow of
confidential talk between these two men.

' I know somebody,' said Lamond, after a little
pause, ' who will be proud of this morning's work.'

' Who is that?'

' Maria.'

And Harry's eyes fell before the glance of Maria's
father.

During the meal there was little mention of the
treasure found in the mosque. Such matters are
better left undiscussed when walls are only canvas.
Harry, moreover, showed little curiosity on the matter. His inclination was rather to set the subject
on one side—on a shelf in his mind, as it were,
where other incidents of his life were stored, and
where the dust of forgetfulness would, perhaps,
mercifully cover them up in time to come. He

never took these mental relics down from their perch and turned them over. Most of us, it is to be feared, have such a shelf of our own, and are no more courageous than Harry Wylam in the presence of our mementos.

'I have got it in a safe place,' Lamond had said carelessly, when he returned—washed and restored to his usual placid self—at breakfast time. 'When the country is settled again we will look into it. I suppose you will trust me to hand over to you your rightful share.'

'Oh, yes,' Harry answered hurriedly, 'that will be all right!' And he turned to the breakfast-table with a deep interest in the simple military fare there displayed.

After breakfast he obeyed an order from headquarters to present himself before one of the chiefs of the staff and report upon his exploit, which was duly noted to his credit, and earned him a company before long. Indeed, his promotion was promised him then and there. He came out of the chief's tent with a beating heart and a hundred good resolutions buzzing through his brain. It was a grand life, this soldiering. And he wondered how it was that he had been content to waste nearly four years in Calcutta when active service could have been had for the asking.

He sought out Phillip Lamond, and imparted the good news to him.

'I'm to get my company,' he said. 'Some of the people who think badly of me will have to acknowledge that there is some good in me yet.'

And Lamond wondered who these people might be. He was not, however, allowed to meditate long, for Harry's hearty hand came down on his shoulder with an affectionate emphasis.

'And I owe it all to you, old chap!' cried the young soldier. 'It was your idea—and your knowledge enabled us to carry it through. I can't think why you will not let me tell them that you were there—that you really did the whole thing!'

'Because,' replied Lamond, with his weary smile, 'I want you to have the whole credit of it. It is nothing to me. I am not a soldier, I am an old chap; while to you it may make a difference. But you didn't mention that we went inside the mosque?'

'No—you told me not to.'

'That's right. Never mention that,' said Lamond, with his pleasant laugh.

CHAPTER XVIII.

WITHIN THE GATES.

THE mutineers in Delhi had a great fear of mines —and the explosion which levelled the obnoxious buildings caused a sort of panic in the city.

' It is,' they said, ' one of the mines that they are building under the city walls.'

And the quick voice of rumour did the rest. During the first part of the day no sortie was made. No daring native sapper could be found to go down and investigate the scene of the explosion in the valley. But as the hours passed by without further alarm, a sortie was at length made, and the true cause of the wreck of the mosque and its surrounding buildings identified.

The charred and shattered remains of the negligent guard were discovered amidst the *débris* of the square house, and two wounded men were brought in. The first of these—a poor water-carrier by trade—had been struck down by a falling stone as he hurried towards the city to raise the alarm. The second was the holy man, who had so courageously

defended the door of the mosque against Harry
Wylam. The fakir was known to some of his res-
cuers, and as they helped him along he told them
how the attack had been made. He himself, he
stated, had heard the shouts of the sepoys defending themselves as best they could in the dark against
the bayonets of the English, and being alarmed,
had run round to the mosque, where he hoped to
conceal himself. But one of the English officers
had followed him and cut him down by a sabre-
stroke over the head, which would most assuredly
have slain him, but for the thickness of his turban.
The skin was not cut, he further told his commiser-
ating countrymen, but the blow had been a severe
one, rendering him insensible during many hours.
A stone from the ruined buildings must, he thought,
have fallen on his ankle, for he could not walk without assistance. So he hobbled towards the city,
painfully and with labour, leaning his spare weight
on the arms of two kind-hearted gunners.

As they passed through the Lahore Gate he gave
a sudden sigh, as of one who had accomplished at
last a task long essayed, and there was a queer light
in his eyes as he looked around upon the wild faces
and the disorderly streets.

'Had he been in Delhi before?' they asked him.

'Oh, yes—but not since the siege!' he replied.

' Friends have I in Benares, where I am known.
But not in Delhi. I feared that some might mistake me for a spy.'

' Ah!' laughed the soldiers of Delhi. ' The English have no spies. They have no one whom they can trust. It is we who have spies—in their camps, waiting at their mess-tables, writing out their official despatches. No—we have no fear of spies, for we have caught and killed the few they had. No doubt they would like to get a man into Delhi, but that they cannot do. Surely you are walking better now.'

' Yes,' answered the fakir slowly, ' the pain has left me a little.'

' It is, perhaps, that you are glad to get inside Delhi—where you are safe?' suggested the other.

' Yes,' replied the holy man with a little sigh, ' I am glad to get inside Delhi. But am I safe? Will the English go away?'

' Yes—of course. They have no more men. There are only women and old men left in England.'

The party were now passing along the chief street of the city, the Chandnee Chouk, the most beautiful street in all India. It cuts the town in two almost from wall to wall, in one unbroken line. For it stretches from the Lahore Gate to the King's

Palace, which stands above the river Jumna. On their right, far above them, gleamed and glittered in the morning sun the domes and minarets of the Jumma Musjid. Before them stretched the long unbroken line of palace and mosque and noble houses, all surrounded by gardens and trees. It was a prospect that pleased, but man was vile, for the roadway was a stream of lowest humanity. Soldiery, drunk with spirits and a great licence, were moving about in parties, while differences of opinion or creed were openly settled with blows and steel. The citizens and shopkeepers kept within doors, where they crouched in fear and trembling. But many of them fell victims to the rapacity and the violence of the disheartened sepoys. These openly defied their officers, and the commander-in-chief, Mirza Moghul, did not dare to enforce a stricter discipline.

This, and more, the soldiers told the wounded priest as they led him towards the quarters of their chief. The information of which he was possessed was naturally of considerable value to the mutineers, and the orders were that all wounded men from the valley should at once be taken to an officer holding a post similar to an English chief of the Intelligence Department.

In due course the fakir was haled to the presence

of the chiefs, and abased himself even to the ground
before these adventurers, who had risen to their
proud position from the humble places of rascaldom, and held their authority in inward fear by
outward bluster. These gentry would fain have
enjoyed a greater state, and sat at a table covered
with papers, bearing arms embossed with gold,
wearing turbans where jewels sparkled. But the
soldiery came and went with a careless gait, having,
apparently, no reverence for the great. It was no
better, they said, at the palace of the poor old king
of Delhi—a mere regal peg upon which adventurers
hitched their ambitions.

' So,' one of them said, speaking harshly in a voice
thick with a long course of Oriental debauchery,
' so you were present at the explosion outside the
gates this morning?'

The fakir acquiesced, with a further abasement of
his spare person.

They heard all that he had to tell them of the
explosion, and of the probable numbers of the
attacking party, which he took care to exaggerate.
Then they showed a desire for more, and the man's
eagerness to impart what he knew had an Oriental
shiftiness in it, which was perfectly understood by
his hearers.

They contradicted him, subjected him to a close

cross-examination, and, indeed, chased him up and down, in and out the paths of truth with considerable zest. For if there is one pastime dearer to the Oriental than lying, it is the discovery of his neighbour's untruth. On one or two points the fakir admitted with a certain coy reluctance that his questioners had caught him tripping, and appeared to be no whit the less esteemed on that account. With regard to other items of news, however, he held his point, and at last one of his interlocutors began to lose his temper.

' Do you mean to say that the Feringhees are not constructing batteries every night, in preparation for the big guns that are coming up from the south?'

' I know of no such batteries, sahib.'

' But they exist—they are now being constructed.'

' No, sahib.'

' Then you lie—you lie in your teeth.'

' No, sahib,' protested the fakir; ' I tell truth—by my mother's——'

' Shabash! We do not want to hear of your mother—I have proofs that you are lying!'

The fakir shrugged his shoulders with true Oriental calm. He was in no wise afraid of the upstart leader—one of many who sprang up in Delhi at this time, and in the morning were cut down. He muttered something in his beard.

'What say you?' cried the soldier.

'I think you have no such proof.'

The soldier leapt to his feet and leaned across the table from whence he had hurriedly snatched up a bundle of papers.

'But what are these?' he cried. 'What are these—lying son of a false mother?'

The fakir took the papers and spread them out on the floor, where he squatted down after the manner of his country. He opened the folded papers one by one—examining them carefully.

'These are plans,' he admitted at last, 'of the British lines, showing the new batteries to be constructed.'

'Yes,' cried the soldier triumphantly, 'and they are drawn up by an Englishman. We do not employ only badmashes as spies, as do the Feringhees. We have better men than that!'

The priest was examining the papers with a glitter beneath his shaggy eyebrows. The plan was in each case explained by the text appended in a fine handwriting. They were on native-made paper, but the work and the handwriting were unmistakably European. The fakir breathed hard, as if with difficulty. He folded the papers and handed them back with a cringing bow. They were plans, sure enough, of British lines and batteries as usually constructed by our engineers.

The chief of the Delhi staff took back the documents with a proud smile of triumphant cunning. He threw them down on the table without taking the precaution of counting them, which was a mistake, for the fakir had one of the papers concealed under his bare foot.

The priest presently went limping out into the busy streets a free man, but in disgrace for an unsatisfactory spy. The roadway was almost impassable by reason of the ill-manners of the sepoys, who rendered miserable the lives of the unarmed citizens of Delhi. It was only when he had passed the bank and found his way to the magazine that the fakir secured that solitude for which his soul seemed to long. He found a quiet spot at last beneath some trees overlooking the Jumna, and here squatted down against the wall of a wrecked house, the recent dwelling of a high English official.

He sat for some time in that Oriental depth of reflection which must assuredly be nearly allied to sleep. Then he began to fumble slowly in the folds of his voluminous and not too clean apparel. Before long he produced the plan of a battery which he had succeeded in purloining from the authorities, and unfolded it with that air of treasuring a trifle

14

which belongs to beggars of all nations. After a
pause he searched a second time amidst the intrica-
cies of his clothing, and produced a second treasure.
It was a note written on the paper of a well-known
Calcutta club. If the fakir was able to decipher
English he might have read as follows:—

'DEAR HARRY,--Heard of a horse that will suit
you down to the ground. Shall I send him round
to your quarters this afternoon?

'Yours ever,

'PHILLIP LAMOND.'

The priest laid the two side by side upon the
ground, and compared them. The letter and the
plan supplied to the mutineers in Delhi were written by the same hand.

With a queer smile the fakir folded them together, and concealed them in his robes. Then he
laid him down in the shadow of the broken wall, and
fell into that profound slumber which sheer weariness lays upon the human brain, even in the midst
of a thousand perils.

Without the city—over the valley upon the
Ridge--a new commander had by now gathered
the reins within his hands. Barnard's successor,
Reed, had retired in favour of Wilson—a fine officer,
who had already made the mutineers fear him. But
the times were bad, and our troops in a worse

strait than ever they had been. For the rainy season had set in, with that sudden violence so characteristic of tropical changes. The weeks wore on,
and nothing was done. These days were not in
truth passed idly, for the attacks were, if anything,
more numerous. The mutineers received daily
reinforcements from the provinces, from Central
India, from every part where garrisons had been
quartered and stationed. And our troops could
only stand and watch the enemy swarm like ants
into the city.

From every part of India, and more especially
from the Punjab, came news almost daily, which
kept the minds of the besiegers actively employed.
It seemed, indeed, that there were giants arising in
the north; for the names of Edwardes, of John
Nicholson—of Frederick Cooper, a deputy commis-
sioner who ordered two hundred and sixty men to
be shot, and personally superintended the execution—were on all lips. Such tales as this went
round the camp, and Harry Wylam hoped that the
gods would give him such a chance of showing that
he would shirk neither danger nor responsibility.

It was soon rumoured that Nicholson was coming
from the Punjab to help them, and with that instinct which flashes through the brain of an army,
as through the mind of one man, the troops on the

Ridge discerned that a great leader was about to take command of them. Through the rank and file there seemed to pass a thrill of hope and energy. This man—the destined conqueror of Delhi—seemed to send before him a mental wave of strength and purpose, generated in the stern depths of his own heart, sweeping out over all who followed him, who came nigh unto him, the genius of command.

At this time also, when hope seemed to have sprung up from nothing on every side, strange rumours were current in the camp. It was known that more reliable news was filtering out of the stronghold of the mutineers—news of confusion and strife within the walls—of failing spirit and internal differences among the leaders of the Mutiny. These voices were vague and indefinite, but with one accord they seemed to whisper that the interior of Delhi and all that was passing there were no longer closed pages to the British leaders.

And suddenly men began to whisper to each other, as they looked across the valley towards the domes and minarets of the impregnable stronghold with a new interest—with a queer longing look of wonder in their weary eyes.

And that which they whispered to each other was:

' There is an Englishman in Delhi! There is an English officer in disguise in Delhi!'

CHAPTER XIX.

WAR.

HARRY had the honour of sitting at table with
Nicholson the night after his arrival from the
north, and talked of the brilliant gathering to the
end of his life. The great commander—not so long
ago a poor captain of the line—was himself the
gravest soldier present, and by his chilly manner
awed even Harry, as he himself confessed, into
silence. There was something lion-like and still,
the subaltern said, about the greatest chief he had
ever served under, something large and strong
which seemed to raise him above his fellows. The
merriest wit, the most reckless young fire-eaters—
and we may be sure that Henry was among these—
were gradually silenced, and that which had begun
a gay feast ended solemnly.

Almost immediately, as if this man had the power
of moving events, a greater activity was noticeable
in Delhi. The siege train was daily expected. At
last this weary delay was to be settled one way or
the other. An assault would be somewhat of a for-

lorn hope, and yet Nicholson seemed just the man
to lead such attempts. Delhi was almost impregnable. But Nicholson was—or seemed to be—
unconquerable. The air was big with coming events.

Within the city it was certain that some great
movement was afoot, and the besiegers listened to
the sounds of the drums and gongs, to the ringing
of the bells, to the rumble of big guns through the
streets, with an increasing uneasiness. Then came
the news, clear and concise, from that unknown
source within the walls, that a great army was to
move out with the object of intercepting the siege-
train. The big guns, it was known, were coming
north with a very insufficient guard. The mutineers soon heard of it, and with one of the strokes
of good generalship which at intervals distinguished
their campaign, determined to take advantage of
the weakness of the British convoy.

It is a matter of history that Nicholson, sure of
the reliability of his information, took two thous-
and men and went out to meet the foe, fighting the
battle of Najufgarh, in which signal victory Harry
was fortunate enough to bear a sword and escape
uninjured.

Early in September the siege-train arrived, and
its advent was celebrated by high and low with wild
excitement. It seemed now certain that General

Wilson would deliver the assault; and first to urge this daring attempt was Baird-Smith, the great chief of the Engineers. The work of constructing new batteries was carried on in face of immense difficulty by night, and under a galling fire by day; and at last, towards the middle of the month, the work, all incomplete and insufficient indeed, was pronounced satisfactory enough for the purpose.

All knew that an end was drawing nigh, and in the city there seemed to dwell a hush as if of misgiving. The guns were worked steadily enough, but the manner of the mutineers' warfare was now more distinctly on the defensive than it ever had been. It was as if they had begun at last to fear their foes.

Harry worked in Brind's Battery—number one—as it was called, and was among those surprised there by the enemy on the morning of September 8, when the dawn found the work incomplete and but one gun mounted. He continued to work under fire, and was again mentioned for his daring and cheerful example to the men.

Finally, on the morning of the fourteenth, he was given a company of Pathans—wild warriors, as fair in face as he himself—with which to play his little part in the assault. He moved out to his place in the third column, trembling with that wild excite-

ment which surely has no equal in human emotions
—the thirst for battle. Under Colonel Campbell,
Harry was ordered to enter the city by the Cashmere Gate, which was to be blown open. This act
of daring was accomplished unseen by Harry, who
himself had volunteered to carry a bag of powder
across the plankless bridge. The explosion was the
signal for the advance, which was greeted with a
wild shout, and Harry found himself at last within
the walls of Delhi. Here in the narrow streets
ensued a fight upon which the historian will scarcely
care to dwell; for the long pent-up fury of the men
broke all bounds of humanity, and their officers
scarce sought to restrain them. Women, indeed,
were spared, but boys and old men, bearing no sort
of arm, were cut down ruthlessly. Peaceful citizens, coming trembling to their doors to welcome
their deliverers from the horrors of anarchy and
licentiousness, were bayoneted on their own thresh-
olds, because their faces were black. It was indeed
impossible to distinguish between friend and foe,
and the deadly fire from the windows of the houses
was some excuse for the bitter retaliation wreaked
upon old and young. A thousand deeds of hero-
ism, as well as many acts of fury and revenge, were
done by individual fighters: for this was a soldier's
battle in the narrow streets of Delhi.

Foremost among the stormers in the third column was Harry Wylam—wild with excitement—hoarse and almost voiceless—his clothes torn, his helmet thrown aside. He had been among the first to pass beneath the ruined gateway, and since then his men had scarce been able to keep pace with him. He could no longer shout to them to come on, for his voice had broken. He swept on—bloodstained, silent—killing—killing all he met, an avenging fury.

The fire of the big guns had ceased, for Nicholson's column was in the Cashmere breach fighting its way into the city. The artillery on the Ridge must needs hold their fire, watching the walls of the city, where the smoke hung motionless like a cloud, where the rattle of musketry fire never ceased.

Campbell's men pressed forward, following their officers towards the Chandnee Chouk—the broadest thoroughfare in the city—where discipline would be able to assert its superiority over untrained numbers.

Harry had left his men some yards behind. He was almost alone at the turning of a long narrow street. He paused, uncertain which might be his way, for he had never been in Delhi before, and as he stood irresolute he saw one of the enemy running towards him sword in hand. In a flash of thought Harry recognised the fakir with whom he had fought at the door of the mosque some weeks earlier.

Harry's blood was up. He was ready for any foe, and this one was worthy of steel that had done such execution during the last half-hour. Without waiting for his men he ran forward to meet his ancient foe, who was waving his sword with a gesture startlingly familiar. It was the infantry signal to halt.

Half blinded by fury Harry ran forward—any black face had the power to make him mad. He raised his sword, and rushed upon the fakir, who turned aside the crashing blow and stepped back.

' Harry—you d——d fool!' he said.

' Marqueray—by Heaven!'

' Yes- of course!' answered the other. ' Where are your men! This way—there are forty pandies in a house down this alley—men from Cawnpore, Harry—come on! They are Cawnpore men!— Cawnpore!'

Harry followed—forgetting his surprise in the mad infection of battle. Marqueray's voice, usually so quiet, had something in it that moved Harry to fierce joy. Here was one who loved fighting as he loved it—whose quiet blood was stirred to a fury as wild as his own.

Followed only by three men they dashed down

the alley and into the house indicated by Marqueray. The three were Englishmen—not of Harry's
company.

When the sepoys, huddled together in one room,
saw Marqueray, followed closely by Harry, they
gave a sort of wail—a cry of abject terror. In that
dwelling in a quiet alley between the Cashmere
Gate and the Chandnee Chouk, those five Englishmen scored out their Cawnpore. When they
emerged from the house and followed the men of
the third attacking column all was still within.

The third column penetrated as far as the great
tree-bordered thoroughfare, where they found themselves alone—almost within musket shot of the magazine and the bank and the king's palace, which
places were held by the enemy for many days longer.
The other assaulting columns had not succeeded so
well—their difficulties had indeed been infinitely
greater. For a few minutes Campbell waited, and
fully aware of the immense peril of his position
retreated at length to the church.

Marqueray had in the meantime disappeared. He
had undertaken the perilous task of penetrating
through the city to Nicholson, the leader of the
assault, to communicate to him the position of the
third column. Harry grumbled loudly enough at
the retreat, which prudent step was by no means

agreeable to many another in the successful detachment. There was, however, no help for it, and as
he reluctantly turned his back upon the enemy, who
kept up a nasty fire from a hundred hidden points
of vantage—he suddenly dropped, hit by a bullet in
the groin.

Marqueray made his way through the terror-
stricken city, with what intrepidity may be imagined,
for at every turn a new danger awaited him. The
sepoys were half-mad with fear, and those who kept
their courage, deeming all law and order at an end,
gave themselves up freely to riot and disorder.

When the Englishman reached the Lahore bastion, whither the sound of continuous firing led him,
he found that strongkold still in the hands of the
enemy, as it remained for some days. Moreover,
he had the mortification of looking upon the backs
of his countrymen as these retreated, abandoning
the attempt to storm the bastion.

By a circuitous route he gained that portion of
the wall held by the British, and hurriedly made
himself known. The first words of his own language to cross his ears were depressing enough—the
hopeless password of the moment.

' Nicholson is dead! Nicholson is killed!'

The first sight he ever had of the great leader
—and the last—was a glimpse obtained of the stern

face and stricken form, as they bore John Nicholson
back to the British lines to die. It would seem that
even the greatest of men are destined to accomplish
no more than half of the tasks they attempt—for
Nicholson, shot through the chest when in the act
of leading a wild dash for the Lahore bastion, fell,
knowing full well that Delhi was not yet taken.
He had, indeed, effected an entry. The assault had
been successful in so far as the Cashmere Gate had
been destroyed and the breach carried. But the
city was not half taken, for the strongest positions
in it were still held by the enemy.

Nicholson—fiery and reckless, a consummate
leader—all-seeing and resourceful, a perfect general
—groaned as they bore him away. He looked
with a sort of wonder in his stricken eyes at the tall
fakir bloodstained, black with powder and dust,
and never knew him for the fellow officer who had
played a great unknown part in the great day's work.

Night came upon the city, and in the dark each
party worked to strengthen its position. Barri-
cades were thrown up by the English—communication was kept open between the various columns.
A footing had been established, a victory, indeed,
gained, but at what a cost! Twelve hundred officers and men had fallen. Nicholson was mortally
wounded. His name is written indelibly in the

history of our Eastern Empire, but because his
wonderful career was short—because he played his
part upon a crowded stage—the record of his
achievements has never been a household story in
England.

In the land of his adoption—the vast state for
which he lived, dared, and died—his name will
never be forgotten. There he is worshipped to-
day, literally as a god. The wild tribesmen of the
frontier tell that the hoof-beat of his horse may
be heard nightly in the Peshawur valley, and the
sound will never cease until the rule of the English
is at an end.

It was only on the third day that Phillip Lamond
succeeded in entering the city. He was in company with other civilians and volunteers, having
business legitimate or otherwise, in Delhi.

His knowledge of the intricate streets was made
known to those in command, and duly turned to
account. In the attack on the bank on the third
day he was deputed to guide an attacking party by
a circuitous route, in order to effect a junction with
the main force at work near the king's palace.

He arrived too late for the first attack, and had
the mortification of seeing the position taken without the aid of the reinforcements under his guidance.
The leaders of the assault came back to report their

success to the General, who stood surrounded by
his staff. Among the victors Lamond perceived
the fakir who had dogged him more than once.

'Here,' cried a staff officer behind Lamond,
'Marqueray, the General wants you!'

It was the fakir who obeyed the call.

'Marqueray!' exclaimed Lamond involuntarily,
a thousand recollections whizzing through his brain.

'Yes, Marqueray!' replied the fakir, pausing for
a moment and looking straight into his eyes.

The others fell back and unconsciously formed in
line—a double line of brilliant soldiers, everyone
of them bearing a name known to history. They
stood forming a lane of bright uniforms, though
some indeed were tarnished, and through this lane
the fakir, Frederic Marqueray, tattered and dust-
stained, footsore and bespattered with blood, passed
in his flowing robes to salute his General.

CHAPTER XX.

HARRY'S wound took him back to Calcutta, and would, moreover, have justified an immediate return to England had he been minded to revisit that shore. But in truth he was not over sure of the reception that awaited him there.

The Doctor spoke vaguely, after the manner of his kind, of the benefits of a sea voyage to one whose blood, being naturally of a high temperature, had become further heated by an indiscreet mode of life, followed closely by the fatigue and hardship of a long campaign.

'Oh, hang it!' cried Harry to his adviser with a feeble reflex of his old masterful manner. 'Shall I get well in this country? Tell me that.'

The man of medicine looked at him.

'Yes,' he answered, 'if you obey my orders.'

Harry made a wry face, for he knew that this meant the satisfying of a thirst very natural in so hot a climate with plain soda-water or such stuff as lemonade.

'There's nobody at home,' he began—and paused, remembering Miriam's last letter, full of prim concern as to his safety, with a very womanly panic peeping out between the close written lines; for the Brighton Academy had not succeeded in quite finishing this faithful heart.

' I am not in good odour at the Horse Guards,' said Harry, correcting himself. ' Got into a devil of a scrape, which they will hardly have forgotten yet.'

Lamond, who had at last returned to Calcutta from the north, where order was almost re-established, counselled Harry very strongly to remain in India, and had a thousand urgent reasons against his returning to England.

So Harry remained in Calcutta, and as his hurt began to mend his wild spirit returned to him. The Mutiny was quelled, and its passage had left a new India—the days of the Company were over, and the Governor-General had become the Queen's Viceroy.

High and low alike had been stepping upward. Promotion seemed to be within reach of all. Marqueray, Harry heard, was now a Colonel, doing great deeds under Sir Colin Campbell in the North-West. Many younger men than Harry were Majors, whilst he remained Captain Wylam.

It was not in his nature to grudge others the

honours they had won by bravery or owed to fortune;
but he aired his own grievances frankly enough.

'Like my luck,' he said. 'Barnard was devilish
fond of me. He would have got me something
good, but he died. The other fellows didn't take
to me. A prim lot they were.'

In the rush of promotion and the general distribu-
tion of honours some thought it rather marked that
Harry Wylam should be overlooked, but the victim
himself swore heartily enough when he thought of
his grievances, and at other times forgot them.

So soon as his health was in part restored to him
he began again his wild ways, and those frequenting
the sporting clubs found him as jolly a companion
as could be desired. For he had money to fling
away, and flung royally on green cloth or sward,
where there were plenty waiting to gather it up.
Nor did these gentlemen pause to inquire the source
from whence Harry's riches came. They did not
even know Phillip Lamond. They were a jolly
open-handed set of fellows, such as in France are
called hardy companions, and scorned all tittle-
tattle that savoured of gossip. When they had
money, which was not often, they spent it freely
enough—when the other fellow had the gold they
took it as happily, and did not care to inquire how
long it would last.

The day came when Harry's portion was again at an end. Lamond had divided with a scrupulous care the proceeds of their joint expedition, and that which fell to Harry's share would have been a moderate fortune to most men. But Harry Wylam was not of those that keep with too close a care either the law, money, or their counsel. And the wealth which the fakir had almost soid his life to defend soon vanished at the gambling table.

' Rum old chap, Marks,' Harry was wont to exclaim at this time, whenever there was mention of that distinguished officer. And the more he thought over the incident at the mosque the less he understood it.

Lamond also seemed shy of referring to that exploit, and was at pains to curb Harry's loquaciousness whenever Delhi came under discussion. The elder man still attempted to exercise some control over the wild young officer, and when he failed, which he invariably did, took his reverse with his usual lazy indifference, as if it did not much matter.

To such a life as Harry was leading there is only one end, and this came soon enough—it was the end of his money. And the watchful Lamond was in the room when Harry threw his last stake upon the table and lost it.

' There,' cried Harry, rising from his chair and

looking down at the eager faces of his fellow-gam-
blers with bloodshot eyes. 'There, I'm cleared
out, that's the last of two fortunes.'

He gave a short reckless laugh and turned away;
for he had too much spirit to grumble at his luck
now. He had played a bold game. Perhaps he
had foreseen the end. At all events he faced it
with the spirit of an Englishman.

There was a little silence. And one thick-voiced
player said, 'Better luck next time, Harry!'

Harry was gone to the window, where he stood
looking out into the night. The dawn was not far
off. He turned, and the play had already begun
again. There was silence in the room; and the
cards, as they lightly fell on the polished table,
seemed to be whispering to each other. Harry
shrugged his shoulders, and walked out of the room
without noticing Lamond, who stood apparently
watching the play at another table. It is to be
feared that the young soldier's gait was not too
steady.

After a minute Lamond followed him, and ten
minutes later, it was Lamond who wrenched a pistol
from Harry's hand, and threw it into the corner of
the comfortless bedroom, whither the young fellow
had gone to hide himself like a stricken dog.

'None of that,' said Lamond, aroused for a

moment only from his impassiveness. 'None of that, my boy.'

'Why not?' muttered Harry, sitting heavily down on his bed, heedless of the mosquito curtain which he tore from its frail fastening, so that it fell over him like a cloak. 'Confound this curtain. Why not? It is nobody's business but my own.'

He held his weary head and looked round the room, which was feebly lighted by a candle flickering in the breeze that was stirring before the dawn. His eyes had no light of comprehension. He was of those who look, but do not perceive. He never saw the faded miniature of Miriam, who smiled, with her head posed conventionally, from a frame suspended on the wall.

Lamond however saw it. It was the first time he had penetrated to Harry's bedroom.

'It is nobody's business but my own,' went on Harry with the dull aggressiveness of one whose brain is no longer to be excited by alcohol.

'We'll talk about that to-morrow,' answered Lamond, who was mixing something in a tumbler at the washing-stand.

'Drink this, and don't make an ass of yourself.'

Harry's dull eyes flashed for a moment. He looked up into the steady quiet face of Phillip Lamond—the man who was never roused—and he

took the draught. It was an opiate, and presently
Harry was sleeping quietly.

Lamond moved about the room, noiselessly
arranging the mosquito curtain over Harry, who lay
all dressed upon his bed. He took the candle and
carried it to the miniature upon the wall, which he
studied with grave face. Then he laid his spare
form down to rest on a long chair, and closed his
eyes.

The morning light found them thus, and Phillip
Lamond's life looked the better of the two. For
Harry was pale with patches of lurid colour in his
cheeks. It is dangerous to play with even the
strongest constitution in India.

Lamond was awake first, and went to the bath-
room adjoining Harry's bedchamber, from which
retirement he presently emerged fresh and alert.
He did not wake Harry, but passed the time in
writing a letter on that young gentleman's note
paper with a pen which scratched aloud, and displayed every sign of displeasure at being thus rudely
set to work after an idle existence.

The missive was addressed to Miss Lamond, and
before Harry groaned and yawned himself into the
consciousness of life, it was speeding down the
river to the hand of Maria.

Harry opened his eyes at length—weary and

bloodshot. They rested on the calm face of Phillip Lamond, without light and void for a few moments.

'Ah!' he said; 'I remember.'

And he looked guiltily in the corner where the pistol still lay. He sat up slowly in bed, and his hand went to his brow.

'You stopped me,' he said, looking with a certain fascination in the direction of the firearm.

'Yes, I stopped you,' answered Lamond, who now picked up the pistol, and removing the percussion cap, slipped it into his pocket

'Then I think it was confoundedly interfering of you,' said Harry, with a mirthless laugh. For his sense of humour never deserted him, even at the gravest moments of his life. Indeed, he had during his thirty years or so of life faced death with an unflinching mien so often that he could contemplate his escape from an ignominious end with recklessness.

It was the other man who wore a grave face, whose eyes bore a certain scared look as of one who had built a high castle and suddenly perceived a flaw in its foundation.

'That may be,' said Lamond seriously; 'but I am not going to stand by idle any longer and see your father's son go to the devil.'

'Then you'll have to shut your eyes,' broke in Harry, who was still in a wild mood. 'for that's the

way I'm going, sure enough. Luck is dead against
me—nobody cares what happens to me, and I'm
d——d if *I* do.'

'That is not the truth,' said Lamond steadily.
'You've plenty of friends who would be ready
enough to help you. If it's money you want, I
have a little of that which is at your disposal. If
it is position you have only to keep steady to secure
that.'

'Thanks, old fellow,' said Harry, suddenly grave.
'You are a trump. I always thought so, though
others didn't.' At which Mr. Lamond shrugged
his shoulders indifferently enough. 'But I'm not
going to take your money. I have not fallen so low
as that yet. I can sell my commission, I suppose—
or at the worst I can blow out my worthless brains.'

'And break a woman's heart,' said Lamond
quietly.

There was a little pause. Harry was sitting on
his bed—a dishevelled, unshaven object—handsome
still, despite his careless dress. For he had slept
in his clothes, and the man who has slept in his
clothes starts the day sorely handicapped. He
looked slowly up into Lamond's face. That gentleman was standing before him—his narrow and
effeminate face a little pallid in the strong light of
the tropic sun.

'A woman's heart—what the devil do you mean?'

There was a little twitch of the elder man's lips, which might have betokened a spasm of honest feeling.

'Ever since you came to this country you have been making love to Maria; not quite the straight thing, unless you meant honestly by an inexperienced young girl.'

For a moment Harry sat in amazement, as well he might. Many of us sit amazed when we see our own actions through the eyes of another. Phillip Lamond had said nothing but the truth, and yet it startled Harry strangely.

'I have no reason to think,' he said doggedly, 'that Maria cares for me any more than a dozen other fellows. What is there to care for in an unlucky beggar like me?'

'Ah, Harry,' answered Lamond with a short laugh, 'women see things in us that are not there. And I suppose we mostly return the compliment.'

He turned away and leant against Harry's somewhat rickety chest of drawers with a graceful nonchalance.

'Of course,' he said, 'I may be mistaken. I almost hope I am. A little over anxiety is perhaps allowable to the father of a motherless girl—she is all I have now.'

And across the river of Death an airy sigh was wafted to the shade of Maria's mother, who had been a barmaid in Calcutta before she married Phillip Lamond, and settled steadily down—to drink.

'Maria has said nothing to me, of course; no girl would,' he went on. He broke off with an easy-going shrug. 'But I suppose young people must settle these things for themselves. Anyway, come down and stay with us a few days. You are in bad health. You are better out of town now that the hot weather is coming on. A little peace and quiet will set you up. I have business in the town. Pack up some traps, and I'll call for you after tiffin.'

With a nod he was gone, leaving Harry somewhat puzzled, and in the grip of a new feeling of shame and discomfort.

The heat of the day was over before Lamond returned in a palanquin. They embarked in his boat, which was waiting in the harbour. On the voyage down the swift stream Harry was silent, and his companion seemed disinclined for conversation. They were both, perhaps, thinking of the first voyage they made together years earlier when Harry returned to India with all the world before him.

The little bungalow looked cool and peaceful in the quiet of the afternoon. In the verandah the

new comers espied a white-clad form, gracefully re-
posing on a long cane chair. It was Maria, who
presently rose and came across the parched lawn
to meet them, looking very pretty, youthful and
happy in the shade of the parasol she carried.

Lamond paused to give some order to his boatmen. Harry and Maria walked slowly back to the
verandah together. With a pretty little movement
of familiarity which was quite sisterly she slipped
her hand within his arm.

' I am so glad you have come to see us again,' she
said.

CHAPTER XXI.

PEACE.

IN the bungalow on the banks of the Hooghly, Phillip Lamond had a room, which was known to the household as his study. It was not even an office, and had no appearance of ledgers and files; but looked innocent and studious enough with a few books and magazines, not always of a recent date, lying on the table.

'Here,' Phillip Lamond was wont to say, 'I transact my small affairs, and here I smoke more than is good for me, as Maria always tells me.'

And indeed the apartment was saturated with a pleasant Bohemian odour of bye-gone Manilla cheroots—a suggestion, as it were, of a harmless easy-going vice indulged in with a very human weakness of mind. There is nothing so innocent as a harmless vice—and most of us cherish one.

'Come into my room,' said Lamond, rising from the breakfast table the next morning, 'and we will have a smoke.'

He stood with his hands thrust into the pockets

of his thin and flowing jacket, looking down at the young people, who were perhaps inclined to linger over the pleasant meal.

Harry was in clean white—he felt indeed cleanly without and within—a pleasant feeling of a new start in life which comes to some in the morning hours when the cool of a long night has soothed the feverish vapours of a forgotten day.

Maria was dressed in spotless cambric, with a pale-blue ribbon at her throat. The season was well advanced, and a daily increasing heat of the atmosphere no doubt accounted for loose and flowing sleeves, from which emerged the whitest round arms in the world. The duties of the breakfast table called forth a considerable display of curved wrist and clever curling fingers. Maria was, withal, of a demure humour this morning, with downcast eyes and a very fascinating shyness which was quite new. She had only monosyllables at her disposal, and never glanced at Harry at all, who, on the contrary, never looked at anything else than herself.

In response to Lamond's invitation Harry slowly rose, with an urgent glance at Maria, who was preparing some crumbs for an imaginary assembly of birds on the verandah, and therefore did not notice the direction of his gaze.

'When Maria considers that we have smoked enough she will come and drag us from our den—eh—my dear?' said Lamond, affectionately. And Harry muttered something to the effect that her task would be an easy one. Indeed, the young fellow's condition was such that a single hair would do the business.

Lamond led the way to his study without appearing to notice that Harry paused on the threshold of the dining-room to look back at Maria, whose pretty head was bent over the table in a vain endeavour to hide a charming blush.

'Well,' said the elder man easily when they were seated, 'have you young people arrived at an understanding yet?'

He was cutting the end of a cigar, and did not look up. It was quite evident that in this, as in all the affairs of his life, he was rather floating with the stream than endeavouring to guide the course of events.

'Yes,' said Harry stoutly; 'and I never thought to be so happy.'

'Ah!' answered Lamond, with an affectionate and tolerant laugh. 'It is well to gather the roses while you may. I suppose I must be content so long as my little girl is happy. I tell you frankly, Harry, that that is what I chiefly want——'

Phillip Lamond paused, cigar in hand, and looked out of the window with a queer suggestion of surprise in his eyes. It seemed almost as if he was astonished at hearing the plain unvarnished truth spoken in his own voice.

' I have not much else to live for,' he went on, ' than Maria. I frankly tell you I hoped she would do better for herself. There are plenty of fellows with money and a good position who have asked me to help them in the matter. But I have always referred them to Maria herself. So long as you care for each other, I suppose I must be content. I can give my girl a little settlement, which should be enough for young people to begin upon——'

He paused again.

'Deuced generous,' muttered Harry, with a shamed face.

'.... And I hope you will get something soon. There are plenty of appointments going begging. Yes, Harry, my boy, we'll pull through somehow. I must make the best of it.'

He gave a little sigh, and lighted a cigar.

' Perhaps the luck will turn,' exclaimed the hopeful young gambler; and in truth the fresh morning air, the brightness of the river, the odorous luxuriance of the Indian garden, and the memory of Maria's last smile, would have instilled a like hopefulness in older hearts than his. ' It's been dead against me up to now, but it must surely have turned when Maria began to care.'

With which excellent, loverlike reflection he lapsed into a happy silence.

' There will,' said Lamond carelessly, after a pause, ' be a little left of the Delhi estate when we can get things settled up.'

' Then I'll settle it on her!' cried Harry, whose spirits were rising, and with them the spontaneous open-handedness which he had not lost with the boyhood and good health that were no longer his. ' I'll settle every halfpenny of it on her,' he said. ' You're half a lawyer—come, let us do it now.'

Lamond laughed in his easy-going way.

' No hurry,' he said, puffing at his cigar.

' Yes—but there is—every hurry. We're going to get married at once.'

' Oh, are you?' laughed Lamond in his tolerant way. ' Have you asked Maria?'

' No,' answered Harry. ' But——'

' You know girls generally want a long time to make up their minds,' broke in the fond father. ' There are a lot of things to be got—clothes, and such things.'

' Yes,' admitted Harry. ' But——'

And he explained no farther, leaving it to be understood that the impatience of so ardent a lover might overcome the coyness of even Maria.

The maiden's father had turned to the table, where he was tentatively fingering a quill.

'It is always better,' he said half to himself, with a pondering, uncertain air, 'to keep the lawyers out of these affairs. So much easier to manage such things amicably between friends.'

Harry consigned all lawyers to perdition in his frank soldierly way, and urged Phillip Lamond to make out what he called a 'chit,' to the effect that he endowed his future wife Maria with all his worldly goods.

'I'll have to do it in the church,' he said, 'why not do it now?'

Lamond laughed, laid aside his cigar, and with much hesitation made out a brief marriage settlement, which, if it lacked legal verbosity, was nevertheless a very binding and masterly organ in its way.

'What I've said is this,' he observed, when he had finished—and he dotted an 'i' here and there with the air of one little accustomed to such work. 'I've said that you settle upon her the estate known as your Delhi estate, with all rents or profits whatsoever, due, overdue, or in accumulation from

16

whatsoever source, the same to be held in trust
for Maria by two persons—say myself and another.
That you hereby relinquish all claim to such estate
and such rents as may have accrued in favour of
the trustees.'

'Hand it over,' cried Harry, seizing a pen and
dipping it in the ink.

Lamond obeyed, and then drew back.

'Wait a minute,' he said, with his fingers in his
thin hair. 'Ought it not to be witnessed?'

He did not give an opinion. He merely asked
Harry's advice upon a point of which he was himself ignorant.

'Perhaps it ought,' said Harry impatiently. His
was the dangerous form of indolence, that has sudden accesses of energy.

But this difficulty was soon overcome by Lamond,
who rang the bell, and sent for Maria's English
maid. Another European witness was found in the
manager of a neighbouring rice mill, who came in
all floury, signed his name and departed, leaving a
faint haze in the atmosphere.

'It isn't much,' said Harry, when all was signed
and sealed. 'What a fool I have been ; what a con-
founded fool—Lamond.'

The elder man laughed in his good-natured
way.

'No. It is practically nothing. But as for
fools, we have all been that in our time,' he
opined with tolerance, as one who did not by any
means pretend to perfection himself. There is
no sinner so hopeless as he who confesses his sins
easily.

It was Maria's voice that diverted Harry's attention from what he had done, and carried his soul at
one flight above such mundane matters as a marriage-settlement—Maria's fresh voice carolling a
song as she glided in and out of the deep shade of
the great banyan tree.   •

'Well,' exclaimed the happy lover, as he rose
and threw his cigar away. 'That is done! I only
wish it was more.'

'Things may turn out better than they seem to
promise,' said Lamond indifferently. 'Let us hope
they will—when the country is settled again. And
in the meantime I can perhaps manage a little ready
money——'

He looked up with his kindly smile, not seeking
to retain Harry. The young fellow came forward
eagerly, and grasped the slim hand in his strong
fingers.

'You're a brick—by Heaven, you're a brick,
Lamond,' he said earnestly.

And Mr. Phillip Lamond was left alone in his

study with a cigar, and the serene consciousness of that reward which is the estate of him who seeks to do good to his neighbour.

Maria, we may be sure, was sufficiently shocked and alarmed at the mere mention of the word ' marriage.' Indeed, she behaved with all the coy trepidation belonging to her new and fluttering state, as understood by maidens at the beginning of the present reign. We can afford to laugh at such to-day, when the fairer sex is advancing and advances, even to the altar-rail, with a calm self-satisfaction and an unfaltering step.

So Maria gave a little gasp of horror when Harry mentioned marriage, and listened nevertheless with a comprehending ear when the word settlement was attached to the alarming syllables.

' But I could never be married,' she cried. ' No, never. It would be so terrible.'

And Harry's re-assurances were necessarily long and comprehensive.

' But we shall have nothing to live upon,' she still protested. ' We shall be poor, and I know you will get tired of me.'

Whereupon she was interrupted by a torrent of protestations and vows, such as many have made and few have kept since the days of Adam.

' Do you think,' said the blushing Maria when

this was over, ' that your guardian will do anything
for us? He is very rich, is he not?'

Harry's face clouded, and a flicker of Maria's
eyelids showed that she had noted the change.

' But I do not mind,' she added quickly. ' I do
not mind being poor, so long as you go on thinking . . . . what you think now.'

' That I am the happiest man in the world,' cried
Harry, the cloud dispersed by a glance of Maria's
dark eyes.

' I do not understand why you are,' she began
with a pretty misgiving.

And the talk thus glided easily into the happy
channel where some of us have trifled in our time,
before wading into the deeper waters of life.

At times they stepped out for a moment and
stood upon the hard strand of practical daily existence. And, singularly enough, it was always Maria
who led the way. Mingled with a high romantic
comprehension of the situation, she seemed to be
endowed with a most estimable recollection of the
fact that the ways and means of existence are necessarily also the ways and means to happiness.

' I wonder,' she said, ' if you will get some good
appointment? They ought to have given you your
majority.'

' Why, Marqueray's a colonel.'

' Yes, but he is a horrid man,' opined Maria by
way of consolation. ' Of course I know nothing of
money matters; but is it not by influence that good
appointments are secured? Can one not buy such
things?'

' If one has the money one can buy anything,'
replied Harry with a laugh. ' But why are you so
anxious for me to get an appointment?'

' Oh,' she answered, with a pretty thoughtfulness,
' it gives one a position, which is so important in
India.'

She was perhaps thinking of a hundred slights—
small feminine slights which men neither see nor
comprehend—put upon the daughter of Phillip
Lamond, who had no position. She glanced at
Harry beneath her lashes. There was something
momentarily suggestive of a sleek cat feeling its way
towards some desired object in that quick glance.

' And of course,' she went on, ' a great deal is
done by home influence. You surely have that.
Could you not write home? If you have quarrelled
with your guardian, why not write to—Miss Gresham? And—tell her at the same time that you are
engaged.'

Harry's face had hardened again quite suddenly.
But Maria was only feminine. She could not keep
her fingers from forbidden things.

' No,' he answered shortly.

' Do you know, Harry,' said the girl coquettishly, ' I am a little jealous of Miss Gresham. Were you fond of her?'

' No—no; drop that,' said Harry almost roughly; and he rose from his seat at Maria's side.

CHAPTER XXII.

THE SUPPRESSED LETTER.

FREDERIC MARQUERAY was advised of Harry's intended marriage by a friendly letter from the happy man himself. This missive was delivered to the rising young commander in his quarters at Cawnpore, and received an immediate answer. Indeed, Marqueray wrote a pressing and urgent letter to his former subaltern before attending to the remainder of his correspondence. In those days the railway did not connect Calcutta and Cawnpore, although the land had been surveyed and plans drawn out. The train came no nearer than half way, from whence the mail service was effected by road. The arrival of letters at their destination was still an uncertain affair, owing to the immense drain upon the resources of the authorities, as regards horseflesh and cartage, which had been made by the military commanders in the forwarding of troops and ammunition.

At this juncture, as in others, Frederic Marqueray acted with promptitude and decision. He wrote a letter to Harry Wylam, which that youth could scarcely have shown to his intended wife, and still less to that fair one's father. For Marqueray knew as much of Phillip Lamond and his daughter as was required to sever the foolish connection into which Harry in his carelessness had drifted. No date had been fixed for the marriage, and the truest friend that Harry possessed in India hoped that the fatal alliance might yet be avoided.

It was only in the evening of the same day—after the despatch of his letter—that Marqueray learnt from a mutual friend, in receipt of later news from Calcutta, that Harry Wylam's wedding had been fixed for an early date.

A hurried calculation showed that Marqueray's letter might, in the course of the mail, as at that time running, reach its destination one day before that, reluctantly and coyly set aside by the bashful bride, for the fulfilment of her lover's happiness.

By riding night and day Marqueray knew that he could overtake the mail and pass it. He set out as the bugles sounded the hour of nine.

Harry had been all for a quiet wedding in the early morning at the Garrison Church, but the bride, who naturally held the casting vote at this time, willed it otherwise.

'I suppose,' said Lamond, with his air of gentle resignation, 'that we had better make a splash.'

And to accomplish this excellent object he contracted with the manager of a large hotel to furnish a wedding breakfast for a number of guests to be thereafter named. The ceremony was to take place in the Cathedral. Invitations were issued to all the persons of position whom the Lamonds knew, and to many they did not.

'Wylam's made an ass of himself again,' his friends said of him at the club, and the servants found several invitation cards in the waste-paper basket.

Maria made a bold attempt to unearth a bishop of some sort to perform the ceremony, feeling no doubt that a higher functionary would naturally tie a closer knot. But the bishop pleaded that indisposition which seems to lurk, in company perhaps with a smile, in lawn sleeves. Harry, however, ordered a new tunic, though the lace on his captain's uniform was still fresh enough; and there was a certain consolation in the brilliancy of its scarlet.

He called in person on Lady Leaguer, who promised to be present.

'I cannot answer for my husband,' she said. 'He may be away from home.'

Harry paused, and drew in his feet rather awk-

wardly. It was a singular thing that Major-General
Sir Thomas Leaguer should never have inquired
after his subaltern. This leader, who had come
through the Mutiny with a whole skin and a brighter
honour, must have had a hundred posts of trust and
danger to assign to the younger men with whose
capabilities he had become acquainted in times of
peace. No such post, no such honour had come
Harry's way. The luck, as he often protested, was
not in his favour. His old leader seemed to have
forgotten him, and yet forgetfulness had never
been a characteristic of the keen-eyed, intrepid
soldier.

'Have you heard from Frederic Marqueray
lately?' inquired my lady, changing the subject
with a haste which almost seemed to anticipate
awkward questions.

'No. I wrote to him, of course, to tell him of
my marriage.'

'And you have had no answer?' asked the lady
casually.

'No. I only wrote a fortnight ago.'

Lady Leaguer glanced at a silver date stand—a
pretty new toy she had lately received from home.
A quick calculation told her that Marqueray's reply
would arrive too late.

She again assured Harry of her intention to be

present at his wedding, and the happy bridegroom withdrew.

Phillip Lamond wrote in confidence a long letter to that upright citizen, John Gresham, in the city of London, wherein he set forth his own objections to the union about to be contracted. He apologised for doing so in the most gentlemanly manner in the world, pleading as excuse the very natural anxiety of a widower whose only child was about to take so momentous a step in life.

' Harry,' he imparted in confidence to one whom, having never seen, he nevertheless ventured to look upon as an old friend—' Harry was,' he feared, ' a wild fellow. He had, it was true, conducted himself with marked valour during the terrible trial through which India had just passed. He had even distinguished himself on more than one occasion under arms.' This, Phillip Lamond was in the happy position of being able to confirm from the evidence of his own eyes, as he, like many another gentleman of middle age, had deemed it his duty to carry a sword in the service of his country in her sore trait. But war was happily not a normal state of existence, and it was chiefly in times of peace that the writer feared for Harry, whose superabundant spirits and energy led him into mischief at that time when our common enemy is especially zealous in finding work for idle hands to do. While allowing anxiety to disturb his nightly repose, Mr. Lamond still hoped for the best, and trusted that, under Providence, his darling child might be enabled to exercise a good influence over her husband, and bring to a higher condition of development those good qualities which were known to exist in Harry's heart by all who loved him. It was, in truth, a beautiful letter, and Phillip Lamond sealed and despatched it with considerable self-satisfaction. One of its chief merits rested upon the fact that long before a reply could reach Calcutta Harry and Maria would be man and wife.

So at last the happy morning dawned, and Harry was as deeply in love as ever. Maria, with all her innocence and the inexperience of which her father could never say enough, had known how to inflame and never allow to diminish the ardour of her lover's passion. The joyful day found Harry in the highest spirits, Maria collected and calm, but determined. At last the object of her ambition was within sight—a position. In a few hours she would be the wife of a captain in her Most Gracious Majesty's Indian Army. Should she go home to England—and who shall say where a maiden's dreams may reach?—she would be entitled to a presentation at Court. She would go home not as the daughter of Phillip Lamond, whose position in Calcutta society was singularly vague and ambiguous, but as the wife of a British officer who had played a gallant part in the glorious capture of Delhi, whose name had been mentioned in despatches, and would be handed down to posterity in the military annals of his country.

So Maria's heart beat high, and the cathedral bells rang out a glad chime. Harry buckled on his sword and cast one last glance around his bedroom. He noted the forlorn furniture taken at a valuation from his predecessor; he smiled at the bruise in the wall made by a flying dumb-bell which had escaped his grip in the early days when he cultivated athletics and attended to the expansion of his chest. He remembered that the fourth castor of his armchair still reposed in the table-drawer instead of adding to the symmetry of the piece of furniture which he had intended to repair any time this last three years. But he never glanced at the miniature on the wall.

The carriages rolled up to the cathedral doors, and the syces, perched on nothing behind their masters, cried frantically to the throng to make room. The imperturbable crowd of turbaned natives stood watching in silence. There were no small boys to cry huzzay—and the small boy who cries huzzay is a very useful adjunct.

The organ pealed out its contribution towards the general stir, and Harry stood with his gloved fingers at his moustache looking anxiously towards the door.

At last Maria came, and a hundred necks were craned. There was no doubt of her beauty at that moment. Through the modest veil, dark eyes flashed and a blush mantled on rounded cheeks. This was her moment of triumph; for she knew as well as any that the multitude had not assembled in their numbers out of love to herself. Half of the women who noted in one comprehensive stare the cut, the material, the general success of her wedding dress, were of that world into which Maria was about to step. She was rising from the ranks, and these kind-hearted ladies had assembled to make her ascent as hard as possible—to rob each step of its little triumph by the discovery of a small mistake.

But Maria Lamond was a clever woman; and her father, still intent on his ' splash,' was easy, indifferent, and quite master of the situation, as he led his daughter, and surreptitiously aided her to drag her weighty train the length of the aisle.

In a loud and ready voice Harry undertook to love, comfort, honour, and keep Maria in sickness and in health, while in a lower tone, as if discounting the necessary promises as much as possible, she expressed her intention of honouring and obeying him.

The clergyman, who was an old-fashioned person, delivered a sermon of considerable length, during which Harry shuffled his feet and sighed impatiently. In the middle of the learned discourse Frederic Marqueray, travel-stained and tired, quietly entered the cathedral—too late.

By some strange instinct Phillip Lamond turned in his seat at the precise moment when Marqueray slipped quietly into a pew at the back of the church, and thus the presence of Harry's former captain and faithful friend became known.

Harry would have it that Marqueray should sign the register, and against a slight protest on the part of his bride sent a messenger summoning his friend to the vestry.

The newcomer was greeted by Harry with effusion and a merry volume of words delivered in a frank and boisterous tone, which made the grave parson raise his eyebrows in mild protest. Maria had lifted her veil aside, her eyes were bright with excitement, her cheeks flushed. She greeted Marqueray in a friendly enough manner, and left him keenly alive to the futility of the letter he had written. What could reason and experience hope to effect against such bright eyes and all-conquering dimples!

' Have you just arrived in Calcutta ? ' she asked.

' Yes. I have come straight from the station.'

' How good of you! ' And Maria looked straight into his eyes with spirit and defiance.

' You two,' broke in Harry with a hand on Marqueray's shoulder, ' will have to be great chums.'

And he looked from one to the other with his jolly laugh. A move was made, for the formalities were over and the parson's fee duly paid.

' Of course,' said Lamond, linking his arm within Marqueray's, ' you will come round to the hotel with us; we've got a little bit of breakfast going there.'

Maria seconded the invitation very prettily, and Marqueray accepted.

' If you will excuse my travel-stained appearance,' he added.

' My dear fellow,' protested Lamond, ' we'll excuse anything in so old a friend.'

Marqueray almost began to think that he was indeed an old friend, so pleasant an air of *camaraderie* Harry's father-in-law assumed in enunciating this. Maria too was kind enough to flash a smile upon him beneath her veil.

At the hotel a merry party crowded into the room where the breakfast was set out. On a side-table the presents were laid out in generous display—as

17

generous a display, that is, as possible, for there were not very many of them. But Harry's gifts to Maria were profuse and lavish enough to make up for any deficiencies displayed by the friends who had won the bridegroom's money in his palmier days. These in truth were the men who opined that Harry had made an ass of himself, and held aloof.

Some of her lover's presents were new to Maria, who duly admired them with little cries of delight and surprise. A number of letters and some telegrams were upon the table, beside the presents awaiting Harry's inspection. Many of his friends with the armies in the north and at Delhi had heard of his marriage, and their letters of congratulation had arrived with the mail by which Frederic Marqueray travelled down to Calcutta.

' Ah!' cried Harry, ' a lot of letters; and here is one from you, Marks!'

' Yes,' said Marqueray, coming forward; and taking the letter from Harry's hand he tore it in shreds.

' Don't do that!' shouted Harry eagerly. ' What was in it ?'

' Nothing.'

And as the tiny pieces fluttered to the ground the bride turned round and looked at Marqueray.

CHAPTER XXIII

NOT long after the wedding Lamond wrote from
Delhi to inform his dear boy that a windfall had
dropped his way. In confirmation of this happy
news he enclosed a draft on a Calcutta bank for a
handsome sum. Harry swore that the luck had
changed at last, as the thin pink paper fluttered to
the ground.

'Four thousand rupees!' he cried, and Maria's
bright eyes took to themselves an additional glitter.
'The luck has changed, old girl—the luck has
changed.' He kissed his wife boisterously, and she
set her hair in order with a little frown. She did
not seem so tolerant of her husband's somewhat
demonstrative affection as she had been when he
was a lover only.

'What will you have? 'Tis six months to-day
that we were married,' continued Harry, waving
the paper across Maria's red lips. 'Say, Maria,
what shall it be?'

'Well,' she answered somewhat curtly; 'of

course we want a brougham of our own, instead of that horrid hired thing that shakes me to bits.'

' Right!' cried Harry, whose fingers seemed ever to be burnt by money, so quickly did he part with it. ' We'll drive in now and buy one.'

Harry had not yet found work to do. He had in truth applied often enough, but no appointment was ever vacant when he sent up his name. Perhaps he applied to the wrong person. Perhaps that unfortunate cloud under which he had left England had been wafted across to India. Who shall say what zephyrs blow our luck hither and thither? Not, assuredly, Harry Wylam. He only cursed his ill-fortune and dropped into the Bohemian, hand-to-mouth mode of life which had obtained in the bungalow across the river.

For they were now in a furnished house in Garden Reach, with hired horses and carriages; and Maria sat in the drawing-room in her new dresses, every afternoon, awaiting the visits of ladies who never came. Harry did not go to his club for nearly three months, but now, at the end of six, dropped in occasionally to see his friends. If the women did not call at the furnished house in Garden Reach, the men did. Harry felt that there was something wrong here, but he did not know what. The callers were not among the most desirable of his friends, but Maria did not seem to notice anything amiss with their manners, and, when Harry suggested this, laughed at him, and called him a jealous old stupid.

Then came a time when Maria could see no visitors, and was impatient and petulant with her husband. Harry's endeavours at this time to please his wife were somewhat pathetic in their clumsy honesty. He did not understand women at all. His comprehension of the situation was limited, and at last he lost patience and went off to the club, leaving Maria hard-faced and sullen in the somewhat dismal house in the quiet suburb.

His idleness seemed to annoy her. His tastes— all for sport and an active open-air life—were not her tastes, a lamentable fact which it is to be feared most young couples come to recognise within a year or so of marriage. Maria taunted her husband with his indolence and his inability to find work for the sword that was rusting in its scabbard—which was a mistake. Harry began to employ himself at the club.

Only two months had elapsed since the purchase of the new brougham, and Harry began to think that the luck had never really turned at all. It had been false to him. Money, indeed, was not at this time wanting. Lamond had remitted further

amounts from Delhi, where things he said were
' looking up.'   Harry did not rightly know—and in
truth scarce cared to inquire—whether these sums
were in the form of a loan, or came to him from the
sale of his estates.

Day by day the furnished house in Garden Reach
saw less of him, and his friends at the club had an
increased enjoyment of his society.   His spirits
were at times as high as ever, but those who knew
him well were of opinion that he made an effort
to appear jolly, and was not naturally so.   He
began to play a little, just to while away the long
evenings.   He knew that if he went home he
would find Maria lying down or already in bed.

In due time Maria had cause to send for him during the day, and he was ushered into her shaded
bedroom.

' A little girl, my good sir,' said the doctor,
pressing his hand.

' A little girl, egad,' repeated Harry stepping
softly, and he looked down at a small bundle in the
smiling ayah's arms.

' Little beggar's a bit highly coloured, eh ?' he
said anxiously, his own face a sudden deep red with
honest pride.

As he stooped to kiss Maria a tear trickled from
his sunburnt cheek, and fell upon her hand.   He

turned again, and looked with a queer pride at the child, whose small face seemed strangely peaceful.

' Her eyes are blue,' whispered the ayah, for the infant was sleeping.

The first money expended upon her had been won at the card-table; for Harry had a run of luck at this time, and he spent his winnings freely enough in gifts for Maria and the little one. So matters progressed while the mother slowly recovered, and the infant grew with an astonishing rapidity which was an ever new delight to Harry.

The first caller was kind Lady Leaguer, drawn towards the young mother in her loneliness and friendlessness. Lady Leaguer was herself a mother, as the Army List testifies to-day, and gave Maria the benefit of her own happy experiences. Others soon followed her ladyship, as was to be expected, for most women are like sheep in their visits, especially if the bell-wether carries a title. Thus the tide flowed for a while in Garden Reach, and Harry —when the cards favoured him—was ready to swear that he was the luckiest man in India. His debts were daily growing in bulk all the while, for when he had money he spent it on his wife and child, and only when he could find nothing more to buy he took it to the card-table. The rent of the furnished house was overdue. He owed money right and left, and no attempt had been made to pay off the debts incurred by Maria's long illness.

Presently the tradespeople began to dun him for a settlement of their bills, and Harry laughingly put them off. Then he borrowed money with which to play—one evening when the luck seemed about to turn. And he was thus fairly embarked upon the easy descent. Maria was stronger now, and began to gather into her own capable hands the strings of their joint fortunes. She found them tangled, as well she might, and turned upon her husband in a fury.

'You are a pauper!' she cried. 'You are practically turned out of the Army, for no commander will have you. You do not attempt to find work, and you are living like a grand gentleman, with your buggy and your club. You are living on us. It is father's money that you are throwing away.'

It was the first time he had seen Maria like this, the first time he had heard in her voice a certain stridency which is not in the tones of ladies born and bred. He had nothing to answer, and he went out thinking of that tone in her voice.

If he could only persevere with the cards, the luck must turn in time. He drove in the buggy mentioned to the club referred to by Maria in her wrath, and there failed to find a lender. They were mostly borrowers there. Then he took another step down the hill. He went to a native money-lender, whose obscure shop was in the China Bazaar.

After considerable trouble he found the house indicated to him by a friend who had had need of financial accommodation—as it is gracefully called by the accommodator—on more than one occasion. He was ushered into an inner room by a bearer, who seemed to serve by merely sitting on the door-step and waiting.

The money-lender was a Parsee of eminently respectable appearance, whose strange headdress imparted an additional blandness to a countenance full of accommodation. This gentleman rose and bowed over a low table. He was not alone. Near him, in the attitude and chair of a visitor, a native, richly dressed and turbaned, sat gravely noting the proceedings. Both these men were evidently of a position and dignity which enabled them to receive the visit of a European with equanimity.

'I want some money,' said Harry, standing squarely in the little room and feeling intensely ashamed of himself. 'My name is Henry Wylam —Captain.'

The Parsee money-lender bowed with a little

smile, which, far from indicating surprise, seemed
to say that Captain Henry Wylam had been expected—sooner or later.   The native gentleman,
however, whose heavy face had merely expressed a
polite patience, turned sharply—as sharply, that is,
as his bulk allowed—in his chair and half rose.   The
rings on his fingers flashed in the subdued light of
the room.

'Captain Henry Wylam?' he said in perfect
English, and a voice that had a pleasant sound in it.

'Yes,' answered Harry, rather stiffly.

'Of Delhi?'

'Of that as much as any place.'

The stout man had risen.   He was as tall as
Harry, and very broad, making a fine dignified
figure in his loose robes and great turban.

'And you want—*money?*' with a little laugh.

'Yes.'

The man shrugged his shoulders.   He bowed
very low with a perfect dignity.

'I am Hajii Alaraka Sajin,' he said, 'of Delhi.'

'Ah!   Glad to make your acquaintance,' said
Harry courteously, for he had learnt the lesson of
the Mutiny, and was naturally of a pleasant address.
But it was evident from his honest face that he had
never heard the name before.

'Mr. Sajin is one of the great bankers of the

Punjab—indeed, of all India,' said the money-
lender in unctuous explanation. 'No native gentleman has helped so much to quell the Mutiny.'

'It is strange that we should meet thus, Captain
Wylam,' said the banker quietly. 'I have only
arrived in Calcutta this morning—the first time for
twenty years. Your father honoured me with his
confidence, and more—with his friendship.'

Harry held out his hand with the frank, almost
boyish, spontaneity to which he owed many a
friendship.

'Then, by gad, sir, I *am* glad to meet you!' he
cried, and the grip he gave Hajii Alaraka Sajin
made that old gentleman wince. The money-lender
—a man of tact—seeing how the land lay, had risen
from his chair.

'Excuse me, sir,' he said punctiliously to Harry;
'perhaps our business can wait. I am wanted elsewhere. I will return soon.'

He glanced at the native banker, who nodded
approvingly, and left the room. For a moment
neither of the remaining occupants of the little
office spoke. Hajii Alaraka Sajin moved somewhat ponderously in his chair, with the help of
his arms, as stout men do.

'So,' he said, thickly, 'you came here for
money?'

' Yes,' admitted Harry, with a laugh which was not quite free from embarrassment.

' Hard up, eh ? '

' Damnably hard up, sir ! '

Harry had seated himself on the corner of the Parsee's writing-table, and was swinging one leg carelessly.

The native banker looked at him with a sort of amusement lurking in the wrinkles beneath his yellow, expressionless eyes. It was a fat, heavy face, with folds of superfluous flesh below the eyes, into which Harry frankly smiled.

' And,' said Sajin, leaning forward and emphasising his points with the tip of his forefinger on the arm of the chair, ' you are the heaviest depositor in my bank—one of the largest native banks in India. Nearly two million rupees to your credit at this moment, and increasing daily, for I carry the interest to your credit at the end of each month.'

' Gammon ! ' said Harry.

' No, but I have it in the books—it is in black and white,' protested the stout man, with that love of the written fact which is natural to his race.

Harry laughed sceptically.

' When you were two years old—nearly thirty years ago now—I received instructions from your guardians through Mr. Lamond, of this city, to remit to England one-half of the proceeds of your estate, the other moiety to remain on deposit in my bank up to a certain sum: namely, two millions of rupees. No more than that amount was to accumulate, and when I thought fit, in consultation with my partners, I had authority to invest the money in safe undertakings—in *India.* For twenty years the firm of Hajii Alaraka Sajin and Co., of Delhi, have administered the proceeds of one-half of your estate.'

' Does Lamond know this ? ' asked Harry with a white face.

' My dear sir—since he instructed us to do it.'

' Ah—of course.'

The native gentleman was leaning forward, looking curiously into Harry's face.

' I understood,' he said, ' that Mr. Lamond was in almost daily communication with you, and that he was reporting to you from time to time our administration of the money, which has thus been allowed to accumulate awaiting your need of it.'

' Yes,' answered Harry vaguely. ' Yes.'

The word ' accumulate ' struck him disagreeably. It figured in the agreement, or the assignment, which he had made before his marriage in the little room that Lamond called his study.

' Mr. Lamond,' went on the native, ' was always

averse to my communicating with you direct. You
did not wish, as I understood, to be troubled with
the minor details of business. You were, if I may
mention it, only spending half your income; the
remainder was accumulating. I had every reason
to suppose that things were going on satisfactorily.'

' Yes,' said Harry, upon whom an unnatural quiet
seemed to have fallen.

' The money was and is quite safe,' said Sajin.
' It can only be released by your written order, bearing your signature. I have the instructions signed
by yourself some years ago when you first returned
to this country.'

' Yes,' answered Harry. ' I have signed many
papers.'

He rose and held out his hand.

' Thank you, Mr. Sajin; you have done well.
Where may I find you should I require your further
advice ? '

' I am staying in Calcutta for a few days—stay, I
will write down the address. Then I return to
Delhi. I have a large business, and cannot allow
myself a long holiday.'

He had written the address as he spoke, and he
handed it to Harry.

' There is nothing I can do for you, Captain
Wylam ? '

'Nothing just now, thank you,' replied Harry, with a queer calm.

He shook hands and went out. The twilight was far advanced, and in the narrow, tortuous streets it was almost dark. Here and there in the mysterious shadows men passed to and fro, silent and furtive, as if ashamed of their transactions.

CHAPTER XXIV.

COMPOUND INTEREST.

As Harry walked towards the club (he had not payment of a palanquin in his pocket) his thoughts went back to the one friend in India whom he could trust in any need and at all times. He thought he remembered that Frederic Marqueray was in Calcutta.

Harry walked slowly with a limp, his souvenir of the Mutiny, which ever grew more noticeable when he was tired or in bad health. His constitution had in truth partly broken down under the strains he continually put upon it. His dress was disordered, and somewhat shabby. No one took much notice of this forlorn figure, this seedy person, who nevertheless had the remains of air and bearing which had once marked the gentleman and the officer.

In the entrance hall of the club he paused and steadied himself with a glass of brandy. Then he went slowly up to the smoking-room, where he knew the members would be assembled, awaiting the dinner-hour and discussing the day's news. The room was full when he entered. Lamond was present, sitting in a deep chair, reading a newspaper.

He looked up, and nodded to Harry with his pleasant smile. One or two men turned and glanced at the newcomer over their shoulders, with that interest which is ever aroused by vice in all its forms. He passed close by some who sniffed the brandy, and exchanged a glance.

Harry went to Lamond and stood before his chair.

" I have just seen Hajii Alaraka Sajin, of Delhi,' he said in a voice that made many turn to look at him.

' Ah,' replied Lamond, suddenly grave. There was that in Harry's face that made his father-in-law glance hurriedly round the room.

' Yes, and I have found out that you are a scoundrel—a d——-d scoundrel—and a thief!'

' Hush, man,' whispered Lamond. ' You're drunk. Don't, for Heaven's sake, make a disturbance here.'

He had risen and laid his hand on Harry's arm. At the moment of Harry's speaking a loud laugh in another quarter of the room had fortunately drowned his voice, which was low and hoarse. No one was taking much notice of them, except indeed one man who was watching them quietly from the

18

other side of the room—Frederic Marqueray—who still had the power that Harry had noticed of passing unheeded among his fellows, though his name had made a stir in India.

'Disturbance!' answered Harry. 'I'll make a disturbance in all Bengal with this. You tricked me over that marriage-settlement. You've been laying by half my money for it for years. I can't think why I have been such a d——d fool all these years not to see what you are!'

'That will do,' said Lamond, in a steady undertone. 'Shut up, you young fool. Don't you see the men beginning to listen?'

'And well they may. I'll give them something to listen to. All Calcutta shall know that you are a swindler!' cried Harry, wheeling round on his heel and facing the rest of the room.

'And all Calcutta shall know that you looted at Delhi,' said Lamond in his ear.

'Listen, you chaps,' cried Harry.

Lamond looked at the door. Marqueray was standing against it.

'Listen to the story of a low swindle,' pealed out Harry's voice, clear and ringing in the silence of the vast room. 'This man, Phillip Lamond, was entrusted by my father on his death-bed with the administration of my affairs. My father treated him

as a friend. God help him! he thought he was an
honourable man. The estate was tied up for me
during my childhood. The trustees were Englishmen in business in London who had never been in
India, and knew nothing of Indian affairs. The
administration of matters in India was entrusted
to Hajii Alaraka Sajin and Co., of Delhi, under the
superintendence of Phillip Lamond.'

He turned and pointed a shaking finger into
Lamond's face, who stood white-lipped but imperturbable still. The man's nerves were of steel
beneath his gentle demeanour. There was not one
friendly glance in the faces confronting him. Frederic Marqueray stood guard over the only exit.
There was another reckoning, perchance, awaiting
him there. Lamond did not open his lips. His
quiet smile was in itself a triumph of intrepidity
and self-assurance.

'These people in Delhi were honest,' went on
Harry with flashing eyes; the old Harry Wylam—
upright, honest, fiery, and noble—seemed to stand
before his friends again. 'He was too cunning to
attempt to buy them. Every anna that passed out
of their hands into his had to be accounted for, so
he thought of a deep scheme. I can't think why I
have been such a d——d fool.'

He gave a reckless little laugh, looking round as

if to seek from others the explanation of his folly.
But none gave it.

'He told them,' he went on clearly enough, for
his eyes were open now—'he told the native bankers
to send home only one-half of the income arising
from the estates left by my father. The remainder
was to be allowed to accumulate in India. He
wanted to keep it within reach. How he obtained
the signature of my guardians to this document
God only knows! In good faith Hajii Alaraka
Sajin and Co. acted according to their instructions,
and fortune favoured Mr. Lamond. I came out to
India. I was a young fool. He flattered my van-
ity. While seeming to be against it, he conceived
the idea that I should marry his daughter. He
knew the fortune that was at my back, but no one
else did. I was, of course, ignorant of it. I went
—wrong, as you all know. That was my own
fault. I do not want to blame anybody else for
that.'

He stopped and looked round, and many of the
faces wore a guilty look, though he blamed no one.

'I was allowed,' he continued, ' to consider myself ruined, to run into debt, to meet a thousand
difficulties. And at the worst, when I was in ill-
health and idle—put aside as a drinker and a gambler—this noble gentleman consented to—nay, he

pushed me into a marriage with his daughter. " Now," he said, " at all events, no one can say that I wanted your money for Maria." '

He paused with the name on his lips, and looked at Frederic Marqueray, by what instinct he could not have told. And then he went on with the story, leaving Maria out of it. What part she had played no one ever knew from Harry, and others also held their peace with a chivalry as generous.

' But he went too far. He went away to Delhi, and left me to go to the devil in my own way. He came back and just saved me from blowing my brains out. He nearly missed his mark after all. Then he practically forced this marriage upon— no, I won't say that. I was willing enough. He drew up a prenuptial marriage-settlement, in which I assigned to his daughter, unconditionally, my Delhi estates and all accumulations of money attaching thereto. A common swindle, gentlemen. And I signed it. The thing never would have been found out until after I had drunk myself into the grave or shot myself, but I went this afternoon to a money-lender's, and in that office I ran against Hajii Alaraka Sajin, of Delhi. It looks like Providence——'

He turned upon Lamond.

' D——d like Providence!' he repeated, with a laugh most unpleasant to the ear.

There was an awkward pause, as when the conversation turns upon a topic to which those assembled have not given a deep consideration. Still Phillip Lamond maintained silence, reserving his fire, as it were, and waiting until the enemy in the heat of his attack should make a false move. Marqueray, from the door, was watching him anxiously. Perhaps the brilliant leader knew somewhat of this man's resources, and dreaded that fire when the guns should open.

'I am not complaining, gentlemen,' went on Harry with a fine dignity, which sat well on him. 'I have no one to blame but myself. I have made mistakes—and worse. I am content to abide by the result. As for the money, I shall make no attempt to recover it. But I tell you this- and must apologise for giving you so wearisome an account of my own affairs— I tell you this, because that man has no place in this room or in any assembly of gentlemen. He is a scoundrel, a common swindler. I will have him hounded out of every club in India——'

He turned and looked at Lamond with flashing eyes—breathless, after his long and passionate declamation. Phillip Lamond, immoveable even now, apparently cold, except indeed that the tendons of his neck were tense beneath the skin, while the jaw-

bone worked convulsively in his hollow cheek, returned the gaze with resolution.

' And I,' he said, speaking so that only Harry
and one or two could hear him, ' will have you
court-martialed.'

Across the room Marqueray seemed to catch the
words—it may have been from the movement of
the thin, bloodless lips—for he left the door and
moved nearer.

Harry, having said all that he had come to say,
was for going to the door, white-faced, and full of
hot rage, when Lamond raised his voice.

' Now it is my turn,' he said, and in the silence
his words carried to the farthest corner of the room,
although he spoke in a quiet voice. ' Since Captain Wylam has elected to settle his domestic affairs
in public, it is only right that the other side of the
question should be heard—if I am not asking too
much——'

He paused, and looked complacently upon a group
of unsympathetic faces. There was not, indeed,
one that seemed to desire the other side of the
question. Not one pair of eyes looked back into
Phillip Lamond's pale, calculating gaze with anything but the coldest disapprobation. For all these
were officers and gentlemen of a certain rank and
position, neither of which he could rightly claim.

They were one and all for Harry, and against Phillip
Lamond.   He had faced the world thus all his life,
conscious that the world's feeling was antagonistic.
He must have taken a wrong turning years before,
and he had never found the way out of the enemy's
country, but had wandered hither and thither in it,
finding no rest.

He stood taking, as it were, the measure of his
hearers—the oldest man in the room. Well-pre-
served, slim and upright, his narrow face, brown and
scarce wrinkled, his smooth hair quite white.   He
belonged to the earlier generation of Anglo-Indians.
His contemporaries were gone home rich men, or
dead.   Phillip Lamond was left, and still fought the
world.

'The accusations brought against me are hardly
worth contradicting,' he said calmly.   'They are
suggested by spite and disappointed cupidity.   This
man, Hajii Alaraka, has a grudge against me because, in the interest of my friend's son, I have
superintended the administration of the boy's estate
with too keen an eye.   Captain Wylam married my
daughter, with my consent, it is true—but a grudg-
ing consent.   No father would be anxious to give
his daughter's life to the care of a drunkard and a
gambler.   I have supplied them with money since
their marriage—but let that pass.   I have done

more, and I now see my error. I have screened this man, because my daughter is his wife—and there I made a mistake. He is unfit to bear the Queen's Commission. I can testify that he looted at Delhi, before the city was taken and during the assault. At the blowing up of the mosque, which was my idea and for which he got the credit, he left his men in a position of imminent peril, and went into the mosque, where he discovered treasure and took possession of it.'

There was an ominous stillness in the room, for Lamond was only giving voice to a whisper that had spread through Northern India. The members present had grouped themselves into an attentive half-circle before the two disputants.

'You all know,' went on Lamond, 'that he came back from Delhi with plenty of money—which has since disappeared, of course. He was in command of the expedition that blew up the mosque. I was nothing in it but an obscure civilian, I had no say in the matter. My small knowledge of the district was found useful, and I placed it at the disposal of the authorities. I was acting as guide. But, even a civilian could see that there was something wrong. Since the question of looting has been investigated —since the recent courts-martial I have understood what was the matter that night before Delhi. It

was not an expedition to serve the British army,
but to enrich Captain Henry Wylam.'

He paused with an indifferent shrug of his shoulders, as of one who has passed beyond all great
interests in life, and seeks only to do the right. His
pale blue eyes scanned the faces in front of him,
and noted a change in the expressions there, for
the faces of a crowd, listening to one man, usually
express one emotion as public speakers know. The
expression was not exactly in his own favour, but it
was less friendly to Harry. For the majority of his
hearers had borne a sword for England, in her great
peril, and having survived, had passed through the
pain which was hers, when certain facts transpired
to tarnish the shield of her glory.

He scanned the faces, then he turned and glanced
at Harry.

'He cannot deny it,' he said less in exultation
than in sorrow.

And, indeed, Harry's drawn face was the picture
of guilt and surprise and consternation.

CHAPTER XXV.

A FRIEND IN NEED.

HARRY was for the moment taken aback, and stood dumb before the jury he had himself selected to hear his case. He was by nature hasty, fiery, and honest. It had ever been with him the habit to give voice to the thought so soon as ever this came to his brain. Concealment was as repugnant to his soul as it was impossible to his countenance. A hasty judgment, a quick word, a sudden repentance and a broken resolution had, alas! been his method of procedure through life. The hidden thought, the slow, snake-like motive were not his, and he could scarce believe them in another. A fair fight of any sort exhilarated him, but an underhand pass with an illegitimate blade made a coward of him. He was afraid now, and he showed it. A wave of doubt swept across the faces before him as the shadow of a cloud across a fair field on a breezy day. Harry Wylam afraid? They had never conceived the thought; and the fact was before them.

' He cannot deny it,' repeated Phillip Lamond,

'No, but others can!' said a voice behind, and
all eyes were fixed on Frederic Marqueray.

'*You!*' retorted Lamond as quick as thought.
'You are the principal witness. You were there
disguised as a fakir. You are the principal witness,
my fine young gentleman.'

'Who saw nothing,' said Marqueray, quietly,
'for you had knocked me senseless with a slash over
the head—from behind.'

Lamond paused for a moment. This was a foe
of different metal.

'My evidence would be quite enough to convict
him,' he said easily.

'Your evidence?'

'Yes, my evidence.'

Marqueray came a little nearer. His long narrow
face—drawn into furrows by the enormous fatigues
of a terrible campaign, twitched nervously—the
only sign he ever gave of anger.

'You will be out of India long before that,' he
said evenly. 'If you are a wise man you will be
out of India to-morrow morning.'

Lamond was looking at him with a sudden nar-
rowing of his gaze. Some, who had seen a tiger
spring, caught their breath. Marqueray's eyes
never left his adversary's face, while he took a paper
from his pocket and unfolded it. It was a piece of

native-made paper, and the soft, clothy sound of it
was the only break to a deathly silence.

Marqueray held it up in front of Lamond's face.
He said some words quickly in a low voice in the
Tamil tongue, and Phillip Lamond drew in a sharp,
choking breath.

'Keep your hands from your pockets,' said Frederic Marqueray, who knew murder in the eyes when
he saw it, 'and go.'

As Phillip Lamond moved towards the door,
Marqueray turned on his heel, facing him as a
crab faces danger, and watched the slim, clenched
hands.

The door was slowly opened. Lamond paused
for a moment with his fingers on the handle, his
foot on the threshold, his back turned towards the
room full of men. He paused as if in thought.
Then he went on, closing the door behind him.
He had played his last card in a long game.

'Poor devil!' said a voice with a queer break in
it. It was the voice of Harry Wylam.

The end of the scene had been so sudden, so
unexpected, so astonishingly dramatic, that for a
few moments the slow-minded Englishmen left
standing in the large room were speechless and, it
seemed, deprived of the power of thought.

The first to speak was a general officer—a white-haired veteran—who, like Marqueray, was versed in many Indian tongues.

He pushed his way forward.

'Marqueray,' he said in an authoritative voice, 'what did you say to that man? I think I have a right to know.'

At all events he had a right to ask, though Marqueray in his discretion would rather have answered the question elsewhere.

Before replying he moved towards the door, where he stood almost in the position which he had held during the dispute.

'I told him,' he said, 'that he was a spy. I showed him a plan of the Ridge batteries supplied by him to the mutineers inside Delhi.'

There was, as the speaker had anticipated, a roar of rage, and many of the younger men made a rush towards the door. But he stood barring it with his outstretched arms. He was their superior officer. None but the general could dispute his word, and that officer perhaps knew better.

'No,' cried Marqueray, 'let him go. We cannot prove it. I have been trying to do so for months.'

They fell back, some murmuring discontentedly, others aghast with surprise and a sort of shame.

'Remember,' said Marqueray, striking the note with a sure touch, 'that he is an Englishman. None know it except ourselves, and we had better forget it.'

'And what about the men who bought him?' cried one passionately. 'What about the mutineers inside Delhi who were in communication with Lamond, and knew him to be an Englishman?'

'I know who they were. They showed me the papers themselves, and I stole one of them,' replied the man who had staked his life for his country's cause. The paper was in his pocket, and many would have liked to see it. But he never raised a hand to satisfy their curiosity.

'But the men have only to produce the rest of the papers and to say whence they got them, and all the world will know,' cried the first speaker angrily. It was not one man's reputation only that was at stake, but the good name of a whole race.

'They will never do that. We killed them all in Delhi—Wylam and I and three troopers. Forty of them.'

A silence followed this plain statement. And, perchance, some in that room recognised what manner of man stood before them. Some, perhaps, caught a glimpse in that drawn and stern face of a whole suppressed record of deeds conceived in cold blood, and carried out with an intrepidity such as is vouchsafed to few. Some, it may be, guessed in

part the sacrifice that Frederic Marqueray had made
when he barred the door behind Phillip Lamond.
For the sake of Englishmen he had connived at the
escape of one who would have dragged the good
name in the lowest depths of treachery and degradation. And, in suppressing the deeds of Phillip
Lamond, he had deliberately struck his own name
out of history. The good and the evil of the great
unstoried intrigues in and around Delhi were so com-
mingled that, if Marqueray had given to the world
a record of his adventures—as many at this time
were engaged in doing—he must have told the
shameful story of Phillip Lamond also. Instead, he
was content that his contemporaries and brother
officers should know him as a good soldier only, and
that history should never tell of a marvellous feat.
He threw the good that he had wrought into the
balance over against Phillip Lamond's evil deeds,
and was content to go his own way, bearing in his
silent heart the knowledge that he was a greater than
many whose names then were, and are to this day,
a pleasant household word for bravery, and the
admiration of every English schoolboy.

' I do not see,' said one of the younger men,
' how you can fail to prove that he did it. You
have the paper. I suppose you can prove that it is
his handwriting.'

'Yes—but we cannot prove that he drew up the plans with the view of selling them to the mutineers,' replied Marqueray. 'We cannot meet his defence that the papers were stolen from him by a native servant. He was an accredited guide to the force before Delhi. He had a perfect right to have the plans in his possession.'

Marqueray moved away from the door. He knew enough, no doubt, of Phillip Lamond, to entrust that gentleman's safety to his own care after the lapse of fifteen minutes, which grace he had now accorded him.

In replying to the arguments, put forth by the younger and hot-headed members, Marqueray displayed no desire to close the question. Rather, indeed, was his manner that of one desirous of giving every information. Nothing arouses curiosity so quickly as the obvious desire to conceal. He moved towards the chair, which he had lately vacated, and there sat down.

'Then,' said the officer, whose perception was keener than his discretion, 'how was it you frightened him so confoundedly?'

'Oh, he thought I could prove it.'

'Bluff?' inquired the sceptic, with a smile full of mutual understanding.

'Bluff,' replied the man, who had been inside

19

Delhi—looking steadily, and as some thought, coldly at his interlocutor.

He took up a pen and wrote something on a large sheet of the club-paper. No one had left the room. Some sat down, but the majority formed themselves into groups and stood discussing this event in whispers. The scratching of Marqueray's pen continued. A member looked at the clock and went to the door, turning the handle and rattling it impatiently.

'This door is locked,' he cried. 'Where is the key?'

'In my pocket,' said Marqueray, turning in his chair. 'I propose that we all sign this paper before anyone leaves the room. General, will you lead off?'

The general took the sheet of foolscap, and read it with a gleam in his fierce old eyes.

'Certainly,' he said. 'D——n it, sir—certainly.'

He took a quill and splashed his name down on the paper, and a great name it was. The others followed suit, as behoved men accustomed to discipline, and thus the undertaking was signed that none should divulge Phillip Lamond's secret.

Harry put his name to the paper the last but one; immediately, in fact, over the signature of his good angel. And the scrawl, a great bold flourish, be-

neath the name of Harry Wylam, touched the top
of the capital letters of a neat and compressed
' Frederic Marqueray.'

The two friends stood side by side for a moment
while Marqueray laid the blotting-paper upon the
writing with a steady hand. Harry gave a gulp.
There were a thousand things he wished to say to
the man who seemed to be ever by his side when
needed. A hundred fair resolutions rose in his
mind, and he wanted to tell Marqueray that his
good offices had not been thrown away upon an
unworthy object, but on one who intended to lead
a new life. But Marqueray, always a little stern
and cold, did not invite such protestations by his
demeanour. Indeed, his own life had been marked
and shaped more by deeds than words, and it is
probable that he failed in part to understand
Harry's impulsive nature—capable enough of good,
but sorely susceptible to the influence of the pass·
ing moment, which is rarely for good and usually
takes its clue from the faultiness of our poor
nature.

So Harry moved away with the rest, and Marqueray folding the paper tucked it into the front of
his tunic. He handed the key to the young fellow
who had wished to have it, and the doors being
thrown open many went about their business, a

prey to that passing emotion which is all we can
give to our neighbours' affairs.

Harry sat despondently down at a table littered
with newspapers, and dragging a journal towards
him set his elbows upon it with a reckless vehe-
mence, as if determined to throw his whole mind
into the perusal of the news.

He sat there, turning his back upon the room, in
dogged silence, and read no word of the print
before him. His eyes were dull with a heavy
despair, his chin thrust forward in mute defiance
of fate. Indeed, the worst seemed to have happened to him. Whichever way he turned disgrace
awaited him.

One by one the members got up and, with some
explanatory word, delivered in a tone of forced
indifference to whoever happened to be near, left
the room. One was going to dinner; another was
engaged to dine with friends, and must repair to his
quarters to dress.

Harry knew where Marqueray was sitting. He
heard that chair pushed back, and its late occupant
walk slowly from the room. He raised his haggard
face from his hand and listened. Marqueray had
gone without a word. This was the sorest blow.
His last friend the man who had stood by him
through thick and thin (and in truth the thick had

outweighed the thin in Harry's life), his good angel
—had gone with the others.

The clock over the door struck seven. It was
long after the hour at which men dined in those
days. Harry could not have eaten a morsel, but
the temptation to drink was upon him. Perhaps
he could gather his wits with the help of a stimulant, and think what must be done. He did not
know that Marqueray was waiting at the foot of
the stairs, having foreseen this danger.

Harry turned and looked over his shoulder. He
was alone in the room with one man—the general who
had forced Marqueray to speak. This was Harry's
general, the commandant of the force in Calcutta.

The old gentleman was reading a newspaper with
marked attention.

Harry rose and moved unsteadily towards the
door, and the newspaper was laid aside.

' Wylam.'

' Yes, sir.'

' I must ask you,' said the general, ' to consider
yourself under arrest. When you have dined
please go to your quarters.'

Harry stood for a moment. The words did not
seem to reach his understanding at once. He
looked at the general, who avoided meeting the
glance. Then he walked slowly from the room.

CHAPTER XXVI

FLIGHT.

PHILLIP LAMOND walked down the broad stairs of the club with composure and a face that was almost serene. Indeed, the servants—who disliked him for a meanness which is commoner than we suspect— noticed nothing.

A wise man conscious of the seed of sudden death in his constitution is often brave enough to make quiet preparations for his departure, so arranging his affairs that he may undertake at a moment's notice and without indecent haste the long journey that must inevitably come.

It is probable that Phillip Lamond, conscious of the instability of his foothold upon the slippery incline of Calcutta society, had foreseen the moment when he would fall. Nay, further; it is probable that in some subtle way he may have been allowed to distinguish, by one of those flashes of foresight which we can only call instinct, the man who was destined at last to trip him up. In his dealings

with Marqueray he had always lacked nerve. In
the valley between the Ridge and the walls of Delhi
he had trembled in the presence of the fakir, whom
he would have killed had Harry Wylam not prevented him. Among our heartstrings there is one
which is only touched by one or two friends and one
or two foes. Lamond had always been conscious of
a thrill of misgiving when in the presence of Frederic Marqueray. There was no feeling of surprise
in his mind now. It all seemed natural and pre-
ordained.

But he was shaken. He was almost sixty years
of age; and a great anger or a heavy fall is dangerous after fifty. His hands were shaking, and he
thrust them into the pockets of the loose jacket
that he always wore. He walked rapidly and rather
unsteadily out of the club compound, where it was
dark, into the dusty street, now crowded with
baboos and their clerks hurrying home from shop
and office. The light of the street lamps or the
glare of a shop-window fell on a face that was aged
and worn. He hurried on into the smaller streets,
and presently entered the house of a native forwarding agent.

It is notable that in his strait this Englishman
went to one who was not of his race.

The night was dark, with a strong breeze that

hummed and moaned through the rigging of the ships lying in the river as Phillip Lamond stepped into his boat ten minutes later. He aroused the boatmen with a sharp word, and took his seat on the luxurious cushion amidships. The four rowers were in the bows; the steersman, lost in the darkness, crouched in the stern. There had been rain up-country, and the river was full. The babble of the water round the mooring chains of the vessels at anchor in the stream told that this was unusually rapid. Lamond, who knew every humour of the great sacred river, who had passed up and down its treacherous waters almost daily for forty years, unlaced his boots. It is said that he who falls into the Hooghly never rises to the surface again, but Lamond had twice swum to the dreary mud-steeped banks—leaving his boatmen, by-the-bye, to drown.

Once out into the stream he bade the oarsmen bend to their work, but these hesitated, and the steersman humbly remonstrated. The night was dark and stormy. It would be impossible to discern other craft at anchor or moving, though of the latter there would scarce be many abroad at such a time. A collision must inevitably mean death. In reply, Phillip Lamond took the steering oar, and sent the pilot into the bows to keep watch there. Thus the little boat sped down stream at a terrific pace.

Every moment was a distinct gain; for nothing could follow them at such a speed, and the road to Garden Reach was in those days sandy, uneven, and unfit for rapid travelling.

Phillip Lamond seemed to know that Marqueray had given him until the morning to make his escape, and of Harry he had no fear. For Harry had proved himself to be as clay in the potter's hands during these last years of gradual degradation.

The steersman brought the boat to a standstill, swinging skilfully in mid-stream, not at the bungalow steps, but across the river at a landing not far removed from the furnished house where Maria awaited her husband's return to dinner.

She was in evening dress, her beautiful white arms gleaming through the delicate muslin, for she thought that Harry might bring some friend to dine. They had begun their married life, observing the little formalities and customs of their station, both scrupulously donning full dress for their *tête-à-tête* evening meal. But of late this excellent practice, serving to maintain a self and mutual respect, as well as to guard intact the barrier of position, had been neglected.

Maria rose from her chair, and looked at her father with a sort of hardness about her lips, which might have indicated anxiety in a softer face.

'Harry?' she exclaimed in a low, interrogative voice.

'No, there is nothing wrong with Harry,' replied Lamond, closing the door carefully.

'But,' he turned and showed her a face that had grown suddenly old, 'it is all up with me.'

'What do you mean?' asked Maria, who was calm and collected enough at this juncture. Indeed, her manner was rather that of a man than of a helpless woman.

'I have been accused of selling information to the mutineers.'

'A spy,' said Maria.

And her father was silent.

'Of course you are innocent,' she said, tossing her head so that the diamonds at her throat (which had never been paid for) glittered in the lamplight.

'Keep your scorn for your husband!' said the fond father.

And Maria knew that he was guilty.

'What does it mean?' she asked. 'What will happen?'

She had risen, white-faced but quite collected; ready for an emergency—her father's daughter.

'God knows,' he answered. 'I mustn't wait to see. If it had not been for Marqueray they would have torn me to pieces.'

He laughed—a scaffold laugh.

' Who found out ? '

Lamond did not answer. He had not played a dangerous game all his life without learning a greater wisdom than that.

' Who accused you ? ' amended Maria.

' Marqueray.'

He repeated the name with something like wonder in his voice, and Maria looked at him. She was a woman, and had not yet parted with the conviction that she could have made Frederic Marqueray love her.

' That is not all,' said her father, looking worn and broken.

Maria waited in a suspense which she held in control with a fine nerve.

' Harry has found out about the money. He met Sajin of Delhi by accident at a money-lender's, and the—the fat was in the fire.'

Lamond, it will be perceived, did not pause to choose his language. There may be honour in certain circles, but there is not always a great refinement of speech.

' But it is settled on me,' cried Maria in a strident voice, a sudden fear in her eyes.

' Yes,' answered her father, with something very like a sneer. And they looked into each other's

faces. This was triumph; this, success. Success is
the hammer with which we strike the world, and
find it hollow.

For years these two had striven to gain that which
was now theirs. Lamond had perhaps little to lose,
but he had risked that little for the attainment of
this end. He had brought Maria up from girlhood
to seek the same goal. Fresh from school she
had come out to him, and he had taught her that
money was the end and aim of human endeavour.
She had proved an apt pupil, and the slowly-laid
seed had borne fruit.

Lamond was of too refined a nature to lay his
scheme before her in its crude form. He had
hinted here, had half exposed a motive there,
and Maria understood. The vilest conspirators
are those who dare not even shape their plot in
words.

These two were too clever to fail, and in the hour
of their triumph they stood facing each other with
white faces and drawn eyes.

'What is to be done?' said Maria. 'We cannot
stay here.'

'No; we must go down to-night to Diamond
Harbour, where I have ascertained that there are
outward-bound vessels at anchor. Marqueray gave
me till to-morrow morning.'

The name made Maria wince.

She, too, had risked something in the great venture—that which women risk, nay, throw away, when
they marry for any other motive than love.

' Where shall you go ? ' she asked.

' I do not know yet,' replied the father, with his
old leisureliness of manner, which his astute daughter probably recognised as a mere trick. ' The old
world will be too hot for me if this comes out, and
Harry is dangerous. I shall probably try the Pacific
slope. You had better go to Ceylon, and there await
developments.'

' And the child ? ' asked Maria, stooping to pick
up her lace pocket handkerchief. She need scarcely
have taken the precaution, for her father did not
look at her.

' Oh, stick to that. It will strengthen your posi-
tion. But they cannot rob you of the money.
That is square enough. I have seen to that, Maria.
And I know my way about.'

He gave a little laugh, rather short and hard for a
laugh of triumph.

' Galle,' he said, ' Galle is the place for you.
Pretty little place. Healthy enough. Nice sea-
breezes. The—er—child mustn't die. I have
friends in Galle who will show you the ropes.'

' Yes, but a friend of yours might show me the

wrong ones,' said the lady who had made herself a position.

Lamond took the filial snub easily enough. He had a special smile for snubs, well known in Calcutta. He reflected for a moment, standing by the open window.

' Yes,' he admitted, quite without rancour. ' Perhaps you had better say nothing about me. Husband on active service. Calcutta not good for the —er—child. Something of that sort.'

With a wave of his hand he indicated what seemed to be a triumphal ascent for Maria, from one position to another in the years to come.

' But I should live at Galle, at any rate for a bit,' he added gravely. It is marvellous how the shady people of the world know where to find the shady spots.

' Will you be ready in an hour ?' he continued. ' Get a bit of dinner and pack your things. Bring the ayah. Tell her there is cholera, or anything. I've got some things to attend to across at the bungalow. Will be back in an hour with the boat.'

Maria, who was as good a campaigner as her father (having no doubt inherited the capacity from the gentleman who had been on active service in life's battle ever since his boyhood), lost no time in repining, but whipped the fittest of her trousseau

into one box, and the best of the wedding presents
into another. She knew that the luggage-carrying
capacities of a Hooghly boat were limited, and
wisely abandoned the plated articles.

'They'll go towards the rent,' she reflected, remembering Harry's impecunious condition and the
last quarter's arrears.

A tiny trunk took all the infant's small belong-
ings, and that diminutive traveller was dragged
rather hastily from her bed to be dressed without
resistance, and half asleep in the complete abandon-
ment of childhood. Verily the second and the third
generation are called upon to pay. This infant's
first journey was a flight.

The embarkation was safely effected about ten
o'clock, at which hour Harry had not yet returned
home. Lamond arrived with the boat and two
men to carry Maria's luggage. These individuals
he introduced by the drawing-room window, which
stood open, and the whole party quietly evacuated
by that exit. A waning moon was just rising
through the smoke of the great city which had
known Lamond's footfall these thirty years, and
was never to know it more.

The river was running as rapidly as earlier in the
evening, but its face was now lighter and the dark
forms of vessels moored by either bank were easily

distinguishable. The rowers took their places, and
the steersman gave the word of departure. There
was, Lamond had commanded, to be no singing.
He sat down by Maria in the stern of the boat,
while the ayah carrying her charge crouched at their
feet.

The boat shot out into mid-stream, where the current caught it and whirled it swiftly and silently
towards the sea. Thus, Phillip Lamond departed
from the scene of his long and fruitful labours.

They reached Diamond Harbour without accident, and crept quietly alongside a steamer moored
there. The boat had left Calcutta that morning on
her way to Bombay, calling at Madras, Pondicherry
Galle, and Goa. Lamond knew her captain, who
was aroused from his slumbers by the anchor-watch,
and drove a shrewd bargain between yawns.

A cabin was at Maria's disposal, with berths for
the baby and the ayah. Lamond saw that all was
arranged for his daughter's comfort.

' And what will you do ? ' she asked.

They were standing on the deck by the rail where
the rope-ladder hung over the side to Lamond's
boat.

He turned and looked at the riding-lights in the
harbour.

' Oh, I shall find a coaster to take me to the Dutch

settlements or to Pondicherry, and after that I shall get away somehow.'

The flickering lamp of the anchor-watch showed whitely on his snow-like hair and moustache, as he clambered over the rail after kissing Maria, who said no word.

' Don't be too hard on me, Maria,' he said, with his feet on the ladder. ' Whatever I did, I did for you.'

And his face disappeared below the bulwarks.

CHAPTER XXVII.

HARRY was fortunate enough to obtain an early
trial, which benefit he owed as much to the influence of friends as to the promptitude of the martial court. Of native evidence there was in this
case fortunately none, and the proceedings of the
court-martial were considerably curtailed by this
omission. The follower of Mohammed in the wit-
ness-box is himself a difficult man to follow.

The trial was a short one, and Harry bore it with
a manly straightforwardness of demeanour, which
went far to win for him the sympathy of his judges.
He pleaded guilty, and spoke the honest truth.
The court, however, seemed to be under the influence of evidence which did not transpire at the trial,
and must therefore have come to their ears before
that event. The evidence of Frederic Marqueray
was carefully taken. All the other witnesses had
perished. Harry refused to plead the extenuating
circumstance, but the court insisted, and Phillip
Lamond's share in the night's work before Delhi

was dragged out into the cold contemplation of Harry's brother officers.

During the long deliberation the prisoner was confined in an adjoining room, and when the court was at length agreed he came back to find his sword lying on the table with the hilt turned towards him. It was the sword that Miriam Gresham had drawn, with a little shudder, from its sheath, for the first time after it came into his possession, in the drawing-room in St. Helen's Place.

The sword was his again, but the reprimand was so severe that all who heard it knew that Harry could never bare the blade in the service of his Queen again.

' I'm only fit for a soldier,' he said to his friends who crowded round him and shook him by the hand, ' and they won't have me.'

He went down to Garden Reach, where he expected to find Maria, to whom he had written many times without reply. But instead of his wife he found the cook's mother in the drawing-room, which ancient Hindu lady was looking over a photograph album in company with a select circle of her friends. It is to be feared that Harry kicked the cook. At all events he attempted to do so, and caused that functionary's mother to display an agility beyond her years.

The servants told him that Maria had left ten days earlier.

' The night of my arrest,' reflected Harry.

' Did the memsahib go away alone ? ' he asked with a sudden fierceness about his lips and eyes. ' No, she went with her father.' And Harry gave a sharp sigh of relief. There is no more suspicious man on earth than the naturally trusting man who has been deceived.

' Where had the memsahib gone ? '

The servants looked at each other with raised shoulders and outspread hands, and the butler was understood to murmur that the wages were overdue.

' Go to the devil,' said Harry, and turning on his heel he faced Marqueray, who was coming into the room.

' Where are the child and Maria ? ' he cried, as soon as he recognized the newcomer. ' This house is deserted. Half the ornaments are gone. The child has disappeared, and Maria. For God's sake tell me where they are, Marks.'

And he strode across the room towards his friend. The long confinement within doors had blanched his usually ruddy face. He was thin and haggard, with dull eyes looking from a countenance that bore the mark of disease and weakness.

' I don't know,' answered Marqueray gently ; ' but

I have a clue. Sit down, and don't agitate yourself.'

The quiet man pushed the servants from the
room and closed the doors. He forced Harry into
a chair.

' You've not been drinking ? ' he inquired in a
hard voice.

' No,' answered Harry, without resentment.
' God! what a hard man you are! ' he added with a
short laugh. And he threw himself back in the
chair, letting his hands fall on the basket-work arms
with a gesture of despair.

Marqueray looked at him, and there was something in his grave eyes that made the impetuous
Harry leap to his feet, and seize the steady brown
hand in both of his.

' No, by God! ' he cried. ' You're the best friend
I've got. I believe you're the best friend a man
ever had.'

He returned to his seat half ashamed of his sudden outburst of feeling, which in truth Marqueray
had received but awkwardly.

' I wonder why you do it ? ' he went on; and the
new suspicion leapt suddenly into his eyes. ' It is
not because you have fallen in love with Maria, like
the rest of them ? '

' No, I hate her,' replied Marqueray.

Harry drew in his feet and leant forward with his elbows on his knees, his eyes fixed on the matting under his feet.

' So do I,' he said, slowly and deliberately; ' but not the child. Funny, isn't it? I can't understand it. Maria can go to the devil, but I want the child.'

He looked up with shining eyes, and was not ashamed now.

' I think,' said Marqueray, ' that you will be able to get the child. I have had but little time this last week to make inquiries '—he did not think it worth mentioning that he had devoted every moment to his hearer's interests—' but it seems certain that they took passage to Ceylon, where you will probably find them.'

Harry's face brightened, and clouded over again almost at once.

' But how am I going to get the child away from her?' he asked hopelessly.

' Money,' returned the cynic; ' money will do it.'

Harry shook his head with a characteristic, reckless laugh.

' I have none,' he said.

' Not in hand,' replied his friend; ' but it is probable that if you went to law you could recover the

whole amount of which you were defrauded. I do
not say it is certain, but it is probable; and Lamond
is not here—cannot come back to fight it. You
have on the other hand no right to the child. You
cannot take it from its mother's custody.'

' It's a she,' broke in Harry, with that irrespon-
sible sense of the humorous which never left him.
' Bless her heart! I don't think Wylam men are
much good.'

' You cannot take her from her mother's custody
without the mother's full consent,' went on Marqueray in his solemn way. Nothing roused him
but the din of battle. ' But if you undertake to
abandon all claim to the money you would probably secure that. You cannot have both.'

' Then I'll have the kid,' said Miss Wylam's
father. And her price was forty thousand pounds.

Harry was all eagerness to start at once, and
indeed would have departed then and there on his
quest had not Marqueray restrained his impatience.
There was much to be considered, and many precautions to be taken.

' A mother's love,' said Marqueray, ' is not a
thing to be trifled with. We must have everything
done decently and in order. Your lawyer must go
with you.'

' Gad! what has a lawyer to do with a mother's

love?' inquired Harry with a laugh, for his face
never lost its power of lighting up at a moment's
notice.   He was ever up or down, in the clouds or
stumbling in the valley of despair.

'A great deal in this case,' answered Marqueray.
'You must make quite sure of the child.'

'Then why not come with me yourself?' cried
Harry excitedly.   'We could have a jolly time
together.   And you're as good as any lawyer.'

He sat up in his chair and clapped his two hands
on his knees, with the eagerness of a schoolboy
planning an escapade.

'I cannot do that,' answered Marqueray with a
queer hesitation.   'I am under orders to go to the
North-West.   They have given me a brigade.'

Harry sprang to his feet.

'A brigade?   Begad!' he shouted.   'A brigade:
and here am I chattering of my own affairs.'

He ran forward and clapped his friend on the
back with vigorous enthusiasm.

'A brigade!' he said again.   'How old are you,
Marks?'

'Forty-one.'

'Forty-one; only a few years older than I am.
Gad! I am glad, old man.'

They were both in uniform, and the colonel's
tunic worn by Marqueray was almost a new one.

Harry's full-dress for the court-martial was old and shabby.

He stood for a moment with his hands on his friend's shoulder, looking over his head out of the window across the silent river. Who shall say what thoughts were passing through his brain? He turned and looked at the two swords lying side by side on the table—the one never to be unsheathed again—and his breath was caught in a sharp sigh. The hand resting on Marqueray's shoulder was clenched.

It was Marqueray who spoke first, in a voice, perhaps intentionally, practical and indifferent.

'I wish I could go with you,' he said; 'but the lawyer will be the better man. You must see that you have entire and complete control of the child for the whole of her minority. It must be set down in black and white.'

Harry walked slowly to the window, where he stood with his back turned towards his companion. Perhaps he would not have been beloved as he was had he not had a heart for sudden remorse and self-abasement.

'And when I have her,' he said, 'what am I to do with her? God knows I'm not fit to be a father. I'm not fit, Marks, to have the care of so much as a kitten.'

There was a long silence, broken at length by the

elder man, who spoke slowly as if some thought or
fear had touched the grave serenity with which he
faced all that came in his path, whether difficulty,
or danger, or responsibility.

' You will have to take her home to England,' he
said. ' There is surely someone there who will
take her in.'

Harry turned slowly, his face drawn with a sort
of fear.

' Someone,' he echoed, in a dull voice. ' Someone—do you mean——?'

' I could only mean one person,' returned Marqueray simply. ' Miss Gresham.'

' But—no by God, I couldn't do that. You don t
understand, Marks. You don't know what a blackguard I've been.'

He sat heavily down with his head in his hands.

' I do not know much about women,' said the
great soldier. ' Have not had much to do with
them—only Lady Leaguer. But if I were in your
place I think I should ask Miss Gresham. We do
not always understand these things. She may want
to do it.'

He sat staring at his own boots, with a puzzled
expression as of one who had dealt in warfare and
the ways of men all his life, but to whom the gen-
tler side of creation was but a closed book.

There was much yet to be arranged, and Marqueray's time was limited. Many precautions were, he thought, necessary to a full and permanent victory over that mother's love, upon which he had set a price in hard rupees.

Harry, in his heedless impetuosity, would have journeyed to Ceylon that same night, taking ship hurriedly as Maria had done before him, in Diamond Harbour. But the cooler head of his friend prevailed, and Harry at last consented to secure the services of a trusty lawyer having knowledge of his affairs, which indeed were by now public property in Calcutta.

Then Marqueray looked at his watch and said that it was time for him to be going.

' When do you take command—when do you leave Calcutta ? ' asked Harry, with a twisted lip, as if endeavouring to smile indifferently.

' To-night,' answered his senior, rising.

' A brigade,' said Harry again, with a sharp sigh. ' And gad! they're right! There is no better man —Marks. And the men know it. They'll follow you to hell if need be, I know; for I followed you through Delhi.'

Marqueray went to the table where he had laid his sword when he unbuckled it. It was a plain, regulation weapon—as bright as a mirror. Harry's was a finer sword, with an engraved scabbard and silver at the hilt.

' Take mine,' said Harry suddenly. ' I shall not want it—again.'

Marqueray paused, with his hand on the table.

' I should like you to have it,' said Harry. ' It is a good sword—for I have tried it. I've nothing else to give you, and you have been the best friend I have had.'

Marqueray took up Harry's sword, and buckled it to his own side. His horse was pawing the gravel outside the window.

' And even you,' went on Harry, ' could not save me from my worst enemy.'

' Your worst enemy——?' inquired Marqueray, holding out his hand.

' Myself,' answered Harry, with a laugh.

CHAPTER XXVIII.

A PURCHASE.

ALTHOUGH Galle has belonged to England these many years there still lingers in its quaint white houses and neat fortifications the touch of the Dutchman's hand. The sea was rippling in before a strong breeze, as Harry's steamer swung round the point, with its lighthouse, which then had a look of 'Mynheer' about it, though to-day a larger structure graces the south-west extremity of Ceylon. It was early afternoon. The steamer which brought Harry was timed to sail again at ten o'clock for Bombay, and he hoped to take passage in her.

The little town of Galle, which since then has bloomed into a port of call only to fade into obscurity again, looked pretty enough this afternoon. Its verdure was restful to eyes accustomed to the glare of Calcutta streets and the brown herbage of India. The harbour was gay with bunting and brightly-painted craft. The catamarans sped hither and thither across the rippled water.

Harry looked at it all moodily enough, and the keen-faced lawyer by his side smoked a cigarette indifferently.

' Do you think we'll get the child ? ' asked Captain Wylam, perhaps for the hundredth time.

' Not a doubt of it,' replied the man of law, who reflected with complacency that his legal match was not to be found south of Madras.

' I'll see her alone—at first,' said Harry.

' Yes—you will be wise to do so. These matters are so often painful.'

So they landed and went to the hotel where, as Marqueray had foretold, they found Maria's name upon the books. The lady was in the verandah of her own room—number fourteen—the servants said. She was entertaining friends.

' Already,' muttered Harry with a frown. ' Show me to the verandah occupied by Mrs. Wylam.'

' Name, sir,' said the obsequious Cingalese waiter.

' Wylam ! '

And the attendant hurried on, followed only by Harry; the lawyer, with the discretion of his craft, remaining in the entrance-hall in company with a long tumbler of brandy and soda-water. His keen eye contracted as he saw the young officer walk away with a peculiar unsteadiness of the limbs.

'In a bad way, that chap,' he muttered, taking up a newspaper.

The first sound that Harry heard as he entered number fourteen was his wife's high-pitched laugh, followed by a masculine and somewhat throaty sound of merriment. Maria was apparently entertaining her friends with considerable success. These, however, on closer investigation, appeared to have existed only in the imagination of the Cingalese servant, for there was but one guest in the verandah, a red-faced, military-looking man, whose merriment vanished as he caught sight of Harry.

'Bay Jove!' the stout man exclaimed, rising hurriedly and dropping his stick. 'Bay Jove—eh?'

And he looked from husband to wife.

Maria had risen also. She was dressed loudly, and wore jewellery at her throat, and bracelets on her white arms, which were bare in open elbow sleeves. Harry wondered whether her style had deteriorated with a strange rapidity, or whether he had hitherto failed to see her as she was. The laugh falling from the red lips now open in a momentary surprise had jarred on his nerves. Maria could not claim immunity from the laws of heredity—her mother had so laughed behind the bars at jokes, no doubt as delicately flavoured as that just compassed by the stout Adonis.

The lady recovered her presence of mind in an instant, as ladies do, being more practised no doubt in the ways of being found out.

' Mr. Smither—my husband,' she said, with an introductory wave of the hand.

Harry bowed silently, while the stout gentleman gathered up his hat and stick.

' How do! eh ? Bay Jove! must be going. D——n those steps, Bay Jove!' muttered Mr. Smither, stumbling backwards down the steps, and vanishing hastily by the garden.

' Well ? ' ejaculated Maria, turning fiercely on her husband.

' Well,' answered Harry, with a calmness which made his wife feel momentarily uneasy.

' What do you want here ? ' she asked, eyeing his shabby clothes with a faint look of scorn. And indeed they compared badly with her own finery.

' Not you,' answered Harry. ' We have done with each other.'

' For ever if my feelings are to be consulted. You are disgraced. It is a degradation to bear your name. A British officer, indeed. A pretty officer you are! Why, you have been turned out of the army.'

This was a guess, for the news, such as it was, could not have reached her. She accompanied the

remark with a quick glance to see if the shot told,
which, indeed, it did, as a shot may that is sent at
random. Harry winced, although the words were
untrue to the letter, but savouring, in the spirit, of
that which had truly happened.

Then she hurled at him such a storm of vituperation as he had never conceived possible from the
lips of a woman. She used words, common enough,
alas! in the mouths of those men who had been his
companions, but of which Harry had deemed all
women—even the lowest—happily ignorant. He
had, doubtless, read in books, as we have, that a
beautiful woman seems invariably to gather additional loveliness from a lapse into sudden passion.
It may be so indeed in books, but not in real life.
At all events, Maria's husband did not think her
beautiful at this moment.

He was more astonished that she should speak
such words than that they should be applied to
him, and in this surprise her abuse lost a part of its
sting. Most of it, indeed, had a modicum of truth
—such a small germ of fact as women know best
how to use, spreading it over a volume of deduc-
tion, so that the whole appears true. Without
drawing upon her imagination, however, Maria
knew quite enough to make Harry quiver with
shame at the memory perhaps of nothing so much

21

as that he had once cared for this woman. The deepest humiliation is the shame of having loved.

He was getting grey-haired, and his face too at this moment looked grey and weary.

' What do you want ? ' cried his wife scornfully. ' Why do you follow me ? I suppose you want money. You look like it; and you haven't shaved this morning. I suppose your hand was too shaky.'

' I want nothing from you that I cannot pay for,' replied Harry in a broken voice. ' I have spoilt your life—perhaps. You may be right, Maria. I am sorry for it. But you have not made mine easy.'

Maria was looking at him with a queer speculation in her eyes. He had mentioned payment. He did not look as if he had money. Neither did she know that she possessed anything for which he might be prepared to offer a price. She was endowed, it will be seen, with a large common-sense, and reflected that it was better to talk things over quietly than to waste breath in vituperation. And although most ladies are constantly protesting that they have no heads for business, results go to prove that they frequently transact their own affairs with a remarkable shrewdness.

Maria's face softened a little.

' Well,' she said, ' what do you want ? '

Harry, primed by the lawyer, opened, as it were, with his heavy guns.

' The settlement I made on you before our marriage was illegal,' said he. ' If I fight it I am, in the opinion of the best lawyers in India, bound to win.'

Maria shrugged her shoulders. What woman is afraid of legal cunning or backward to pit her own against it ?

' The wording of the assignment as drawn up by your father,' said Harry, remembering his lesson as best he could, ' is not sound. And even if it were, the fact of its being drawn by him with the knowledge that he undeniably possessed at the time is sufficient to impair its validity.'

' Then you are going to fight ? ' Maria sneered, with a gleam of her pretty white teeth.

' Unless you agree to my proposal.'

Whereat Maria laughed scornfully, which served to conceal the curiosity she felt.

' I do not suppose I shall do that,' she said, with a great air of indifference, arranging the lace at her sleeve. ' I am not to be frightened by mere threats. What is your proposal ? '

' I want the child,' replied Harry, who was too simple to carry concealment further. He trembled as he said it, and Maria, wondering a little at such

feeling, of which the counterpart was doubtless
excluded from her own heart by the strong common-sense which we have noticed, scarce believed
him. To set a great price upon the possession of
such an encumbrance as was at that moment sleeping on the floor of the next room under the dark
eyes of the ayah seemed preposterous.

' What for ? ' she asked. For, with the simple,
even cunning people are sometimes caught indulg-
ing in simplicity.

' To bring her up like a lady,' replied Harry,
looking into her eyes. And she, with a self-com-
mand that did her credit, restrained the very obvious retort which was no doubt on the tip of so
quick a tongue.

' You may have the child and welcome,' she said,
' on the terms you propose—but it must all be down
in black and white,' added she, true to her father's
teaching.

Harry thanked her clumsily enough, with a very
honest joy glistening in his eyes as he rang the bell.
When the servant appeared, which he did with singular rapidity, Harry instructed him to ask the gentleman who was waiting in the hall to come to
number fourteen.

' We can settle it outright,' he said to his wife,
with such evident delight that Maria began to won-

der whether she ought to have held out for better
terms. But she doubtless consoled herself with
the reflection that Harry had nothing more to give.

'I have a lawyer here,' explained he further,
'who has made out the necessary agreements, and
will witness the signature.'

The man of deeds appeared at this moment on
the threshold and bowed to Maria, with whom he
had danced many times in Calcutta.

Maria had, indeed, numbered him, in her maiden
meditations, among her many admirers, and had
even informed herself of the prospects of a rising
solicitor in India. His manner at this moment was
full of promise for his future, inasmuch as he
showed himself master of a most delicate situation.
The bow on the threshold combined professional
severity with personal admiration. As a lawyer he
was strong, as a man he tacitly admitted to Maria
that he was weak, and therefore enthralled by her
beauty. With a strict faithfulness to his client he
managed to convey to Maria a subtle regret that he
had been engaged, as it were, on the other side.

Thus this clever young man arranged a difficult
matter with an apparent ease and the pleasantest
manner in the world. At the same time the contract, which may or may not have been strictly legal,
was very effectually executed.

He laid the blotting-paper almost affectionately upon Maria's name, and then stood upright,
looking calmly at his client through a single eyeglass.

' And now,' he said softly, ' the child's ayah.'

The two men went into an adjoining room where
they found the gentle native nurse seated on the
floor beside her charge, and slowly waving a fan
over the peaceful little head. The woman raised
her glance for a moment only—indeed, there is no
nurse so faithful as an ayah—and seeing Harry her
deep, melancholy eyes lighted. She drew aside the
lace covering with that soft touch which is so full
of knowledge, and which black fingers can compass
every whit as tenderly as the hand of an enlight-
ened Christian mother.

Harry knelt down and buried his red face in the
soft coverings, with an impetuous disregard for
observation, which the single eyeglass contemplated
with the large tolerance of one who has many cli-
ents, and sees them in unguarded moments.

The lawyer began at once a conversation with the
ayah, but found that until he had taken notice of the
baby he could make but little progress. Even this
he did with a certain *savoir-faire*, and returned to
the charge. The matter did not take many minutes, and it is probable that one so acute and dis-

criminating as Harry's legal adviser avoided the
mistake of attributing to his own eloquence the
ayah's decision to accompany her small charge to
that cold grey country of the north, where she
would have to brave curiosity and rudeness wherever
she went.

' There, my dear sir,' said the lawyer to Harry in
the hall, ' I think everything is fixed up. Do not
lose that agreement. My fee is two hundred rupees.
And I will be off to the harbour and find some
thing to take me up to Madras.'

Harry paid him the two hundred rupees, and
sent a message by him to the captain of the steamer,
by which he intended to take passage for himself
and his little daughter to Bombay, *en route* for the
native country which he had left under a cloud
more than five years earlier. The cloud in truth
had spread and thickened until it obscured almost
the entire heaven, but he felt, nevertheless, some
exultation as he thought of home.

There remained one duty—to bid his wife farewell.

He found Maria in number fourteen in the act of
locking away in her jewel-case the agreement signed
by Harry.

' I've come,' he said slowly, ' to say good-bye.'

' Oh! good-bye,' Maria answered carelessly, and

the jewel-case shut with a snap, closing upon the result of Maria Lamond's first venture in life. ' I suppose,' she went on, ' you will take the child home to your—Miss Gresham ? '

And Harry went out of the room, wondering why she supposed that.

ALMOST the last words of Frederic Marqueray to Harry on his departure had been urging him to go home and start the world afresh. Such false beginnings as Harry had made have indeed been retrieved frequently enough; and men have risen who, when they first took the road, had every appearance of going down hill.

Harry sailed from Bombay in the fine ship *Constance*, of nine hundred tons burthen, with his baby daughter and her native nurse. And after such varieties of fair and foul weather as have caused poets and others to liken a sea-voyage to a human life, they anchored off Gravesend, at which town the passengers were set ashore.

The day happened to be a Sunday. There was but one train, late in the evening. It was the month of November, and a river fog hung on the shipping at anchor. Harry was a stranger in this town, and knew not where to pass the time until the departure of the London train. The little party went therefore to the railway station, and there found refuge in a dismal waiting-room. The ayah was abashed by so many new sights, dazed by strange sounds, and shivering with cold. The child whimpered in its soft shawls, with a mournful little voice that would not cease complaining.

Such was the fresh start in life. And but for the little whimpering voice Harry would have sought consolation where he knew he could find it, at least for a time. But that small voice had a power over him, which Marqueray and other strong men had failed to exercise. Harry drew himself up, in his thin and somewhat shabby Indian tweeds, and would not give way to the temptation that flared across the road from the open door of a hotel. It was a mere railway tavern, where he could not find asylum for his child.

He had been dreading that which he knew must come to-morrow, with the slowly increasing fear that belongs to remorseful anticipation. He had at first reflected that he should see Miriam in perhaps three months. The months had slipped away, in the enforced idleness of the sea-voyage, until the dread moment lay a few weeks ahead. In less than twenty-four hours he must face Miriam now—and the man who had shown his courage among the heroes of the Mutiny, who had dared death a hun-

dred times with a shout of exultation and a dauntless bearing, found himself face to face at last with
abject fear.

During the miserable railway journey he sat in
silence, and there doubtless fell about his ears during this time of retrospection the ruins of those vast
edifices which we all build in the air when we are
young, and of which the broken remains hinder our
footsteps in later life.

At eleven o'clock the next morning Harry Wylam
passed through the iron gateway of St. Helen's
Place, which he had entered years earlier with his
first black-eye slowly swelling—his heart hot with
the wild exultation of his first fight. He had
fought, Heaven knows, many a fight since then, and
had not always won. It was his heart that was
swelling now, and not with pride. A few alterations caught his attention, but he did not heed
them. Some of the quiet houses had been given
over to the speculator to be converted into offices.
But the porter's lodge was there, as, indeed, it is
to-day, and Harry dared not give so much as a passing glance at the little square window where the
gold-laced hat dimly notified the presence of the
janitor. He walked on as if in a dream, or more,
perhaps, as if half awakened from a long sleep full
of evil visions.

He glanced up at the window of Mr. Gresham's house, just as he had glanced, not so many years ago, to see if Miriam were there to note the grandeur of his new uniform and the swing of his great sword. He raised his hand to the knocker, and gave a sudden gulp at the sound it made. The door was opened with a swing, and half-closed again at the sight of this shabby visitor. The man stood in the opening looking, not at Harry, but at his clothes.

' Well, young man,' he said.

It was Parks, who had helped him out of many a scrape, and connived in many a practical joke. Parks, who had brought him home from Chatham, adventurous and unashamed, who now did not recognise him.

' Mr. Gresham in ? ' asked Harry in a voice that he need not have attempted to disguise. His life had done that as effectually as it had altered his face.

' No! Mr. Gresham is gone to his office.' And the door was closed a little further.

' Miss Miriam in ? '

' Yes,' answered the butler, ' but she won't see the likes of you. What is your business ? What's yer name, anyway ? '

' Harry Wylam.'

The door was slowly opened, and the old man

backed against the wall, where he stood a broken figure, with his white head bowed.

' Beg pardon, Mr. Harry,' he said; ' I didn't recognise yer, not just at first. I see it's you, now, sir. But —— '

' All right, Parks,' said Harry, holding out his hand and taking the frail fingers in his. He did not wait for a further explanation; indeed, would have none of it. ' Is Miss Miriam in the drawing-room ? '

' Yes, sir.'

The old servitor led the way upstairs. It seemed to Harry that nothing was altered in the house. He remembered the sense of cleanliness, the faint odour of furniture polish that had hovered on the stairs before he could walk them. As they mounted, the sound of the piano came to their ears. It was Miriam's hour for practising. Her father still liked to hear her play the piano her mother had touched, after he had eaten his good dinner and solemnly sipped his two glasses of '32 port.

The butler opened the door and went in.

' Miss Miriam,' he said, and that was all. But it was almost a cry.

Harry followed, and as the butler closed the door Miriam rose from the piano with a puzzled look. What struck Harry at once was her youth. He seemed to have lived so long—to be so old. And here was Miriam, youthful still, standing in a girlish attitude with one hand at the piano, it seemed on the threshold of life. Her poor face was of a piteous white. Thus they stood through interminable moments looking at each other. She knew him— had known him instantly—would have known him had his hair been white instead of grey, had he looked a hundred times shabbier and poorer and more broken.

Then suddenly he went forward and, casting himself on a sofa, buried his face in his arms, as Miriam had seen him do a dozen times in some boyish disgrace.

'Oh—Mim!' he cried in a broken voice. And that was all his greeting.

She stood at the piano shaking like a leaf, and spoke no word. She waited for him to lift that poor grey head, and who shall say what a wealth of pity and tenderness and love, ay! and of that forgiveness which only women compass, must have been hidden in her heart.

It was Harry who spoke first.

'I have left Ma—my wife,' he said. 'She—I couldn't live with her any longer. It is a miserable story, and very little of it is fit for your ears.'

He sat with dull eyes, to which the tears never came, looking round the room, of which the very

atmosphere seemed to breathe of goodness and
purity. Indeed, such a story as he had to tell was
sadly out of place in this spot, and his lips were
sealed by a sort of shame. All that had touched
his life to mar it and stain it was irrevocably shut
out from this pure house.

' No doubt it was a great deal my own fault,' he
went on, in a quiet voice. ' But I have been punished for it, God knows.'

There was a little movement at the piano, where
he would not look.

' I ought never to have married her,' he continued.
' I do not know why I did, and I suppose I have
ruined your life.'

' No, you must not say that,' she protested, in a
voice that had a strange ring—one would almost
have thought of joy—in it. For a woman knows
when he who speaks to her loves her, and gathers
not always that knowledge from the words he says.

' I seem to be—possessed of a devil,' he said,
with a sudden harsh laugh. ' I bring trouble to all
who come near me.'

Miriam shook her head with a queer little smile,
as if she had knowledge of some future which was
withheld from him.

' And I have not come home alone,' he said; ' I
have brought home my little girl.'

'Why?' asked Miriam, after a long pause, almost the question that Maria had asked. Harry made no answer, but sat with lowered eyes. And some woman's instinct told her the answer to the question she had put.

'Do you want me to take care of her, Harry?' asked she, in a low voice; and Harry nodded.

'I cannot think how I can ask you to do it,' he muttered, staring at the carpet, and biting his thumb. 'But she is so helpless.'

'Yes, I know,' answered Miriam, in a voice which thrilled with heaven only knows what woman's dreams. For it is to heaven that such dreams belong, and the realisation of them on earth must, it seems, be part of Paradise. 'Where is she?'

'At the Golden Cross in Trafalgar Square.'

'Then I will go and bring her here,' said Miriam, going towards the door which he held open for her to pass out as if she had been a queen.

When she returned to the drawing-room she found it vacant, and on inquiring learnt that Harry had gone to Eastcheap to seek his guardian there.

Thither indeed he had hastened with a new dawn of hope in his heart. As he walked along the familiar streets through which he had passed as a boy on his way to school four times a day, there arose in his heart a strange inexplicable sense of exultation, the same sense that had made itself heard in Miriam's voice. A note as it were of joy in a chord of grief. Let those explain it who can.

Harry remained in the outer office, sending in a note by a new clerk, whose face was unfamiliar. There were many at the desks whom Harry knew. They seemed to be sitting in the same attitudes, writing in the same books, with the same pens. Some perchance might have known him had they looked up or had he emerged from the shadowy corner near the door which he had selected with the purpose of remaining unrecognised. He was kept waiting a long time, during which, no doubt, in the quiet of his own room, the stout old British merchant was waging a tough fight. For he had bidden this scapegrace go away never to return.

' Will you step this way ? ' said the new clerk, and Harry followed through the dimly-lighted passage where the letter-books were stored on shelves near the ceiling.

Mr. Gresham, unaltered, save that perhaps he was a little stouter, stood gravely by his writing-table awaiting his visitor. He shook hands in silence and motioned Harry to a chair.

' I have seen Miriam,' blurted out Harry honestly. ' I went there first.'

Mr. Gresham's kind face hardened a little.

22

'Ah,' he said, 'you used not to be a coward,
Harry.'

'No, but I am now.'

He sat somewhat heavily on the chair reserved for
influential business callers, and told Mr. Gresham
the story he had not told Miriam.   He told it as
man to man, without extenuation, hiding nothing,
suppressing nothing.   And Mr. Gresham, leaning
back in his chair with finger-tips pressed together—
his attitude when puzzling out some commercial
problem—wondered whether he had made some
mistake far back at the beginning of Harry's education which had turned the whole life astray.

He listened to it all with a wonderful patience,
and a tolerance which, like his frame, had grown
broader with advancing years.   He only made one
comment.

'Your friend, Colonel Marqueray,' he said, ' must
be worthy of all esteem.'

Then he asked one question.

'Where is the child ?'

'Miriam has gone to fetch it from the Golden
Cross Hotel,' Harry answered, looking anxiously
at his guardian's face.   But Mr. Gresham made no
comment.

'You have no money ?'

'None,' was the answer.

Mr. Gresham's cheque-book lay by his hand. He opened it, and signed a cheque for one hundred pounds.

'You will want money,' he said. 'You require new clothes.'

Harry blushed. He bent forward and took the money almost with eagerness. There was a queer light in his eyes, and his hand was unsteady.

'You will come to St. Helen's Place again,' said Mr. Gresham, with a largeness of heart which was not lost upon his hearer.

'No,' answered Harry quickly; 'I am not going there again. She thinks I am going back again—at once—this evening. But I am not.'

'She?' questioned Mr. Gresham.

'Miriam,' explained Harry with wavering glance. 'I am not going back to St. Helen's Place. I am going away from England at once.'

'Where to?'

'Oh—anywhere. The Cape will do.'

'And why are you going?' asked the old man with a cold wonder.

'I don't know.'

Harry rose, and held out his hand to say farewell.

'I don't know,' he repeated.

CHAPTER XXX

WHEN a man quits his native land and journeys in difficulty to a new country, with the comment that it ' will do,' it may be surmised that he leaves his heart behind him. Such a fresh start in life did Harry Wylam set about to compass from the moment that he was assured of his child's welfare in the house which had been his own childhood's home. Whether he returned to England with the decision already matured of quitting it again immediately seems doubtful. It is more probable that he acted thus, as at most junctures of his life, on the impulse of the moment. As a man journeys on through his years of existence he learns to know himself, if it so be that he fails—as many of us do—to form a new man of some sort or other. Harry knew his own nature well enough to be aware of the fact that in sudden temptation he usually succumbed. His was not a nature which may face temptation and take a Spartan pleasure in resisting it. He had failed so often that he now knew himself. The interview in the drawing-room of St. Helen's Place had convinced him in one flash of self-knowledge that he had awakened from the bad dream of his life in India to find that his real self was quite other, and that the one love of his life was, and ever would be, Miriam Gresham.

' No! By God!' he said to himself as he stepped on board the vessel in which he had taken passage to the Cape of Good Hope, ' I'll be a gentleman this time!'

Those who have had the patience to follow this record so far will not be surprised to hear that before the voyage was ended Harry had recovered his wild spirits in a great degree, and only at times gave way to humours of melancholy and depression. He soon became a favourite among his fellow-passengers, and his jolly laugh resounded sometimes through the ship.

At Cape Town he remained a few weeks, and there found a remittance awaiting him, forwarded in the kind forethought of his guardian (for so he continued to call honest John Gresham) by a steamer sailing after his vessel, and arriving at her destination a few weeks earlier. Harry wrote letters full of hope and cheery anticipation. The climate suited him ; his health was already more satisfactory ; it seemed probable that he would find work without

difficulty. He would write once a week. And at
the end of a fortnight he drifted northward with the
scum that ever floats on the wave of civilisation,
and forgot his promise.

During the following five years those who watched
and waited for news at home heard but little of him,
and, indeed, such advices as they received scarce
whetted their thirst for more. That perfect con-
tentment with the interests in the immediate
vicinity, which marks a shallow nature, seemed to
increase its hold upon Harry as he grew older. His
letters, never conspicuously coherent, or indeed
notable for any one of the epistolary arts, made
constant reference at this time to persons totally
unknown to the recipients of the communications,
and in such manner as to convey the impression
that he was almost absorbed in the sayings and
doings of those around him.

It was Mr. Gresham who heard from a trusted
business connection in the Republic of Argentina,
that a young lady of the name of Maria Lamond,
whose father lived in a lordly fashion at the city of
Rio de Janeiro, had married a general of renown in
South America, who was spoken of as the future
president of the Spanish colony. After a mature
consideration, the City merchant forwarded this
information to Harry, but refrained at that time

from telling Miriam. Harry received the letter in
due course, and laughed recklessly at its news. He
was at that time working as team-driver to a
Dutch farmer, and having recovered his strength,
was deemed a man of some importance in a land
where physical power, a great courage, and fault-
less marksmanship were held in highest esteem.

It was shortly after this that he fell seriously ill,
and once more approached the threshold of death.
His employers treated him with a great kindness
which was not entirely attributable to the fact that
Mr. Gresham's remittances of money still came to
hand regularly, to be spent lavishly at once. The
daughter of his employer—a heavy-faced Dutch
maiden who, perhaps, possessed a warm heart—was
especially devoted to his welfare, never leaving his
bedside by night or day until the danger was
overpast.

The team-driver, whose name was a byeword for
all that was wild and reckless and daring, recovered
therefore his strength, and had been at work some
days when his employer called him aside.

' When are you going to marry that girl ? ' he
asked in a thick voice, standing squarely in front of
Harry.

' Never,' Harry returned stoutly.

' You'll marry that girl.'

' I'm d——d if I do,' retorted Harry with a laugh, whereat the farmer struck at him heavily, and announced his intention of killing him.

So Harry, half recovered from his sickness, fought the Dutch farmer, and whipping him, left him lying insensible before his own door.

Again he drifted northwards, whither the tide of rascaldom seemed ever flowing, and the whole of his next remittance from London was sent back to the Dutch farmer, who accepted the gift with the strong common-sense that so often overrules pride. A portion of the money was spent in a new dress of the brightest magenta for the girl whose cause had been so stoutly upheld by her father, and doubtless brought much consolation to that maiden. Even a broken heart may beat at the sight of a new bonnet.

Two years after this an enthusiastic young colonial bishop, making his way northward, like a sleuth-hound on the scent of sin, met in the open veldt a single waggon slowly moving southward. As ships upon the sea meeting in mid-ocean joyfully clew up sails and pause to exchange news of the busy world, so the waggons on the great plains of Southern Africa naturally made halt, and the travellers drew together.

The bishop, with his rifle on his shoulder, his jacket pockets impartially stuffed with cartridges and tracts, went forward on foot to meet the small waggon, which seemed to be in the sole charge of a native driver.

After the customary greetings the divine turned his thoughts to the business that called him to wander, not disdaining in his young enthusiasm to cast seed on the wayside. He was searching among his store of devotional literature for something suitable for a native team-driver who could not read, when the curtain of the tent was drawn aside, and the face of a white man appeared in the dim recesses of the interior.

' Whom have you there ? ' asked the bishop.

'The man that breaks the stones for the road up at Happywith, the next station. He's mighty sick, that man. I'm taking him down to Oomstrand to the doctor.'

The bishop went forward to the waggon.

' Are you an Englishman ? ' he asked.

' Yes, are you a doctor ? '

' No, I'm only a parson. Can I do anything for you ? '

The man shook his head. ' Not yet,' he answered with a laugh. ' But I think I shall have something in your line before long, unless we get to Oomstrand pretty quickly.'

The bishop, with somewhat boyish activity

hoisted himself up to the shaft of the waggon,
where he sat with his legs dangling.

' Excuse me,' said he, with the quiet assurance of
his cloth, ' but it seems to me that you are a gentleman.'

' Was once,' the sick man answered, passing a
thin hand over his brow and curly hair that was
almost white. ' I was in the army, and fought in
the Mutiny. My name is Harry Wylam. I was
cashiered for looting.'

' And were you guilty ? ' asked the man of God.

' Yes.'

Harry was lying back on his rough bed, with
parted lips and half-closed eyes. The excitement
of this little incident, common enough on the waggon track, seemed to have overpowered him. Presently his eyes closed, and the bishop slipped quietly
to the ground. An hour and more elapsed before
Harry stirred. And when he did so, the kind English voice aroused him to a full consciousness.

' Here—wake up—I have some strong soup waiting for you. There's brandy in it. It will do you
good. I have turned my waggon round and am
going back to Oomstrand with you. You are one
of my parishioners, you know.'

After the soup Harry seemed stronger, and even
showed some inclination to talk. The afternoon

was wearing on, and in the cool of the evening it was the bishop's intention to make a move. The oxen were feeding with that contemplative calm which belongs to the bovine race, while the native teamsman slept in the shadow of the waggons.

The bishop, having despatched a hearty meal while Harry slept, now lighted his pipe, and climbed to the shaft of the waggon.

' Better now ? ' he inquired cheerily.

' Yes,' answered Harry, with a look of rest in his eyes.

' Funny thing we've never met before,' went on the other; ' I have been up and down this country these last two years.'

' I have seen you pass—when I was breaking stones on the road,' said Harry with his laugh, which sounded strange enough from such blanched lips.

' Have you no friends at home to whom I could write and tell your state ? You will not be fit to work for some months. Surely your people at home would be glad to hear of you, or sorry to hear of your sickness,' said the good Samaritan, without taking his pipe from his lips, and bluffly and honestly as man to man.

Harry made no answer, but lay back on his rough pillows deep in thought.

'Parents dead?' inquired the younger man.

'Yes,' Harry answered. 'Thank God, they died when I was a child.'

'Is there nobody, then?'

Harry did not speak for some time. He turned over and found that his face was close to his companion's elbow, who sat smoking and gazing abstractedly out over the rolling veldt now shimmering in the sunshine.

'Did you ever hear of John Gresham of St. Helen's Place, in London?' asked the sick man.

'Yes,' answered the other, 'I was curate in a City church before I came here, and I met Mr. Gresham then.'

'Will you write to him—when we get to Oomstrand?'

The bishop was silent for some moments. Then he laid his strong brown hand on Harry's shoulder. 'Mr. Gresham died two years ago—when I was last in England.'

Harry turned away, so that his face was hidden against the canvas of the waggon-cover, and his companion sat smoking and looking out over the veldt.

'And his daughter?' said Harry suddenly in a broken voice.

'She was well. I knew her only by sight. I

used to see her in church, when by chance I offi-
ciated at St. Helen's. I did so when I was last in
England. And there was a child—a little girl
adopted by Mr. Gresham, I believe.'

' What was she like—the little girl—was she
dark ? ' asked the broken voice.

' No; she was fair, with blue eyes.'

The sick man gave a queer laugh, which set his
companion thinking.

' Was Miss Gresham going to be married?' asked
the bishop's patient after a pause.

' No; her friends say she will never marry.'

The two men were silent for some time, and
presently the bishop noticing that Harry had fallen
asleep, himself laid down in the shadow of the waggon, and rested during the heat of the afternoon.
He was astir again before sunset, and aroused the
men.

When Harry awoke from his slumber his new
found friend was sitting beside him, and again
offered him food, which in pure exhaustion the sick
man swallowed.

' Did you ever hear the name of Marqueray ? '
Harry asked of the only gentleman with whom he
had conversed for many years.

' All Englishmen know that name,' was the reply.
' He is one of the great commanders out in India.'

' Only man I was ever afraid of,' commented Harry with a little laugh, and turning over he fell asleep again.

He did not stir when, at sunset, a start was made; and during the journey across the moonlit veldt, which lasted until dawn, he made no answer when addressed by his companions.

It was nearly daylight when the waggons reached the small town of Oomstrand, and drew up before the only inn.

The bishop went to Harry's vehicle, and un-strapped the flap of the covering which had been closed against the heavy dew. He drew aside the soaking canvas, and found that that which had been adrift so long had reached the shore at last.

THE END

MESSRS. LONGMANS, GREEN, & CO.'S
CLASSIFIED CATALOGUE

OF

WORKS IN GENERAL LITERATURE.

History, Politics, Polity, Political Memoirs, &c.

Abbott.—A HISTORY OF GREECE. By EVELYN ABBOTT, M.A., LL.D.
Part I.—From the Earliest Times to the Ionian Revolt. Crown 8vo., 10s. 6d.
Part II.—500-445 B.C. Cr. 8vo., 10s. 6d.

Acland and Ransome.—A HAND-BOOK IN OUTLINE OF THE POLITICAL HISTORY OF ENGLAND TO 1894. Chronologically Arranged. By A. H. DYKE ACLAND, M.P., and CYRIL RANSOME, M.A. Cr. 8vo., 6s.

ANNUAL REGISTER (THE). A Review of Public Events at Home and Abroad, for the year 1895. 8vo., 18s.

Volumes of the ANNUAL REGISTER for the years 1863-1894 can still be had. 18s. each.

Armstrong.—ELIZABETH FARNESE; The Termagant of Spain. By EDWARD ARMSTRONG, M.A. 8vo., 16s.

Arnold (T., D.D.), formerly Head Master of Rugby School.
INTRODUCTORY LECTURES ON MODERN HISTORY. 8vo., 7s. 6d.
MISCELLANEOUS WORKS. 8vo., 7s. 6d.

Bagwell.—IRELAND UNDER THE TUDORS. By RICHARD BAGWELL, LL.D. 3 vols. Vols. I. and II. From the first Invasion of the Northmen to the year 1578. 8vo., 32s. Vol. III. 1578-1603. 8vo., 18s.

Ball.—HISTORICAL REVIEW OF THE LEGISLATIVE SYSTEMS OPERATIVE IN IRELAND, from the Invasion of Henry the Second to the Union (1172-1800). By the Rt. Hon. J. T. BALL. 8vo., 6s.

Besant.—THE HISTORY OF LONDON. By Sir WALTER BESANT. With 74 Illustrations. Crown 8vo., 1s. 9d. Or bound as a School Prize Book, 2s. 6d.

Brassey (LORD).—PAPERS AND ADDRESSES.
NAVAL AND MARITIME, 1872-1893. 2 vols. Crown 8vo., 10s.
MERCANTILE MARINE AND NAVIGATION, 1871-1894. Crown 8vo., 5s.
IMPERIAL FEDERATION AND COLONISATION FROM 1880 to 1894. Cr. 8vo., 5s.
POLITICAL AND MISCELLANEOUS, 1861-1894. Crown 8vo., 5s.

Bright.—A HISTORY OF ENGLAND. By the Rev. J. FRANCK BRIGHT, D.D.
Period I. MEDIÆVAL MONARCHY: A.D. 449 to 1485. Crown 8vo., 4s. 6d.
Period II. PERSONAL MONARCHY: 1485 to 1688. Crown 8vo., 5s.
Period III. CONSTITUTIONAL MONARCHY: 1689 to 1837. Cr. 8vo., 7s. 6d.
Period IV. THE GROWTH OF DEMOCRACY: 1837 to 1880. Cr. 8vo., 6s.

Buckle.—HISTORY OF CIVILISATION IN ENGLAND AND FRANCE, SPAIN AND SCOTLAND. By HENRY THOMAS BUCKLE. 3 vols. Crown 8vo., 24s.

Burke.—A HISTORY OF SPAIN, from the Earliest Times to the Death of Ferdinand the Catholic. By ULICK RALPH BURKE, M.A. 2 vols. 8vo., 32s.

Chesney.—INDIAN POLITY: a View of the System of Administration in India. By General Sir GEORGE CHESNEY, K.C.B., M.P. With Map showing all the Administrative Divisions of British India. 8vo., 21s.

Creighton.—HISTORY OF THE PAPACY DURING THE REFORMATION. By MANDELL CREIGHTON, D.D., LL.D., Bishop of Peterborough. Vols. I. and II., 1378-1464, 32s. Vols. III. and IV., 1464-1518, 24s. Vol. V., 1517-1527. 8vo., 15s.

History, Politics, Polity, Political Memoirs, &c.—*continued.*

Cuningham.—A SCHEME FOR IM-
PERIAL FEDERATION: a Senate for the
Empire. By GRANVILLE C. CUNING-
HAM, of Montreal, Canada. Cr. 8vo.,
3s. 6d.

Curzon.—PERSIA AND THE PERSIAN
QUESTION. By the Right Hon. GEORGE
N. CURZON, M.P. With 9 Maps, 96
Illustrations, Appendices, and an Index.
2 vols. 8vo., 42s.

De Tocqueville.— DEMOCRACY IN
AMERICA. By ALEXIS DE TOCQUE-
VILLE. 2 vols. Crown 8vo., 16s.

Dickinson.—THE DEVELOPMENT OF
PARLIAMENT DURING THE NINE-
TEENTH CENTURY. By G. LOWES
DICKINSON. M.A. 8vo. 7s. 6d.

Ewald.—THE HISTORY OF ISRAEL. By
HEINRICH EWALD, Professor in the
University of Göttingen. 8 vols. 8vo.,
Vols. I. and II., 24s. Vols. III. and IV.,
21s. Vol. V., 18s. Vol. VI., 16s. Vol.
VII., 21s. Vol. VIII., 18s.

Follett.—THE SPEAKER OF THE HOUSE
OF REPRESENTATIVES. By M. P.
FOLLETT. With an Introduction by
ALBERT BUSHNELL HART, Ph.D. of
Harvard University. Crown 8vo., 6s.

Froude (JAMES A.).

THE HISTORY OF ENGLAND, from the
Fall of Wolsey to the Defeat of the
Spanish Armada. 12 vols. Cr. 8vo.,
3s. 6d. each.

THE DIVORCE OF CATHERINE OF ARA-
GON. Crown 8vo., 6s.

THE SPANISH STORY OF THE ARMADA,
and other Essays. Cr. 8vo., 3s. 6d.

THE ENGLISH IN IRELAND IN THE
EIGHTEENTH CENTURY.

Cabinet Edition. 3 vols. Cr. 8vo., 18s.

"*Silver Library*" Edition. 3 vols.
Cr. 8vo., 10s. 6d.

ENGLISH SEAMEN IN THE SIXTEENTH
CENTURY. Crown 8vo., 6s.

THE COUNCIL OF TRENT. Cr. 8vo., 6s.

SHORT STUDIES ON GREAT SUBJECTS.
4 vols. Cr. 8vo., 3s. 6d. each.

CÆSAR: a Sketch. Cr. 8vo., 3s. 6d.

Gardiner (SAMUEL RAWSON, D.C.L.,
LL.D.).

HISTORY OF ENGLAND, from the Accession of James I. to the Outbreak of
the Civil War, 1603-1642. 10 vols.
Crown 8vo., 6s. each.

HISTORY OF THE GREAT CIVIL WAR,
1642-1649. 4 vols. Cr. 8vo., 6s. each.

HISTORY OF THE COMMONWEALTH
AND THE PROTECTORATE, 1649-1660.
Vol. I., 1649-1651. With 14 Maps.
8vo., 21s.

THE STUDENT'S HISTORY OF ENGLAND,
With 378 Illustrations. Cr. 8vo., 12s.

Also in Three Volumes, price 4s. each.

Greville.—A JOURNAL OF THE REIGNS
OF KING GEORGE IV., KING WILLIAM
IV., AND QUEEN VICTORIA. By
CHARLES C. F. GREVILLE, formerly
Clerk of the Council.

Cabinet Edition. 8 vols. Crown 8vo.,
6s. each.

"*Silver Library*" Edition. 8 vols.
Crown 8vo., 3s. 6d. each.

Hearn.—THE GOVERNMENT OF ENG-
LAND: its Structure and its Development.
By W. EDWARD HEARN. 8vo., 16s.

Historic Towns.—Edited by E. A.
FREEMAN, D.C.L., and Rev. WILLIAM
HUNT, M.A. With Maps and Plans.
Crown 8vo., 3s. 6d. each.

Bristol. By the Rev. W. Hunt.	London. By Rev. W. J. Loftie.
Carlisle. By Mandell Creighton, D.D.	Oxford. By Rev. C. W. Boase.
Cinque Ports. By Montagu Burrows.	Winchester. By Rev. G. W. Kitchin, D.D.
Colchester. By Rev. E. L. Cutts.	York. By Rev. James Raine.
	New York. By Theodore Roosevelt.
Exeter. By E. A. Freeman.	Boston (U.S.). By Henry Cabot Lodge.

Joyce.—A SHORT HISTORY OF IRELAND,
from the Earliest Times to 1608. By
P. W. JOYCE, LL.D. Cr. 8vo., 10s. 6d.

Kaye (SIR JOHN W.), **and Malleson**
(COL. G. B.).

HISTORY OF THE SEPOY WAR IN INDIA.
1857-1858. By Sir JOHN W. KAYE,
K.C.S.I., F.R.S. 3 vols. 8vo. Vol.
I. 18s.: Vol. II. 20s.: Vol. III. 20s.

History, Politics, Polity, Political Memoirs, &c.—*continued*.

Kaye (Sir John W.), and **Malleson** (Col. G. B.)—*continued*.

HISTORY OF THE INDIAN MUTINY, 1857-1858. Commencing from the close of the Second Volume of Sir John W. Kaye's 'History of the Sepoy War.' By Colonel G. B. MALLESON, C.S.I. 3 vols. 8vo. Vol. I., with Map, 20s.; Vol. II., with 4 Maps and Plans, 20s.; Vol. III., with 4 Maps, 20s.

ANALYTICAL INDEX TO Sir John W. KAYE'S 'HISTORY OF THE SEPOY WAR' AND Col. G. B. MALLESON'S 'HISTORY OF THE INDIAN MUTINY,' (Combined in one volume.) By FREDERIC PINCOTT. 8vo., 10s. 6d.

KAYE AND MALLESON'S 'HISTORY OF THE INDIAN MUTINY, 1857-1858.' (Being a Cabinet Edition of the above Works.) Edited by Colonel G. B. MALLESON. With Analytical Index by FREDERIC PINCOTT, and Maps and Plans. 6 vols. Cr. 8vo., 6s. each.

Knight.—MADAGASCAR IN WAR TIME: the Experiences of *The Times* Special Correspondent with the Hovas during the French Invasion of 1895. By E. F. KNIGHT. With 16 Illustrations and a Map. 8vo., 12s. 6d.

Lang (ANDREW).

PICKLE THE SPY. Disclosing the Treasons of A—— M——, Esq., of G——; also of James Mohr Macgregor, and Macallester, an Irishman. With the Secret Amours and Misfortunes of H.R.H. Charles P—— of W——. Drawn from the Cabinets of the late Elector of Hanover, and of their French and Prussian Majesties. With Portraits and Illustrations. 8vo., 18s. (and for Crown 8vo. Edition also).

ST. ANDREWS. With 8 Plates and 24 Illustrations in the Text. 8vo., 15s. net.

Laurie.—HISTORICAL SURVEY OF PRE-CHRISTIAN EDUCATION. By S. S. LAURIE, A.M., LL.D. Crown 8vo., 12s.

Lecky (WILLIAM EDWARD HARTPOLE).

HISTORY OF ENGLAND IN THE EIGHTEENTH CENTURY.
Library Edition. 8 vols. 8vo., £7 4s.
Cabinet Edition. ENGLAND. 7 vols. Cr. 8vo., 6s. each. IRELAND. 5 vols. Crown 8vo., 6s. each.

HISTORY OF EUROPEAN MORALS FROM AUGUSTUS TO CHARLEMAGNE. 2 vols. Crown 8vo., 16s.

Lecky (WILLIAM EDWARD HARTPOLE)—*continued*.

HISTORY OF THE RISE AND INFLUENCE OF THE SPIRIT OF RATIONALISM IN EUROPE. 2 vols. Crown 8vo., 10s.

DEMOCRACY AND LIBERTY. 2 vols. 8vo., 36s.

THE EMPIRE: its Value and its Growth. An Address delivered at the Imperial Institute. Crown 8vo., 1s. 6d.

Macaulay (LORD).

COMPLETE WORKS.
Cabinet Ed. 16 vols. Post 8vo., £4 16s.
Library Edition. 8 vols. 8vo., £5 5s.
'*Edinburgh Edition*.' 8 vols. 8vo., 6s. each.

HISTORY OF ENGLAND FROM THE ACCESSION OF JAMES THE SECOND.
Popular Edition. 2 vols. Cr. 8vo., 5s.
Student's Edit. 2 vols. Cr. 8vo., 12s.
People's Edition. 4 vols. Cr. 8vo., 16s.
Cabinet Edition. 8 vols. Post 8vo., 48s.
Library Edition. 5 vols. 8vo., £4.

CRITICAL AND HISTORICAL ESSAYS, WITH LAYS OF ANCIENT ROME, in 1 volume.
Popular Edition. Crown 8vo., 2s. 6d.
Authorised Edition. Crown 8vo., 2s. 6d., or 3s. 6d., gilt edges.
Silver Library Edition. Cr. 8vo., 3s. 6d.

CRITICAL AND HISTORICAL ESSAYS.
Student's Edition. 1 vol. Cr. 8vo., 6s.
People's Edition. 2 vols. Cr. 8vo., 8s.
Trevelyan Edit. 2 vols. Cr. 8vo., 9s.
Cabinet Edition. 4 vols. Post 8vo., 24s.
Library Edition. 3 vols. 8vo., 36s.

ESSAYS which may be had separately, price 6d. each sewed, 1s. each cloth.

Addison and Walpole.	The Earl of Chatham(Two Essays).
Frederick the Great.	Ranke and Gladstone.
Lord Bacon.	
Croker's Boswell's Johnson.	Milton and Machiavelli.
Hallam's Constitutional History.	Lord Byron, and The Comic Dramatists of the Restoration.
Warren Hastings.	
Lord Clive.	

MISCELLANEOUS WRITINGS AND SPEECHES.
Popular Edition. Cr. 8vo., 2s. 6d.
Cabinet Edition. Including Indian Penal Code, Lays of Ancient Rome, and Miscellaneous Poems. 4 vols. Post 8vo., 24s.

SELECTIONS FROM THE WRITINGS OF LORD MACAULAY. Edited, with Occasional Notes, by the Right Hon. Sir G. O. Trevelyan, Bart. Cr. 8vo., 6s.

History, Politics, Polity, Political Memoirs, &c.—*continued*.

Mackinnon.—THE UNION OF ENG-LAND AND SCOTLAND: a Study of International History. By JAMES MAC-KINNON, Ph.D., Examiner in History to the University of Edinburgh. 8vo., 16s.

May.—THE CONSTITUTIONAL HISTORY OF ENGLAND since the Accession of George III. 1760-1870. By Sir THOMAS ERSKINE MAY, K.C.B. (Lord Farnborough). 3 vols. Crown 8vo., 18s.

Merivale (The Very Rev. CHARLES, late Dean of Ely).
HISTORY OF THE ROMANS UNDER THE EMPIRE. 8 vols. Cr. 8vo., 3s. 6d. each.
THE FALL OF THE ROMAN REPUBLIC: a Short History of the Last Century of the Commonwealth. 12mo., 7s. 6d.

Montague.—THE ELEMENTS OF ENG-LISH CONSTITUTIONAL HISTORY. By F. C. MONTAGUE, M.A. Cr. 8vo., 3s. 6d.

O'Brien.—IRISH IDEAS. REPRINTED ADDRESSES. By WILLIAM O'BRIEN. Crown 8vo., 2s. 6d.

Richman.—APPENZELL: Pure Democracy and Pastoral Life in Inner-Rhoden. A Swiss Study. By IRVING B. RICHMAN Consul-General of the United States to Switzerland. With Maps. Crown 8vo., 5s.

Seebohm (FREDERIC).
THE ENGLISH VILLAGE COMMUNITY Examined in its Relations to the Manorial and Tribal Systems, &c. With 13 Maps and Plates. 8vo., 16s.
THE TRIBAL SYSTEM IN WALES: being Part of an Inquiry into the Structure and Methods of Tribal Society. With 3 Maps. 8vo., 12s.

Sharpe.—LONDON AND THE KINGDOM: a History derived mainly from the Archives at Guildhall in the custody of the Corporation of the City of London. By REGINALD R. SHARPE, D.C.L., Records Clerk in the Office of the Town Clerk of the City of London. 3 vols. 8vo. 10s. 6d. each.

Sheppard.—MEMORIALS OF ST. JAMES'S PALACE. By the Rev. EDGAR SHEPPARD, M.A., Sub-Dean of the Chapels Royal. With 41 full-page Plates (8 photo-intaglio), and 32 Illustrations in the Text. 2 Vols. 8vo. 36s. net.

Smith.—CARTHAGE AND THE CARTHA-GINIANS. By R. BOSWORTH SMITH, M.A., Assistant Master in Harrow School. With Maps, Plans, &c. Cr. 8vo., 3s. 6d.

Stephens.—A HISTORY OF THE FRENCH REVOLUTION. By H. MORSE STEPHENS, Balliol College, Oxford. 3 vols. 8vo. Vols. I. and II., 18s. each.

Stubbs.—HISTORY OF THE UNIVERSITY OF DUBLIN, from its Foundation to the End of the Eighteenth Century. By J. W. STUBBS. 8vo., 12s. 6d.

Sutherland.—THE HISTORY OF AUSTRALIA AND NEW ZEALAND, from 1606 to 1890. By ALEXANDER SUTHER-LAND, M.A., and GEORGE SUTHER-LAND, M.A. Crown 8vo., 2s. 6d.

Taylor.—A STUDENT'S MANUAL OF THE HISTORY OF INDIA. By Colonel MEADOWS TAYLOR, C.S.I., &c. Cr. 8vo., 7s. 6d.

Todd.—PARLIAMENTARY GOVERNMENT IN THE BRITISH COLONIES. By ALPHEUS TODD, LL.D. 8vo., 30s. net.

Vincent.—THE LAND QUESTION IN NORTH WALES: being a Brief Survey of the History, Origin, and Character of the Agrarian Agitation, and of the Nature and Effect of the Proceedings of the Welsh Land Commission. By J. E. VINCENT. 8vo., 5s.

Wakeman and Hassall.—ESSAYS INTRODUCTORY TO THE STUDY OF ENGLISH CONSTITUTIONAL HISTORY. Edited by HENRY OFFLEY WAKEMAN, M.A., and ARTHUR HASSALL, M.A. Crown 8vo., 6s.

Walpole.—HISTORY OF ENGLAND FROM THE CONCLUSION OF THE GREAT WAR IN 1815 TO 1858. By SPENCER WALPOLE. 6 vols. Crown 8vo., 6s. each.

Wolff.—ODD BITS OF HISTORY: being Short Chapters intended to Fill Some Blanks. By HENRY W. WOLFF. 8vo., 8s. 6d.

Wood-Martin.—PAGAN IRELAND: an Archaeological Sketch. A Handbook of Irish Pre-Christian Antiquities. By W. G. WOOD-MARTIN, M.R.I.A. 412 Illustrations. 8vo., 15s.

Wylie.—HISTORY OF ENGLAND UNDER HENRY IV. By JAMES HAMILTON WYLIE, M.A., one of H. M. Inspectors of Schools. 3 vols. Crown 8vo. Vol. I., 1399-1404, 10s. 6d. Vol. II., 15s. Vol. III., 15s. [Vol. IV. *in the press.*

Biography, Personal Memoirs, &c.

Armstrong.—THE LIFE AND LETTERS OF EDMUND J. ARMSTRONG. Edited by G. F. ARMSTRONG. Fcp. 8vo., 7s. 6d.

Bacon.—LETTERS AND LIFE OF FRANCIS BACON, INCLUDING ALL HIS OCCASIONAL WORKS. Edited by J. SPEDDING. 7 vols. 8vo., £4 4s.

Bagehot.—BIOGRAPHICAL STUDIES. By WALTER BAGEHOT. Cr. 8vo., 3s. 6d.

Blackwell.—PIONEER WORK IN OPENING THE MEDICAL PROFESSION TO WOMEN : Autobiographical Sketches. By ELIZABETH BLACKWELL. Crown 8vo., 6s.

Boyd (A. K. H.). ('A.K.H.B.').

TWENTY-FIVE YEARS OF ST. ANDREWS. 1865-1890. 2 vols. 8vo. Vol. I., 12s. Vol. II., 15s.

ST. ANDREWS AND ELSEWHERE : Glimpses of Some Gone and of Things Left. 8vo., 15s.

THE LAST YEARS OF ST. ANDREWS : September 1890 to September 1895. 8vo., 15s.

Brown.—THE LIFE OF FORD MADOX BROWN. By FORD MADOX HUEFFER. With 49 Plates and 7 Illustrations in the Text, being reproductions of the Artist's Pictures.

Buss.—FRANCES MARY BUSS AND HER WORK FOR EDUCATION. By ANNIE E. RIDLEY. With 5 Portraits and 4 Illustrations. Crown 8vo., 7s. 6d.

Carlyle.—THOMAS CARLYLE : a History of his Life. By JAMES A. FROUDE. 1795-1835. 2 vols. Crown 8vo., 7s. 1834-1881. 2 vols. Crown 8vo., 7s.

Digby.—THE LIFE OF SIR KENELM DIGBY, by one of his Descendants. By the Author of 'The Life of a Conspirator,' 'A Life of Archbishop Laud,' etc. With Illustration. 8vo.

Erasmus.—LIFE AND LETTERS OF ERASMUS. By JAMES A. FROUDE. Crown 8vo., 6s.

Fox.—THE EARLY HISTORY OF CHARLES JAMES FOX. By the Right Hon. Sir G. O. TREVELYAN, Bart., M.P.

Library Edition. 8vo., 18s.

Cabinet Edition. Crown 8vo., 6s.

Granville.—LETTERS OF HARRIET, COUNTESS GRANVILLE, 1810-1845. Edited by her son, the Hon. F. LEVESON-GOWER. With Portrait. 2 Vols. 8vo., 32s.

Halford.—THE LIFE OF SIR HENRY HALFORD, Bart., G.C.H., M.D., F.R.S. By WILLIAM MUNK, M.D., F.S.A. 8vo., 12s. 6d.

Hamilton.—LIFE OF SIR WILLIAM HAMILTON. By R. P. GRAVES. 8vo. 3 vols. 15s. each. ADDENDUM. 8vo., 6d. sewed.

Havelock.—MEMOIRS OF SIR HENRY HAVELOCK, K.C.B. By JOHN CLARK MARSHMAN. Crown 8vo., 3s. 6d.

Haweis.—MY MUSICAL LIFE. By the Rev. H. R. HAWEIS. With Portrait of Richard Wagner and 3 Illustrations. Crown 8vo., 7s. 6d.

Holroyd.—THE GIRLHOOD OF MARIA JOSEPHA HOLROYD (Lady Stanley or Alderly), as told in Letters of a Hundred Years Ago, from 1776 to 1796.

Luther.—LIFE OF LUTHER. By JULIUS KÖSTLIN. With Illustrations. Crown 8vo., 7s. 6d.

Macaulay.—THE LIFE AND LETTERS OF LORD MACAULAY. By the Right Hon. Sir G. O. TREVELYAN, Bart., M.P.

Popular Edit. 1 vol. Cr. 8vo., 2s. 6d.
Student's Edition. 1 vol. Cr. 8vo., 6s.
Cabinet Edition. 2 vols. Post 8vo., 12s.
Library Edition. 2 vols. 8vo., 36s.
'Edinburgh Edition.' 2 vols. 8vo., 6s. each.

Marbot.—THE MEMOIRS OF THE BARON DE MARBOT. Translated from the French by ARTHUR JOHN BUTLER, M.A. Crown 8vo., 7s. 6d.

Nansen.—FRIDTIOF NANSEN, 1861-1893. By W. C. BRÖGGER and NORDAHL ROLFSEN. With an Introductory Poem by BJÖRNSTJERN BJÖRNSON. Translated by WILLIAM ARCHER. With numerous Illustrations, Portraits and Maps.

Romanes.—THE LIFE AND LETTERS OF GEORGE JOHN ROMANES. M.A., LL.D. Written and Edited by his Wife. With Portrait and 2 Illustrations. 8vo., 15s.

Biography, Personal Memoirs, &c.—*continued*.

Seebohm.—The Oxford Reformers —John Colet, Erasmus and Thomas More : a History of their Fellow-Work. By Frederic Seebohm. 8vo., 14s.

Shakespeare.—Outlines of the Life of Shakespeare. By J. O. Halliwell-Phillipps. With numerous Illustrations and Fac-similes. 2 vols. Royal 8vo., £1 1s.

Shakespeare's True Life. By Jas. Walter. With 500 Illustrations by Gerald E. Moira. Imp. 8vo., 21s.

Stephen.—Essays in Ecclesiastical Biography. By Sir James Stephen. Crown 8vo., 7s. 6d.

Turgot.—The Life and Writings of Turgot, Comptroller-General of France, 1774-1776. Edited for English Readers by W. Walker Stephens. 8vo., 12s. 6d.

Verney.—Memoirs of the Verney Family.

Vols. I. and II. During the Civil War. By Frances Verney. With 38 Portraits. Royal 8vo., 42s.

Vol. III. During the Commonwealth. 1650-1660. By Margaret M. Verney. With 10 Portraits, &c. 8vo., 21s.

Wellington.—Life of the Duke of Wellington. By the Rev. G. R. Gleig, M.A. Crown 8vo., 3s. 6d.

Wolf.—The Life of Joseph Wolf, Animal Painter. By A. H. Palmer, With 53 Plates and 14 Illustrations in the Text. Royal 8vo, 21s.

Travel and Adventure, the Colonies, &c.

Arnold (Sir Edwin, K.C.I.E.).

Seas and Lands. With 71 Illustrations. Cr. 8vo., 3s. 6d.

Wandering Words. With 45 Illustrations. 8vo., 18s.

East and West. With 41 Illustrations by R. T. Pritchett. 8vo., 18s.

AUSTRALIA AS IT IS, or Facts and Features, Sketches and Incidents of Australia and Australian Life, with Notices of New Zealand. By A Clergyman, thirteen years resident in the interior of New South Wales. Cr. 8vo., 5s.

Baker (Sir Samuel White).

Eight Years in Ceylon. With 6 Illustrations. Crown 8vo., 3s. 6d.

The Rifle and the Hound in Ceylon. 6 Illustrations. Cr. 8vo., 3s. 6d.

Bent (J. Theodore).

The Ruined Cities of Mashonaland ; being a Record of Excavation and Exploration in 1891. With 117 Illustrations. Crown 8vo., 3s. 6d.

The Sacred City of the Ethiopians; being a Record of Travel and Research in Abyssinia in 1893. With 8 Plates and 65 Illustrations in the Text. 8vo., 10s. 6d.

Bicknell.—Travel and Adventure in Northern Queensland. By Arthur C. Bicknell. With 24 Plates and 22 Illustrations in the text. 8vo. 15s.

Brassey.—Voyages and Travels of Lord Brassey, K.C.B., D.C.L., 1862-1894. Arranged and Edited by Captain S. Eardley-Wilmot. 2 vols. Cr. 8vo., 10s.

Brassey (The late Lady).

A Voyage in the 'Sunbeam'; Our Home on the Ocean for Eleven Months.
Library Edition. With 8 Maps and Charts, and 118 Illustrations. 8vo., 21s.
Cabinet Edition. With Map and 66 Illustrations. Crown 8vo., 7s. 6d.
Silver Library Edition. With 66 Illustrations. Crown 8vo., 3s. 6d.
Popular Edition. With 60 Illustrations. 4to., 6d. sewed, 1s. cloth,
School Edition. With 37 Illustrations. Fcp., 2s. cloth, or 3s. white parchment.

Sunshine and Storm in the East.
Library Edition. With 2 Maps and 141 Illustrations. 8vo., 21s.
Cabinet Edition. With 2 Maps and 114 Illustrations. Crown 8vo., 7s. 6d.
Popular Edition. With 103 Illustrations. 4to., 6d. sewed, 1s. cloth.

Travel and Adventure, the Colonies, &c.—*continued.*

Brassey (The late LADY)—*continued.*

IN THE TRADES, THE TROPICS, AND THE ' ROARING FORTIES'.

Cabinet Edition. With Map and 220 Illustrations. Crown 8vo., 7s. 6d.

Popular Edition. With 183 Illustrations. 4to., 6d. sewed, 1s. cloth.

THREE VOYAGES IN THE ' SUNBEAM'. Popular Edition. 346 Illustrations. 4to., 2s. 6d.

Browning.—A GIRL'S WANDERINGS IN HUNGARY. By H. ELLEN BROWNING. With Illustrations. 8vo.

Froude (JAMES A.).

OCEANA : or England and her Colonies. With 9 Illustrations. Crown 8vo., 2s. boards, 2s. 6d. cloth.

THE ENGLISH IN THE WEST INDIES : or the Bow of Ulysses. With 9 Illustrations. Cr. 8vo., 2s. bds., 2s. 6d. cl.

Howitt.—VISITS TO REMARKABLE PLACES, Old Halls, Battle-Fields, Scenes illustrative of Striking Passages in English History and Poetry. By WILLIAM HOWITT. With 80 Illustrations. Crown 8vo., 3s. 6d.

Knight (E. F.).

THE CRUISE OF THE ' ALERTE ': the Narrative of a Search for Treasure on the Desert Island of Trinidad. 2 Maps and 23 Illustrations. Cr. 8vo., 3s. 6d.

WHERE THREE EMPIRES MEET: a Narrative of Recent Travel in Kashmir, Western Tibet, Baltistan, Ladak, Gilgit, and the adjoining Countries. With a Map and 54 Illustrations. Cr. 8vo., 3s. 6d.

THE ' FALCON' ON THE BALTIC: being a Voyage from London to Copenhagen in a Three-Tonner. With 10 Full-page Illustrations. Crown 8vo., 3s. 6d.

Lees and Clutterbuck.—B. C. 1887: A RAMBLE IN BRITISH COLUMBIA. By J. A. LEES and W. J. CLUTTERBUCK. With Map and 75 Illustrations. Cr. 8vo., 3s. 6d.

Murdoch.—FROM EDINBURGH TO THE ANTARCTIC: An Artist's Notes and Sketches during the Dundee Antarctic Expedition of 1892-93. By W. G. BURN MURDOCH. With 2 Maps and numerous Illustrations. 8vo., 18s

Nansen (Dr. FRIDTJOF).

THE FIRST CROSSING OF GREENLAND. With numerous Illustrations and a Map. Crown 8vo., 3s. 6d.

ESKIMO LIFE. Translated by WILLIAM ARCHER. With 31 Illustrations. 8vo., 16s.

Peary.—MY ARCTIC JOURNAL: a Year among Ice-Fields and Eskimos. By JOSEPHINE DIEBITSCH-PEARY. With 19 Plates, 3 Sketch Maps, and 44 Illustrations in the Text. 8vo., 12s.

Quillinan. — JOURNAL OF A FEW MONTHS' RESIDENCE IN PORTUGAL, and Glimpses of the South of Spain. By Mrs. QUILLINAN (Dora Wordsworth). New Edition. Edited, with Memoir, by EDMUND LEE, Author of 'Dorothy Wordsworth,' etc. Crown 8vo., 6s.

Smith.—CLIMBING IN THE BRITISH ISLES. By W. P. HASKETT SMITH. With Illustrations by ELLIS CARR.

Part I. ENGLAND. 16mo., 3s. 6d.

Part II. WALES AND IRELAND. 16mo., 3s. 6d.

Part III. SCOTLAND. [*In preparation.*

Stephen. — THE PLAYGROUND OF EUROPE. By LESLIE STEPHEN, formerly President of the Alpine Club. New Edition, with Additions and 4 Illustrations. Crown 8vo., 6s. net.

THREE IN NORWAY. By Two of Them. With a Map and 59 Illustrations. Cr. 8vo., 2s. boards, 2s. 6d. cloth.

Tyndall.—THE GLACIERS OF THE ALPS: being a Narrative of Excursions and Ascents. An Account of the Origin and Phenomena of Glaciers, and an Exposition of the Physical Principles to which they are related. By JOHN TYNDALL, F.R.S. With numerous Illustrations. Crown 8vo., 6s. 6d. net.

Whishaw.—THE ROMANCE OF THE WOODS : Reprinted Articles and Sketches. By FRED. J. WHISHAW. Crown 8vo., 6s.

Sport and Pastime.

THE BADMINTON LIBRARY.

Edited by HIS GRACE THE DUKE OF BEAUFORT, K.G.

Assisted by ALFRED E. T. WATSON.

Crown 8vo.   Price 10s. 6d. each Volume, Cloth.

•.• *The Volumes are also issued half-bound in Leather, with gilt top.   The price can be had from all Booksellers.*

ARCHERY. By C. J. LONGMAN and Col. H. WALROND. With Contributions by Miss LEGH, Viscount DILLON, Major C. HAWKINS FISHER, Rev. EYRE W. HUSSEY, Rev. W. K. R. BEDFORD, J. BALFOUR PAUL, and L. W. MAXSON. With 2 Maps, 23 Plates, and 172 Illustrations in the Text. Crown 8vo., 10s. 6d.

ATHLETICS AND FOOTBALL. By MONTAGUE SHEARMAN. With an Introduction by Sir RICHARD WEBSTER, Q.C., M.P., and a Contribution on Paper-chasing by WALTER RYE. With 6 Plates and 52 Illustrations in the Text from Drawings by STANLEY BERKELEY, and from Instantaneous Photographs by G. MITCHELL. Crown 8vo., 10s. 6d.

BIG GAME SHOOTING. By CLIVE PHILLIPPS-WOLLEY.

Vol. I. AFRICA AND AMERICA. With Contributions by Sir SAMUEL W. BAKER, W. C. OSWELL, F. J. JACKSON, WARBURTON PIKE, and F. C. SELOUS. With 20 Plates and 57 Illustrations in the Text by CHARLES WHYMPER, J. WOLF, and H. WILLINK, and from Photographs. Crown 8vo., 10s. 6d.

Vol. II. EUROPE, ASIA, AND THE ARCTIC REGIONS. With Contributions by Lieut.-Colonel R. HEBER PERCY, Arnold PIKE, Major ALGERNON C. HEBER PERCY, W. A. BAILLIE-GROHMAN, Sir HENRY POTTINGER, Bart., Lord KILMOREY, ABEL CHAPMAN, WALTER J. BUCK, and St. GEORGE LITTLEDALE. With 17 Plates and 56 Illustrations in the Text by CHARLES WHYMPER, and from Photographs. Cr. 8vo., 10s. 6d.

BILLIARDS. By Major W. BROADFOOT, R.E. With Contributions by A. H. BOYD, SYDENHAM DIXON, W. J. FORD, DUDLEY D. PONTIFEX, RUSSELL D. WALKER, and REGINALD H. R. RIMINGTON-WILSON. With 11 Plates by LUCIEN DAVIS, R.I., 19 Illustrations in the Text from Photographs, and numerous Diagrams and Figures. Crown 8vo., 10s. 6d.

BOATING. By W. B. WOODGATE. With an Introduction by the Rev. EDMOND WARRE, D.D., and a Chapter on 'Rowing at Eton' by R. HARVEY MASON. With 10 Plates, 39 Illustrations in the Text, after Drawings by FRANK DADD, and from Instantaneous Photographs, and 4 Maps of the Rowing Courses at Oxford, Cambridge, Henley, and Putney. Crown 8vo., 10s. 6d.

COURSING AND FALCONRY.

COURSING. By HARDING COX.

FALCONRY. By the Hon. GERALD LASCELLES. With 20 Plates and 56 Illustrations in the Text by JOHN CHARLTON, R. H. MOORE, G. E. LODGE, and L. SPEED.

Crown 8vo., 10s. 6d.

CRICKET. By A. G. STEEL, and the Hon. R. H. LYTTELTON. With Contributions by ANDREW LANG, R. A. H. MITCHELL, W. G. GRACE, and F. GALE. With 12 Plates and 52 Illustrations in the Text, after Drawings by LUCIEN DAVIS, and from Photographs. Crown 8vo., 10s. 6d.

CYCLING. By the EARL OF ALBEMARLE, and G. LACY HILLIER. With 19 Plates and 44 Illustrations in the Text by the EARL OF ALBEMARLE, JOSEPH PENNELL, S. T. DADD, and GEORGE MOORE. Crown 8vo., 10s. 6d.

Sport and Pastime—*continued.*

THE BADMINTON LIBRARY—*continued.*

DANCING. By Mrs. LILLY GROVE, F.R.G.S. With Contributions by Miss MIDDLETON, The Honourable Mrs. ARMYTAGE, The COUNTESS OF ANCASTER, and Mrs. WORDSWORTH. With Musical Examples, and 38 Full-page Plates and 93 Illustrations in the Text. Crown 8vo., 10s. 6d.

DRIVING. By His Grace the DUKE OF BEAUFORT, K.G. With Contributions by other Authorities. With Photogravure Intaglio Portrait of His Grace the DUKE OF BEAUFORT, and 11 Plates and 54 Illustrations in the Text, after Drawings by G. D. GILES and J. STURGESS, and from Photographs. Crown 8vo., 10s. 6d.

FENCING, BOXING, AND WRESTLING. By WALTER H. POLLOCK, F. C. GROVE, C. PREVOST, E. B. MITCHELL, and WALTER ARMSTRONG. With 18 Intaglio Plates and 24 Illustrations in the Text. Crown 8vo., 10s. 6d.

FISHING. By H. CHOLMONDELEY-PENNELL, Late Her Majesty's Inspector of Sea Fisheries.

Vol. I. SALMON AND TROUT. With Contributions by H. R. FRANCIS, Major JOHN P. TRAHERNE, FREDERIC M. HALFORD, H. S. HALL, and THOMAS ANDREWS. With Frontispiece, 8 Full-page Illustrations of Fishing Subjects by C. H. WHYMPER and CONWAY LLOYD-JONES, and very numerous Illustrations of Tackle, &c. Crown 8vo., 10s. 6d.

Vol. II. PIKE AND OTHER COARSE FISH. With Contributions by the MARQUIS OF EXETER, WILLIAM SENIOR, G. CHRISTOPHER DAVIES, H. R. FRANCIS, and R. B. MARSTON. With Frontispiece, 6 Full-page Illustrations of Fishing Subjects by C. H. WHYMPER and CONWAY LLOYD-JONES, and very numerous Illustrations of Tackle, &c. Crown 8vo.,

GOLF. By HORACE G. HUTCHINSON. With Contributions by the Rt. Hon. A. J. BALFOUR, M.P., Sir WALTER SIMPSON, Bart., LORD WELLWOOD, H. S. C. EVERARD, ANDREW LANG, and others. With 25 Plates and 65 Illustrations in the Text by THOMAS HODGE and HARRY FURNISS, and from Photographs. Cr. 8vo., 10s. 6d.

HUNTING. By His Grace the DUKE OF BEAUFORT, K.G., and MOWBRAY MORRIS. With Contributions by the EARL OF SUFFOLK AND BERKSHIRE, Rev. E. W. L. DAVIES, DIGBY COLLINS, ALFRED E. T. WATSON, Sir MARTEINE LLOYD, GEORGE H. LONGMAN, and J. S. GIBBONS. With 5 Plates and 54 Illustrations in the Text by J. STURGESS, J. CHARLTON, G. D. GILES, and A. C. SEALY. Crown 8vo., 10s. 6d.

MOUNTAINEERING. By C. T. DENT, With Contributions by W. M. CONWAY, D. W. FRESHFIELD, C. E. MATHEWS, C. PILKINGTON, Sir F. POLLOCK, H. G. WILLINK, and an Introduction by Mr. JUSTICE WILLS. With 13 Plates and 95 Illustrations in the Text by H. G. WILLINK, &c. Crown 8vo., 10s. 6d.

RACING AND STEEPLE-CHASING.

RACING. By the EARL OF SUFFOLK AND BERKSHIRE and W. G. CRAVEN. With a Contribution by the Hon. F. LAWLEY.

STEEPLE-CHASING. By ARTHUR COVENTRY and ALFRED E. T. WATSON With Coloured Frontispiece and 56 Illustrations in the Text by J. STURGESS. Crown 8vo., 10s. 6d.

RIDING AND POLO.

RIDING. By Captain ROBERT WEIR, Riding Master, R.H.G. With Contributions by the DUKE OF BEAUFORT, the EARL OF SUFFOLK AND BERKSHIRE, the EARL OF ONSLOW, E. L. ANDERSON, and ALFRED E. T. WATSON.

POLO. By J. MORAY BROWN. With 18 Plates and 41 Illustrations in the Text by G. D. GILES, FRANK DADD, and F. STUART ALLAN.

Sport and Pastime —*continued.*

THE BADMINTON LIBRARY—*continued.*

SEA FISHING. By JOHN BICKERDYKE. With Contributions on Whaling, by Sir H. W. GORE-BOOTH ; Tarpon, by ALFRED C. HARMSWORTH ; Antipodean and Foreign Fish, by W. SENIOR. With 22 Full-page Plates and 175 Illustrations in the Text, by C. NAPIER HEMY, R. T. PRITCHETT, W. W. MAY, and others. Crown 8vo., 10s. 6d.

SHOOTING.

Vol. I. FIELD AND COVERT. By LORD WALSINGHAM and Sir RALPH PAYNE-GALLWEY, Bart. With Contributions by the Hon. GERALD LASCELLES and A. J. STUART-WORTLEY. With 11 Full-page Illustrations and 94 Illustrations in the Text by A. J. STUART-WORTLEY, HARPER PENNINGTON, C. WHYMPER, G. E. LODGE, J. H. Oswald BROWN, Sir R. FRANKLAND, and from Photographs. Crown 8vo., 10s. 6d.

Vol. II. MOOR AND MARSH. By LORD WALSINGHAM and Sir RALPH PAYNE-GALLWEY, Bart. With Contributions by LORD LOVAT and LORD CHARLES LENNOX KERR. With 8 Full-page Illustrations and 57 Illustrations in the Text by A. J. STUART-WORTLEY, HARPER PENNINGTON, C. WHYMPER, J. G. MILLAIS, C. E. LODGE, and from Photographs. Crown 8vo., 10s. 6d,

SKATING. By J. M. HEATHCOTE and C. G. TEBBUTT. Figure-Skating. By T. MAXWELL WITHAM. With Contributions on Curling (Rev. JOHN KERR), Tobogganing (ORMOND HAKE), Ice-Sailing (HENRY A. BUCK), Bandy (C. G. TEBBUTT). With 12 Plates and 272 Illustrations and Diagrams in the Text, by C. WHYMPER and Capt. R. M. ALEXANDER. Crown 8vo., 10s. 6d.

SWIMMING. By ARCHIBALD SINCLAIR and WILLIAM HENRY, Hon. Secs. of the Life-Saving Society. With 13 Plates and 136 Illustrations in the Text by S. T. DADD and from Photographs by G. MITCHELL. Crown 8vo., 10s. 6d.

TENNIS, LAWN TENNIS, RACQUETS, AND FIVES. By J. M. and C. G. HEATHCOTE, E. O. PLEYDELL-BOUVERIE, and A. C. AINGER. With Contributions by the Hon. A. LYTTELTON W. C. MARSHALL, L. DOD, H. W. W. WILBERFORCE, H. F. LAWFORD, SPENCER W. GORE, R. D. SEARS, and HERBERT CHIPP. With 12 Plates and 67 Illustrations in the Text by LUCIEN DAVIS, C. M. NEWTON, and from Photographs. Crown 8vo., 10s. 6d.

YACHTING.

Vol. I. INTRODUCTION, CRUISING, CONSTRUCTION OF YACHTS, YACHT RACING RULES, FITTING-OUT, &c. By Sir EDWARD SULLIVAN, Bart., LORD BRASSEY, K.C.B., C. E. SETH-SMITH, C.B., G. L. WATSON, R. T. PRITCHETT, Sir GEORGE LEACH, K.C.B., Vice-President V.R.A., 'THALASSA,' THE EARL OF PEMBROKE AND MONTGOMERY, E. F. KNIGHT, and Rev. G. L. BLAKE. With 21 Plates and 93 Illustrations in the Text by R. T. PRITCHETT, G. L. WATSON, J. M. SOPER, &c., and from Photographs. Crown 8vo., 10s. 6d.

Vol. II. YACHT CLUBS, YACHTING IN AMERICA AND THE COLONIES, YACHT RACING, &c. By R. T. PRITCHETT, the MARQUIS OF DUFFERIN AND AVA, K.P., JAMES McFERRAN, Rev. G. L. BLAKE, T. B. MIDDLETON, EDWARD WALTER CASTLE and ROBERT CASTLE, G. CHRISTOPHER DAVIES, LEWIS HERRESHOFF, THE EARL OF ONSLOW, G.C.M.G., H. HORN, and Sir GEORGE LEACH, K.C.B., Vice-President V.R.A. With 35 Plates and 160 Illustrations in the Text by R. T. PRITCHETT, G. L. WATSON, J. M. SOPER, &c., and from Photographs. Crown 8vo., 10s. 6d.

Sport and Pastime—*continued.*

FUR AND FEATHER SERIES.

Edited by A. E. T. WATSON.

Crown 8vo., 5*s*. each Volume

* *The Volumes are also issued half-bound in Leather, with gilt top. The price can be had from all Booksellers.*

THE PARTRIDGE. Natural History, by the Rev. H. A. MACPHERSON; Shooting, by A. J. STUART-WORTLEY; Cookery, by GEORGE SAINTSBURY. With 11 Illustrations and various Diagrams. Crown 8vo., 5*s*.

THE GROUSE. Natural History by the Rev. H. A. MACPHERSON; Shooting, by A. J. STUART-WORTLEY; Cookery, by GEORGE SAINTSBURY. With 13 Illustrations and various Diagrams. Crown 8vo., 5*s*.

THE PHEASANT. Natural History by the Rev. H. A. MACPHERSON; Shooting, by A. J. STUART-WORTLEY; Cookery, by ALEXANDER INNES SHAND. With 10 Illustrations and various Diagrams. Crown 8vo., 5*s*.

THE HARE. Natural History by the Rev. H. A. MACPHERSON; Shooting, by the Hon. GERALD LASCELLES; Coursing, by CHARLES RICHARDSON; Hunting, by J. S. GIBBONS and G. H. LONGMAN; Cookery, by Col. KENNEY HERBERT. With 9 Illustrations. Cr. 8vo., 5*s*.

WILDFOWL. By the HON. JOHN SCOTT MONTAGU, M.P., &c. [*In preparation.*

THE RED DEER. By CAMERON OF LOCHIEL, LORD EBRINGTON, &c.
       • [*In preparation.*

BADMINTON MAGAZINE (THE) OF SPORTS AND PASTIMES, THE. Edited by ALFRED E. E. WATSON ('Rapier'). With numerous Illustrations, 1*s*. Monthly.

Vol. I., August to December, 1895. 6*s*.

Vol. II., January to June, 1896. 6*s*.

Bickerdyke.—DAYS OF MY LIFE ON WATERS FRESH AND SALT; and other Papers. By JOHN BICKERDYKE. With Photo-Etched Frontispiece and 8 Full-page Illustrations. Crown 8vo., 6*s*.

DEAD SHOT (THE): or, Sportsman's Complete Guide. Being a Treatise on the Use of the Gun, with Rudimentary and Finishing Lessons on the Art of Shooting Game of all kinds. By MARKSMAN. With 13 Illustrations. Crown 8vo., 10*s*. 6*d*.

Ellis.—CHESS SPARKS; or, Short and Bright Games of Chess. Collected and Arranged by J. H. ELLIS, M.A. 8vo., 4*s*. 6*d*.

Falkener.—GAMES, ANCIENT AND ORIENTAL, AND HOW TO PLAY THEM. By EDWARD FALKENER. With numerous Photographs & Diagrms. 8vo., 21*s*.

Ford.—THE THEORY AND PRACTICE OF ARCHERY. By HORACE FORD. New Edition, thoroughly Revised and Rewritten by W. BUTT, M.A. With a Preface by C. J. LONGMAN, M.A. 8vo., 14*s*.

Francis.—A BOOK ON ANGLING: or Treatise on the Art of Fishing in every Branch; including full Illustrated List of Salmon Flies. By FRANCIS FRANCIS. With Portrait and Plates. Cr. 8vo., 15*s*.

Gibson.—TOBOGGANING ON CROOKED RUNS. By the Hon. HARRY GIBSON. With Contributions by F. DE B. STRICKLAND and 'LADY-TOBOGGANER'. With 40 Illustrations. Crown 8vo., 6*s*.

Graham.—COUNTRY PASTIMES FOR BOYS. By P. ANDERSON GRAHAM. With numerous Illustrations from Drawings and Photographs. Crown 8vo., 6*s*.

Sport and Pastime—*continued.*

Lang.—ANGLING SKETCHES.   By A. LANG. With 20 Illus. Cr. 8vo., 3s. 6d.

Longman.—CHESS OPENINGS. By FRED. W. LONGMAN. Fcp. 8vo., 2s. 6d.

Maskelyne.—SHARPS AND FLATS : a Complete Revelation of the Secrets of Cheating at Games of Chance and Skill. By JOHN NEVIL MASKELYNE. With 62 Illustrations. Crown 8vo., 6s.

Park.—THE GAME OF GOLF.   By WILLIAM PARK, Junr., Champion Golfer, 1887-89.   With 17 Plates and 26 Illustrations in the Text.   Crown 8vo., 7s. 6d

Payne-Gallwey (Sir RALPH, Bart.).

LETTERS TO YOUNG SHOOTERS (First Series). On the Choice and Use of a Gun. With 41 Illustrations. Cr. 8vo., 7s. 6d.

LETTERS TO YOUNG SHOOTERS. (Second Series). On the Production, Preservation, and Killing of Game, With Directions in Shooting Wood-Pigeons and Breaking-in Retrievers. With 104 Illustrations. Crown 8vo., 12s. 6d.

Pole (WILLIAM).

THE THEORY OF THE MODERN SCIENTIFIC GAME OF WHIST. Fcp. 8vo., 2s. 6d.

THE EVOLUTION OF WHIST. Cr. 8vo., 6s.

Proctor.—HOW TO PLAY WHIST: WITH THE LAWS AND ETIQUETTE OF WHIST. By RICHARD A. PROCTOR. Crown 8vo., 3s. 6d.

Ronalds.—THE FLY-FISHER'S ENTOMOLOGY. By ALFRED RONALDS With 20 Coloured Plates. 8vo., 14s.

Wilcocks. THE SEA FISHERMAN : Comprising the Chief Methods of Hook and Line Fishing in the British and other Seas, and Remarks on Nets, Boats, and Boating. By J. C. WILCOCKS. Illustrated. Crown 8vo., 6s.

Veterinary Medicine, &c.

Steel (JOHN HENRY).

A TREATISE ON THE DISEASES OF THE DOG. 88 Illustrations. 8vo., 10s. 6d.

A TREATISE ON THE DISEASES OF THE OX. With 119 Illustrations. 8vo., 15s.

A TREATISE ON THE DISEASES OF THE SHEEP. With 100 Illustrations. 8vo., 12s.

OUTLINES OF EQUINE ANATOMY : a Manual for the use of Veterinary Students in the Dissecting Room. Crown 8vo., 7s. 6d.

Fitzwygram.—HORSES AND STABLES. By Major-General Sir F. FITZWYGRAM, Bart. With 56 pages of Illustrations. 8vo., 2s. 6d. net.

"Stonehenge."—THE DOG IN HEALTH AND DISEASE.   By "STONEHENGE". With 78 Illustrations 8vo., 7s. 6d.

Youatt (WILLIAM).

THE HORSE. With 52 Illustrations. 8vo., 7s. 6d.

THE DOG.   With 53 Illustrations. 8vo., 6s.

Mental, Moral, and Political Philosophy.
LOGIC, RHETORIC, PSYCHOLOGY, ETC.

Abbott.—THE ELEMENTS OF LOGIC. By T. K. ABBOTT, B.D. 12mo., 3s.

Aristotle.

THE POLITICS: G. Bekker's Greek Text of Books I., III., IV. (VII.), with an English Translation by W. E. BOLLAND, M.A. ; and short Introductory Essays by A. LANG, M.A. Crown 8vo., 7s. 6d.

Aristotle.—*continued.*

THE POLITICS: Introductory Essays. By ANDREW LANG (from Bolland and Lang's 'Politics'). Cr. 8vo., 2s. 6d.

THE ETHICS: Greek Text, Illustrated with Essay and Notes. By Sir ALEXANDER GRANT, Bart. 2 vols. 8vo., 32s.

Mental, Moral and Political Philosophy—*continued.*

Aristotle.—*continued.*

AN INTRODUCTION TO ARISTOTLE'S ETHICS. Books I.-IV. (Book X. c. vi.-ix. in an Appendix.) With a continuous Analysis and Notes. By the Rev. E. MOORE, D.D. Cr. 8vo., 10s. 6d.

Bacon (FRANCIS).

COMPLETE WORKS. Edited by R. L. ELLIS, J. SPEDDING, and D. D. HEATH. 7 vols. 8vo., £3 13s. 6d.

LETTERS AND LIFE, including all his occasional Works. Edited by JAMES SPEDDING. 7 vols. 8vo., £4 4s.

THE ESSAYS: with Annotations. By RICHARD WHATELY, D.D. 8vo., 10s. 6d.

THE ESSAYS: Edited, with Notes. By F. STORR and C. H. GIBSON. Cr. 8vo., 3s. 6d.

THE ESSAYS. With Introduction, Notes, and Index. By E. A. ABBOTT. D.D. 2 vols. Fcp. 8vo., 6s. The Text and Index only, without Introduction and Notes, in One Volume. Fcp. 8vo., 2s. 6d.

Bain (ALEXANDER).

MENTAL SCIENCE. Crown 8vo., 6s. 6d.

MORAL SCIENCE. Crown 8vo., 4s. 6d.

The two works as above can be had in one volume, price 10s. 6d.

SENSES AND THE INTELLECT. 8vo., 15s.

EMOTIONS AND THE WILL. 8vo., 15s.

LOGIC, DEDUCTIVE AND INDUCTIVE. Part I., 4s. Part II., 6s. 6d.

PRACTICAL ESSAYS. Crown 8vo., 2s.

Bray (CHARLES).

THE PHILOSOPHY OF NECESSITY: or Law in Mind as in Matter. Cr. 8vo., 5s.

THE EDUCATION OF THE FEELINGS: a Moral System for Schools. Crown 8vo., 2s. 6d.

Bray.—ELEMENTS OF MORALITY, in Easy Lessons for Home and School Teaching. By Mrs. CHARLES BRAY. Cr. 8vo., 1s. 6d.

Davidson.—THE LOGIC OF DEFINITION, Explained and Applied. By WILLIAM L. DAVIDSON, M.A. Crown 8vo., 6s.

Green (THOMAS HILL). The Works of. Edited by R. L. NETTLESHIP.

Vols. I. and II. Philosophical Works. 8vo., 16s. each.

Vol. III. Miscellanies. With Index to the three Volumes, and Memoir. 8vo., 21s.

LECTURES ON THE PRINCIPLES OF POLITICAL OBLIGATION. With Preface by BERNARD BOSANQUET. 8vo., 5s.

Hodgson (SHADWORTH H.).

TIME AND SPACE: a Metaphysical Essay. 8vo., 16s.

THE THEORY OF PRACTICE: an Ethical Inquiry. 2 vols. 8vo., 24s.

THE PHILOSOPHY OF REFLECTION. 2 vols. 8vo., 21s.

Hume.—THE PHILOSOPHICAL WORKS OF DAVID HUME. Edited by T. H. GREEN and T. H. GROSE. 4 vols. 8vo., 56s. Or separately, Essays. 2 vols. 28s. Treatise of Human Nature. 2 vols. 28s.

Justinian.—THE INSTITUTES OF JUSTINIAN: Latin Text, chiefly that of Huschke, with English Introduction, Translation, Notes, and Summary. By THOMAS C. SANDARS, M.A. 8vo., 18s.

Kant (IMMANUEL).

CRITIQUE OF PRACTICAL REASON, AND OTHER WORKS ON THE THEORY OF ETHICS. Translated by T. K. ABBOTT, B.D. With Memoir. 8vo., 12s. 6d.

FUNDAMENTAL PRINCIPLES OF THE METAPHYSIC OF ETHICS. Translated by T. K. ABBOTT, B.D. (Extracted from 'Kant's Critique of Practical Reason and other Works on the Theory of Ethics.' Cr. 8vo., 3s.

INTRODUCTION TO LOGIC, AND HIS ESSAY ON THE MISTAKEN SUBTILTY OF THE FOUR FIGURES. Translated by T. K. ABBOTT, and with Notes by S. T. COLERIDGE. 8vo., 6s.

Mental, Moral and Political Philosophy—*continued.*

Killick.—HANDBOOK TO MILL'S SYSTEM OF LOGIC. By Rev. A. H. KILLICK, M.A. Crown 8vo., 3s. 6d.

Ladd (GEORGE TRUMBULL).

PHILOSOPHY OF MIND: an Essay on the Metaphysics of Physiology. 8vo., 16s.

ELEMENTS OF PHYSIOLOGICAL PSYCHOLOGY. 8vo., 21s.

OUTLINES OF PHYSIOLOGICAL PSYCHOLOGY. A Text-Book of Mental Science for Academies and Colleges. 8vo., 12s.

PSYCHOLOGY, DESCRIPTIVE AND EXPLANATORY : a Treatise of the Phenomena, Laws, and Development of Human Mental Life. 8vo., 21s.

PRIMER OF PSYCHOLOGY. Crown 8vo., 5s. 6d.

Lewes.—THE HISTORY OF PHILOSOPHY, from Thales to Comte. By GEORGE HENRY LEWES. 2 vols. 8vo., 32s.

Max Müller (F.).

THE SCIENCE OF THOUGHT. 8vo., 21s.

THREE INTRODUCTORY LECTURES ON THE SCIENCE OF THOUGHT. 8vo., 2s. 6d.

Mill.—ANALYSIS OF THE PHENOMENA OF THE HUMAN MIND. By JAMES MILL. 2 vols. 8vo., 28s.

Mill (JOHN STUART).

A SYSTEM OF LOGIC. Cr. 8vo., 3s. 6d.

ON LIBERTY. Cr. 8vo., 1s. 4d.

ON REPRESENTATIVE GOVERNMENT. Crown 8vo., 2s.

UTILITARIANISM. 8vo., 2s. 6d.

EXAMINATION OF SIR WILLIAM HAMILTON'S PHILOSOPHY. 8vo., 16s.

NATURE, THE UTILITY OF RELIGION, AND THEISM. Three Essays. 8vo., 5s.

Mosso.—FEAR. By ANGELO MOSSO. Translated from the Italian by E. LOUGH and F. KIESOW. With 8 Illustrations. Crown 8vo., 7s. 6d.

Romanes.—MIND AND MOTION AND MONISM. By GEORGE JOHN ROMANES, M.A., LL.D., F.R.S. Crown 8vo., 4s. 6d.

Stock.—DEDUCTIVE LOGIC. By ST. GEORGE STOCK. Fcp. 8vo., 3s. 6d.

Sully (JAMES).

THE HUMAN MIND : a Text-book of Psychology. 2 vols. 8vo., 21s.

OUTLINES OF PSYCHOLOGY. 8vo., 9s.

THE TEACHER'S HANDBOOK OF PSYCHOLOGY. Crown 8vo., 5s.

STUDIES OF CHILDHOOD. 8vo. 10s. 6d.

Swinburne.—PICTURE LOGIC : an Attempt to Popularise the Science of Reasoning. By ALFRED JAMES SWINBURNE, M.A. With 23 Woodcuts. Post 8vo., 5s.

Weber.—HISTORY OF PHILOSOPHY. By ALFRED WEBER, Professor in the University of Strasburg, Translated by FRANK THILLY, Ph.D. 8vo., 16s.

Whately (ARCHBISHOP).

BACON'S ESSAYS. With Annotation. By R. WHATELY. 8vo., 10s. 6d.

ELEMENTS OF LOGIC. Cr. 8vo., 4s. 6d.

ELEMENTS OF RHETORIC. Cr. 8vo., 4s. 6d.

LESSONS ON REASONING. Fcp. 8vo., 1s. 6d.

Mental, Moral and Political Philosophy—*continued.*

Zeller (Dr. EDWARD, Professor in the University of Berlin).

THE STOICS, EPICUREANS AND SCEP-TICS. Translated by the Rev. O. J. REICHEL, M.A. Crown 8vo., 15s.

OUTLINES OF THE HISTORY OF GREEK PHILOSOPHY. Translated by SARAH F. ALLEYNE and EVELYN ABBOTT. Crown 8vo., 10s. 6d.

Zeller (Dr. EDWARD)—*continued.*

PLATO AND THE OLDER ACADEMY. Translated by SARAH F. ALLEYNE and ALFRED GOODWIN, B.A. Crown 8vo., 18s.

SOCRATES AND THE SOCRATIC SCHOOLS. Translated by the Rev. O. J. REICHEL, M.A. Crown 8vo., 10s. 6d.

MANUALS OF CATHOLIC PHILOSOPHY.

(Stonyhurst Series.)

A MANUAL OF POLITICAL ECONOMY. By C. S. DEVAS, M.A. Cr. 8vo., 6s. 6d.

FIRST PRINCIPLES OF KNOWLEDGE. By JOHN RICKABY, S.J. Crown 8vo., 5s.

GENERAL METAPHYSICS. By JOHN RICKABY, S.J. Crown 8vo., 5s.

LOGIC. By RICHARD F. CLARKE, S.J. Crown 8vo., 5s.

MORAL PHILOSOPHY (ETHICS AND NATURAL LAW). By JOSEPH RICKABY, S.J. Crown 8vo., 5s.

NATURAL THEOLOGY. By BERNARD BOEDDER, S.J. Crown 8vo., 6s. 6d.

PSYCHOLOGY. By MICHAEL MAHER, S.J. Crown 8vo., 6s. 6d.

History and Science of Language, &c.

Davidson.—LEADING AND IMPORTANT ENGLISH WORDS: Explained and Exemplified. By WILLIAM L. DAVIDSON, M.A. Fcp. 8vo., 3s. 6d.

Farrar.—LANGUAGE AND LANGUAGES. By F. W. FARRAR, D.D., F.R.S., Cr. 8vo., 6s.

Graham.—ENGLISH SYNONYMS, Classified and Explained: with Practical Exercises. By G. F. GRAHAM. Fcap. 8vo., 6s.

Max Müller (F.).

THE SCIENCE OF LANGUAGE, Founded on Lectures delivered at the Royal Institution in 1861 and 1863. 2 vols. Crown 8vo., 21s.

BIOGRAPHIES OF WORDS, AND THE HOME OF THE ARYAS. Crown 8vo., 7s. 6d.

Max Müller (F.)—*continued.*

THREE LECTURES ON THE SCIENCE OF LANGUAGE, AND ITS PLACE IN GENERAL EDUCATION, delivered at Oxford, 1889. Crown 8vo., 3s.

Roget. — THESAURUS OF ENGLISH WORDS AND PHRASES. Classified and Arranged so as to Facilitate the Expression of Ideas and assist in Literary Composition. By PETER MARK ROGET, M.D., F.R.S. Recomposed throughout, enlarged and improved, partly from the Author's Notes, and with a full Index, by the Author's Son, JOHN LEWIS ROGET. Crown 8vo., 10s. 6d.

Whately.—ENGLISH SYNONYMS. By E. JANE WHATELY. Fcap. 8vo., 3s.

Political Economy and Economics.

Ashley.—ENGLISH ECONOMIC HISTORY AND THEORY. By W. J. ASHLEY, M.A. Crown 8vo., Part I., 5s. Part II., 10s. 6d.

Bagehot.—ECONOMIC STUDIES. By WALTER BAGEHOT. Cr. 8vo., 3s. 6d.

Barnett.—PRACTICABLE SOCIALISM : Essays on Social Reform. By the Rev. S. A. and Mrs. BARNETT. Cr. 8vo., 6s.

Brassey.—PAPERS AND ADDRESSES ON WORK AND WAGES. By Lord BRASSEY. Crown 8vo., 5s.

Devas.—A MANUAL OF POLITICAL ECONOMY. By C. S. DEVAS, M.A. Crown 8vo., 6s. 6d. (*Manuals of Catholic Philosophy.*)

Dowell.—A HISTORY OF TAXATION AND TAXES IN ENGLAND, from the Earliest Times to the Year 1885. By STEPHEN DOWELL (4 vols. 8vo.) Vols. I. and II. The History of Taxation 21s. Vols. III. and IV. The History of Taxes, 21s.

Macleod (HENRY DUNNING, M.A.). BIMETALISM. 8vo., 5s. net. ELEMENTS OF BANKING. Cr. 8vo., 3s. 6d. THE THEORY AND PRACTICE OF BANKING. Vol. I. 8vo., 12s. Vol. II. 14s.

Macleod (HENRY DUNNING)—*cont.* THE THEORY OF CREDIT. 8vo. Vol. I. 10s. net. Vol. II., Part I., 10s. net. Vol II. Part II., 10s. 6d.

A DIGEST OF THE LAW OF BILLS OF EXCHANGE, BANK NOTES, &c. [*In the press.*]

Mill.—POLITICAL ECONOMY. By JOHN STUART MILL. *Popular Edition.* Crown 8vo., 3s 6d. *Library Edition.* 2 vols. 8vo., 30s.

Symes.—POLITICAL ECONOMY : a Short Text-book of Political Economy. With Problems for Solution, and Hints for Supplementary Reading ; also a Supplementary Chapter on Socialism. By E. J. SYMES, M.A. Crown 8vo., 2s. 6d.

Toynbee.—LECTURES ON THE IN-DUSTRIAL REVOLUTION OF THE 18th CENTURY IN ENGLAND. By ARNOLD TOYNBEE. With a Memoir of the Author by BENJAMIN JOWETT, D.D. 8vo., 10s. 6d.

Webb.—THE HISTORY OF TRADE UNIONISM. By SIDNEY and BEATRICE WEBB. With Map and full Bibliography of the Subject. 8vo., 18s.

STUDIES IN ECONOMICS AND POLITICAL SCIENCE.

Issued under the auspices of the London School of Economics and Political Science.

THE HISTORY OF LOCAL RATES IN ENG-LAND : Five Lectures. By EDWIN CANNAN, M.A., Balliol College, Oxford. Crown 8vo., 2s. 6d.

SELECT DOCUMENTS ILLUSTRATING THE HISTORY OF TRADE UNIONISM. 1. The Tailoring Trade. Edited by F. W. GALTON. With a Preface by SIDNEY WEBB, LL.B. Crown 8vo., 5s.

DEPLOIGE'S REFERENDUM EN SUISSE. Translated with Introduction and Notes, by P. C. TREVELYAN, M.A. [*In preparation.*]

SELECT DOCUMENTS ILLUSTRATING THE STATE REGULATION OF WAGES. Edited, with Introduction and Notes, by W. A. S. HEWINS, M.A., Pembroke College, Oxford ; Director of the London School of Economics and Political Science. [*In preparation.*]

HUNGARIAN GILD RECORDS. Edited by Dr. JULIUS MANDELLO, of Budapest. [*In preparation.*]

THE RELATIONS BETWEEN ENGLAND AND THE HANSEATIC LEAGUE. By Miss E. A. MACARTHUR, Vice-Mistress of Girton College, Cambridge. [*In preparation.*]

Evolution, Anthropology, &c.

Babington.—FALLACIES OF RACE THEORIES AS APPLIED TO NATIONAL CHARACTERISTICS. Essays by WILLIAM DALTON BABINGTON, M.A. Crown 8vo., 6s.

Clodd (EDWARD).

THE STORY OF CREATION : a Plain Account of Evolution. With 77 Illustrations. Crown 8vo., 3s. 6d.

Evolution, Anthropology, &c.—*continued.*

Clodd (EDWARD)—*continued.*

A PRIMER OF EVOLUTION: being a Popular Abridged Edition of 'The Story of Creation'. With Illustrations. Fcp. 8vo., 1s. 6d.

Lang.—CUSTOM AND MYTH: Studies of Early Usage and Belief. By ANDREW LANG, M.A. With 15 Illustrations. Crown 8vo., 3s. 6d.

Lubbock.—THE ORIGIN OF CIVILISATION and the Primitive Condition of Man. By Sir J. LUBBOCK, Bart., M.P. With 5 Plates and 20 Illustrations in the Text. 8vo. 18s.

Romanes (GEORGE JOHN).

DARWIN, AND AFTER DARWIN: an Exposition of the Darwinian Theory, and a Discussion on Post-Darwinian Questions.

Part I. THE DARWINIAN THEORY. With Portrait of Darwin and 125 Illustrations. Crown 8vo., 10s. 6d.

Part II. POST-DARWINIAN QUESTIONS: Heredity and Utility. With Portrait of the Author and 5 Illustrations. Cr. 8vo., 10s. 6d.

AN EXAMINATION OF WEISMANNISM. Crown 8vo., 6s.

Classical Literature and Translations, &c.

Abbott.—HELLENICA. A Collection of Essays on Greek Poetry, Philosophy, History, and Religion. Edited by EVELYN ABBOTT, M.A., LL.D. 8vo., 16s.

Æschylus.—EUMENIDES OF ÆSCHYLUS. With Metrical English Translation. By J. F. DAVIES. 8vo., 7s.

Aristophanes.—The ACHARNIANS OF ARISTOPHANES, translated into English Verse. By R. Y. TYRRELL. Cr. 8vo., 1s.

Becker (Professor).

GALLUS: or, Roman Scenes in the Time of Augustus. Illustrated. Cr. 8vo., 3s. 6d.

CHARICLES; or, Illustrations of the Private Life of the Ancient Greeks. Illustrated. Cr 8vo., 3s. 6d.

Cicero.—CICERO'S CORRESPONDENCE. By R. Y. TYRRELL. Vols. I., II., III. 8vo., each 12s. Vol. IV., 15s.

Farnell.—GREEK LYRIC POETRY: a Complete Collection of the Surviving Passages from the Greek Song-Writing. By GEORGE S. FARNELL, M.A. With 5 Plates. 8vo., 16s.

Lang.—HOMER AND THE EPIC. By ANDREW LANG. Crown 8vo., 9s. net.

Lucan.—THE PHARSALIA OF LUCAN. Translated into Blank Verse, with some Notes. By EDWARD RIDLEY, Q.C., sometime Fellow of All Souls College, Oxford.

Mackail.—SELECT EPIGRAMS FROM THE GREEK ANTHOLOGY. By J. W. MACKAIL. 8vo., 16s.

Rich.—A DICTIONARY OF ROMAN AND GREEK ANTIQUITIES. By A. RICH, B.A. With 2000 Woodcuts. Crown 8vo., 7s. 6d.

Sophocles.—Translated into English Verse. By ROBERT WHITELAW, M.A., Assistant Master in Rugby School: late Fellow of Trinity College, Cambridge. Crown 8vo., 8s. 6d.

Tacitus.—THE HISTORY OF P. CORNELIUS TACITUS. Translated into English, with an Introduction and Notes, Critical and Explanatory, by ALBERT WILLIAM QUILL, M.A. T.C.D., sometime Scholar of Trinity College, Dublin. 2 Vols. Vol. I 8vo., 7s. 6d., Vol. II., 12s. 6d.

Tyrrell.—TRANSLATIONS INTO GREEK AND LATIN VERSE. Edited by R. Y. TYRRELL. 8vo., 6s.

Virgil.—THE ÆNEID OF VIRGIL. Translated into English Verse by JOHN CONINGTON. Crown 8vo., 6s.

THE POEMS OF VIRGIL. Translated into English Prose by JOHN CONINGTON. Crown 8vo., 6s.

THE ÆNEID OF VIRGIL, freely translated into English Blank Verse. By W. J. THORNHILL. Crown 8vo., 7s. 6d.

THE ÆNEID OF VIRGIL. Books I. to VI. Translated into English Verse by JAMES RHOADES. Crown 8vo., 5s.

Wilkins.—THE GROWTH OF THE HOMERIC POEMS. By G. WILKINS. 8vo., 6s.

Poetry and the Drama.

Acworth.—BALLADS OF THE MARATHAS. Rendered into English Verse from the Marathi Originals. By HARRY ARBUTHNOT ACWORTH. 8vo., 5s.

Allingham (WILLIAM).

BLACKBERRIES. Imperial 16mo., 6s.

IRISH SONGS AND POEMS. With Frontispiece of the Waterfall of Asaroe. Fcp. 8vo , 6s

LAURENCE BLOOMFIELD. With Portrait of the Author. Fcp. 8vo., 3s. 6d.

FLOWER PIECES; DAY AND NIGHT SONGS; BALLADS. With 2 Designs by D. G. ROSSETTI. Fcp. 8vo., 6s. ; large paper edition, 12s.

LIFE AND PHANTASY: with Frontispiece by Sir J. E. MILLAIS, Bart., and Design by ARTHUR HUGHES. Fcp. 8vo., 6s. ; large paper edition, 12s.

THOUGHT AND WORD, AND ASHBY MANOR: a Play. Fcp. 8vo., 6s. ; large paper edition, 12s.

Sets of the above 6 vols. may be had in uniform half-parchment binding, price 30s.

Armstrong (G. F. SAVAGE).

POEMS: Lyrical and Dramatic. Fcp. 8vo., 6s.

KING SAUL. (The Tragedy of Israel, Part I.) Fcp. 8vo. 5s.

KING DAVID. (The Tragedy of Israel, Part II.) Fcp. 8vo. 6s.

KING SOLOMON. (The Tragedy of Israel, Part III.) Fcp. 8vo., 6s.

UGONE: a Tragedy. Fcp. 8vo., 6s.

A GARLAND FROM GREECE: Poems. Fcp. 8vo., 7s. 6d.

STORIES OF WICKLOW: Poems. Fcp. 8vo., 7s. 6d.

MEPHISTOPHELES IN BROADCLOTH: a Satire. Fcp. 8vo., 4s.

ONE IN THE INFINITE: a Poem. Cr. 8vo., 7s. 6d.

Armstrong.—THE POETICAL WORKS OF EDMUND J. ARMSTRONG. Fcp. 8vo., 5s.

Arnold (Sir EDWIN).

THE LIGHT OF THE WORLD: or, the Great Consummation. Cr. 8vo., 7s. 6d. net.

THE TENTH MUSE, AND OTHER POEMS. Crown 8vo., 5s. net.

POTIPHAR'S WIFE, and other Poems. Crown 8vo., 5s. net.

ADZUMA: or, the Japanese Wife. A Play. Crown 8vo., 6s. 6d. net.

Beesly.—BALLADS, AND OTHER VERSE. By A. H. BEESLY. Fcp. 8vo., 5s.

Bell (Mrs. HUGH).

CHAMBER COMEDIES: a Collection of Plays and Monologues for the Drawing Room. Crown 8vo., 6s.

FAIRY TALE PLAYS, AND HOW TO ACT THEM. With numerous Illustrations by LANCELOT SPEED. Crown 8vo.

Carmichael.—POEMS. By JENNINGS CARMICHAEL (Mrs. FRANCIS MULLIS). Crown 8vo., 6s. net.

Christie.—LAYS AND VERSES. By NIMMO CHRISTIE. Crown 8vo., 3s. 6d.

Cochrane (ALFRED).

THE KESTREL'S NEST, and other Verses. Fcp. 8vo., 3s. 6d.

LEVIORE PLECTRO: Occasional Verses. Fcp. 8vo., 3s. 6d.

Florian.—THE FABLES OF FLORIAN. Done into English Verse by Sir PHILIP PERRING, Bart. Crown 8vo., 3s. 6d.

Goethe.

FAUST, Part I., the German Text, with Introduction and Notes. By ALBERT M. SELSS, Ph.D., M.A. Cr. 8vo., 5s.

FAUST. Translated, with Notes. By T. E. WEBB. 8vo., 12s. 6d.

Gurney.—DAY DREAMS: Poems. By Rev. ALFRED GURNEY, M.A. Crown 8vo., 3s. 6d.

Poetry and the Drama—*continued*.

Ingelow (JEAN).

POETICAL WORKS. 2 vols. Fcp. 8vo., 12*s.*

LYRICAL AND OTHER POEMS. Selected from the Writings of JEAN INGELOW. Fcp. 8vo., 2*s.* 6*d.*; cloth plain, 3*s.* cloth gilt.

Lang (ANDREW).

BAN AND ARRIÈRE BAN. A Rally of Fugitive Rhymes Fcp. 8vo., 5*s.* net.

GRASS OF PARNASSUS. Fcp. 8vo., 2*s.* 6*d.* net.

BALLADS OF BOOKS. Edited by ANDREW LANG. Fcp. 8vo., 6*s.*

THE BLUE POETRY BOOK. Edited by ANDREW LANG. With 12 Plates and 88 Illustrations in the Text by H. J. FORD and LANCELOT SPEED. Crown 8vo., 6*s.*

Lecky.—POEMS. By W. E. H. LECKY. Fcp. 8vo., 5*s.*

Lindsay.—THE FLOWER SELLER, and other Poems. By LADY LINDSAY. Crown 8vo., 5s.

Lytton (THE EARL OF) (OWEN MEREDITH).

MARAH. Fcp. 8vo., 6*s.* 6*d.*

KING POPPY: a Fantasia. With 1 Plate and Design on Title-Page by Sir ED. BURNE-JONES, A.R.A. Crown 8vo., 10*s.* 6*d.*

THE WANDERER. Cr. 8vo., 10*s.* 6*d.*

LUCILE. Crown 8vo., 10*s.* 6*d.*

SELECTED POEMS. Cr. 8vo., 10*s.* 6*d.*

Macaulay.—LAYS OF ANCIENT ROME, &c. By Lord MACAULAY.

Illustrated by G. SCHARF. Fcp. 4to., 10*s.* 6*d.*

—————————— Bijou Edition. 18mo., 2*s.* 6*d.*, gilt top.

—————————— Popular Edition. Fcp. 4to., 6*d.* sewed, 1*s.* cloth.

Illustrated by J. R. WEGUELIN. Crown 8vo., 3*s.* 6*d.*

Annotated Edition. Fcp. 8vo., 1*s.* sewed, 1*s.* 6*d.* cloth.

Macdonald.—A BOOK OF STRIFE, IN THE FORM OF THE DIARY OF AN OLD SOUL: Poems. By GEORGE MAC-DONALD, LL.D. 18mo., 6*s.*

Morris (WILLIAM).

POETICAL WORKS. LIBRARY EDITION. Complete in Ten Volumes. Crown 8vo., price 6*s.* each.

THE EARTHLY PARADISE. 4 vols. 6*s.* each.

THE LIFE AND DEATH OF JASON. 6*s.*

THE DEFENCE OF GUENEVERE, and other Poems. 6*s.*

THE STORY OF SIGURD THE VOLSUNG, and the Fall of the Niblungs. 6*s.*

LOVE IS ENOUGH: or, The Freeing of Pharamond: a Morality; and POEMS BY THE WAY. 6*s.*

THE ODYSSEY OF HOMER. Done into English Verse. 6*s.*

THE ÆNEIDS OF VIRGIL. Done into English Verse. 6*s.*

———

Certain of the Poetical Works may also be had in the following Editions :—

THE EARTHLY PARADISE.
Popular Edition. 5 vols. 12mo., 25*s.*; or 5*s.* each, sold separately.

The same in Ten Parts, 25*s.*; or 2*s.* 6*d.* each, sold separately.

Cheap Edition, in 1 vol. Cr. 8vo., 7*s.* 6*d.*

LOVE IS ENOUGH; or, The Freeing of Pharamond: a Morality. Square crown 8vo., 7*s.* 6*d.*

POEMS BY THE WAY. Square crown 8vo., 6*s.*

** For Mr. William Morris's Prose Works, see p. 31.

Murray.—(ROBERT F.), Author of 'The Scarlet Gown'. His Poems, with a Memoir by ANDREW LANG. Fcp. 8vo., 5*s.* net.

Nesbit.—LAYS AND LEGENDS. By E. NESBIT (Mrs. HUBERT BLAND). First Series. Crown 8vo., 3*s.* 6*d.* Second Series, with Portrait. Crown 8vo., 5*s.*

Poetry and the Drama—*continued*.

Peek (HEDLEY) (FRANK LEYTON).

SKELETON LEAVES: Poems. With a Dedicatory Poem to the late Hon. Roden Noel. Fcp. 8vo., 2s. 6d. net.

THE SHADOWS OF THE LAKE, and other Poems. Fcp. 8vo., 2s. 6d. net.

Piatt (SARAH).

POEMS. With Portrait of the Author. 2 vols. Crown 8vo., 10s.

AN ENCHANTED CASTLE, AND OTHER POEMS: Pictures, Portraits and People in Ireland. Crown 8vo., 3s. 6d.

Piatt (JOHN JAMES).

IDYLS AND LYRICS OF THE OHIO VALLEY. Crown 8vo., 5s.

LITTLE NEW WORLD IDYLS. Cr. 8vo., 5s.

Rhoades.—TERESA AND OTHER POEMS. By JAMES RHOADES. Crown 8vo., 3s. 6d.

Riley (JAMES WHITCOMB).

OLD FASHIONED ROSES: Poems. 12mo., 5s.

POEMS HERE AT HOME. Fcap. 8vo., 6s. net.

Shakespeare.—BOWDLER'S FAMILY SHAKESPEARE. With 36 Woodcuts 1 vol. 8vo., 14s. Or in 6 vols. Fcp 8vo., 21s.

THE SHAKESPEARE BIRTHDAY BOOK. By MARY F. DUNBAR. 32mo., 1s. 6d.

Sturgis.—A BOOK OF SONG. By JULIAN STURGIS. 16mo., 5s.

Works of Fiction, Humour, &c.

Alden.—AMONG THE FREAKS. By W. L. Alden. With 55 Illustrations by J. F. SULLIVAN and FLORENCE K. UPTON. Crown 8vo, 3s. 6d.

Anstey (F.), Author of 'Vice Versâ'.

VOCES POPULI. Reprinted from 'Punch'. First Series. With 20 Illustrations by J. BERNARD PARTRIDGE. Cr. 8vo., 3s. 6d.

THE TRAVELLING COMPANIONS. Reprinted from 'Punch'. With 25 Illus, by J. B. PARTRIDGE. Post 4to., 5s.

THE MAN FROM BLANKLEY'S: a Story in Scenes, and other Sketches. With 24 Illustrations by J. BERNARD PARTRIDGE. Post 4to., 6s.

Astor.—A JOURNEY IN OTHER WORLDS. a Romance of the Future. By JOHN JACOB ASTOR. With 10 Illustrations Cr. 8vo., 6s.

Baker.—BY THE WESTERN SEA. By JAMES BAKER, Author of 'John Westacott'. Crown 8vo., 3s. 6d.

Beaconsfield (THE EARL OF).

NOVELS AND TALES. Complete in 11 vols. Cr. 8vo., 1s. 6d. each.

Vivian Grey.	Sybil.
The Young Duke, &c.	Henrietta Temple
Alroy, Ixion, &c.	Venetia.
Contarini Fleming, &c.	Coningsby.
Tancred.	Lothair.
	Endymion.

NOVELS AND TALES. The Hughenden Edition. With 2 Portraits and 11 Vignettes. 11 vols. Cr. 8vo., 42s.

Works of Fiction, Humour, &c.—*continued*.

Dougall (L.).

BEGGARS ALL. Crown 8vo., 3s. 6d.

WHAT NECESSITY KNOWS. Crown 8vo., 6s.

Doyle (A. CONAN).

MICAH CLARKE: a Tale of Monmouth's Rebellion. With 10 Illustrations. Cr. 8vo., 3s. 6d.

THE CAPTAIN OF THE POLESTAR, and other Tales. Cr. 8vo., 3s. 6d.

THE REFUGEES: a Tale of the Huguenots. With 25 Illustrations. Crown 8vo., 3s. 6d.

THE STARK-MUNRO LETTERS. Cr. 8vo., 6s.

Farrar (F. W., Dean of Canterbury).

DARKNESS AND DAWN: or, Scenes in the Days of Nero. An Historic Tale. Cr. 8vo., 7s. 6d.

GATHERING CLOUDS: a Tale of the Days of St. Chrysostom. Crown 8vo., 7s. 6d.

Fowler.—THE YOUNG PRETENDERS. A Story of Child Life. By EDITH H. FOWLER. With 12 Illustrations by PHILIP BURNE-JONES. Crown 8vo., 6s.

Froude.—THE TWO CHIEFS OF DUNBOY: an Irish Romance of the Last Century. By J. A. FROUDE. Cr. 8vo. 3s. 6d.

Haggard (H. RIDER).

SHE. 32 Illustrations. Cr. 8vo., 3s. 6d.

ALLAN QUATERMAIN. With 31 Illustrations. Crown 8vo., 3s. 6d.

MAIWA'S REVENGE. Crown 8vo., 1s. boards; 1s. 6d. cloth.

COLONEL QUARITCH, V.C. Cr. 8vo., 3s. 6d.

CLEOPATRA. With 29 Illustrations Crown 8vo., 3s. 6d.

Haggard (H. RIDER)—*continued*.

BEATRICE. Cr. 8vo., 3s. 6d.

ERIC BRIGHTEYES. With 51 Illustrations. Cr. 8vo., 3s. 6d.

HEART OF THE WORLD. With 15 Illustrations, Crown 8vo., 6s.

JOAN HASTE. With 20 Illustrations. Cr. 8vo., 6s.

THE PEOPLE OF THE MIST. With 16 Illustrations. Crown 8vo., 6s.

MONTEZUMA'S DAUGHTER. With 24 Illustrations. Crown 8vo., 3s. 6d.

NADA THE LILY. With 23 Illustrations. Cr. 8vo., 3s. 6d.

ALLAN'S WIFE. With 34 Illustrations. Crown 8vo., 3s. 6d.

THE WITCH'S HEAD. With 16 Illustrations. Crown 8vo., 3s. 6d.

MR. MEESON'S WILL. With 16 Illustrations. Crown 8vo., 3s. 6d.

DAWN. With 16 Illustrations. Crown 8vo., 3s. 6d.

Haggard and Lang.—THE WORLD'S DESIRE. By H. RIDER HAGGARD and ANDREW LANG. With 27 Illustrations Crown 8vo., 3s. 6d.

Harte.—IN THE CARQUINEZ WOODS, and other Stories. By BRET HARTE. Cr. 8vo., 3s. 6d.

Hope.—THE HEART OF PRINCESS OSRA. By ANTHONY HOPE. With 9 Illustrations by JOHN WILLIAMSON. Crown 8vo., 6s.

Hornung.—THE UNBIDDEN GUEST. By E. W. HORNUNG. Cr. 8vo., 3s. 6d.

Lang.—A MONK OF FIFE: a Romance of the Days of Jeanne D'Arc. By ANDREW LANG. With Illustrations and Initial Letters by SELWYN IMAGE. Crown 8vo., 6s.

Works of Fiction, Humour, &c.—*continued*

Lyall (EDNA).
THE AUTOBIOGRAPHY OF A SLANDER.
Fcp. 8vo., 1s. sewed.
Presentation Edition. With 20 Illustrations. Cr 8vo., 2s. 6d. net.
THE AUTOBIOGRAPHY OF A TRUTH.
Fcp. 8vo., 1s. sewed ; 1s. 6d. cloth.
DOREEN : The Story of a Singer. Cr.
8vo., 6s.

Magruder.—THE VIOLET. By JULIA
MAGRUDER. With Illustrations by C.
D. GIBSON. Crown 8vo.

Matthews.—HIS FATHER'S SON : a
Novel of the New York Stock Exchange. By BRANDER MATTHEWS.
With Illus. Cr. 8vo., 6s.

Melville (G. J. WHYTE).
The Gladiators.   Holmby House.
The Interpreter.   Kate Coventry.
Good for Nothing.   Digby Grand.
The Queen's Maries.   General Bounce.
Cr. 8vo., 1s. 6d. each.

Merriman.—FLOTSAM : The Study of
a Life By HENRY SETON MERRIMAN. With Frontispiece and Vignette
by H. G. MASSEY, A.R.E. Cr. 8vo., 6s.
THE WELL AT THE WORLD'S END.
2 vols. 8vo. 24s.

Morris (WILLIAM).
THE WELL AT THE WORLD'S END. 2
vols., 8vo., 24s.
THE STORY OF THE GLITTERING PLAIN,
which has been also called The Land
of the Living Men, or The Acre of
the Undying. Square post 8vo., 5s.
net.
THE ROOTS OF THE MOUNTAINS,
wherein is told somewhat of the Lives
of the Men of Burgdale, their Friends,
their Neighbours, their Foemen, and
their Fellows-in-Arms. Written in
Prose and Verse. Square cr. 8vo., 8s.
A TALE OF THE HOUSE OF THE WOLFINGS, and all the Kindreds of the
Mark. Written in Prose and Verse.
Second Edition. Square cr. 8vo., 6s.
A DREAM OF JOHN BALL, AND A
KING'S LESSON. 12mo., 1s. 6d.
NEWS FROM NOWHERE ; or, An Epoch
of Rest. Being some Chapters from
an Utopian Romance. Post 8vo.,
1s. 6d.
** For Mr. William Morris's Poetical
Works, see p. 19.

Newman (CARDINAL).
LOSS AND GAIN : The Story of a Convert. Crown 8vo. Cabinet Edition
6s. ; Popular Edition, 3s. 6d.

Newman (CARDINAL)—*continued.*
CALLISTA : A Tale of the Third Century. Crown 8vo. Cabinet Edition,
6s. ; Popular Edition, 3s. 6d.

Oliphant.—OLD MR. TREDGOLD. By
Mrs. OLIPHANT. Crown 8vo., 6s.

Phillipps-Wolley. SNAP; a Legend
of the Lone Mountain. By C. PHILLIPPS-WOLLEY. With 13 Illustrations
by H. G. WILLINK. Cr. 8vo., 3s. 6d.

Quintana.—THE CID CAMPEADOR :
an Historical Romance. By D.
ANTONIO DE TRUEBA Y LA QUINTANA.
Translated from the Spanish by Henry
J. Gill, M.A., T.C.D. Crown 8vo, 6s.

Rhoscomyl (OWEN).
THE JEWEL OF YNYS GALON. With
12 Illustrations. Crown 8vo., 6s.
BATTLEMENT AND TOWER: a Romance.
Crown 8vo., 6s.

Robertson.—NUGGETS IN THE DEVIL'S
PUNCH BOWL, and other Australian
Tales. By ANDREW ROBERTSON. Cr.
8vo., 3s. 6d.

Rokeby.—DORCAS HOBDAY. By
CHARLES ROKEBY.

Sewell (ELIZABETH M.).
A Glimpse of the World. | Amy Herbert.
Laneton Parsonage. | Cleve Hall.
Margaret Percival. | Gertrude.
Katharine Ashton. | Home Life.
The Earl's Daughter. | After Life.
The Experience of Life. | Ursula. Ivors.
Cr. 8vo., 1s. 6d. each, cloth plain. 2s. 6d.
each, cloth extra, gilt edges.

Stevenson (ROBERT LOUIS).
THE STRANGE CASE OF DR. JEKYLL
AND MR. HYDE. Fcp. 8vo., 1s.
sewed, 1s. 6d. cloth.
THE STRANGE CASE OF DR. JEKYLL
AND MR. HYDE ; with Other Fables
Crown 8vo., 3s. 6d.
MORE NEW ARABIAN NIGHTS—THE
DYNAMITER. By ROBERT LOUIS
STEVENSON and FANNY VAN DE
GRIFT STEVENSON. Crown 8vo.,
3s. 6d.
THE WRONG BOX. By ROBERT LOUIS
STEVENSON and LLOYD OSBOURNE.
Crown 8vo., 3s. 6d.

Suttner.—LAY DOWN YOUR ARMS
Die Waffen Nieder: The Autobiography
of Martha Tilling By BERTHA VON
SUTTNER. Translated by T. HOLMES.
Cr. 8vo., 1s. 6d.

Works of Fiction, Humour, &c.—*continued.*

Trollope (ANTHONY).

THE WARDEN. Cr. 8vo., 1s. 6d.

BARCHESTER TOWERS. Cr. 8vo., 1s. 6d.

TRUE (A) RELATION OF THE TRAVELS AND PERILOUS ADVENTURES OF MATHEW DUDGEON, Gentleman : Wherein is truly set down the Manner of his Taking, the Long Time of his Slavery in Algiers, and Means of his Delivery. Written by Himself, and now for the first time printed Cr. 8vo., 5s.

Walford (L. B.).

Mr SMITH : a Part of his Life. Crown 8vo., 2s. 6d.

THE BABY'S GRANDMOTHER. Crown 8vo., 2s. 6d.

COUSINS. Crown 8vo. 2s. 6d.

TROUBLESOME DAUGHTERS. Crown 8vo., 2s. 6d.

PAULINE. Crown 8vo. 2s. 6d.

DICK NETHERBY. Crown 8vo., 2s. 6d.

THE HISTORY OF A WEEK. Crown 8vo. 2s. 6d.

A STIFF-NECKED GENERATION. Crown 8vo. 2s. 6d.

NAN, and other Stories. Cr. 8vo., 2s. 6d.

Walford (L. B.)—*continued*

THE MISCHIEF OF MONICA. Crown 8vo., 2s. 6d.

THE ONE GOOD GUEST. Cr. 8vo. 2s. 6d.

'PLOUGHED,' and other Stories. Crown 8vo., 6s.

THE MATCHMAKER. Cr. 8vo., 6s

West (B. B.).

HALF-HOURS WITH THE MILLIONAIRES : Showing how much harder it is to spend a million than to make it. Cr. 8vo., 6s.

A FINANCIAL ATONEMENT. Cr. 8vo., 6s.

SIR SIMON VANDERPETTER, AND MINDING HIS ANCESTORS. Two Reformations. Crown 8vo., 5s.

Weyman (S. J.).

THE HOUSE OF THE WOLF. Cr. 8vo., 3s. 6d.

A GENTLEMAN OF FRANCE. Cr. 8vo., 6s.

THE RED COCKADE. Cr. 8vo., 6s.

Whishaw.—A BOYAR OF THE TERRIBLE : a Romance of the Court of Ivan the Cruel, First Tzar of Russia. By FRED. WHISHAW. With 12 Illustrations by H. G. MASSEY, A.R.E. Cr. 8vo., 6s.

Popular Science (Natural History, &c.).

Butler.—OUR HOUSEHOLD INSECTS. An Account of the Insect-Pests found in Dwelling-Houses. By EDWARD A. BUTLER, B.A., B.Sc. (Lond.). With 113 Illustrations. Crown 8vo., 3s. 6d.

Furneaux (W.).

BUTTERFLIES AND MOTHS (British). With 12 coloured Plates and 241 Illustrations in the Text. Crown 8vo., 12s. 6d.

THE OUTDOOR WORLD; or, The Young Collector's Handbook. With 18 Plates, 16 of which are coloured, and 549 Illustrations in the Text. Crown 8vo., 7s. 6d.

Hartwig (Dr. GEORGE).

THE SEA AND ITS LIVING WONDERS. With 12 Plates and 303 Woodcuts. 8vo., 7s. net.

THE TROPICAL WORLD. With 8 Plates and 172 Woodcuts. 8vo., 7s. net.

THE POLAR WORLD. With 3 Maps, 8 Plates and 85 Woodcuts. 8vo., 7s. net.

THE SUBTERRANEAN WORLD. With

Hartwig (Dr. GEORGE)—*continued.*

THE AERIAL WORLD. With Map, 8 Plates and 60 Woodcuts. 8vo., 7s. net.

HEROES OF THE POLAR WORLD. 19 Illustrations. Crown 8vo., 2s.

WONDERS OF THE TROPICAL FORESTS 40 Illustrations. Crown 8vo., 2s.

WORKERS UNDER THE GROUND, 29 Illustrations. Crown 8vo., 2s.

MARVELS OVER OUR HEADS. 29 Illustrations. Crown 8vo., 2s.

SEA MONSTERS AND SEA BIRDS. 75 Illustrations. Crown 8vo., 2s. 6d.

DENIZENS OF THE DEEP. 117 Illustrations. Crown 8vo., 2s. 6d.

VOLCANOES AND EARTHQUAKES. 30 Illustrations. Crown 8vo., 2s. 6d.

WILD ANIMALS OF THE TROPICS. 66 Illustrations. Crown 8vo., 3s. 6d.

Hayward.—BIRD NOTES. By the late JANE MARY HAYWARD. Edited by EMMA HUBBARD. With Frontispiece and 15 Illustrations by G. E. LODGE. Cr. 8vo., 6s.

Helmholtz.—POPULAR LECTURES ON SCIENTIFIC SUBJECTS. By HERMANN VON HELMHOLTZ. With 68 Woodcuts.

Popular Science (Natural History, &c.).

Hudson.—BRITISH BIRDS. By W. H. HUDSON, C.M.Z.S. With a Chapter on Structure and Classification by FRANK E. BEDDARD, F.R.S. With 17 Plates (8 of which are Coloured), and over 100 Illustrations in the Text. Crown 8vo., 12s. 6d.

Proctor (RICHARD A.).

LIGHT SCIENCE FOR LEISURE HOURS. Familiar Essays on Scientific Subjects. 3 vols. Crown 8vo., 5s. each.

ROUGH WAYS MADE SMOOTH. Familiar Essays on Scientific Subjects. Crown 8vo., 3s. 6d.

PLEASANT WAYS IN SCIENCE. Crown 8vo., 3s. 6d.

NATURE STUDIES. By R. A. PROCTOR, GRANT ALLEN, A. WILSON, T. FOSTER and E. CLODD. Crown 8vo., 3s. 6d.

LEISURE READINGS. By R. A. PROCTOR, E. CLODD, A. WILSON, T. FOSTER, and A. C. RANYARD. Cr. 8vo., 3s. 6d.

. *For Mr. Proctor's other books see Messrs. Longmans & Co.'s Catalogue of Scientific Works.*

Stanley.—A FAMILIAR HISTORY OF BIRDS. By E. STANLEY, D.D., formerly Bishop of Norwich. With Illustrations. Cr. 8vo., 3s. 6d.

Wood (Rev. J. G.).

HOMES WITHOUT HANDS: a Description of the Habitation of Animals, classed according to the Principle of Construction. With 140 Illustrations. 8vo., 7s. net.

Wood (Rev. J. G.)—*continued.*

INSECTS AT HOME: a Popular Account of British Insects, their Structure, Habits and Transformations. With 700 Illustrations. 8vo., 7s. net.

INSECTS ABROAD: a Popular Account of Foreign Insects, their Structure, Habits and Transformations. With 600 Illustrations. 8vo., 7s. net.

BIBLE ANIMALS: a Description of every Living Creature mentioned in the Scriptures. With 112 Illustrations. 8vo., 7s. net.

PETLAND REVISITED. With 33 Illustrations. Cr. 8vo., 3s. 6d.

OUT OF DOORS; a Selection of Original Articles on Practical Natural History. With 11 Illustrations. Cr. 8vo., 3s. 6d.

STRANGE DWELLINGS: a Description of the Habitations of Animals, abridged from 'Homes without Hands'. With 60 Illustrations. Cr. 8vo., 3s. 6d.

BIRD LIFE OF THE BIBLE. 32 Illustrations. Crown 8vo., 3s. 6d.

WONDERFUL NESTS. 30 Illustrations. Crown 8vo., 3s. 6d.

HOMES UNDER THE GROUND. 28 Illustrations. Crown 8vo., 3s. 6d.

WILD ANIMALS OF THE BIBLE. 29 Illustrations. Crown 8vo., 3s. 6d.

DOMESTIC ANIMALS OF THE BIBLE. 23 Illustrations. Crown 8vo., 3s. 6d.

THE BRANCH BUILDERS. 28 Illustrations. Crown 8vo., 2s. 6d.

SOCIAL HABITATIONS AND PARASITIC NESTS. 18 Illustrations. Crown 8vo., 2s.

Works of Reference.

Longmans' GAZETTEER OF THE WORLD. Edited by GEORGE G. CHISHOLM, M.A., B.Sc., Fellow of the Royal

Maunder (Samuel)—*continued.*

TREASURY OF GEOGRAPHY, Physical, Historical, Descriptive and Political.

Works of Reference—continued.

Maunder's (Samuel)—continued.
TREASURY OF KNOWLEDGE AND LIBRARY OF REFERENCE. Comprising an English Dictionary and Grammar, Universal Gazeteer, Classical Dictionary, Chronology, Law Dictionary, &c. Fcp. 8vo., 6s.

SCIENTIFIC AND LITERARY TREASURY. Fcp. 8vo., 6s.

THE TREASURY OF BOTANY. Edited by J. LINDLEY, F.R.S., and T. MOORE, F.L.S. With 274 Woodcuts and 20 Steel Plates. 2 vols. Fcp. 8vo., 12s.

Roget.—THESAURUS OF ENGLISH WORDS AND PHRASES. Classified and Arranged so as to Facilitate the Expression of Ideas and assist in Literary Composition. By PETER MARK ROGET, M.D. F.R.S. Crown 8vo., 10s. 6d.

Willich.—POPULAR TABLES for giving information for ascertaining the value of Lifehold, Leasehold, and Church Property, the Public Funds, &c. By CHARLES M. WILLICH. Edited by H. BENCE JONES. Crown 8vo., 10s. 6d.

Children's Books.

Crake (Rev. A. D.).
EDWY THE FAIR; or, the First Chronicle of Æscendune. Crown 8vo., 2s. 6d.

ALFGAR THE DANE: or, the Second Chronicle of Æscendune. Cr. 8vo., 2s. 6d.

THE RIVAL HEIRS: being the Third and Last Chronicle of Æscendune. Crown 8vo., 2s. 6d.

THE HOUSE OF WALDERNE. A Tale of the Cloister and the Forest in the Days of the Barons' Wars. Crown 8vo., 2s. 6d.

BRIAN FITZ-COUNT. A Story of Wallingford Castle and Dorchester Abbey. Crown 8vo., 2s. 6d

Lang (ANDREW).
THE BLUE FAIRY BOOK. With 138 Illustrations. Crown 8vo., 6s.

THE RED FAIRY BOOK. With 100 Illustrations. Crown 8vo., 6s.

THE GREEN FAIRY BOOK. With 101 Illustrations. Crown 8vo., 6s.

THE YELLOW FAIRY BOOK. With 104 Illustrations. Crown 8vo., 6s.

THE BLUE POETRY BOOK. With 100 Illustrations. Crown 8vo., 6s.

THE BLUE POETRY BOOK. School Edition, without Illustrations. Fcp. 8vo., 2s. 6d.

THE TRUE STORY BOOK. With 66 Illustrations. Crown 8vo., 6s.

Lang (ANDREW)—continued.
THE RED TRUE STORY BOOK. With 100 Illustrations. Crown 8vo., 6s.

THE ANIMAL STORY BOOK. With 67 Illustrations. Crown 8vo., 6s.

Meade (L. T.).
DADDY'S BOY. With Illustrations. Crown 8vo., 3s. 6d.

DEB AND THE DUCHESS. With Illustrations. Crown 8vo., 3s. 6d.

THE BERESFORD PRIZE. With Illustrations. Crown 8vo., 3s. 6d.

THE HOUSE OF SURPRISES. With Illustrations. Crown 8vo., 3s. 6d.

Molesworth. — SILVERTHORNS. By Mrs. MOLESWORTH. With Illustrations. Crown 8vo., 5s.

Stevenson.—A CHILD'S GARDEN OF VERSES. By ROBERT LOUIS STEVENSON. Small fcp. 8vo., 5s.

Upton (FLORENCE K., and BERTHA).
THE ADVENTURES OF TWO DUTCH DOLLS AND A 'GOLLIWOGG'. Illustrated by FLORENCE K. UPTON, with Words by BERTHA UPTON. With 31 Coloured Plates and numerous Illustrations in the Text. Oblong 4to., 6s.

Children's Books—*continued.*

Upton (FLORENCE K., and BERTHA)—
continued.

THE GOLLIWOGG'S BICYCLE CLUB.
Pictures by FLORENCE K. UPTON.
Words by BERTHA UPTON. With
Coloured Plates and numerous Illus-
trations in the Text. Oblong 4vo. 6s.

Wordsworth.—THE SNOW GARDEN,
and other Fairy Tales for Children. By
ELIZABETH WORDSWORTH. With Illustrations by TREVOR HADDON.
Crown 8vo., 5s.

Longmans' Series of Books for Girls.

Crown 8vo., price 2s. 6d. each

ATELIER (THE) DU LYS: or an Art
Student in the Reign of Terror.

BY THE SAME AUTHOR.

Mademoiselle Mori.
That Child.
Under a Cloud.
The Fiddler of
Lugau.

A Child of the Revolu-
tion.
Hester's Venture.
In the Olden Time.
The Younger Sister.

ATHERSTONE PRIORY. By L. N. COMYN.

THE THIRD MISS ST. QUENTIN. By
Mrs. MOLESWORTH.

THE PALACE IN THE GARDEN. By
Mrs. MOLESWORTH. Illustrated.

THE STORY OF A SPRING MORNING, &c.
By Mrs. MOLESWORTH. Illustrated.

NEIGHBOURS. By Mrs. MOLESWORTH.

VERY YOUNG; and QUITE ANOTHER
STORY. By JEAN INGELOW.

CAN THIS BE LOVE? By Louis A. Parr.

KEITH DERAMORE. By the Author of
' Miss Molly '.

SIDNEY. By MARGARET DELAND.

AN ARRANGED MARRIAGE. By DORO-
THEA GERARD.

LAST WORDS TO GIRLS ON LIFE AT
SCHOOL AND AFTER SCHOOL. By
MARIA GREY.

STRAY THOUGHTS FOR GIRLS. By
LUCY H. M. SOULSBY. 16mo.,
1s. 6d. net.

The Silver Library.

CROWN 8vo. 3s. 6d. EACH VOLUME.

Arnold's (Sir Edwin) Seas and Lands.
With 71 Illustrations. 3s. 6d.

Bagehot's (W.) Biographical Studies.
3s. 6d.

Bagehot's (W.) Economic Studies. 3s. 6d.

Bagehot's (W.) Literary Studies. 3
vols. 3s. 6d. each.

**Baker's (Sir S. W.) Eight Years in
Ceylon.** With 6 Illustrations. 3s. 6d.

**Baker's (Sir S. W.) Rifle and Hound in
Ceylon.** With 6 Illustrations. 3s. 6d.

**Baring-Gould's (Rev. S.) Curious Myths
of the Middle Ages.** 3s. 6d.

**Baring-Gould's (Rev. S.) Origin and
Development of Religious Belief.** 2
vols. 3s. 6d. each.

Becker's (Prof.) Gallus: or, Roman Scenes
in the Time of Augustus. Illus. 3s. 6d.

Becker's (Prof.) Charicles: or, Illustra-
tions of the Private Life of the Ancient
Greeks. Illustrated. 3s. 6d.

Bent's (J. T.) The Ruined Cities of Ma-
shonaland: being a Record of Excavation and Exploration in 1891.
With 117 Illustrations. 3s. 6d.

Brassey's (Lady) A Voyage in the 'Sun-
beam '. With 66 Illustrations. 3s. 6d.

**Butler's (Edward A.) Our Household
Insects:** an Account of the Insect-
Pests found in Dwelling-Houses.
With 7 Plates and 113 Illustrations in
the Text.

The Silver Library—*continued*.

Clodd's (E.) Story of Creation : a Plain Account of Evolution. With 77 Illustrations. 3*s.* 6*d.*

Conybeare (Rev. W. J.) and Howson's (Very Rev. J. S.) Life and Epistles of St. Paul. 46 Illustrations. 3*s.* 6*d.*

Dougall's (L.) Beggars All; a Novel. 3*s.* 6*d.*

Doyle's (A. Conan) Micah Clarke : a Tale of Monmouth's Rebellion. 10 Illus. 3*s.* 6*d.*

Doyle's (A. Conan) The Captain of the Polestar, and other Tales. 3*s.* 6*d.*

Doyle's (A. Conan) The Refugees : A Tale of The Huguenots. With 25 Illustrations, 3*s.* 6*d.*

Froude's (J. A.) The History of England, from the Fall of Wolsey to the Defeat of the Spanish Armada. 12 vols. 3*s.* 6*d.* each.

Froude's (J. A.) Short Studies on Great Subjects. 4 vols. 3*s.* 6*d.* each.

Froude's (J. A.) The English in Ireland. 3 vols. 10*s.* 6*d.*

Froude's (J. A.) The Spanish Story of the Armada, and other Essays. 3*s.* 6*d.*

Froude's (J. A.) Cæsar : a Sketch. 3*s.* 6*d.*

Froude's (J. A.) Thomas Carlyle a History of his Life.
1795-1835. 2 vols. 7*s.*
1834-1881. 2 vols. 7*s.*

Froude's (J. A.) The Two Chiefs of Dunboy : an Irish Romance of the Last Century. 3*s.* 6*d.*

Gleig's (Rev. G. R.) Life of the Duke of Wellington. With Portrait. 3*s.* 6*d.*

Greville's (C. C. F.) Journal of the Reigns of King George IV., King William IV., and Queen Victoria. 8 vols, 3*s.* 6*d.* each.

Haggard's (H. R.) She : A History of Adventure. 32 Illustrations. 3*s.* 6*d.*

Haggard's (H. R.) Allan Quatermain. With 20 Illustrations. 3*s.* 6*d.*

Haggard's (H. R.) Colonel Quaritch, V.C. : a Tale of Country Life. 3*s.* 6*d.*

Haggard's (H. R.) Cleopatra. With 29 Full-page Illustrations. 3*s.* 6*d.*

Haggard's (H. R.) Eric Brighteyes. With 51 Illustrations. 3*s.* 6*d.*

Haggard's (H. R.) Beatrice. 3*s.* 6*d.*

Haggard's (H. R.) Allan's Wife. With 34 Illustrations. 3*s.* 6*d.*

Haggard's (H. R.) The Witch's Head. With Illustrations. 3*s.* 6*d.*

Haggard's (H. R.) Mr. Meeson's Will. With Illustrations. 3*s.* 6*d.*

Haggard's (H. R.) Dawn. With 16 Illustrations. 3*s.* 6*d.*

Haggard's (H. R.) Montezuma's Daughter. With 25 Illustrations.

Haggard's (H. R.) Nada the Lily. With Illustrations by C. H. M. KERR. 3*s.* 6*d.*

Haggard's (H. R.) and Lang's (A.) The World's Desire. With 27 Illus. 3*s.* 6*d.*

Harte's (Bret) In the Carquinez Woods, and other Stories. 3*s.* 6*d.*

Helmholtz's (Hermann von) Popular Lectures on Scientific Subjects. With 68 Woodcuts. 2 vols. 3*s.* 6*d.* each.

Hornung's (E. W.) The Unbidden Guest. 3*s.* 6*d.*

Howitt's (W.) Visits to Remarkable Places. 80 Illustrations. 3*s.* 6*d.*

Jefferies' (R.) The Story of My Heart : My Autobiography. With Portrait. 3*s.* 6*d.*

Jefferies' (R.) Field and Hedgerow. With Portrait. 3*s.* 6*d.*

Jefferies' (R.) Red Deer. 17 Illus. 3*s.* 6*d.*

Jefferies' (R.) Wood Magic : a Fable. 3*s.* 6*d.*

Jefferies' (R. The Toilers of the Field. With Portrait from the Bust in Salisbury Cathedral. 3*s.* 6*d.*

Knight's (E. F.) The Cruise of the 'Alerte' : a Search for Treasure on the Desert Island of Trinidad. 2 Maps and 23 Illustrations. 3*s.* 6*d.*

Knight's (E. F.) Where Three Empires Meet : a Narrative of Recent Travel in Kashmir, Western Tibet, etc. With a Map and 54 Illust. 3*s.* 6*d.*

Knight's (E. F.) The Falcon on the Baltic : A Coasting Voyage from Hammersmith to Copenhagen in a Three-Ton Yacht. With Map and 11 Illustrations. 3*s.* 6*d.*

Lang's (A.) Angling Sketches. 20 Illus. 3*s.* 6*d.*

The Silver Library—*continued.*

Lang's (A.) Custom and Myth : Studies of Early Usage and Belief. 3s. 6d.

Lang's (A.) Cock Lane and Common-Sense. With a New Preface.

Lees (J. A.) and Clutterbuck's (W.J.) B.C. 1887, A Ramble in British Columbia. With Maps and 75 Illustrations. 3s. 6d.

Macaulay's (Lord) Essays and Lays of Ancient Rome. With Portrait and Illustrations. 3s. 6d.

Macleod's (H. D.) The Elements of Banking. 3s. 6d.

Marshman's (J. C.) Memoirs of Sir Henry Havelock. 3s. 6d.

Max Müller's (F.) India, what can it teach us? 3s. 6d.

Max Müller's (F.) Introduction to the Science of Religion. 3s. 6d.

Merivale's (Dean) History of the Romans under the Empire. 8 vols. 3s. 6d. ea.

Mill's (J. S.) Political Economy. 3s. 6d.

Mill's (J. S.) System of Logic. 3s. 6d.

Milner's (Geo.) Country Pleasures. 3s. 6d.

Nansen's (F.) The First Crossing of Greenland. With Illustrations and a Map. 3s. 6d.

Phillipps-Wolley's (C.) Snap: a Legend of the Lone Mountain. With 13 Illustrations. 3s. 6d.

Proctor's (R. A.) The Orbs Around Us. Essays on the Moon and Planets, Meteors and Comets, the Sun and Coloured Pairs of Suns. 3s. 6d.

Proctor's (R. A.) The Expanse of Heaven. Essays on the Wonders of the Firmament. 3s. 6d.

Proctor's (R. A.) Other Worlds than Ours. 3s. 6d.

Proctor's (R. A.) Other Suns than Ours. 3s. 6d.

Proctor's (R. A.) Rough Ways made Smooth. 3s. 6d.

Proctor's (R. A.) Pleasant Ways in Science. 3s. 6d.

Proctor's (R. A.) Myths and Marvels of Astronomy. 3s. 6d.

Proctor's (R. A.) Nature Studies. 3s. 6d.

Proctor's (R. A.), Clodd (Edward), &c. Leisure Readings. With Illustrations.

Rossetti's (Maria F.) A Shadow of Dante: an Essay towards studying Himself, his World and his Pilgrimage. 3s. 6d.

Smith's (R. Bosworth) Carthage and the Carthaginians. 3s. 6d.

Stanley's (Bishop) Familiar History of Birds. 160 Illustrations. 3s. 6d.

Stevenson's (R. L.) The Strange Case of Dr. Jekyll and Mr. Hyde; with other Fables. 3s. 6d.

Stevenson (Robert Louis) and Osbourne's (Lloyd) The Wrong Box. 3s. 6d.

Stevenson (Robt. Louis) and Stevenson's (Fanny van de Grift) More New Arabian Nights.—The Dynamiter. 3s. 6d.

Weyman's (Stanley J.) The House of the Wolf: a Romance. 3s. 6d.

Wood's (Rev. J. G.) Petland Revisited. With 33 Illustrations. 3s. 6d.

Wood's (Rev. J. G.) Strange Dwellings. With 60 Illustrations. 3s. 6d.

Wood's (Rev. J. G.) Out of Doors. 11 Illustrations. 3s. 6d.

Cookery, Domestic Management, &c.

ACTON.—MODERN COOKERY. By ELIZA ACTON. With 150 Woodcuts. Fcp. 8vo., 4s. 6d.

Bull (THOMAS, M.D.).

HINTS TO MOTHERS ON THE MANAGEMENT OF THEIR HEALTH DURING THE PERIOD OF PREGNANCY. Fcp. 8vo., 1s. 6d.

THE MATERNAL MANAGEMENT OF CHILDREN IN HEALTH AND DISEASE. Fcp. 8vo., 1s. 6d.

De Salis (Mrs.).

CAKES AND CONFECTIONS À LA MODE. Fcp. 8vo., 1s. 6d.

DOGS: a Manual for Amateurs. Fcp. 8vo., 1s. 6d.

DRESSED GAME AND POULTRY À LA MODE. Fcp. 8vo., 1s. 6d.

DRESSED VEGETABLES À LA MODE. Fcp. 8vo., 1s. 6d.

Cookery, Domestic Management, &c.—*continued.*

De Salis (Mrs.)—*continued.*

DRINKS À LA MODE. Fcp. 8vo., 1s. 6d.

ENTRÉES À LA MODE. Fcp. 8vo., 1s. 6d.

FLORAL DECORATIONS. Fcp. 8vo., 1s. 6d.

GARDENING À LA MODE. Part I. Vegetables, 1s. 6d.; Part II. Fruits, 1s. 6d.

NATIONAL VIANDS À LA MODE. Fcp. 8vo., 1s. 6d.

NEW-LAID EGGS: Hints for Amateur Poultry Rearers. Fcp. 8vo., 1s. 6d.

OYSTERS À LA MODE. Fcp. 8vo., 1s. 6d.

PUDDINGS AND PASTRY À LA MODE. Fcp. 8vo., 1s. 6d.

SAVOURIES À LA MODE. Fcp 8vo., 1s. 6d.

SOUPS AND DRESSED FISH À LA MODE. Fcp. 8vo., 1s. 6d.

SWEETS AND SUPPER DISHES À LA MODE. Fcp. 8vo., 1s. 6d.

De Salis (Mrs.)—*continued.*

TEMPTING DISHES FOR SMALL INCOMES. Fcp. 8vo., 1s. 6d.

WRINKLES AND NOTIONS FOR EVERY HOUSEHOLD. Cr. 8vo., 1s. 6d.

Lear.—MAIGRE COOKERY. By H. L. SIDNEY LEAR. 16mo., 2s.

Poole.—COOKERY FOR THE DIABETIC. By W. H. and Mrs. POOLE. With Preface by Dr. PAVY. Fcp. 8vo., 2s. 6d.

Walker (JANE H.)

A HANDBOOK FOR MOTHERS: being Simple Hints to Women on the Management of their Health during Pregnancy and Confinement, together with Plain Directions as to the Care of Infants. Cr. 8vo., 2s. 6d.

A BOOK FOR EVERY WOMAN. Part I. The Management of Children in Health and out of Health. Crown 8vo., 2s. 6d.

Miscellaneous and Critical Works.

Allingham.—VARIETIES IN PROSE. By WILLIAM ALLINGHAM. 3 vols. Cr. 8vo, 18s. (Vols. 1 and 2, Rambles, by PATRICIUS WALKER. Vol. 3, Irish Sketches, etc.)

Armstrong.—ESSAYS AND SKETCHES. By EDMUND J. ARMSTRONG. Fcp. 8vo., 5s.

Bagehot.—LITERARY STUDIES. By WALTER BAGEHOT. With Portrait. 3 vols. Crown 8vo., 3s. 6d. each.

Baring-Gould.—CURIOUS MYTHS OF THE MIDDLE AGES. By Rev. S. BARING-GOULD. Crown 8vo., 3s. 6d.

Baynes.—SHAKESPEARE STUDIES, AND OTHER ESSAYS. By the late THOMAS SPENCER BAYNES, LL.B., LL.D. With a biographical Preface by Prof. LEWIS CAMPBELL. Crown 8vo., 7s. 6d.

Boyd (A. K. H.) ('A.K.H.B.'). And see MISCELLANEOUS THEOLOGICAL WORKS, p. 32.

AUTUMN HOLIDAYS OF A COUNTRY PARSON. Crown 8vo., 3s. 6d.

Boyd (A. K. H.). ('A.K.H.B.')—*continued.*

COMMONPLACE PHILOSOPHER. Crown 8vo., 3s. 6d.

CRITICAL ESSAYS OF A COUNTRY PARSON. Crown 8vo., 3s. 6d.

EAST COAST DAYS AND MEMORIES. Crown 8vo., 3s. 6d.

LANDSCAPES, CHURCHES AND MORALITIES. Crown 8vo., 3s. 6d.

LEISURE HOURS IN TOWN. Crown 8vo., 3s. 6d.

LESSONS OF MIDDLE AGE. Cr. 8vo., 3s. 6d.

OUR LITTLE LIFE. Two Series. Cr. 8vo., 3s. 6d. each.

OUR HOMELY COMEDY: AND TRAGEDY. Crown 8vo., 3s. 6d.

RECREATIONS OF A COUNTRY PARSON. Three Series. Cr. 8vo., 3s. 6d. each. Also First Series. Popular Ed. 8vo., 6d.

Miscellaneous and Critical Works—*continued.*

Butler (SAMUEL).

EREWHON. Cr. 8vo., 5s.

THE FAIR HAVEN. A Work in Defence of the Miraculous Element in our Lord's Ministry. Cr. 8vo., 7s. 6d.

LIFE AND HABIT. An Essay after a Completer View of Evolution. Cr. 8vo., 7s. 6d.

EVOLUTION, OLD AND NEW. Cr. 8vo., 10s. 6d.

ALPS AND SANCTUARIES OF PIEDMONT AND CANTON TICINO. Illustrated. Pott 4to., 10s. 6d.

LUCK, OR CUNNING, AS THE MAIN MEANS OF ORGANIC MODIFICATION? Cr. 8vo., 7s. 6d.

EX VOTO. An Account of the Sacro Monte or New Jerusalem at Varallo-Sesia. Crown 8vo., 10s. 6d.

Gwilt.—AN ENCYCLOPÆDIA OF ARCHITECTURE. By JOSEPH GWILT, F.S.A. Illustrated with more than 1100 Engravings on Wood. Revised (1888), with Alterations and Considerable Additions by WYATT PAPWORTH. 8vo., £2 12s. 6d.

Hamlin.—A TEXT-BOOK OF THE HISTORY OF ARCHITECTURE. By A. D. F. HAMLIN, A.M., Adjunct-Professor of Architecture in the School of Mines, Columbia College. With 229 Illustrations. Crown 8vo., 7s. 6d.

Haweis.—MUSIC AND MORALS. By the Rev. H. R. HAWEIS. With Portrait of the Author, and numerous Illustrations, Facsimiles, and Diagrams. Crown 8vo., 7s. 6d.

Indian Ideals (No. 1)—

NĀRADA SŪTRA: An Inquiry into Love (Bhakti-Jijnāsā). Translated from the Sanskrit, with an Independent Commentary, by E. T. STURDY. Crown 8vo., 2s. 6d. net.

Jefferies (Richard).

FIELD AND HEDGEROW. With Portrait. Crown 8vo., 3s. 6d.

THE STORY OF MY HEART: With Portrait and New Preface by C. J. LONGMAN. Crown 8vo., 3s. 6d.

Jefferies (Richard)—*continued.*

RED DEER. 17 Illustrations. Crown 8vo., 3s. 6d.

THE TOILERS OF THE FIELD. With Portrait. Crown 8vo., 3s. 6d.

WOOD MAGIC. With Frontispiece and Vignette by E. V. B. Cr. 8vo., 3s. 6d.

THOUGHTS FROM THE WRITINGS OF RICHARD JEFFERIES. Selected by H. S. HOOLE WAYLEN. 16mo., 3s. 6d.

Johnson.—THE PATENTEE'S MANUAL: a Treatise on the Law and Practice of Letters Patent. By J. & J. H. JOHNSON, Patent Agents, &c. 8vo., 10s. 6d.

Lang (ANDREW).

LETTERS TO DEAD AUTHORS. Fcp. 8vo., 2s. 6d. net.

LETTERS ON LITERATURE. Fcp. 8vo., 2s. 6d. net.

BOOKS AND BOOKMEN. With 19 Illustrations. Fcp. 8vo., 2s. 6d. net.

OLD FRIENDS. Fcp. 8vo., 2s. 6d. net.

COCK LANE AND COMMON SENSE. Crown 8vo., 3s. 6d.

Macfarren.—LECTURES ON HARMONY. By Sir GEO. A. MACFARREN. 8vo., 12s.

Max Müller (F.).

INDIA: WHAT CAN IT TEACH US? Cr. 8vo., 3s. 6d.

CHIPS FROM A GERMAN WORKSHOP.

Vol. I., Recent Essays and Addresses. Cr. 8vo., 6s. 6d. net.

Vol. II., Biographical Essays. Cr. 8vo., 6s. 6d. net.

Vol. III., Essays on Language and Literature. Cr. 8vo., 6s. 6d. net.

Vol. IV., Essays on Mythology and Folk Lore. Crown 8vo., 8s. 6d. net.

Milner. — COUNTRY PLEASURES: the Chronicle of a Year chiefly in a Garden. By GEORGE MILNER. Cr. 8vo., 3s. 6d.

Miscellaneous and Critical Works—*continued.*

Morris (WILLIAM).

SIGNS OF CHANGE. Seven Lectures delivered on various Occasions. Post 8vo., 4s. 6d.

HOPES AND FEARS FOR ART. Five Lectures delivered in Birmingham, London, &c., in 1878-1881. Crown 8vo., 4s. 6d.

Orchard.—THE ASTRONOMY OF 'MILTON'S PARADISE LOST'. By THOMAS N. ORCHARD, M.D., Member of the British Astronomical Association. With 13 Illustrations. 8vo., 15s.

Poore.—ESSAYS ON RURAL HYGIENE. By GEORGE VIVIAN POORE, M.D., F.R.C.P. With 13 Illustrations. Cr. 8vo., 6s. 6d.

Proctor. — STRENGTH: How to get Strong and keep Strong, with Chapters on Rowing and Swimming, Fat, Age, and the Waist. By R. A. PROCTOR. With 9 Illustrations. Cr. 8vo, 2s.

Richardson.—NATIONAL HEALTH. A Review of the Works of Sir Edwin Chadwick, K.C.B. By Sir B. W. RICHARDSON, M.D. Cr. 8vo., 4s. 6d.

Rossetti.—A SHADOW OF DANTE: being an Essay towards studying Himself, his World, and his Pilgrimage. By MARIA FRANCESCA ROSSETTI. Cr. 8vo., 3s. 6d.

Solovyoff.—A MODERN PRIESTESS OF ISIS (MADAME BLAVATSKY). Abridged and Translated on Behalf of the Society for Psychical Research from the Russian of VSEVOLOD SERGYEEVICH SOLOVYEFF. By WALTER LEAF, Litt. D. With Appendices. Crown 8vo., 6s.

Stevens.—ON THE STOWAGE OF SHIPS AND THEIR CARGOES. With Information regarding Freights, Charter-Parties, &c. By ROBERT WHITE STEVENS, Associate Member of the Institute of Naval Architects. 8vo. 21s.

West.—WILLS, AND HOW NOT TO MAKE THEM. With a Selection of Leading Cases. By B. B. WEST. Fcp. 8vo., 2s. 6d.

Miscellaneous Theological Works.

** For Church of England and Roman Catholic Works see MESSRS. LONGMANS & CO.'s *Special Catalogues.*

Balfour.—THE FOUNDATIONS OF BE-LIEF: being Notes Introductory to the Study of Theology. By the Right Hon. ARTHUR J. BALFOUR, M.P. 8vo., 12s. 6d.

Bird (ROBERT).

A CHILD'S RELIGION. Crown 8vo., 2s.

JOSEPH THE DREAMER. Cr. 8vo., 5s.

JESUS, THE CARPENTER OF NAZARETH. Crown 8vo, 5s.

To be had also in Two Parts, 2s. 6d. each.

Part. I.—GALILEE AND THE LAKE OF GENNESARET.

Part II.—JERUSALEM AND THE PERÆA.

Boyd (A. K. H.). ('A.K.H.B.').

COUNSEL AND COMFORT FROM A CITY PULPIT. Crown 8vo., 3s. 6d.

SUNDAY AFTERNOONS IN THE PARISH CHURCH OF A SCOTTISH UNIVERSITY CITY. Crown 8vo., 3s. 6d.

CHANGED ASPECTS OF UNCHANGED TRUTHS. Crown 8vo., 3s. 6d.

GRAVER THOUGHTS OF A COUNTRY PARSON. Three Series. Crown 8vo., 3s. 6d. each.

PRESENT DAY THOUGHTS. Crown 8vo., 3s. 6d.

SEASIDE MUSINGS. Cr. 8vo., 3s. 6d.

Miscellaneous Theological Works—*continued*.

Boyd (A. K. H.) (**'A.K.H.B.'**)—*cont.*

'TO MEET THE DAY' through the Christian Year ; being a Text of Scripture, with an Original Meditation and a Short Selection in Verse for Every Day. Crown 8vo., 4s. 6d.

OCCASIONAL AND IMMEMORIAL DAYS. Cr. 8vo., 7s. 6d.

De La Saussaye.—A MANUAL OF THE SCIENCE OF RELIGION. By Prof. CHANTEPIE DE LA SAUSSAYE. Crown 8vo., 12s. 6d.

Gibson.—THE ABBÉ DE LAMENNAIS AND THE LIBERAL CATHOLIC MOVEMENT IN FRANCE. By the HON. W. GIBSON.

Kalisch (M. M.).

BIBLE STUDIES. Part I. The Prophecies of Balaam. 8vo., 10s. 6d. Part II. The Book of Jonah. 8vo., 10s. 6d.

COMMENTARY ON THE OLD TESTAMENT: with a new Translation. Vol. I. Genesis. 8vo., 18s. Or adapted for the General Reader. 12s. Vol. II. Exodus. 15s. Or adapted for the General Reader. 12s. Vol. III. Leviticus, Part I. 15s. Or adapted for the General Reader. 8s. Vol. IV. Leviticus, Part II. 15s. Or adapted for the General Reader. 8s.

Macdonald (GEORGE, LL.D.).

UNSPOKEN SERMONS. Three Series. Crown 8vo., 3s. 6d. each.

THE MIRACLES OF OUR LORD. Crown 8vo., 3s. 6d.

Martineau (JAMES, D.D., LL.D.).

HOURS OF THOUGHT ON SACRED THINGS : Sermons. 2 Vols. Crown 8vo. 3s. 6d. each.

ENDEAVOURS AFTER THE CHRISTIAN LIFE. Discourses. Cr. 8vo., 7s. 6d.

THE SEAT OF AUTHORITY IN RELIGION. 8vo., 14s.

ESSAYS, REVIEWS, AND ADDRESSES. 4 Vols. Crown 8vo., 7s. 6d. each. I. Personal ; Political. II. Ecclesiastical ; Historical. III. Theological ; Philosophical. IV. Academical ; Religious.

HOME PRAYERS, with Two Services for Public Worship. Crown 8vo. 3s. 6d.

Max Müller (F.).

HIBBERT LECTURES ON THE ORIGIN AND GROWTH OF RELIGION, as illustrated by the Religions of India. Crown 8vo., 7s. 6d.

INTRODUCTION TO THE SCIENCE OF RELIGION : Four Lectures delivered at the Royal Institution. Cr. 8vo., 3s. 6d.

NATURAL RELIGION. The Gifford Lectures, delivered before the University of Glasgow in 1888. Cr. 8vo., 10s. 6d.

PHYSICAL RELIGION. The Gifford Lectures, delivered before the University of Glasgow in 1890. Cr. 8vo., 10s. 6d.

ANTHROPOLOGICAL RELIGION. The Gifford Lectures, delivered before the University of Glasgow in 1891. Cr. 8vo., 10s. 6d.

THEOSOPHY OR PSYCHOLOGICAL RELIGION. The Gifford Lectures, delivered before the University of Glasgow in 1892. Cr. 8vo., 10s. 6d.

THREE LECTURES ON THE VEDANTA PHILOSOPHY, delivered at the Royal Institution in March, 1894. 8vo., 5s.

Phillips.—THE TEACHING OF THE VEDAS. What Light does it Throw on the Origin and Development of Religion ? By MAURICE PHILLIPS, London Mission, Madras. Crown 8vo., 6s.

Romanes.—THOUGHTS ON RELIGION. By GEORGE J. ROMANES. Crown 8vo., 4s. 6d.

SUPERNATURAL RELIGION : an Inquiry into the Reality of Divine Revelation. 3 vols. 8vo., 36s.

REPLY (A) TO DR. LIGHTFOOT'S ESSAYS. By the Author of 'Supernatural Religion'. 8vo., 6s.

THE GOSPEL ACCORDING TO ST. PETER : a Study. By the Author of 'Supernatural Religion'. 8vo., 6s.

Vivekananda.—YOGA PHILOSOPHY : Lectures delivered in New York, Winter of 1895-6, by the Swami Vivekananda, on Raja Yoga : or, Conquering the Internal Nature ; also Patanjali's Yoga Aphorisms, with Commentaries. Crown 8vo., 3s. 6d.